TORN BETWEEN WORLDS

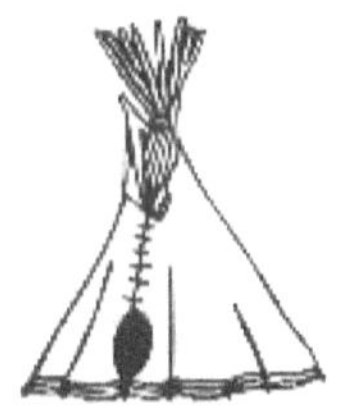

A Western Historical Romance Novel

Linda Chalk

Elizabeth Rose Press

i

ACKNOWLEDGEMENTS

I want to thank my family, especially my husband, for their support and patience while I closeted myself in my office to write, often at the expense of other household duties.

I also want to thank my writer friends and "support group" members of the OVRWA (Ohio Valley Romance Writers Association) with whom I have learned so very much, through workshops and conferences and 'brain picking' about the world of writing. I would not have been able to publish *Torn Between Worlds* without them.

Thank you to all of those who shared their support and encouragement during the final weeks as I prepared for publication.

Since there are many people who had a hand in this work, and I'm sure I will forget someone, I will not mention individual names. You all know who you are.

AUTHOR'S NOTE

This book is a work of fiction. The names, characters, incidents and places are products of the author's imagination, or have been used fictitiously and are not to be construed as real. Many of the resources, including personal diaries and trail guidebooks, used in the creation of this book were written by immigrants who actually experienced the overland trail and reflect the prejudices and conditions of the time.

During my research and writing, I gained admiration for the families who at great peril, crossed the prairie in search of a better life. When my travels take me across the prairie states, in our modern RV with microwave oven and running water, highway rest stops and fast food, I think about the immigrants of 1849 chased by cholera, who slept in the rain and drove wagons containing all their worldly goods through rushing rivers.

CHAPTER 1

September 1848
Possum Hollow Missouri

Lydia Whitley tied her horse, Sunshine, to the hitching post, half-expecting some drunk to stagger out of the saloon to greet her with obscene remarks. She hated going into the one road, pimple of a town, with its reputation for gunfights and skirmishes, but she'd promised to purchase some baking soda at the General Store for Agnes Applegate.

The old woman was like a grandmother to Lydia. And Mrs. Applegate was dying.

On this particular afternoon, Lydia found the town unusually calm, with few people on the street. Laughter drifted from the saloon and the clang of metal reverberated from the smithy's shop. Like a line of hornets, the Kincaid brothers were coming and going with supplies from the General Store. Always ready for a fight, the oldest brother was jabbing at the younger two, who were doing the heavy work of loading barrels into their wagon.

Lydia was considering hiding until they left and she could cross the street and enter the store without risk of harassment, when two beefy arms came from behind and snatched her into a dark passageway next to the smithy's.

Where no one could hear her scream.

She doubled over and tugged against the iron-like grip around her waist, the odor of her attacker's unwashed body stealing her breath. Blindly, she kicked backwards, heels striking solid muscle. She clawed at the calloused hands. The attempt at escape only brought a low rumble of laughter and he swung her around to face him. A large hand pinned her wrists behind her as he dropped her feet to the ground.

"Ain't you a feisty squaw?"

Lydia cringed at his liquor-fouled breath. It was the Kincaid cousin, Willie. He'd shown up in town only recently, to stir up trouble, no doubt. Rumor was he'd shot someone before fleeing to Possum Hollow. There was no proof to the story. Willie couldn't have been more than eighteen years old, yet he was fully a man and towered over Lydia. A ghoulish scar ran the length of his left cheek.

"Let me go!" A barefooted kick to his right shin was ineffective and only brought a deep-throated laugh.

He dragged his tongue over his lips.

Lydia gulped and tried to pull away.

He snatched a handful of her hair that was pinned at the nape of her neck and tugged fiercely, his thin smile turning into an evil smirk. Lydia screamed as he forced her head into a backwards tilt, immobilizing her. He paused only a moment before ensnaring her mouth with his, bruising her lips and squelching her scream. She gagged on his fouled breath.

Lydia squirmed to pull her mouth from his, the effort further exciting him. He pulled her closer, flattening her breasts against his granite-like chest until she nearly suffocated. Willie devoured her lips with violent intent, his tongue thrust between her teeth, ruthlessly probing her mouth. He writhed against her in a pulsating rhythm, as if he were some wild boar. Bile percolated into her throat and she thought she would vomit.

Terror drove Lydia's defense. She clamped her teeth shut with all of her might. Not until she tasted blood did she open them again.

Willie jerked back and released her with a demonic roar. Then he examined the damage to his tongue with the tips of two grimy fingers and glared.

Lydia staggered backwards and spat out the awful taste of liquor and blood. She froze only long enough to witness her attacker swing his fist to strike. A lifetime of farm work and flight within the forest and hills of Possum Hollow had made Lydia agile, so she easily evaded the blow of the mountain-sized man whose reflexes had slowed with liquor. She ran back onto the walkway of the main street and into another alley.

Her back pressed against the log-hewn wall, all senses were alert. Her eyes darted right and left to catch any movement. The sound of her pounding heart, and her blood swishing in her ears, nearly masked the street sounds. She'd lost him. A figure passed along the front walk between the two buildings. Was it him? She sucked in air and pressed closer to the wall. No. The figure was too short. She breathed out.

Lydia had barely caught her breath before Willie entered the passageway from the rear of the buildings. Perhaps he thought to confuse and corner her by approaching from a different direction. Lydia screamed as he swung at her with a broken piece of wood. She dodged his attack and bolted onto the wooden walkway along the store fronts. From there, she could cross the street, weave her way past the Kincaids and find safety in the General Store.

The street crossing was within view, when a couple of wild pigs scrambled in front of her, nearly causing her to trip before they squealed and scurried away. Those extra seconds were costly. An instant later, as she was about to leap into the street, a stinging pain shot through her. The solid blow across her back knocked her forward.

She tumbled face first into the muddy street as a shrill whinny drew her attention. An imposing black stallion reared up within inches of her. To avoid its flailing hooves, she summersaulted into a chuckhole, her hands coming forward to protect her face as she splashed into the sun-warmed mud. A grunt escaped as she landed on her injured shoulder.

Still rearing, the startled horse whinnied again, its rider fighting to control his mount and to keep from being thrown. By the time Lydia had pushed herself onto her knees in the sticky goo, she found the horse standing quietly, staring down at her as if to question her bizarre situation. Towering above her, the stallion was the most terrifying and magnificent animal she'd ever seen. Its well-defined muscles exuded raw power. His smooth coat and long silky mane glistened.

"Damn it woman! Are you trying to get us killed?" A male voice boomed.

Behind her, the wooden plank again made contact with her backside. She yelped and curled up protectively.

"What the hell!" The man on the horse shouted. "Get away from her! What kind of a man are you to hit a lady?"

Willie laughed with a deep throaty sound. "She's not a lady. She's a savage."

Lydia turned her head in the direction of Willie. Squinting against the bright sun and the muddy water dripping from her hair and into her eyes, she could only discern him as a shadowy figure. He was still clutching the plank.

"This ain't none of your business. I can handle this, stranger."

"Leave her alone." The rider's deep voice held a challenge.

Lydia recognized the click of a hammer being pulled back on a pistol behind her.

"Who the hell are you?" Willie growled. "What right do you have comin' into town on your throne of a horse and tellin' me what to do?"

"The pistol is pointed at you. Not me."

She should have known that a man with a ghoulish scar would argue with a loaded gun. By now the scuffle had attracted attention. Bystanders were lining up along the street. Most were men, in town to drink and gamble. She wondered who they were rooting for, probably taking bets on the outcome. Never mind the squaw lying in the street. She was little more than a prop for their entertainment.

The pistol went off behind her, wringing a cry from her throat. She stiffened as if she were about to be hit. The bullet whizzed to her left and landed in the mud, inches from Willie's feet.

Willie cursed. He stood there for a long moment before throwing down the piece of plank and stomping away. The crowd dispersed, grumbling that the entertainment was over, most likely disappointed at the swift outcome of the dispute.

Lydia shielded her eyes from the sun and gazed at the lean man sitting in the saddle. A ray of light reflecting off his polished boots convinced her he must be wealthy. Shoes and boots were too expensive for everyday use, except in the coldest weather. Lydia shivered as she watched him return the pistol to his hip, its leather holster worn smooth. Only gun-fighters and outlaws wore pistols so comfortably. Rolled up shirtsleeves revealed sun bronzed, well-muscled arms. This out-of-towner was cleaner and better groomed than any of the local men.

"Can you speak?" The rider dismounted and came alongside her, the muddy street obviously not giving him pause. "Are you all right?" he asked with more compassion.

At that moment, Lydia couldn't be certain. Willie had hit her twice, her back and shoulder throbbed. Whether or not the horse had struck her, she was too stunned to discern. She blinked at the man before pushing herself to a seated position with the palms of her hands. The next moment, one of his lean arms came around her back. The other arm slid beneath her legs.

"Wha… What are you doing?"

She was suddenly cocooned in raw muscle and strength. The heat of the man sent a shock wave spiraling from her head to her toes, knotting in her throat and sending her dazed mind into further turmoil. She squirmed to free herself from the wall of chest and arms, the handle of his pistol grinding into her hip. Had she fled the clutches of one brute to be entrapped by another?

"For crying out loud. I might drop you." He tightened his grip and carried her to more solid ground.

When the hot bands of arms eased her to the wooden planks and released her, her shaky legs kept her from escaping. Her knees buckled. But his big hands snatched her arms and steadied her.

"I… I'm fine, sir." Her voice trembled as much as her body. Her heart raced and she panted like a winded greyhound. Maybe if she backed away. Could she dart past him without being snatched again?

"Really? You can't stand by yourself."

As he assessed her, Lydia backed away, knowing she would eventually be trapped against the smithy shop. *Think Lydia! Think!* Panic rose in her throat like bile. She wasn't going to let him touch her again. With each step she took, he moved toward her, until he reached out and seized her arm. A ray of sun slipped under the brim of his hat and she came face to face with the brightest blue eyes she had ever seen.

"For crying out loud! I'm not going to hurt you! You're as skittish as an unbroken mustang." He retrieved a clean handkerchief from his shirt pocket and dabbed at her face.

"Wha… What are you doing?"

"I'm cleaning the mud from your face. Hold still."

When his arm came around to hold her in place against him, she gasped. Her wet dress provided little barrier from the heat of his body.

"Why was that man beating you?"

She looked into his blue eyes, silently pleading for him to release her. The mix of male scents, musk and horse and leather, made her head spin.

When he finished wiping her face, he tucked his handkerchief into a pocket and gazed at her as if truly noticing her for the first time. "I didn't know any Indians lived in these parts. I thought the Osage were driven from Missouri years ago."

Lydia swallowed down a lump in her throat. What did he know about Indians? Only Agnes Applegate, ever spoke of Indians. When he brushed aside a strand of hair from her cheek, a tremor shot through her. With a renewed surge of determination, Lydia caught the man off guard and pulled away from his embrace. Just as quickly, he grabbed her arm and held her fast. His fingers seemed to sear her flesh through the long sleeve of her dress.

"Why are you in such a hurry?" He stared into her face, his eyes absorbing her into their deep blue depths. "I can't let you run off without making sure you're all right and offering you a ride. You're so wobbly, I'm afraid you'll collapse."

Her legs wobbled because of his close proximity, not because of any injury. "I'll be fine." Lydia pulled her shoulders back to stand more proudly and erectly. "I'm not in the habit of accepting rides from strangers."

His smile widened, reached his eyes and illuminated his face. "Then allow me to introduce myself. I'm Joseph Brice."

The audacity! Introductions alone hardly kept them from being strangers. She did not ride off with strange men. *And what else might he have planned for her? Out in the woods. Alone. And he expected her to go willingly? Did he think her a fool or a whore?*

"Are you going to tell me who you are so we can stop the formalities?"

"No," Lydia answered more sharply than she'd intended. "You've helped me enough."

He seemed surprised at her response. "I can't just leave you in the road."

Anyone else would.

He continued to study her, but he must have been satisfied with whatever he was contemplating because he let her go. Finally free, she gathered up enough strength to put her legs into motion. She hurried to retrieve Sunshine, as the voice of Joseph Brice trailed off. "You didn't tell me your name..."

CHAPTER 2

Lydia nearly flew through town before she disappeared into the forest. The cool damp air descended upon her, calmed her nerves and eased the queasiness that was like a knot in her gut. This was Lydia's world, as familiar to her as her own skin. Safe and secure, she could slip into the shadows and disappear.

Lydia slumped over Sunshine's neck, the adrenaline slowly ebbing. She had been grabbed and groped by other men, who thought her Indian blood put her at a lower status, as if she were a free whore for the taking. Most were drunk and she could easily fend off their clumsy attacks, but Lydia had never encountered a man as barbaric as Willie.

Then, there was that stranger, Joseph Brice. The intensity of his eyes, as bright and blue as the noon sky. The memory of his scrutiny made her shiver with goose bumps. In those brief moments when they had touched, she'd felt his gentleness. She'd sensed the power of his lean muscles, restrained and controlled; power to protect, not to dominate or demean. She'd never experienced anything like it. And it left her bewildered. Her face grew hot at the memory of his big hands scooping her from the mud, the contact with his body inappropriate at best. And then he'd wiped her face with a caring touch.

A slight stumble by Sunshine brought Lydia back to the present and to the sound of hooves crunching leaves. Dappled light blinked like shutters through the forest canopy. She needed to pay attention. They were approaching the turn, which led to the Applegate farm, about two miles away, at the top of the ridge, a rugged piece of ground.

She'd heard complaints from others often enough about traveling through the Missouri Ozarks, with its maze of deep valleys and sharp ridges, but Lydia knew this stretch almost like the back of her hand. As she ascended the rocky cliff, she pondered with continued amazement on stories which Agnes had shared. How she and her husband, long ago, had climbed these cliffs, barefoot with pack mules and three small children from Kentucky to 'get away from the confines of society'. They'd hacked a path through the thick forest to set up a home.

Families, like the Applegates who settled on the ridges, lived off the land by hunting or trapping and trading for what they needed. Homesteads, in the hollows, like that of Lydia's parents', with soil and fresh springs could support a cash crop. But few could afford luxuries, like shoes, and winter for everyone in a drafty cabin was an endless source of misery.

One of the first settlers in Possum Hollow, the venerated old mid-wife and self-proclaimed doctor had 'birthed' all the babies until she no longer had the strength.

Lydia slowed as she approached the Applegate place. After the property was no longer farmed, the natural growth of brush and poison vines had taken over what had once been a small field in the front. The moss covered cabin sat against the hillside under a canopy of trees. The sunken porch roof sagged to one side on rotting support beams. Its front door drooped on rusty hinges to leave a small gap at the top. The wisp of smoke rising from the chimney provided a welcome greeting.

By the time Lydia arrived at the cabin, the mud had dried and cracked on her feet and ankles. The front of her dress had stiffened. She felt a rush of embarrassment that she was visiting the woman in such a poor state.

She hopped down from Sunshine and tied her horse to a post several yards from the front door at a watering trough. The trough was strategically placed to collect rain and had a bucket hanging from it on a nail for hauling wash water. Lydia rinsed her soiled feet and hands, then used a clean portion of her skirt hidden beneath her apron to dry them.

Lydia walked past two rocking chairs, which with their broken posts, were only fit for firewood. The butter churn sat between them. Lydia had spent many hours sitting on that porch churning butter as Agnes Applegate told stories of pioneer days gone by. They'd lived in harmony with the Osage Indians. "Not until them land greedy Easterners come and threaten the tribes and took away their lands was there any uprisings."

Lydia had only taken a couple of steps inside, her eyes not yet adjusted to the dark interior when she nearly bumped into the old woman, who was stooped over, shuffling toward the door.

"Mrs. Applegate! I thought you'd taken ill. What are you doing out of bed?"

"Harrumph," she answered and turned back toward where she had come. "I heard somebody out there nosin' around." Lydia noticed with concern, the wheezing in Agnes's chest.

"It was just me." Lydia took a firm hold of the woman's upper arm and led her to her rocker by the fire. Agnes needed her rest and to stay warm to keep the phlegm loose.

The rocker creaked as Lydia helped to ease the woman into the chair. Then she draped a thin, worn quilt over her lap. When the woman was seated, she looked at Lydia as though just noticing her. "Lordy child, ain't you a sight for sore eyes! What in tarnation you been into?"

Lydia glanced down at the front of her muddy dress. "Oh… I had a bit of an accident."

"Come. Sit here with me."

Lydia pulled up a footstool and sat down with a sigh and let her eyes adjust to the dim interior. Other than the beams of light creeping through the small windows, a couple of table lamps and the fire were all that illuminated the cabin. She settled into the warm familiar surroundings and breathed in the scented collection of herbs and spices.

The earthen storage jars containing medicinal herbs were arranged neatly on shelves along one wall. Other herbs hung in bunches from the ceiling beams to dry. Moldy bread, some wilted vegetables and a jug of whiskey sat on the scarred kitchen table. The fresh cutting of lavender was no doubt a gift from someone to help cover the odor of sickness. The dark smoky walls, the distinctive smells of simmering chicken, onion and thyme emanating from a cooking pot welcomed her.

Deciding to examine the simmering dish, Lydia snatched up a ladle and went to the iron pot hanging over the fire. She stirred the rich golden broth with bits of herbs and carrots that bobbed in the bubbly soup. The small hunks of chicken were brown and nearly ready to eat.

"Who made you supper?" Lydia asked.

"I can still fend for myself," Agnes answered crisply. "So long as the boys stop by to cut up wood." She paused and smoothed out the quilt on her lap. "Wilma Kincaid brought me the chicken."

"Mama said you refused to see Doctor Adams."

"You know I don't want no Yankee Quack a messin' with me. I done docter'n longer than any a them highfalutin college fellers." Agnes broke into a spastic cough. She doubled over, gasping for breath, drained of what little strength remained in her shriveled frame.

"Shh." Lydia offered the woman some water from the pitcher on her side table, which she refused. "How about some horehound tea to help your cough? I can make you some."

"You sit right there." Agnes studied her. "Tell me what you been doin'." She reached out with her wrinkled hand, skin as thin as paper, and patted Lydia on the arm. "Did you get me some baking soda?"

"No," Lydia answered bashfully. "Next time." Then she started with the story of how she had stumbled into the street and soiled her dress, omitting her encounter with Willie. She told of how she'd run into the stranger with the magnificent stallion. As Lydia spoke, Agnes relaxed somewhat, sinking deeper into her rocker.

"Ain't heard of no Joseph Brice. What's he like?"

"He's a stranger. Probably just passing through."

"He strong and beautiful? Like his horse?"

"Strong and beautiful? Mrs. Applegate!" Lydia's face warmed. Not wanting to meet Agnes's wise old eyes, she gazed into the lamp illuminating the side table. "He's just a man."

No, he wasn't just any man. He had broad shoulders and muscles that strained against his shirt. He was rugged and moved with confidence. Her heart gave a rush as she remembered his caring touch. She noticed that some strands of hair had slipped from where she'd pinned them at the nape of her neck and now fell below her shoulders. Somewhere she had lost her bonnet. Lydia squirmed self-consciously and fumbled to secure the long strands.

"Tell me what he looks like, in case he comes around here, I'll know who he is."

The old mid-wife knew everyone in Possum Hollow. There was no need to describe Joseph Brice. She would know he was a stranger if she saw him. But since it meant keeping the woman quiet and resting, Lydia continued to talk.

"Well… his voice is deep and silky. His eyes are the color of the sky and sparkle with mischief. His smile is broader than Possum Creek. And he's clean too."

"You makin' this up?" Agnes peered at Lydia through one open eye. "No."

"Maybe you wantin' to see more of this man, eh?" Agnes grinned her toothless smile.

"Mrs. Applegate!" Although this woman was the only person in the world with whom she could engage in such a personal conversation, Lydia grew increasingly uncomfortable. She left the woman's side to poke the fire. "Certainly not! He's strong willed and audacious. And he carries a pistol like some criminal."

"Strong willed means he be a strong man. You wouldn't want no weakling. And my Charlie carried a pistol. Didn't bother me none. He weren't no criminal."

And the stranger made her feel…

She couldn't define how he made her feel, not after experiencing the horror of Willie. She tried to shake off thoughts of both men.

"I see that far off look on your face." Agnes chuckled, until she began to cough uncontrollably.

Lydia managed to get some water down the woman's throat. When the back of her hand brushed her cheek, Lydia noticed that Agnes was burning up. "Enough talking. You need to rest. You're feverish."

"All this talk about this feller of yours, is gettin' me all heated up. I ain't had me a man for more years than I can remember. Not since my Charlie died."

"He's not my feller! Besides, you know no man will want me."

"Don't be so hard on yourself, child." Agnes fought the wheezing to catch her breath. "You've got lots to offer a man. You're good-hearted and mighty purty. Hard workin' too. Don't you listen to what other folks is sayin'."

Lydia wanted to believe her friend's words. But the cruel words of others were difficult to ignore. *Indians are savage. They raid white settlements, scalp their victims and rape the women.* Lydia strove to abide by her mother's teachings, as if proper manners and carriage would erase signs of her heritage, so she could be accepted into society. In her heart, she knew that would never happen in Possum Hollow.

"I'll make some willow bark tea for you, to help with the fever." Mentored by the old healer for as long as Lydia could remember, she was the only other resident in Possum Hollow who knew the secrets of her medicinal teas. Until most recently, along with her mid-wife duties, Agnes had made a living by weaving and spinning and selling the medicinal potions she concocted from the herbs she gathered.

Lydia returned the kettle of water from the cooler part of the fireplace to an area of hot coals and went in search of willow bark within the extensive collection of medicines. She located the small jar she was looking for, carefully labeled with scratches. Agnes had never learned to read or write, so she had invented her own way of labeling her medicines with symbols resembling tiny pictures of the plant's leaves or berries.

Lydia was crushing some of the bark into a mug when the front door burst open. She turned in the direction. "Wilma Kincaid…" The name escaped Lydia's throat as if her stomach had been punched. None hated her more than the Kincaids.

"What are you doin' here?" Wilma growled.

"Visiting." Lydia fought to keep her voice from trembling as she stared at the snake faced woman whose wide girth filled the doorway.

"We don't need your kind here. Go back to that rock you crawled out from under."

"Wilma! Leave the child be!" Agnes ordered in a raspy voice.

Wilma lumbered into the kitchen. She ducked in an attempt to avoid a large kettle hanging from a ceiling beam. A clang said she failed. She growled in response and rubbed her forehead. Her foul mood intensified, she snapped again at Lydia who was standing over the mug of crushed bark. "What are you fixin'?"

"Some tea, for her fever."

Wilma snatched the mug from Lydia's hand and smelled the contents. "She don't need any of your poison. I'm here. Now scat!" She waved her big flabby arm toward the door.

Lydia, who had every right to visit her friend, considered arguing with the intruder. A confrontation would only upset the ailing woman. Lydia hugged her good-bye, noting how alarmingly frail and thin she had become. "I'll come back as soon as I can," she whispered.

In the confined space of the kitchen, Lydia was forced to brush past Wilma, the woman's sour odor making Lydia gag. She moved straight to the door, feeling Wilma's glare as sharp as daggers in her back. Outside, one of the Kincaid boys was setting up to split wood. He only gave her a glance as she untied Sunshine and rode away.

That night, Lydia lay restless in her loft beneath the pounding rain and thunder, the wind so violent, she feared the roof would rip away. Curled under the quilt with a pillow over her head did little to block the outside turmoil, and even less to ease her inner turmoil and endless stream of nightmares. The horror of Willie Kincaid played over and over. The puckered flesh of his scar, the way his unshaven stubble scratched her face as he sought to capture her mouth with his. There was something different about Willie Kincaid. His powerful limbs seemed to feel no pain, making him more brutish. A sort of unfathomable madness lay deep in his dark vacuous eyes that turned her blood to ice.

She battled to focus on the memory of blue eyes and strong arms until a warm glow flowed through her and melted the icy fear in her veins. As the wind blew and the rain pounded, her heart beat wildly. The thunder became like drums and another nightmare rushed in…

She could feel the warmth as if she were actually there, watching them strut around the crackling fire, some with their arms flailing, wailing, twisting their bodies in rhythm to the low beat of the drums. Dark skinned people wrapped in large animal skins or only a strip of leather to cover their loins, the women in shirt-like dresses with leather pieces covering their legs from their moccasins to the fringe of their dresses. Then there was screaming. Women and small children running….

Lydia awoke with a start, disoriented, the thunder and rain drowning her screams.

Eventually the storm moved on, and a ray of sun sneaked through the tiny window of her loft and warmed her face. The night was over. Not quite ready to rise and begin her day after a night of restlessness, Lydia retrieved the quilt from where she had kicked it on the floor, rolled over and curled up under its protection.

"Dagnabbit!" She heard her father exclaim from below. He slammed the door and scrapped his feet on the entry rug as he came inside.

"I thought you and Amos had gone hunting," her mother said. "Lydia! Are you up?"

"Yes Mama!" Lydia was instantly out of bed and splashing cold water on her face from a bowl on her dresser, the pain from the sudden movement reminding her of the blows she had received from Willie Kincaid. A wide red welt stretched across her hip and lower back, a purple bruise forming below the surface. No doubt there was a similar one where she couldn't see. She grit her jaw against the pain and reached for the clean dress hanging nearby, glancing at the mud-soiled garment she had worn the previous day.

"You'll be rubbing your knuckles raw to get the stains out," her mother had scolded her when she'd arrived home. "A lady doesn't wallow in the mud like some wild animal."

Lydia knew she deserved a scolding for probably ruining her dress; yet her mother's words made her cringe. She could never be a lady. No matter how much effort she put toward appearances, there was one thing she could never alter. She was Indian, forever marked with copper skin, black hair and black eyes. There was no denying it. One look and anyone could tell.

She fastened the line of buttons that reached to her neck, then covered the front of the simple brown homespun with a crisp white apron. After securing her long hair into a tight bun at the nape of her neck, she descended the ladder to the main room of the cabin. Except for the four small windows, two in the front and one on each side-wall, which allowed in rays of light, the cabin was dark. Her mother was poking at some coals in the fireplace. Despite cooking on a stove, her mother always liked to have a fire going, except on the hottest of days. "It was life and light," she would say.

Lydia blinked through sleepy eyes to stare at Amanda and Edward Whitley, the white couple who had adopted her so long ago. She did not remember that day or any day before they found her roaming in the woods. According to their story, she'd been thin and malnourished without clothing to protect her. They'd cleaned her crusty wounds, and nursed her back to health.

"An angel sent you," her mother, never blessed with her own children, had once told her.

"You know that dead oak," her father's voice broke through Lydia's thoughts. "I've talked about cutting it down for years. Finally uprooted. Took a good corner of the barn with it. Horses kicked their way out and ran off."

"The horses ran off, Papa?" Lydia's throat constricted.

The family owned three horses, which were used for a variety of farm tasks as well as riding. Sunshine had been a gift from her father. The friendship between Lydia and Sunshine was uncommon. While riding bareback–without a side saddle, when her mother wasn't looking–she felt as one with the horse. Each perceived the other's thoughts through a flexing muscle.

"What about Gertie?" Lydia asked.

"Goat's gone, too. Fortunately, the tree missed the hog pen or they might be gone too."

Terrible things could have happened to the animals. There were coyotes and other hungry creatures lurking about.

"Their prints lead up the hillside. Hard telling how far they've wandered. I might be out there all day fetching them."

Her father had looked forward to going on a hunting trip with his closest friend, Amos Crenshaw. He certainly didn't need the stress and aggravation of having to search for lost animals along with preparations for the coming winter. Lydia watched as he dug through the stash of jerky he always took hunting.

"I can help too, Papa." Lydia hurried to the entry to grab her cloak.

"No. You stay home and help your Mama. Amos is here. And his nephew, who took off after some tracks up the hillside."

"His nephew? I don't remember Amos mentioning a nephew," her mother said. She went to the front window and pulled aside the muslin curtain.

"He's come from out west somewhere to lead Amos and Esther on that fool's mission to California."

"It's not a fool's mission." Amos Crenshaw strode in the front door and wiped his feet on the rug. He was a spectacle wearing the traditional hunting garb, sweat stained from years of use. Made of soft durable deerskin, the wide-bodied shirt with oversized sleeves and a full cape drawn in at the waist by a wide leather belt, fell loosely half way down his thighs to overlap the fringed leggings. Her father had never stuck to such tradition.

Lydia's mind flashed to the day last spring when Amos had shown them the newspaper article announcing the discovery of gold at Sutter's mill, proclaiming that he was going out there to get rich and urged them to come along. Her father had laughed at first, thinking the idea a joke. Her mother sat down and sobbed at the prospect of her best friend, Esther moving away. The topic continued as a source of conflict between the men.

"Rheumatism," Amos defended, closing the door behind him. "Doc Adams agreed the warmer climate would help my rheumatism. 'Sides, crops ain't been good the past couple of years. Esther and me is little better off than when we first come to Possum Holler. Californy's got gold nuggets bigger than a fist!" He waved clenched knuckles at her father to demonstrate. "I can buy me some land in that there, Sac-something valley."

"Sacramento."

"Yeah. That's it."

"How about some hot coffee?" her mother was obviously hoping to diffuse the situation.

"I'll get some…" Lydia offered, and turned toward the kitchen.

"No time," her father replied. He stuffed a canteen into his leather bag and left with Amos Crenshaw at his heels.

While cleaning up from a breakfast of bacon and eggs and biscuits, Lydia said, "Mama, after I feed the chickens, I'd like to check on Mrs. Applegate."

"You visited her yesterday. I need you to bring in the rest of the apples. Too many have already fallen and are starting to turn to vinegar, and with that wind storm last night who knows how many more we might lose if we wait."

"I hoped I could see her today. I think her cough has gotten worse."

"From what I hear, Wilma Kincaid has been tending to her. Let her do it. She has a brood to help her at home. I only have you."

Lydia's shoulders sagged.

"When you're done with the apples, if there's still daylight, then you can see her."

Lydia knew her mother was right, preserving the fruit for winter was critical. But no one else knew how to use Mrs. Applegate's healing herbs. Worry pressed on Lydia as she navigated her way to the barn. She stepped over small branches which had been snapped from trees during the storm, green leaves still clinging. She stopped by the chicken coop, releasing the boisterous birds into their yard and spreading out some feed.

Lydia gasped as she approached the barn. Her father had not exaggerated the damage. The monster oak, with its termite-eaten trunk, maybe three feet wide, and decayed roots, was parallel to the ground, crushing nearly a quarter of the building. Bare branches splayed across the yard or clung to the brittle siding of the building. Only a miracle could have kept animals from being killed.

The hogs snorted and squealed as Lydia came alongside their outdoor pen on the opposite side of the barn. The door between their indoor and outdoor enclosures hung wide open, but the animals were safely contained. She glanced inside the barn to confirm that the interior was empty. A hollow feeling swept over her. Until that moment, she'd foolishly hoped that an animal or two might not have run off. Sunshine maybe, or Gertie. Since the main door was useless, Lydia picked her way through the debris. Inside the barn, she retrieved the baskets and tools she needed for picking apples.

The small orchard helped sustain the family through winter, often with surplus for trade or cash. Lydia had to sort the fallen apples, selecting the best from those with bruises or insects, each to serve their own purpose for cider, pies, or drying, or boiling down for applesauce. The remainder would be raked into the compost or processed into vinegar, her least favorite task. Just the memory of the acrid odor of rotting apples made her face scrunch.

Lydia frowned when she realized she wouldn't be finishing what needed to be done before sunset. As much as she wished to have joined her father's search, or to visit with Mrs. Applegate, she recognized the importance of the harvest. This year's was a success with enough to sell and trade with their neighbors. And although sweat dripped from her brow and the sun beat down mercilessly, the heavy labor left her to her thoughts.

Light was waning when her mother's voice pulled Lydia's attention away. She realized then, how her hands and wrists ached from snapping the fruit from branches. Her arms throbbed from moving the ladder, and her back from stooping, the pain worsened by the injuries inflicted by Willie. She tossed the apples she'd been holding into a basket and moved like an old woman to the cabin.

Her father was sitting atop a draft horse with Amos Crenshaw ambling closely behind on another. The animals were muddy with matted hair and burrs, but they seemed no worse from their adventure. Although relieved that the draft horses had been located, her heart sank. She did not see Sunshine or Gertie. Taking a few steps toward the men she caught sight of a swish of dark horse tail. Partially obscured by a stand of trees her beloved Sunshine was tethered behind a black stallion. Realization brought a rush of excitement and a tingle of fear. She recognized that horse with the mane that cascaded in waves.

CHAPTER 3

Sitting broad shouldered and confident atop the stallion, his hat slightly askew, was Joseph Brice, the man who had nearly run her down. The man who had bathed her with intimate tenderness. "Your daughter?" he spoke to her father.

"Yes." Her father waved an arm toward her. "Lydia, this is Joseph Brice, Amos's nephew."

Lydia nearly choked. *Amos's nephew?*

"And this is my wife, Amanda." By now her mother, wiping her hands on her apron front, had joined the group.

"Nice to meet you," she said.

"Likewise." Joe tipped his hat toward the ladies before pulling up alongside Lydia. He leaned over the saddle. "When Edward said he had a daughter, you weren't quite what I expected."

Of course not. No one expected a white couple in Missouri to call an Indian – daughter. No doubt he had expected her to be the wife of a grizzled old fur trapper, like so many others she met. She swallowed down the bitter taste and scowled.

"Lydia, aren't you going to thank him for returning your horse?" Her mother admonished.

She left her ill-tempered thoughts. "Thank you."

"You're welcome." His lips turned into a smile that brightened his eyes.

"Sorry we're so late," her father said. "I didn't want to leave any of them out all night, not with that pair of coyotes I spotted the other day. We saw fresh tracks along Possum Creek."

"You found them all?" her mother asked.

"All except for Gertie."

"Poor Gertie," Lydia sighed. If the sun weren't so near the horizon, she'd search for the goat herself. Wandering the hills at night was a dangerous prospect even for someone who knew them as well as she did. She shivered as she imagined the defenseless goat, lying wounded and bloody in the undergrowth.

"When she gets hungry for a decent meal, she'll come home." Joe's voice pulled Lydia from her terrifying vision. "I bet you'll find her waiting out here for breakfast in the morning."

"I'm sure Joe's right," her father agreed.

"So, this is your nephew?" her mother asked Amos, studying the two men. "I don't see a resemblance."

Lydia noted the differences too. Amos was a plain man of medium height and build, with dark graying hair. He resembled every other man who dwelled in Possum Hollow. Joseph Brice, however, displayed a rare breed of masculinity. He sat erect in his saddle; muscles filled his shirt. The long sturdy legs pressed against his mount exuded control and confidence over the beast. Realizing she'd been staring, and not liking the direction of her thoughts, she returned her gaze to Amos, her face growing hot.

"He's the son of my sister Irene. He's spent most of his life out west. Learned to be quite a tracker." Amos smiled with pride. "Spitting image of his father. You remember his father, Jackson, don't you?"

"No. I don't believe I've met his father," her mother said.

Lydia noted the tightening of Joe's jaw. There was no missing the glare he shot toward his uncle. "I picked up some tracking tricks from a few Arapaho braves."

Joe knew some Indians? Despite her fatigue, Lydia's attention perked up. *How exciting it must have been to live out west.* More than anything, she wanted to learn about Indians. She often pondered on her heritage and the Indian family she didn't remember. Where were they? Were they alive, or dead? When she'd questioned her adoptive parents about Indians or her heritage, they rebuked her, insisting she focus on the future and not on the past, telling that where she came from no longer mattered. Eventually, she learned not to speak of Indians.

To find answers to her questions, to find the missing pieces of her life, Lydia knew she would have to leave Possum Hollow, to abandon the parents who had given her a home.

"Lydia," her mother said, "why don't you set the table while the men wash up for supper. We've got ham and greens with boiled potatoes and apple pie."

"That's mighty thoughtful of you. Don't think I'll be staying though," Amos said. "Esther will be waitin'. Sides, my rheumatism is actin' up."

"Mr. Brice, how about you?"

"No thanks. I'll probably retire early. We'll need an early start tomorrow, if we're going to get that barn back into shape."

Tomorrow? Joseph Brice was coming back tomorrow? A tremor ran through her.

***

The following morning, when Joe arrived at the Whitley's, he was disappointed to discover that Lydia had sequestered herself sorting and picking apples in the orchard. Only when she carried full baskets of fruit into the barn, dumping them into storage barrels did their paths cross. And then only rarely. His polite nods elicited no response. More than once he considered joining her in the orchard, but she remained elusive, disappearing into the camouflage of trees.

It was nearly noon when Joe finally caught up to her. She was heading into the barn dragging her long skirt through the muddy yard, the full basket slapping against her hip. When she paused for a moment to wipe sweat from her brow with the cuff of her old brown dress and to swat a pesky fly, he swept in beside her. She must not have seen him approach because he easily managed to clutch the handles of the basket.

"Let me help you."

She stared back at him with those wide dark eyes as if she were prey frozen in the sights of a predator. Then, she surrendered the heavy basket with a meek, "Thank you."

He had dumped the apples into the designated barrel before she reached out to retrieve the basket. But Joe kept it from her, speaking before setting it on the ground. "Your mother needs you."

She didn't look back as he followed her into the cabin, swinging the door wide. He had to smack his hand against the door to keep it from slapping him in the face and wondered at the cause of her irritation. Was she just rude? She turned only briefly and without apology before going to the stove where her mother was stirring something in an iron pot. The smell of chicken and onion permeated the room.

Joe paused to remove his hat as he entered the cabin. His Aunt Esther had mentioned that the Whitley's were well-mannered and well-kept. The plank floor and iron cook stove indicated that they were better off than most, although with its compact kitchen and sitting area, the cabin was typical for the backwoods. One corner of the main room served as a bedroom with dresser and a small bedside table with lamp. A frayed quilt adorned the bed. A ladder led to a loft containing a small bed and dresser, no doubt Lydia's quarters. The well-crafted clock placed on the rustic mantle with a bearskin rug on the hearth was a surprising contrast.

From what Joe had seen so far, Edward was much like the other backwoodsmen of Possum Hollow, self-sufficient, proud of home and family. Amanda looked of sturdy stock, built from hard living. Most frontier women had little concern for their appearance, and came across as rough, but Amanda's dress, although threadbare taffeta, and her carriage, hinted at a previous life of sophistication. Lydia was a mystery. His aunt hadn't told him of her background or her race. Why would this white couple have an Indian for a daughter?

"I see he found you," Amanda said, glancing over her shoulder. "I thought you might like to serve our guest a piece of pie. Lunch won't be for a little while yet. I'm going to the smoke house, so keep an eye on this pot, will you?" Amanda hesitated before putting down her wooden spoon, as if she had second thoughts about leaving her daughter alone with him.

"Where's Papa?"

"He rode to the Smithy's to pick up some new hinges for the broken barn door." Amanda wiped her hands on her white apron and departed.

Joe was suddenly alone with Lydia Whitley.

Silence engulfed the place.

"I'll get some wash water." Her soft voice barely penetrated the silence. She poured fresh water into a porcelain bowl and handed him a clean cloth. When his hand inadvertently touched hers, she jerked back, then turned away and smoothed her hand along her apron.

When he finished washing, she took her turn and then served him a piece of apple pie. "How do you like your coffee, Mr. Brice?" she asked softly, her eyes downcast.

"Just black. And please, stop this mister stuff. Call me Joe."

He studied her while she stirred the pot. She wore an ill-fitting homespun dress of unflattering style. Only the apron tied around her provided evidence of the female shape he remembered. As he'd pulled her from the street, his hands had easily slipped around her slim waist. The severe knot of hair emphasized her pinched expression. Yet, her prominent cheekbones and full rosy lips revealed her undeniable beauty. Was her tall, straight stature from pride or self-confidence? Her skittishness hinted at something different. After he'd released her, she'd retreated, quick and agile, like a wild doe, captured and then granted its freedom.

"Aren't you going to have some pie?" he peered over his cup. Steam drifted upwards from the coffee. "It's very good. Your mother said you baked it."

"No." She kept her side toward him as she continued to stir the pot.

"You didn't bake it?"

"I baked it. I just don't want any."

Joe detected a momentary shift in her posture, as if hunching under the weight of his continued gaze. A knife twisted through him. He knew that dispirited expression. He'd seen it too often on his mother's face. She'd worn blisters on her hands by day as a washwoman, and worked herself to the grave serving drinks to men in the tavern by night. She'd been a beautiful woman before she'd been chewed up and spit out by an abusive husband. His father, Jackson Brice.

"Please," Joe said. "I can't enjoy this while you're standing over there with your total attention on that pot. Whatever's in there isn't going to scorch that fast. Sit down and join me."

Lydia shook her head.

"Have some coffee."

"I don't like coffee."

After serving herself pie, she plopped into the chair across from him. For a moment, their gazes met until she stiffened and returned her attention to the food in front of her. She cut a tiny piece with her fork and lifted it daintily into her mouth.

"How are you doing?" he asked. When she didn't answer, he continued. "You seem to be managing well after that man attacked you in the street." She had to be bruised and sore, although her movements revealed little discomfort. All morning, he'd wanted to question her, wondering how she could work with such vigor after receiving the vicious blows. How could she so easily disregard such treatment? And what about her parents? Did they provide no protection?

"I'm fine," she answered curtly and glanced at the stove.

"I wish I could have helped you sooner. Why was he beating you?" The man didn't have any authority over Lydia and now seeing her in this situation, in this cozy cabin with loving parents, Joe didn't believe she was a thief who had been caught stealing. Not that theft would justify her beating.

She seemed to withdraw even further from him. Her lower jaw thrust forward, her lips pinched. She hunched over her plate as if closing in on herself and to shut out the world. Joe said nothing while they ate a few more bites of pie, but he didn't want her to return to inward solitude.

"You'd be much prettier if you let your hair out of that severe bun and let it fall around your shoulders," Joe said.

A choke brought her hand over her mouth. She jerked to her feet so quickly the chair rocked precariously. She groped for the pitcher of water and a cup, coughing and splashing the fluid down the front of her dress before Joe could reach her.

"Are you all right?" he asked, handing her a towel.

"It was stupid of me," she croaked, dabbing at her bodice. She didn't meet his eyes. After she tended to her dress, she tossed the towel aside and returned to her place at the table. Joe politely waited for her to sit before he took his seat.

He continued his scrutiny. "How old are you?" There was much he wanted to learn about this curious woman. Her homespun dress and lack of shoes conformed to the local culture, but her quiet speech and proper manners conveyed intelligence that went beyond the locals' lack of sophistication.

"I don't know," she answered, without looking at him.

"You don't know?"

Lydia put down the bite she was lifting to her mouth and pushed away her plate. "I've had fifteen anniversaries, since they found me." She looked at him boldly, but her voice was almost inaudible. "I think I'm somewhere around nineteen or twenty."

Joe's eyes widened. "Nineteen or twenty?" She moved with the dexterity of someone much younger. "That makes you only about five or six years younger than me. I thought you were much younger, maybe fifteen."

"Fifteen? I assure you, I'm quite the spinster."

"So who found you? Edward and Amanda Whitley?"

"Yes." Lydia stood and returned to the pot on the stove.

"Tell me more."

"I don't remember any more."

"Strange," Joe said, studying her intently. "You don't look like Missouri Osage. Your facial features remind me of plains Indians-- Arapaho or Sioux maybe. Your height and slender bones…" She was the most intriguing woman he'd ever met. She aroused something deep inside him. Something he had never felt before, something that warmed his heart.

Lydia dropped the wooden spoon from between shaky fingers. Wringing her hands, she peered out the kitchen window. "I wonder what's taking Mama so long."

"Has no one ever told you that you're pretty?" Joe finished the last of his coffee and leaned back in his chair. "Perhaps if you smiled more." He hadn't meant to say that aloud. He'd only seen her smile once, and only fleetingly, when he'd returned her missing horse. He'd loved to see her smile again.

Lydia wheeled on her heels, fists clenched. She scowled at him. "And what do you know, Mr. Brice?" she lashed out.

"Call me Joe," he said as she scrambled toward the cabin door, brushing past her mother, who was returning with a hunk of salted pork.

His mouth curved in amusement. *She does have fire.*

CHAPTER 4

Early the following morning, the Whitleys were finishing up breakfast when a knock on the cabin door made Lydia jump. It was Joe. She glanced up at him bashfully, her heart catapulting as her father invited him in and Joe greeted the family. She was grateful that he was giving another day of much needed help to her father, but was relieved when he politely turned down her mother's offering of coffee and the two men quickly departed.

After meal clean up and starting the bread to rise for the day, Lydia performed her usual farm chores. It was late morning before she had collected a small sack of apples to take to Mrs. Applegate.

"Be sure to come back in the early afternoon," her mother said, as Lydia placed the cloth sack into her saddle bag and secured it onto the back of Sunshine.

"Yes, Mama."

She didn't like keeping watch on the time when she visited her friend. Lydia always found something that the feeble woman needed help with and she couldn't leave undone. Or Lydia would simply get caught up in one of Agnes's stories and lose track of time. She understood her mother's request. Lydia had a reputation of dallying longer than she planned, whether it was in town or visiting with her friend.

When she found the door to Agnes's cabin hanging open, Lydia's stomach went to her throat. Something was wrong. She dismounted Sunshine and did not bother to tether the horse.

"Mrs. Applegate!" Pricked with fear, Lydia rushed inside the dark cabin.

The woman would never leave her door open, even on a hot day. "Too many varmints," Agnes had often reminded her. If it weren't bears, cougars or raccoons searching for dinner, it was the flies or mosquitos searching for blood.

Lydia's eyes were beginning to adjust to the dim light of a single lantern when a large figure approached her.

"Go! We don't need you here." The woman growled and waved her flabby arms toward the door. Wilma Kincaid.

"I've come to visit." Lydia couldn't keep the fear from her voice. Not so much from the sudden appearance of Wilma Kincaid, but from the growing dread, that something was terribly wrong. "Mrs. Applegate!" She called out to the old woman. If all was well, her friend would greet her and scold Wilma.

When there was no response, Lydia scanned the room. The rocker next to the fire was empty and the rumpled bed clothes showed no evidence of occupancy.

In Lydia's urgency to push past the large woman and the kitchen table, she nearly stumbled over a firm, yet malleable object on the floor. Her heart leaping into her throat, Lydia bent down to discover Agnes crumpled up, right hip and elbow pressed into the floor.

"Mrs. Applegate. What happened?" She turned to the other woman. "Help me get her up!" *What was wrong with Wilma Kincaid? Why was she just standing there?*

"She's dead!" Wilma growled.

"She can't be." With rising panic and disbelief Lydia brushed the strands of long white hair away from the old woman's face to reveal eyes opened and unfocused. Her gnarled hand was cold to the touch.

"It's that poison, what done it," Wilma said, pointing to Agnes's body.

Poison? What was she talking about? Lydia then noticed the mug containing willow bark from her last visit, the mug shattered near the body of her friend, the bark scattered on the floor like dust. Lydia's throat constricted as she fought to hold back tears. Had Agnes collapsed from fever? Is that why she was reaching for the mug? Lydia should have checked on her sooner.

"It's willow bark. For the fever," Lydia said quietly.

She flinched as Wilma Kincaid snatched her upper arm, scraggly nails gouging through the thin fabric of her sleeve. Using her larger girth and brute strength, the woman dragged Lydia, still on her knees, across the plank floor toward the door. Lydia squirmed to stand, clawing at the hand that clutched her arm, but her feet got tangled up in the hem of her dress. A second later, as Lydia was being shoved outside, she grabbed the shredded doorframe, the skin ripping across her palm. She'd barely pulled back her torn hand when the closing door filled her vision.

Through eyes stinging with tears, Lydia staggered to where Sunshine was grazing on a green patch of ground. Drained of all physical and mental energy, Lydia strained to pull herself up on her horse. She slumped over the beast, wrapping her arms around Sunshine's neck and let the horse take her home. As soon as Lydia was near enough to her family's cabin, she slid from her horse and collapsed to the ground, gut wrenching sobs wracking her.

Joe found her. He bent down and leaned in close. "Lydia, what happened? What's wrong?"

Lydia palmed away her tears, unknowingly smearing blood from her hand onto her face. She looked up at him. "I don't need your help. Leave me alone," she choked.

She needed solitude in her aching grief, to wrap herself in a cocoon. She didn't need Joe standing over her, adding to her misery with the jitteriness he caused.

"You're hurt." He reached out to her check. Then he realized it was her hand that was injured. "We should get that cleaned and dressed. I've seen infections…"

"She's dead," Lydia ground out. "Agnes Applegate is dead."

"Who is Agnes Applegate?"

At that moment, her mother rushed from the house, wiping her hands on her apron. "Lydia, are you hurt?" she asked with alarm.

Lydia showed her mother the palm of her hand where she had ripped it open on the door frame. The pain of her physical injury was almost imperceptible compared with the anguish tightening like a noose around her heart. "Agnes Applegate is dead."

Her mother sucked in her breath, her hand flying to her heart. "Dear Lord, what happened?"

"I found her on the floor. Collapsed from fever..." Lydia broke out into sobs again. "I think... Why didn't I check on her sooner?" she cried into her hands.

"Did you leave her lying there? I'll get your father." Her mother took a couple of determined steps toward the barn.

"No!" Lydia shouted and pushed herself to her feet. "The Kincaids!" Then she fled away from the cabin and her mother and Joseph Brice.

She didn't stop running until she had passed through the floral meadow and reached her favorite spot on the edge of her father's property, where the wooden footbridge stretched over Possum Creek. The smell of damp loamy earth greeted her and the forest scooped her into its embrace. The birds and other little animals kept her company here. Unlike people who shunned her and made her feel alone, the animals were Lydia's friends. They did not care that she was an Indian.

Lydia ambled onto the old footbridge, knowing that each step could bring the bridge crashing into the creek. Frayed rope and broken boards needed replacement. It bowed beneath her weight. Lydia didn't care. She sat and dangled her feet over the water, desolation filling her. Face in her cupped hands, she wailed her grief until there were no more tears. Then she stared dry-eyed into the creek, watching a floating leaf journey along the gentle current toward the Mississippi and the sea. Somewhere in the overhead canopy of trees, a blue jay squawked.

A squirrel approached her on the bridge and sat down a few feet away, flicking its bushy gray tail and twitching its nose. She snatched up an acorn which had dropped onto the bridge and showed the tiny creature what she offered. The squirrel sat up, alert, front paws off the ground and eyed the acorn. Lydia lured the squirrel to her outstretched hand, where after seizing the acorn, the animal rolled it between tiny front paws to investigate the quality with teeth and tongue.

A twig snapped and frightened away the squirrel.

Lydia jerked toward the sound to discover Joe staring at her, legs spread in a relaxed stance, hands shoved into his pockets. Goose bumps prickled along her neck as a sudden breeze swept along the forest floor.

"How did you do that?" Joe asked with obvious amazement.

"You made him leave," she croaked, wishing more than anything to be left alone.

"I'm sorry. I didn't mean to frighten him. I can't believe that you fed a wild squirrel right out of your hand."

"You've been spying? How long have you been standing there?"

Lydia couldn't shake the unsettling feeling that this person had sneaked up on her, catching her unaware. What if it had been someone who meant her harm? What if *he* meant her harm? While she stared at him, her chaotic mind weeded through the possible dangers and whether she should flee in cowardice or self-protection.

He moved toward her and stumbled, the swaying bridge, obviously catching him off guard. It moaned and bowed under his added weight. He managed to sit next to her.

Too close.

"I've only been here a moment. I came to tell you your father left for your friend's cabin. He told me where I could find you."

Her father told him? This bridge was her private place. "There is nothing he can do. The Kincaids will take care of things."

"You mentioned the Kincaids earlier. I've heard that name before. They're the ones hosting the corn shuckin' in a few days."

"Wilma Kincaid was at Mrs. Applegate's when I found her. She blames me for the death." Lydia didn't know what made her blurt that out.

"Your mother told me Agnes Applegate was an old woman. Her health had been failing for some time. Why would this Kincaid woman blame you?"

"I don't want to talk about the Kincaids."

The direction of the conversation made Lydia squirm. It was humiliating to talk of how others shunned her or treated her cruelly because she had dark hair and skin and forced her to live in a sort of isolation. To protect her parents from the pain the knowledge would bring, Lydia hid much of the abuse from her parents. She made excuses for her injuries as clumsiness or simple accidents.

Lydia braced against the bridge with her hand and started to rise. She certainly did not want to discuss something so personal with this man. But Joe's strong fingers came around her arm and pressed her back down.

"Then we'll talk about something else." He looked at her without expression before pulling a black string from his pocket. "Licorice?"

"No, thank you."

While Joe pulled off a piece of licorice between his front teeth. Lydia turned her interest to the flow of water passing from under the bridge, hoping it would distract her from the man filling the space next to her. Several inches were between them, but Lydia could feel the heat emanating from his thighs.

Her mind drifted back to their encounter in her parent's kitchen, where she had wished he would choke on pie. Telling her she should smile more and let her hair down, while his eyes caressed her like fingers on naked flesh. The queasiness in the pit of her stomach had kept her from eating more of the pie. The blue tin plate, at which she'd stared only reminded her of Joe's blue eyes, studying her from across the table.

Even now, he continued to stare at her as though she were some newly discovered species. What had he said? Something about knowing Arapaho braves? Lydia knew that braves were Indian warriors. Joe had obviously seen others with copper skin and dark eyes. She'd never met a more exasperating man. And rude! He didn't know her, or her situation.

She swatted at a gnat, which approached her nose.

"Here. Wipe your face and tell me about Agnes Applegate." He handed her a handkerchief to clean away the blood and dirt and tears.

Lydia scowled at him and took the handkerchief. She cleaned her face and returned the soiled cloth before returning her attention to the passing current and a stick bobbing in the water. A second blue jay joined the squawking.

"Talking about her might help with your grief. I didn't have anyone to share my grief with when my mother died. I was alone with her, beside her bed. She said good-bye, said she loved me, and then closed her eyes and was gone."

"You saw your mother die?" Lydia swallowed a lump. "I can't imagine such a terrible thing as watching someone die."

"Yes. Such a thing can change a person."

Lydia thought she detected a catch in his voice. "What did you do then?"

Joe paused. His pursed lips and pulsing temples told her he was as uncomfortable talking about his past as she was about hers. "I was only eight. My father was away ... on business. I waited in the shabby little apartment we occupied, surviving as best I could. My mother kept a cookie jar hidden away with a small emergency fund. When the money was used up and the landlord kicked me out, I begged for a few odd jobs until my father returned from his long absence. We lived on the road as he pursued his business endeavors. Later, I traveled with my paternal grandfather, trapping in the mountains."

Lydia looked at him. "Your mother must have been young then; you being only eight. I'm sorry. At least Mrs. Applegate lived to a ripe old age." Lydia resumed her study of the creek as it played upon the rocks in the southward bend. "No one knew exactly how old, she always told people it was 'none a their business' and that a number didn't 'make no difference no how'."

Lydia paused, her mouth set in a fine line. "She was like a grandmother. She taught me about herbs and healing because none of her daughters were interested. Besides, they all got married and moved away. Mrs. Applegate told me stories of the early days when the area was raw and primitive." *And when white people lived in harmony with the native Indians.*

Several minutes passed. Joe remained planted alongside her, while Lydia silently dredged up memories of Agnes Applegate until the tears started to build and she was again sucked into the anguish of grief.

"She was so sick." Lydia drew in a quick, gasping breath, fighting to contain the tears. "I last saw her the day…" She turned to look at him. "The day you and I met. She was burning up with fever." Then the flood of tears came and she made a choked sound. "I should have checked on her again!" Struggling with a great panic to breathe, she sucked in several shallow, quick gasps. "Those stupid apples…" The words came out like cursing.

Joe's comforting arm came around her, and without even thinking, she slumped against his chest, raining tears to dampen his shirt until her sobs became a dry and hacking cough. Slowly she became aware of the solid footbridge beneath her, and her cramped legs and the aching back where Willie had struck her. When she heard the blue jay squawk and felt the rise and fall of the muscled chest beneath her cheek, the startling realization of how easily she had accepted Joe's comfort bolted her upright.

She needed to get away.

When she looked into his face, she knew she had erred. Her heart catapulted to her throat as the liquid pools of his eyes drew her to him. Calloused, gentle hands cupped her cheeks and wiped away her tears.

"I'm so sorry," he said.

He stared at her with an expression so tender Lydia shivered and her cheeks grew hot. She knew her pulsing temples were certain to betray her nervousness. How could she go so quickly from sorrow to this? What was this she was feeling? She had no name for it. The sudden upsurge of excitement was both exhilarating and terrifying. Drowning in the depths of his eyes, the forest and the sound of rushing water disappeared. He filled her senses with maleness and licorice and the raw heat of his flesh.

Then his mouth touched hers. It was warm and moist, and the contact startled her. She pulled her lips away, but remained close enough for their noses to nearly touch.

"Wha… what are you doing?"

"Kissing you." His lips tickled hers as he spoke. And then his mouth covered hers again and his hands came up on her shoulders.

The contact stirred something deep and alarming. Like white lightening, liquid fire burned a trail along every nerve to her core. The few men who had dared to force their mouth upon her, did so as an act of violence, for power. How could her body react to Joe with anything other than revulsion? How could she yearn for more of him?

A rush of pure terror shot through her and she jerked away, pushing herself to her feet.

Joe raised his arms in a kind of surrender, as she passed along behind him to stand on the bank. He was slower to get to his feet.

Arms in front of her, poised for defense, Lydia contemplated her best way of escape. Her feet cautiously sought softer ground as she backed away from the bridge and away from Joe. When her bare heel came down on a sharp rock, she nearly tumbled before quickly regaining her balance. She was adept at such moves.

Joe finally stepped toward her. "I'm sorry. I'm not going to hurt you." Ropes and wood of the old bridge creaked a warning under his shifting weight.

Lydia wondered if she could outrun Joe and lose him in the woods. He did not know these mountains or the terrain as well as she did. Then there was the water. Could he swim? She snatched up a meaty tree branch and swung it threateningly like a club.

As he looked at her with a mix of hurt and surprise, she continued to wave the club in front of her as if it were protecting against the man rather than from her own body's treacherous yearnings. How could a simple kiss have ignited such a fire inside her?

She dropped the club and fled.

"Lydia…" he called into the wind.

***

Applesauce kept Lydia occupied the next day. She slipped out of the cabin before dawn to attend to her farm duties. She had a breakfast of eggs and bacon prepared before her mother and father arose, which was well before Joe arrived to resume the repairs to the barn. She was grateful to spend her day inside or close to the house, helping her mother peel apples and hoped the activity would keep her mind away from the death of her friend and away from Joe.

But just the knowledge of Joe's close proximity was a distraction. Several times she caught herself looking out the kitchen window, hoping to catch a glimpse of him at work, until her mother scolded her for not paying enough attention to the apples and removing too much fruit along with the peel. When Lydia missed an apple with her knife and sliced her thumb, putting a short halt to her work, her mother admonished her for her carelessness.

At the mid-day meal, Lydia made excuses for not joining her mother and the men, choosing instead to gather some wild onions from a patch in the meadow.

Alone, under an oak tree, she devoured an apple, a few bites of bread and some goat's cheese. The pungent cheese, aged perfectly, reminded Lydia of Gertie, and of the wonderful milk she gave. Three days had passed since Gertie had been swallowed up by the forest. Lydia fought back tears as memories of her sweet tempered goat added to her melancholy.

After a week of her father being pulled from his normal farm duties to repair the barn, Lydia could finally relinquish the extra chores she had taken on as a result. When Esther Crenshaw stopped by with two bushels of green beans on her way to a quilting bee with her mother, Lydia took a break from heavy farm work. But Lydia would not be attending the bee.

Lydia had quit participating in such social events years ago. The rare times she had let her mother talk her into attending one, the intense atmosphere had been unmistakable. The discomfort of the other attendees had been reflected in awkward and mundane topics of conversation. Lydia hadn't imagined the sighs of relief when she and her mother departed. The gatherings had not been a relaxing time of gossip and camaraderie as her mother promised.

Lydia had more pressing tasks ahead of her than a quilting bee with gossips. She decided to ride to Mrs. Applegate's to retrieve what cache of herbs she could. Since no one else knew their purpose, they would surely be discarded. The woman had no family in the area, so within a few weeks her belongings would be picked over and come winter, a squatter would more than likely take up residence.

When Lydia arrived, the home site was deserted. No smoke wafted from the chimney to greet her. The cabin door had been pulled closed as much as possible, with a gap on top, hanging at an angle on a rusty hinge. Inside, the cabin was stone quiet. No squeak from Agnes's rocker. No mound beneath the bed quilts. Except for the remnants of the shattered mug having been swept away, the contents of the cabin remained untouched.

The ashes in the fireplace were cold and gray. Without a fire, there was no sense of life in the place, except for a trail of mouse droppings around the crusty bread, green with mold. She glanced past the once fragrant lavender, now dry and brown and wrinkled her nose at the abandoned pot of congealed stew. Although the cabin was warm, Lydia shivered. A feeling of cold and death seeped into her bones.

She stuffed as many of Agnes's medicines and storage pots as she could carry into her saddlebags, only passing on those rarer items for which she had little or no knowledge. She regretted not having devoted more time to learning about healing. For Agnes, doctoring had been a gift.

She knew how to bring life into the dyeing and knew little-discussed secrets of how to prevent pregnancy.

Lydia's lip quivered as she took one final look into the cabin and closed the door behind her. She loaded up Sunshine before strolling to the Applegate family cemetery where Lydia found what she expected, a fresh mound of dirt atop the hill overlooking Possum Creek.

The community had wasted no time putting the woman to rest alongside her husband, Charlie, who had died some twenty years earlier of a cougar attack. Lydia counted eight graves. Agnes would be pleased at the speed of her burial. She had often expressed distain at how the community could make a mockery of death, everyone attending the funeral, whether or not they knew the deceased. Attendees would come to eat and drink and sell their wares.

Lydia knelt over the fresh mound of dirt, a brief smile coming to her face as she remembered Agnes's sunny laughter and toothless smile. Always feisty. Not long ago she had been strong and robust. Although her face had turned pale and drawn, her body shriveled and frail, her courage and determination had never diminished. In the end, the fiercely independent woman had been unable to help herself. All of the known herbs and treatments had done nothing to improve her condition.

Lydia wiped away the tears that had trickled down her cheeks and turned away.

Gone was the last pioneer.

***

Lydia was pulling the last steamy pie from the oven when her mother returned home. The aroma of baked apples, cinnamon and nutmeg filled the cabin. "Those smell wonderful," her mother said.

Lydia agreed. No smell was more comforting than that of fresh baked goods, except for the aroma of vegetable soup welcoming her inside on a dreary winter day.

"Did you have a good time with your friends?" Lydia asked.

"Yes. The quilt is progressing nicely." Her mother hung her shawl on a peg alongside the door. "Peggy Sue Phillips is expecting her third child. Allison Kincaid Seavers announced that her year of mourning her husband, Derek is over."

That meant Allison, who was close to Lydia's age was available for a second husband.

"Seems like just last week when Derek died… and losing everything in that awful housefire. Betsy's mother announced her daughter's engagement to Claude Fields. Don't know what she sees in that lazy man." Her mother leaned a palm against the table, as if to brace herself from a sudden fatigue or the ache of her own aging. "Thirteen and already engaged."

Until that moment, Lydia hadn't paid any mind to the drawn expression on her mother's face, the pinched mouth, the wrinkles around her eyes. "Each year the brides seem to get younger and younger."

Whether deliberate or not, her mother's words stung. As the brides got younger, Lydia got older. And with each passing day, her choices narrowed. Women in the Ozarks usually married well before the age of eighteen, quickly filling a modest cabin with their own brood, continuing the cycle of eking out a living in the harsh mountains. The lucky ones moved from the hollow, maybe east to a city to make their future.

There were even less choices for a woman in Lydia's position, an adopted Indian daughter of a poor farmer. Of course Lydia wanted a husband and a family, but as long as she remained in Possum Hollow, she could never marry and start a family of her own. Lydia wanted to believe Mrs. Applegate's words of encouragement, 'You've got lots to offer a man. You're good-hearted and mighty purty. Hard workin' too'.

But there would never be a quilting bee for Lydia.

No man wanted an Injun for a wife.

CHAPTER 5

It was dusk when Joe and other neighbors trickled onto the Kincaid homestead. Dew had cooled and refreshed the air like a cleansing spring rain. The once brilliant sun, now a ball of muted orange, hung lazily above the horizon in a gray and foggy sky. Dogs ran between legs and nipped at ankles, their echoing bays filling the hollow. Laughter and conversation met Joe's ears.

The corn shuckin' was the last large social event before winter. Participants had every intention of enjoying it to the fullest, to renew and seal old friendships. Whole families arrived by wagon, with babies swaddled in blankets. Some children fussed and clung to their mother's skirts while others, such as a group on a grassy area, joined their friends in chase or kick ball.

Joe's aunt and uncle, who arrived by wagon, parted ways; Esther to her tight knit group of women, Amos to join the men. Joe followed his uncle after corralling his horse. Already, the whisky was being passed among the guests, who swigged directly from the jug. Even the women indulged.

Joe learned that a variety of activities followed the work of shuckin' the corn. There were kissing games, arm wrestling, log sawing contests, foot races. Fights often broke out and made a source of entertainment and cheering. Despite some protests, a few neighbors arrived with chickens equipped with spurs to gamble on the cruel sport of cockfights.

Joe's uncle had told him that the corn shuckin' was a contest and that competition was fierce. The first team to shuck all of the corn in their pile and toss it into the crib won. Before the contest began, the team captains alternated in selecting members for their team. Those who were known to shuck corn the quickest or could cheat most effectively were selected first. To be selected first was an honor. Joe, an unknown, was one of the last to be selected – just before a couple of scrawny youths.

The women did not participate in the process of selection or in the shuckin'. Neither did the host. They stood on the sidelines to cheer for their favorite participants.

Before the pistol recoiled, signaling the race to begin, a rush of bodies dived into the two piles of corn. Young boys, striving to be the best, to one day be chosen first to join a team, moved with speed and agility. Hands, agile from seasoned expertise stripped off the ripened coverings to bare the yellow ears. Fine strands of corn silk floated in the air. Women and children strained their throats to cheer on their favorite team. Voices carried for miles, echoing throughout the hills.

Unlike the locals who cared about winning and rank, Joe didn't take the competition seriously. Because competition was fierce, with a person's reputation being at stake, cheating was intense. Joe chuckled as he witnessed numerous participants on both teams casually toss un-shucked corn into the crib or the competitor's side.

Joe stripped off a dried husk and threw another ear into the crib. Already sweat dripped from his brow. Husking corn was strenuous, especially at the required speed. "Hey!" someone shouted from behind Joe. "I saw you toss that over here!"

Thinking he was being accused of cheating, Joe jerked his head around to confront the man.

"I ain't no cheat!" someone shouted back.

"Liar!"

Joe watched his teammate shove the other backwards, beginning the brawl. No one bothered to halt the exchange of blows as the two men tumbled into the pile of corn. The cheers of the crowd intensified with the added entertainment.

Joe stole another glance into the crowd, wondering where Lydia might be. He hadn't spoken to any of the Whitleys since arriving with his aunt and uncle, having been swept immediately into the melee and team selection. The last he had seen of his uncle, he was wiping his drippy chin after gulping back a swig of local whiskey. Joe had nearly choked on the poisonous fluid that burned a trail of fire down his gullet.

Mindlessly, Joe picked up another ear and stripped it clean. Paying little attention, he almost tossed away the ear, like the countless others, until he noticed its small size and strange reddish color.

"Hey," the young man next to him nudged his elbow. "You best put that in your pocket, so's the others can't see."

"What?"

"Put that away. Some other feller might steal it. Don't you know whoever has luck enough to find a red ear gets his choice of the women? For the dancing, that is." He winked.

Joe raised an eyebrow. "The choice of anyone?" His uncle hadn't explained this idiosyncrasy of the game. A doe-eyed young Indian came to mind.

"That's right, any gal. Can even kiss her if'n you want to." The teammate's grin revealed a missing front tooth.

Joe smiled and stuffed the ear into his pocket.

"If'n I was you, I'd take that Seavers gal. Ain't no man who don't want under her skirts."

"Seavers?"

"Allison Kincaid Seavers, the redhead. Her year of mourning her husband is over; she's a bitch in heat."

Joe smiled with amusement as he remembered the exuberant woman who'd deliberately bumped into him his first day in town. Her approach had been anything but subtle, swooping in on him like a vulture on carrion. He'd witnessed it many times, lips parted, darting tongue of invitation. "Yeah, we've met."

Their team captain shouted for them to get back to work, so the two men resumed their neglected duty.

***

Meanwhile, Lydia stood in a small stand of trees watching the activities and then the celebration of the winning team. Any closer than fifteen or twenty yards away, she risked being seen. Small bright fires encircling the area illuminated individual faces. The winning captain was lifted onto the shoulders of steady teammates and carried through the uproarious crowd. She spotted her father standing nearby, swigging from a jug of whiskey. This was one of the rare occasions when he indulged in drink.

Lydia was filled with unexpected pride that Joe was on the team celebrating victory. Then as quickly, her joy deflated. Allison stepped from the crowd, her focus clearly on Joe. She was the most sought after woman in Possum Hollow. No one had a fairer complexion or more perfect curves. Hair of fire, burned in flames across her shoulders. Even at a distance, Lydia could see Allison touch Joe on the arm as she spoke and leaned into him so closely that her breasts brushed him. With a lusty grin, he regarded her cleavage for longer than was appropriate. Lydia's heart constricted.

With the crowd breaking up from the center of activity, hiding would become more difficult. She left her place of darkness under the trees to weave her way among the shadows of the outbuildings. The barn in sight, she nearly stumbled into a couple of burly men in what had become more than a wrestling match. She swallowed a gasp and jumped backward after recognizing Willie Kincaid, who was pounding his frustrations into the man who lay curled up at his feet.

Lydia found her way to an empty stall with the help of firelight filtering in between the slats of the barn. She sat down with legs crossed in the sweet smelling hay alongside the basket of food she had stashed. She would eat supper while her mother and the other women served up the burgoo, a stew like dish, prepared from a conglomeration of meats and vegetables, contributed by the guests. As much as Lydia would like to sample the burgoo, she would rather eat alone than endure the hostile environment her presence created. Or worse, allow her mother to witness the situation.

Lydia withdrew a hunk of ham, cheese and corn bread, remnants from the previous evening's supper. Breaking off a piece of bread, she took a bite of what remained of Gertie's cheese, resigning herself to never seeing the goat again.

She washed down the food with a swallow from a skin of cider before switching to more pleasant thoughts of contests and activities that would take place that evening. She never got very close to the games, but she watched the dancing and listened to the lively music, which always lightened her spirit.

After having her fill, Lydia crept outside, on alert and ready to evade anyone who might cross her path. While she flitted in the shadows between activities, few people she encountered paid her any attention or were too drunk to follow through on any threats. Several little boys threw handfuls of stones at her, but she managed to skitter away from them without harm.

Lydia found Joe at a shooting competition with a group of young women surrounding him. They pushed and shoved one another to get closer to this newcomer, like fresh meat tossed to the wolves, to attract his attention. Officiants scolded the disruptive women, warning them to keep their distance from the shooting range. Joe obviously relished the attention; his gaze and roguish smile seemed to linger on each of the women and he laughed at their jokes. Lydia tried to shrug off the growing jealousy. Would he pair-off with someone this evening? The idea chafed her. She knew she shouldn't care. Any man who ogled women as he did was not a gentleman.

***

Allison Kincaid Seavers stood on the sidelines boiling with outrage. How could these plain, shapeless females, in their worn linsey-woolsey dresses, think Joseph Brice would accept their offers in the kissing game, after *she'd* been rejected? Allison had taken extra care in primping for the evening, donning her best calico, the green accentuating the color of her eyes. She had curled her hair and left it to hang in a flirtatious length, rather than pulled tight at the nape or hidden under a bonnet. Yet she had elicited no special attention from Joseph Brice.

She tried to shake off the sickening vision of him cleaning the face of the Whitley Injun, while her mud soaked dress pressed intimately into his chest. Gun fire had pulled Allison from inside the General Store to its front window in time to witness the newcomer scooping up Lydia from where she cowered in the quagmire, like an animal.

He'd cradled her in his arms with such unmasked tenderness that Allison's stomach had bottomed out. His hands moved along her back with seemingly sensual familiarity, the pulsing movements of his fingers like caresses. For the Injun to receive such attention from this magnificent, well-carved man was perverse.

Allison was standing on the sidelines trying to imagine Joe's hands moving along her own back, when the starry-eyed Jimmy Evers invited her to join him at the edge of the wood. She agreed. She'd show that Joseph Brice how much other men wanted her.

After Jimmy sat down with his back against a tree, Allison joined him, sitting between his outstretched legs, her back turned toward his chest. She closed her eyes and sighed as Jimmy began his routine of unbuttoning the front of her dress so he could fondle her breasts. When his hands slid over her shoulders and across her upper back, she gasped.

"God, no," the low timber of his voice showed concern. She flinched as he eased down the neck of her dress and stared at the welts across her back. The heat of shame rushed over her. It wasn't the first time Jimmy had discovered evidence of her beatings, but the shame of their discovery never went away.

"Your brother?" Anger put an edge to his voice.

"Half-brother." She wouldn't allow the tears to form.

Jimmy kissed the smooth skin between the welts. More than once over the years he had threatened to kill the man, for what he did to her. Then she'd married Derek Seavers, a newcomer to the area, who within a matter of weeks had pulled her from her situation.

Allison had courted many men before marriage, always returning to Jimmy. After two serious relationships that ended in rejection, a new determination had filled her. From then on, she would do the jilting. She would not be the victim. She would be the puppeteer and they the marionette.

With seduction and whispered promises, she lured men in and then left them begging and wanting, the sadistic satisfaction fueling her need for control. Her reputation of being loose was actually false. Few she granted more than a kiss. Men bragged of being beneath her skirts, until no man could admit having been denied.

None knew Allison better than Jimmy, including her late husband Derek. No other had Jimmy's privileges. He was a tall scrawny thing, rather plain looking, with dull brown hair. She and Jimmy had grown up together, practicing on one another and awakening early sexual desires.

Distracted by thoughts of how to ensnare Joe, Allison gave little if any response to the young man, who nibbled her neck and teased her nipples between his fingers. *Short of swooning at Joe's feet…*

"Stop it!" she scolded when Jimmy tried to reach under her dress. Somehow he had managed to wad it to her knees.

He pulled his hands away from her. "What's a matter with you? It ain't no fun if you don't writhe and groan."

"What do you mean? Ain't nothin' the matter." She tossed back a handful of curls in a gesture of defiance.

"Why ain't you lettin' me touch you?"

Allison shoved her skirts back over her legs.

"What you doin' now?" he whined.

"What's it look like?" she snapped. "I'm leavin'."

"Leavin'?"

Allison stood up to finish buttoning her dress.

"Then why'd you meet me here, if you ain't gonna let me finish?" Jimmy's growl laid bare his ache of desire. "It's that Brice feller ain't it? That newcomer." He came to his feet and spat.

Allison felt her face warm with guilt. "Joseph Brice? What gave you that idea?"

"The way you been lookin' at him all night, like with Derek Seavers when he come to town. You only come here with me 'cause Joe wouldn't take you."

Allison slapped Jimmy across the face.

He grunted and snatched her arm as she attempted to slip past him.

"You know I love you, more than anything else," Jimmy said. "You walk now Allison, and you and me is finished." His normally warm liquid eyes had turned to ice. His face twisted into a snarl.

Fear, then fury swelled within her. She couldn't believe her gentle Jimmy was treating her so horribly. "Let me go! You're hurting me." She strained against the grip of his hand. "I'll scream."

When he thrust her away, she tumbled backwards and landed with indignity on her rump, legs splayed in front. Jimmy loomed over her, legs spread wide, fists clenched, his chest heaving from breathlessness. "Don't expect to come back to me!" I'm tired o' waitin' for you to love me. I ain't gonna be here for you no more." He stomped past her and out of sight.

Allison picked herself up and brushed off her dress. "Discard *me* will you? No one discards *me*."

His words cut deep. And his rejection hurt, as if everything in her life had been stripped away and she was alone in the world. She had always depended on Jimmy, but she could never marry him. He was a hillbilly. Same as all the others.

***

Lydia dashed across the grounds to hide against a small outbuilding, which was as close as she dared get to the area encircled with torches and covered with hay for the square dancing. Two locals were playing a fiddle and a banjo.

Lydia imagined that a handsome gentleman chose her from among dozens of young women to partner with him. She curtsied and graciously accepted his invitation. His face appeared from the shadows of her mind, strong square jaw set perfectly and eyes as blue as the daytime sky. They danced together expertly, lightly on their feet, as if controlled by some magical force. Spectators commented on what a fine looking couple they made.

With a start, Lydia realized her daydreaming had propelled her into the flickering light of torches, which were spreading like fingers across the grounds. She prayed no one had seen her making a fool of herself. A whimsical child with a make believe dance partner. Then, she noticed Joseph Brice standing alone in the crowd, apparently looking for something, or someone. When his gaze fell upon her, she sucked in air and slipped into the shadows, pressing her back against the building as if she could simply disappear. Heart racing, she wondered if he could hear the blood rushing into her ears. She prayed for him to pass.

"Hello, Lydia," Joe's deep voice greeted her.

She turned to find him standing within inches of her. A soft ray of moonbeam fell across his face. The urge to flee was instinctive and overwhelming, but she was paralyzed.

"I haven't seen you all evening." His voice was low and silvery. He pressed his elbow to the wall and leaned into her, magnifying his presence. "I was hoping you'd join me for a dance."

"Uh," Lydia stammered. It was if she had been punched. No one had ever asked her to dance, certainly never the most handsome and eligible man in Possum Hollow. Other women would be elated. But there was no way she was going to enter the circle of guests. "I can't."

"You have no choice," Joe said with a wry grin. "I was told I have the pick of any gal I want, and she can't refuse." With finesse, he withdrew the small red ear of corn from his pocket and presented it to her.

Lydia gulped. Joe was right. Although she never participated in the festivities, she knew the rules of the corn shuckin'. Just thinking of joining the others sent a cold chill of terror through her and made her shiver. "I can't dance."

"From what I saw, you do just fine." Joe's lips curved in amusement. He grabbed her right wrist and started to pull her toward the group of dancers.

When she resisted him, he stopped tugging on her.

"What will happen to my reputation if the others find out you refused me? I'll be the laughing stock."

Lydia stiffened at his humiliating blow. Would Joe be the laughing stock because an Indian had refused him, or because it was assumed no women could ever refuse him?

Turning on his heels, he urged her into the firelight and into the crowd of people. A tune was already in progress, so they would have to wait for the next one.

Lydia tried to cower away, breaking into beads of sweat as she tugged unsuccessfully to escape Joe's grip, working to pry off his fingers with her free hand. Her heart threatened to pound out of her chest, her blood pulsing with a deafening swish within her ears. The air was stagnant with sweaty bodies, and smoke and liquor. And somewhere nearby was the distinct odor of vomit. Waves of darkness like shutters crossed her vision, as if she were going to faint. When she opened her mouth to scream at this Joseph Brice, only a dry croaking sound came out. He didn't seem to notice.

From within the crowd, she heard the twang of Allison Seaver's shrill voice. "What a hoot. Joe is teasin' us by showin' up with that Injun."
Laughter broke out in the crowd.
"Which one of us gals are you really pickin'?" a female voice asked.
All eyes fell upon Lydia and Joe.
Then the fiddler stopped.

CHAPTER 6

"He's got a lot a nerve bringin' that Injun to the dancin'!" another young woman shouted.

"And how dare she accept him!"

It seemed that her presence was of most concern to the young women, who like a hive of bees swarmed outward from the crowd, their voices buzzing in Lydia's ears. The meaning of their words was incomprehensible. Distorted faces sneered at her.

"That savage ain't gonna be dancin' here!" Wilma Kincaid stepped forward from the crowd, her eyes flashing contempt at Lydia. "Not after she poisoned poor ole Agnes."

"Poisoned?" A handful of others chimed in.

"Mama, you never told us she was poisoned," Lucy Kincaid, the youngest of the clan said.

"That savage put some kind a dried up leaves in her mug," Wilma said.

"What the hell?" Joe's voice pulled Lydia from the turmoil of her mind and she stared at his lips curled back in revulsion.

How could Joe believe these women? After he had sat with her on the bridge and drawn out intimate, personal thoughts from her and let her grieve and wiped her tears? And… kissed her? She knew he was no gentleman, but to convict her without evidence. What a fool she had been, and weak, to succumb to his spell. To grant him access into the fortress she had so diligently built to protect herself from the world.

She was drowning, fighting for breath, still tugging against the grip of the monster who had dragged her into this nightmare. She dug deep within her being, against waves of panic and cold shaking dread to provide her own defense.

"I didn't poison her!" Lydia's voice came out shrill and otherworldly and she did not recognize it as her own. "It was willow bark..." the words faded into her throat as the returning grief and sadness for the loss of Mrs. Applegate sought to overpower her bravado.

"That black poison was spilt all over her." Waving her big flabby arms, Wilma turned to face the crowd.

"Hasn't Mrs. Applegate ever given you willow bark… for a fever?" Lydia's voice cracked with desperation to acquit herself. "Any of you?" She scanned the sea of faces.

The women looked at each other blankly, shrugged, and returned their stare at Lydia.

"Ain't heard o' no willow bark." The group's spokeswoman and Lydia's chief adversary stated matter-of-factly. Her mouth twisted into a sneer, proclaiming her superiority.

Could these women be that stupid? Either they were actually unintelligent and unaware of the mid-wife's healing herbs, or were cowards to risk opposing Wilma Kincaid. Lydia knew she could never win an argument with fools. Her shoulders slumped in defeat.

"She ain't welcome," Wilma Kincaid said crisply.

"What do you mean, she's not welcome?" Joe's deep voice held a challenge. His eyes narrowed.

A towering man with a jagged scar strode forward through the crowd, meeting Joe's challenge. The sight of Willie sent a shiver through Lydia. "Like Wilma said, the savage ain't welcome! Not at the dancin'." He spread his legs with hands on hips, daring Joe to argue further.

Joe released her wrist, which Lydia brought against her chest protectively, as if it were broken. She paused to stare at the crowd still watching her through the flickering lights of the torches. The invisible force of their accusations fueled with either stupidity, cowardice, or pure meanness drove her away.

She knew there was no use in fighting this terminal battle. Her whole body trembled. All energy had been sucked from her. These people would believe what they wanted or simply use the words against her. She turned her back to them and bounded into the darkness. Lydia sensed Joe following her. She ran like a gazelle, weaving her way between buildings.

When he caught up to her, Joe grabbed her arm and jerked her to a stop to face him. "What the hell's going on here?" His harsh words and tone showed no compassion for what he had subjected her to.

"You're hurting me," she said. "Let me go."

"Damn it!" he growled, and released her. "Is it always like this?"

Surely, he had to have known. How could he not have known? In answer, she blinked at the dark, shadowy face hovering within inches of hers. She would have recognized him even if he hadn't spoken. She breathed in his man scent of soap and sweat that was uniquely him. The heat of his body radiated outward to ease the chill of the evening breeze.

"Don't your parents know what's going on?" He continued to look at her, waiting for an answer. "Where the hell are they, anyway?"

She remembered seeing her Mama and Esther Crenshaw together a few hours back, but her parents and the Crenshaws always left after supper.

***

Joe's heart ached. She looked so vulnerable standing there, so alone. It suddenly dawned on him what she must have endured, not only during this one evening at the dancing, but over a lifetime. She had tried to tell him, as he'd pulled her into the crowd, in her shy way of self-protection, by holding hurtful words and thoughts to herself. As if by speaking them, she would acknowledge any truth they might contain and therefore, shame her.

What a cad he'd been, normally so observant, a skill required to survive alone in the wild open country. This quiet Indian maiden who should have only been a passing figment in this backwoods town distracted him and scrambled his thinking.

"I'm sorry, Lydia," his voice was almost a whisper. "If I had known…" He put his hands upon her shoulders, stared down into her face and breathed in the blend of sweet and earthy scents that was Lydia. Despite the sense that she might flee and disappear, he put his arms around her and drew her close. She melted into him, sliding her arms hesitantly around his waist.

Joe sighed, discovering more pleasure in her acceptance of his advances than he had expected. In turn, he tightened his grip on her, letting her know in no uncertain terms that he wanted her, that it didn't matter what others thought of her. He brushed his cheek along the top of her bonnet covered head and held her for a long while as both remained silent.

Then he released his hold on her and cupped her chin in the palm of his hands. Her breath wafted softly across his cheek as he gazed into her face, her eyes like deep shimmering pools reflecting the moon light. He knew the attraction was perilous, but Joe didn't hesitate to lower his lips upon hers. He heard her breath catch before their brief touching. Then her body tensed and she pulled away.

"Lydia, you don't have to, if you don't want to."

"It's that… Willie… he forced a kiss on me. He was vile and disgusting," her voice was a shrill thread of a sound.

The thought of anyone hurting her wounded him. He unconsciously clenched his jaw and tightened his hands into balls. With what little he had witnessed in the last few days, he could only imagine the nightmares that burdened her.

"Willie Kincaid. The man who beat you. Did he…"

She shook her head and wrapped her arms around herself protectively. "He tried to, but…" The look she gave him was a mix of gratitude and adoration.

Joe knew. He'd thwarted the attacker. He should have killed the man. Right there on the street. "Oh Lydia," he moaned and wrapped her in his arms. Her misery was so intense, he felt the pain as acutely as if he had taken a knife to his own gut. "You must know that a kiss or touch from a man can be a good thing."

"No. I don't," she confessed and pulled away. "I've never been kissed before, except for what Willie did."

If it weren't for the darkness, Joe was certain he would have seen her blush.

"Then let me show you that a kiss can be a pleasant thing."

As he took her into his arms again, she shivered, whether from trepidation or from the same exquisite expectancy which now commanded him. He could not be sure. She allowed him to kiss her, gliding his lips slowly over hers without much pressure, in unhurried sensuous exploration. Her frozen, motionless lips under most circumstances would have been considered a signal of unwillingness, but he knew her inexperience and uncertainty.

"Try moving your lips with mine."

Lydia tried, but was concentrating so much on what she was doing with her lips that her body remained stiff and inflexible. He slid his hands down her back and pulled her closer. When her firm breasts made full contact with his chest, Joe felt a tugging in his loins. Increasing his ardor with a roughness and hunger, he pressed his tongue against her clenched teeth, urging her to open for him. When no amount of coaxing dismantled the barrier, he pulled away slightly.

Lydia's eyes popped open, her lashes fluttering against his cheek, her lips quivering.

"Open your mouth some," he murmured.

Lydia grunted, "Uh, uh," and shook her head. "I can't."

He smiled into her eyes, until a lone tear trickling down her cheek made him frown.

"Please don't cry." He wiped away the dampness with an index finger. "I won't force you to do something you don't want to."

Her head tilted back and the tip of her tongue peeked from between moist lips. She stared at him through deep dark orbs, full of innocence and trust. He kissed her again, tenderly, their tongues touching slightly, until she slid her arms around his neck, molding her body to his, her mouth reaching. He slid his tongue along the fleshy inside of her upper lip, probing and toying, bringing a soft moan bubbling from her throat. She moved onto tiptoes and pressed herself closer to him.

Kissing Lydia was like tasting the sweet nectar of forbidden fruit. Her innocence and purity were more enticing to him than experienced women who flirted and clawed. Lydia was an unspoiled beauty, like a fresh, dewy rose. An attraction like no other. He eased her to the cool soft ground and laid her next to him. As his hands explored the hollows of her back, the rigidity ebbed from her body. She clung to him, arching her back, pressing her breasts into him. He took what she offered, cupping one in his hand.

"No. No more," she moaned breathlessly. She made a weak attempt to push Joe away. "This is wrong."

"Wrong?" His voice was husky. He was looking at her through eyes glazed soft with passion. "We're only kissing."

His mouth returned to hers, provoking a shudder from her. Then he traced along her cheek and down her neck, his tongue leaving a trail of steamy moisture that made her quiver. She tilted her head back, allowing him to nuzzle and bite her neck.

"To feel this way… it's sinful… it's savage."

"Whoever told you such a thing?" Joe nibbled at an exposed earlobe.

"I'm… I'm a lady."

"I know," he grinned. Then he kissed her lips, long and sensuously. After coming up for air, he said, "Why don't you tell me how you feel and I'll let you know if it's wrong."

"Huh?"

"What are you feeling right now?"

"All warm and tingly inside."

"That doesn't sound wrong or sinful to me. Does it to you?" Joe gently stroked her cheek. "I'll tell you a secret," he whispered. "I feel that way too."

Lydia's smile brought gentle laughter from Joe's throat.

"Joe? Is that you I hear?" A woman's voice wrenched the couple from their ecstasy.

Feet shuffling along the fallen leaves drew closer.

"Joe?"

Allison!

Startled back to reality, Joe released Lydia the same instant she scrambled backwards like a crab on her heels. Her eyes flashed shock and outrage, and she was panting. Her bonnet hung on the back of her neck. Locks of hair hung in wild disarray about her shoulders. Her swollen lips glistened in the faint moon light, betraying the heat of her desire. She'd never looked more irresistible.

As if slowly regaining sobriety, Joe stood with the stiffness of an old man, watching the ghost-like image flee into the darkness.

"There you are. I thought I'd seen you." Allison stopped alongside Joe with arms on hips, heaving breasts thrust forward. "You ain't danced with me yet."

CHAPTER 7

After a day of hauling and boiling water, and pounding soiled garments, Lydia's body ached clear to her toes. She'd thrown herself at a frenzied pace into the detestable chore of laundry, hoping that intense physical exertion would relieve her mental anguish. By late afternoon, she was totally exhausted, wanting nothing more than a hot meal and to crumple into a bed of soft quilts. The activity had done little to quell her tumultuous thoughts.

She'd spent a restless night tossing in her bed with visions of blue eyes and strong arms, reliving… In her dream, she'd clung to him, molding her body to his, arching her back, pressing her breasts into his cupped hand. His tongue and hands had been everywhere as if they had multiplied a hundredfold. And the more the strange and pleasurable throbbing between her legs intensified, the more she wanted!

She arose that morning, lips pink and swollen, aware of where every one of his fingers had caressed the contours of her hips and waist, the deep unceasing ache unsatisfied. How could she have allowed herself to be swept up in that wild alien force that had taken control of her body? To lay with a man in the grass and let him kiss her? Nothing she had seen or heard had taught her that passion was a virtue.

"A lady only kisses to please her husband," her mother had said often enough.

She'd behaved wild and savage. No different than a brood mare toward a stallion. It only proved what people said. No matter what her upbringing, Lydia could not be a true lady.

She had sought refuge from her shame in heavy chores. But not even isolation from her parents had eased her torture of self-deprecation.

Lydia tossed the last of the clean laundry into a basket when a man reined his stallion up alongside her. She didn't need to turn her head to recognize the rider or his mount. Her prickling nerves were an indication.

"Hello, Lydia." Joe slid from his horse.

Fear of betraying the strange ache of desire that smoldered deep inside her, she turned her shoulder to him and picked up the basket of laundry.

"Can we talk?" Joe wrapped his big calloused hands around hers and easily pulled the basket away. He set it on the ground in front of them.

Lydia snatched her hands away as if she'd been touched by a hot branding iron. She wanted him to touch her everywhere. And yet she didn't. "You shouldn't come here like this anymore," she said.

"Why not?"

"Because…" she fumbled for an excuse. She couldn't tell him she wanted nothing more than to have him hold her in his arms, to fan and extinguish the fire, that only he could have ignited and which she knew only he could extinguish. She couldn't tell him she didn't want to see him anymore because it hurt too much to be with him and to know he was leaving in a few months, and when he left for California her heart would break. "You've finished the repairs for my father," was her best excuse. Her gaze swept his face before she looked away.

Joe stood unmoving, staring down at her. "I wanted to tell you again how sorry I am for last night."

Her heart gave a queer lurch. "Sorry for what?" Sorry that he had dragged her to the dancing? Sorry that he had kissed her? Sorry that he had rejected her to slip away with Allison? Lydia couldn't be sure which cut more deeply, the shock of Allison's discovery or Joe's rejection.

"I guess I was too blind or too stupid… You tried to tell me. I shouldn't have insisted you join the dancing." Joe scratched his head as he searched for the words. "It's obvious now. Since last night. I've added a few things up. It can't be easy for an Indian to live in this backward society. People hate them here."

Lydia felt the blood drain from her face. Hearing Joe state the words so bluntly, stung her. Even the perceptive Agnes Applegate, who knew Lydia better than anyone else, had never been so direct.

"Have you ever thought of leaving Possum Hollow?" he asked.

Lydia took in a quick sharp breath and her body stiffened. When she didn't answer, Joe repeated the question.

Of course the idea had crossed her mind. Many times. She was from a poor family, with few resources or opportunity. And how could she abandon her parents to run the farm by themselves? They had done so much for her. "This is my home."

"Is it really your home? Are you content, happy here?"

Lydia frowned, not liking his implications. Long ago she had accepted her situation. Although, she was not of these people, the culture, the hills, and valleys around Possum Hollow, deep within the Missouri, Ozarks was all she knew.

"You're beaten, wrongly accused of a crime and bullied. I can only imagine the other humiliations. Your mother and father might be fooled, or refuse to see what's going on, but I'm not."

Lydia's face burned as if she'd been caught in a lie. Keeping secrets from her parents. Wanting to protect them from the same humiliation which she suffered. Goose bumps prickled along her arms until the intensity of Joe's gaze seemed to pierce through her flesh. Hoping to deflate the intense moment, she strolled to where his horse munched on fresh grass. "I don't think you've ever introduced me to your horse."

"I haven't? How shameful." Joe came alongside her and smiled. "His name is Zeus."

"He's a lovely horse." She had to reach up to stroke his nose. He was the largest, most muscular horse she'd ever seen. Joe's affection for him was obvious from the care he provided. The animal was always clean and brushed to a shine. "Zeus is the name of a mythical god, isn't it?"

"Yes, chief of the other gods. I named him for his strength and courage. He's gotten me through some pretty tough scrapes."

"You must love him very much." She wove her fingers through his silky mane.

"Yes, I do. He's my best friend." Joe patted Zeus's belly with affection. "At times when I'm alone on the prairie, or in the mountains with no other human being, Zeus is my only friend."

Lydia understood the sentiment, perhaps better than anyone else. She had often felt that way about Sunshine.

"You're quite good with him, you know." The curve of Joe's mouth held amusement. The usual roguish sparkle had returned to his eyes. "Zeus is normally very skittish around strangers. Would you like to ride him?"

Lydia jerked her hand back. "Oh no, I don't think so."

"I know he's tall. I'll ride with you and help control him until you get used to each other."

Accepting Joe's invitation was not a good idea. She'd promised herself to stay away from him. The more she saw of him, the more painful her life became. She bit her lip and stared at the beautiful horse with strong lines and sinewy muscles that mimicked his owner. To be able to control such a beast…

"You're not chicken are you?"

"Of course not."

"Then hop on." Joe patted the horse's back.

"All right. But first I have to hang up the laundry."

Joe agreed with a nod and his big sunny smile that warmed Lydia inside. Then he snatched up the basket of clean laundry.

Lydia thanked him in a soft voice, then took Zeus by the reins. He didn't hesitate to walk with her to the house where the sun shone along the fence line, where laundry was hung to dry. While Lydia tied Zeus to the hitching post, Joe withdrew a pair of trousers from the basket.

"What are you doing?" she exclaimed.

"I assure you. I'm completely competent." Ignoring her horrified expression, he shook out the trousers and hung them over the split rail fence. "I've done this many times."

"But…" Lydia couldn't tell him she was embarrassed to have him rummage through the family's things: nightgowns and petticoats and the like. She was probably being silly. It made her feel as though every bit of clothing she owned was in the basket and she were standing before him, stark naked.

He picked up a cotton dress and casually draped it over the fence.

Lydia decided it best to finish the job as quickly as possible. The easiest part of doing laundry was turning out to be the most unbearable. She dug into the bottom of the basket to retrieve a nightgown she didn't want Joe messing with and hung it alongside the dress.

Joe picked up her mother's petticoat and when Lydia glanced his way he held it in front of himself, making a curtsey.

"Stop that!" Lydia snatched the petticoat. "What would Mama think if she saw you?"

Joe laughed deeply. Then he picked up a flannel shirt and spread it over the fence.

As they were emptying the basket, her mother stepped from the house. "Lydia, who are you talking… Mr. Brice, I didn't know you were here. You should have come in to say hello."

"Hello, Mrs. Whitley," Joe grinned and tipped his hat.

"We… I finished the laundry," Lydia stammered. "I'll be in soon to help with supper. Joe… er Mr. Brice is taking me for a ride on Zeus."

"Zeus?"

"His stallion."

Joe led the horse to where Lydia stood. His hands came around her waist to lift her effortlessly and thankfully, sideways, as was proper for a lady, onto Zeus. She choked back an involuntary moan when Joe mounted behind her and pressed against her back. Why had she agreed to ride with him? She hadn't considered the lack of room for two. He now sat unsuitably close, his arm wrapped around her waist, and right in front of her mother!

As Joe clicked the horse forward, Lydia turned to wave good-bye to her mother, who did not return the greeting. Nor did she smile.

The thrill of being in Joe's arms distracted Lydia from the pleasure of riding Zeus. Each forward stride of Zeus drove Joe's man parts firmly against her and his arm tighter around her. They were so bonded that Lydia became convinced that surely there was no barrier of cloth between them.

When they arrived at Lydia's favorite meadow, Joe abruptly reined the horse to a stop and then hopped down. "It's your turn." He handed her the reins.

"Would you mind if I...?" Lydia hesitated. "I know it's not proper for a lady, but I'd like to swing my leg over."

Before she finished speaking, Joe was laughing at her.

She furrowed her brow. "What's so funny?"

"You," he said. "I wouldn't think you'd worry about what's "proper" right now. Last night wasn't exactly proper, nor is being here alone with me now. I'm surprised your mother didn't stop us." Joe continued to laugh. "I half expected to see daggers shoot from her eyes."

Lydia scowled. She threw her leg over the other side of Zeus to sit astride. An instant later, she was galloping into the woods, leaving an awestruck Joe in a whirlwind.

***

Joe had guessed at Lydia's skill, but seeing her dodge massive oaks with speed few could achieve was more than he expected. She was like a vision in a dream or something only to be imagined. He blinked his eyes and she was gone.

When Lydia re-entered the meadow, Joe was leaning against a maple tree, chewing a string of licorice. He restrained a gasp as the lovely figure, flushed and out of breath, halted before him, her dress hiked up to her knees to reveal shapely calves and slender ankles. Her long sleek hair tumbled around her to mingle with Zeus's mane. Her smile and lively dancing eyes sparked a flame inside him. Lydia was magnificently suited to sit atop the stallion. The radiant beauty was a far cry from the shy woman he'd first laid eyes on. She was utterly bewitching.

His eyes clinging to the vision, he stuffed the licorice into his back pocket and beamed with joy. While taking her hand and sliding his arm around her to help her down, the strangest feeling came over him. Should he sweep her into his arms or bow down and worship her? His hand lingered briefly at the small of her back.

"Zeus is the finest horse I've ever ridden." She giggled and hugged the horse's neck. Zeus nickered and nuzzled her in return. "Don't tell Sunshine I told you that."

"You've turned my stallion into mush," Joe declared. He loved seeing Lydia so carefree. And it was so rare. The bright, coy expression of any other woman would clearly have been construed as flirtatious. But Lydia was too innocent. She didn't know how she affected him.

***

"I must look a fright," Lydia ran her hands self-consciously along the folds of her dress. Why, when it never mattered before, was she suddenly concerned about her appearance? Maybe the way Joe's eyes roamed over her made her feel exposed. She started to coil up her hair. "It seems I'm always struggling to keep my hair tucked away."

"Don't." The word came out harsh as he reached out to stop her hand. "Please, I like it down." With his thumb he stroked her knuckles and her palm, made rough from farm work. He traced her earlier injury, its jagged edge slowly healing inward. Then he lifted her hand to his lips and kissed it lightly.

His touch was a seductive caress. She gazed at Joe with her heart in her throat and a knot in her stomach. Then she pulled her hand away.

His palm slid up her neck and settled along her ear. "Your hair is like silk," he said, curling his fingers into her hair.

The sound of the whippoorwill faded and the whole world disappeared except for Joe. His bright, lively eyes were so full of... longing? Did she see desire there? Her heart gave a rush and at the same moment, Joe's arms came around her and pulled her close against him. His manly scent of leather filled her nostrils. Then his warm moist lips were upon hers, jolting her as lips touched lips.

Lydia responded with an ardent pressure of her own lips and roving tongue. She slipped her arms around his neck, pulling his head down to her and molding herself to him. Each time they kissed was better than the last and her passion, like a geyser gushed more freely. Oh, how she wanted him.

Then, Joe pulled his mouth away from hers and a chill rushed crossed her face and pulled her from her euphoria.

"Lydia," he murmured breathlessly, "come to California with me." His whisper-soft words were urgent and did not disguise his passion.

"California?" It took Lydia a few moments to churn the meaning of what he was asking. Could she hope that he felt the same growing attraction she felt for him: that he needed her more and more each day; that he couldn't leave her? Could Joe be the man she had always dreamed of? She dared to ask. "Why do you want me to go to California?"

"Haven't you ever wondered about other places?"

She should have expected no other answer. Not wanting to reveal the pain she knew was in her eyes, Lydia pulled from his arms and turned away. "I've never left Possum Hollow. I know no place else."

"Surely you've wondered about Indians or where you were born, how they live?" Joe turned Lydia around by the shoulders to look at her face.

"Of course." She hungered for the truth about Indians. Not words of hate.

"Now is your chance Lydia. I can show you all that. West of Missouri is a big wide world, full of adventures. I can take you to new territory where people aren't so judgmental and are more accepting."

Could Joe be right? Could this be her chance? How could she trust him? She had reason to trust few. And he had said nothing about his feelings for her. He certainly couldn't expect her to travel as his companion, unwed? That would be unseemly. What did he expect of her?

"Possum Hollow is my home."

"No, Lydia. You don't belong here."

"Who are you to know where I belong?" She snapped. *Why was he doing this?* She wanted to shut him out.

"I know your situation here is little better than miserable. Why won't you admit it? You have no future here. You're a woman, yet you live more like a child. You deserve better."

"You do not know what I deserve." She tried to pull away from him, but his grasp on her shoulders was too tight. "I have copper skin and black hair. I am Indian. I am loathsome."

"Is that what you think, that you are loathsome? You are Indian, but you are not loathsome. If only you knew how…" his throat tightened as he stared down at her. Then he released her and stepped back, as if he too believed her words. "I've got some business in Independence this winter." The muscle of his jaw tensed as he spoke. "I'll be leaving in a couple of days. Think on what I've said. Talk with your parents while I'm gone."

His words cut deep and ripped open secrets she had kept hidden. The words and actions of others had helped to form her. She could not be so easily remolded, her path not easily changed.

CHAPTER 8

The pungent odor of sweat and tobacco greeted Joseph Brice and Amos Crenshaw as they entered the dingy saloon. They wove their way past the scattering of spittoons to join Edward Whitley who was seated at a crudely built table. A couple of men in dusty, sweat stained clothes were leaning against the bar engaged in conversation.

Amos introduced his nephew to the stocky, balding proprietor, Chester Curtis, who made a point of meeting everyone in the community. The man served up the usual whiskey for Amos and with a nod of approval from Joe, poured him the same.

The liquor was strong and warmed a path down Joe's throat, catching him off guard. He'd expected some cheap watered down version of liquor masquerading as whiskey.

"So, you're that nephew who's leading a caravan to California," Chester said. "Amos, you're really serious. I figured you'd come to your senses by now."

Amos glared at the man's back as he turned to attend another patron settling in at a table.

"By the way," Amos turned to Edward. "We checked out that story we heard at the corn shuckin'."

"What story?" Edward tossed back the remainder of his drink.

"About the Smithy seeing a goat wander into town," Joe answered.

"Oh. That story." Edward rubbed his forehead. "I don't remember much of last night. Got a bodacious headache."

"Turns out, the smithy saw a lamb, not a goat. Anyway, he and his wife had lamb chops that evening for supper," Amos said.

"Dagnabbit! That goat cost me a heap o' corn." Edward pounded a fist into the bar, the alcohol revealing itself.

"We asked around. No one's seen the goat." Joe wanted to witness the smile that would light Lydia's face if her goat were returned.

"Somebody probably made goat chops outta Gertie anyway," Edward said, before shouting at Chester for another round of drinks.

"You oughta pack up Amanda and Lydia and get outta this stink hole," Amos suggested.

"You know how I feel about leaving," Edward scowled.

"Listen. I'll be selling out in the spring. No reason you can't too. Right, Joe?"

Edward gulped down his drink in one swallow. "You're in your fifties. A man your age shouldn't be traipsing around the wilderness. Younger, stronger men," his voice thickened, "drown in rivers."

"Yes, your brother. Raft got swept up in the Arkansas rapids and pulled under. I'm sorry. But we ain't goin' on the Arkansas. 'Sides we've got Joe here." He threw his arm around Joe's shoulder in a fatherly embrace and grinned.

Joe thought his uncle sounded as if he were proud of him, but in those days of living with his father and later with his paternal grandfather, Amos hadn't been proud enough to claim Joe as his nephew. And where was his uncle during those years of Irene's suffering at the hand of a gambling, womanizing husband?

"After my sister Irene passed – God rest her soul – Joe was practically raised in the Rockies, trapping with his grandfather, Augustus Brice. Joe knows the passes. He'll get us through."

Joe's fingers knotted around his whiskey glass. "I was never much of a fur trapper. After Grandfather died, I worked at Fort Kearney running the travel register for a while, giving out directions and what not." There was no need to mention the period he spent with his father on less legitimate business. The years he wanted to forget.

"You've made no mention of a wife or children," Edward looked at Joe . "A young man like you should be settled down. Not helping gray haired men sow their wild oats."

Joe chafed. He didn't need to defend his way of life. He'd also tried to talk his uncle out of the mission. "He's left me no choice. Over the years,

I've rescued dozens of emigrants who'd been led astray on nonexistent short-cuts by some self-proclaimed expert who'd never stepped west of Missouri. I've seen many die of starvation. Aunt Esther deserves better." He frowned at his uncle for putting him in this awkward position: for leaving him no choice. For putting him in the middle of a conflict with his friend.

"See, even Joe agrees. I've read news stories about little children getting squershed under wagons or buffalo stampedes. When supplies run out, families eat insects or acorns."

"Ain't nothing here for me no more," Amos answered. "I'm tired 'o working my fingers to the bone in this mountain rock, and gettin' nothing better for it. Now, I can buy me some land in that there fertile, Sac-something valley."

"Sacramento Valley," Joe said.

"Yeah, Sacramento. That's it."

Joe swigged the last of his whiskey, but the fluid was ineffective at easing the bitterness of the dispute. Then he tossed a coin onto the table.

"Where you going?" his uncle asked.

"I'm going to see if I can find that goat." It was a ridiculous excuse to leave the place. He'd no sooner turned to leave than Edward tossed out stories of the Donner party snowbound back in '46 turned cannibals. Joe sighed with relief when Edward and Amos's voices faded into the din of the saloon as he stepped outside.

Outside the dark and stuffy saloon, the sun shone brightly, although a chilly wind was kicking up some debris. Joe squinted his eyes to protect them from the intense light and from the swirling dust, so he didn't see the young woman approach him.

"Howdy Joe," the sweet, fluid voice startled him. "I was thinkin' that was your stallion I saw."

Joe managed to open his eyes to a pinhole and caught a glimpse of her wild mop of red hair. There was no missing the identity. "Hello." He tried to keep the irritation from his voice. He was in no mood for conversation with the flirtatious Allison.

"I hear you been looking for a goat," she said with a purr.

"Yes. Have you seen it?" He sounded too eager.

"There's one out at my Pa's place. Wandered in a few days ago. Come look at it yourself. I'll be in Pa's barn after supper."

"How about tomorrow morning instead?" That would give him time to find out what the goat looked like. Maybe bring his uncle in on it.

"Can't." She turned in a movement to scamper away. "Pa's gonna shoot him." She tossed the words over her shoulder.

As the day wore on, Joe debated about forgetting the errand. He knew it would be a foolish waste of time. But he couldn't erase the image of bringing a smile to Lydia's face when he reunited her with the goat. When last they departed, Lydia's eyes had been dark and shadowed with pain, her lips pressed into a tight line. If there was any hope of finding the goat, he had to go to the Kincaid's.

Joe was unable to talk to his uncle about his thoughts on the missing goat because the argument with Edward had left him short-tempered. Then after supper, Amos complained about his rheumatism and went to bed early. So, when Esther settled in to her sewing beside the fire, Joe made excuses to leave without the discussion he had planned.

"Where are you going at such a late hour?" she asked.

Although Joe welcomed the warm bed and hot meals his aunt and uncle provided, he couldn't remember the last time when he'd had no sense of freedom or had his comings and goings questioned.

"I won't be out late." The confinement was making him want to crawl out of his skin. Evenings spent gathered around a fire in a tiny cabin only increased his restlessness. The outdoors was his living space, the stars his nightlight.

Joe rode Zeus at a brisk pace in the growing darkness, both breathing hard when they arrived at the Kincaid's. Dark and quiet, the place looked eerie without the crowds gathered around torches or the sound of laughter at the corn shuckin'. Except for the dim light shining inside the cabin and a waft of smoke from the chimney proving occupancy, Joe would have thought the property currently vacant. He reined up near the barn, as a couple of sleepy hounds yawned and ran up to meet him.

"Hello boys," Joe said, slipping from his saddle. He let the dogs sniff his left hand while he slid his right over the butt of his gun, an unconscious act of reassurance. The weapon was secure in the holster and at the ready. If fired upon, Joe had little recourse. Even with Allison's invitation, his presence there could be construed as trespassing.

The hairs on the back of Joe's neck prickled, encouraging him to leave. This situation wasn't right. Halfway to the Kincaids he'd almost turned Zeus around. He didn't understand his compulsion to reunite Lydia with her goat. Nothing else seemed to matter except seeing her face light up. Nothing would give him greater joy at that moment.

A few steps from Zeus, Joe considered just walking up to the cabin and knocking. There was no need for this clandestine stuff. When he heard a shrill cry coming from the barn, he returned his attention there. *Was the sound human or animal?* Whatever it was, it sounded as if it was in pain.

Joe entered the barn via a creaky door, which set his nerves on edge. The animals, bedded down for the night, snorted and stirred at his entry. The sweet smell of fresh straw mingled with the usual odor of animals. All else was still and silent in the dim glow of a lantern, which hung conveniently at the entrance. The flickering lantern light crept like fingers along shadows toward the inky darkness further into the barn where the sudden sound of whimpering caught his attention.

"Allison!" He shook off the prickly sense of warning that crawled along his skin. He snatched the lantern from its nail and turned up its tired flame to scan the stalls ahead. Only animal eyes reflected back at him.

The whimpering continued, then what sounded like the crack of a whip.

"That your lover?" The angry voice of a man carried from a rear stall. "Slut!" Then another crack of the whip.

Joe hurried in the direction of the sounds until he reached the rear corner of the barn where a tiny glow shone across the floor. He paused, before stepping around the corner to draw his gun from its holster. At the ready, he revealed himself.

Joe's breath caught in his throat as his gaze skipped past the discarded dress and undergarments to where the pathetic lantern illuminated a woman. She sat with knees tucked to her chest. Her long lean fingers clung protectively to a tattered blanket, which she had drawn up to meet her chin. Wild red hair splayed out to frame her face and tumbled down shoulders glistening with sweat.

Dark eyes stared back, wide with torment.

Joe tightened his lips into a hard line as his gaze met where the blanket had pulled away from her leg to reveal a naked calf marred with fresh welts.

A gray ghostly figure of a man stood in the shadows, a whip dangling from his right hand.

"What the hell?" A muscle in Joe's jaw twitched.

"Joseph Brice," the man said smoothly. "This ain't none of your business."

"Allison, what's going on here?" Joe's brain churned with a myriad of explanations, hoping for an alternate to his first conclusion. They all came back to one thing; Joe had caught Otis, Allison's half-brother whipping her. And her submission told Joe that this was not the first time.

"I suggest you leave. Before there's trouble," Otis said.

"Trouble for you just walked in the door. Give me one good reason why I shouldn't blow your head off," Joe said. He pulled back the hammer, the resounding click penetrating the air. He pointed it directly at the other man's head. Joe had learned well from his father, how to hide his tells during poker. The same stony face worked well when Joe drew his gun. He had no intention of shooting the man in cold blood. This was Allison's half-brother, after all.

The two men stared at each other, assessing, Joe unflinching. Otis shifted his weight, beads of sweat breaking out onto his greasy forehead. Finally, realizing a firearm trumped a bullwhip, Otis conceded.

He took Allison by the arm and jerked her to her feet. "Let's go to the house, where you can clean up."

Allison, who still clung to the whip-shredded blanket, stumbled passed Joe, eyes focused on the ground. He turned and watched them depart. Allison's backside was uncovered; fresh red welts were rising up to mingle with the old. Joe let out his breath, feeling emotionally drained by what he had witnessed and wished that he had not. Anger shook him. Although, there was nothing to compare to a brother beating his sister, Allison had clearly set Joe up. She must have been lying in wait, naked, to seduce him. Her brother had encountered her first and ended her plan.

"Seems I'm the only goat here," Joe said.

CHAPTER 9

Every time Joe passed through Independence Missouri, the town seemed larger and busier than the time before. October of 1848 was no exception. Hammers echoed from every block with new construction. People crowded onto the streets. Long trains of ox teams and freighters splashed unwary pedestrians with muck as they passed.

Catching the unexpected scent of baked goods as he strolled along the wooden sidewalk, reminded Joe of his hunger. His stomach growled. Hot coffee and pastry sounded appealing after his long ride, but he would stick with his plan to dine after stopping at the Regency Hotel. He'd already seen to the needs of Zeus, depositing him at a public stable.

Like the other hotels in town, the Regency was little more than a boarding house, but Joe preferred it because it offered private rooms and was usually clean. At first glance, he thought he was at the wrong place. The entire front facade had been updated and a huge addition built onto the side. The building was at least twice the size of the hotel he remembered from a couple of years ago. Under the familiar Regency Hotel sign swinging in the breeze, Joe spotted the words *Under New Management*.

Joe was shocked to find an overcrowded lobby with guests standing elbow to elbow either trying to squeeze into the saloon or waiting their turn in the new dining room with its shiny chandelier. Respectable looking guests, women wearing fashionable dresses, and clean-cut men in tailored waistcoats, stood out against the usual sort of trail worn travelers and transients, who were dirty and sweat-stained from long days on horseback. Joe wondered what had caused the sudden influx of this more respectable class of people. Over the expected odor of leather and unwashed bodies Joe detected the smell of fresh paint and woodwork.

Joe picked his way through the mass of people in the lobby to an older gentleman at the front desk. "A room please."

"You're lucky," the clerk said, removing a key from a pegboard behind him. "Stage just come in. Only got one room left. Ain't the best. It's at the end of the hall in the old section. Kind of drafty."

"I suppose I can't be too choosy."

"You gonna be staying long?"

"I've got business through the winter."

"I bet you're going to California."

"How'd you know?"

The clerk motioned with his arm. "Everybody's a gold digger."

"Everybody?" Joe's jaw dropped. He'd anticipated the number of people heading west to leap, due to the discovery of gold at Sutter's Mill, but not by the amount this one jumping off place indicated. And spring was still months away, when everyone would be gathering to leave.

"More or less." The clerk shrugged.

"Well, I'm not exactly a miner. I'm setting up a caravan of settlers to California. And by the looks of these people," Joe motioned at the lobby, "I doubt most know how to properly outfit for the trip. I bet many could use my help."

"You had much experience at that sort of thing?"

"I've lived most of my life out west trapping and working the travel registries at the forts. I know the passage through the Rockies and the overland route to California. I know what it takes to live out there."

The clerk handed Joe the key and pointed to the registration book. "Well, if anybody's interested, I'll send 'em your way."

"I'd appreciate that."

The clerk watched Joe sign in. "You know, if I was a younger man, I'd join your caravan and set me up a hotel in California to make my gold."

"You'd probably do better than most of these would-be miners." Joe withdrew a coin from his pocket and tossed it onto the registration desk. "That should take care of tonight."

When the clerk quoted the price, Joe nearly fell over. "That's highway robbery," he burst out. "That's more than twice what I paid the last time. I can stay at the Continental for less than that."

"Not anymore you can't. These gold miners gone and pushed up prices."

Joe tossed a few more coins at the clerk and walked away, deciding to stay only until he could find a decent rooming house.

***

Lydia decided to freshen up in Possum Creek, one warm afternoon after helping her mother cut up tomatoes to dry. Mid October was transforming the hillsides from deep greens to a quilted patchwork of reds, yellows and browns. The nights were turning sharply colder as the days shortened, the noon sun riding lower in the sky. Too soon, the warm days would turn bitter cold, the creek made silent and frozen.

Eager for the privacy at her retreat, Lydia practically skipped to the meadow, pausing only to watch a pair of young does graze among the feathery blooms of goldenrod. At the bridge, Lydia dropped her bag of bathing supplies on a drier portion of the damp bank where the sun etched its way through the trees to the forest floor. She had spread a blanket on that very spot, many times, to enjoy a picnic.

Her bathing spot was isolated, deep in the woods, so she rarely encountered anyone there, lost youngsters, or a hunter tracking game along the other side of the creek. She glanced around to be certain it was void of other humans before undressing. The thought of being caught naked was horrifying.

Lydia's throat tightened as she pondered on her encounter with Joseph Brice at that spot. The memory of his kiss warmed her cheeks. She smiled and put a finger to her lips. Any man, especially a stranger, within a close distance left her cold and shaky, her heart pounding in her chest. Joe's presence sparked a different kind of pounding heart. Excitement.

And he'd asked her to go to California with him.

Could Joe be the one? Words of caring and his kiss had pierced her self-made prison.

Mrs. Applegate's words came to mind. *"Don't be so hard on yourself, child. You've got lots to offer a man. Don't you listen to what other folks is sayin'."*

Joe never stated his feelings for her.
It wouldn't be proper.
She could never leave her parents.
Possum Hollow was the only place she knew.
There were no guarantees of a better life elsewhere.
Life was full of no guarantees.
Finding her Indian family was only a foolish, childish dream.

Lydia slipped out of her dress and eased herself down the slippery embankment with the aid of some low hanging branches and thick roots. The water was colder than expected. She sucked in air and tightened her stomach before swimming toward the middle of the creek. A natural swimmer, Lydia was not afraid of water over her head. Unlike her mother, who preferred sponge baths to washing in the creek, Lydia would bathe in Possum Creek until near winter.

Unable to resist the urge to stretch out, she sighed and leaned back, bringing her toes and chest to the water's surface. With eyes closed in contentment, her mind drifted to earlier days when she'd frolicked in the woods and picked wild flowers on warm summer days.

Warm summer days... She could feel the warmth as if she were actually there, in the summer, watching them strut around the crackling fire. Dark skinned people wrapped in large animal skins, the men wearing only a strip of leather to cover their loins. The women in shirt-like dresses with leather pieces covering their legs from their moccasins to the fringe of their dresses. Long shiny hair flowed down their backs or were restrained in braids with feathers and beads and other ornaments. Dancers flailed their arms. Wailing. Twisting their bodies in rhythm to the low beat of the drums. Then the women and children began running and screaming.

Suddenly, there was blood everywhere! Blood splattered on teepees. It puddled on the ground. It puddled beneath bodies lying wounded and bleeding.

A vise-like fear griped Lydia's chest. The very real images startled her into awareness. For a second she had felt a strange bond with those people, like she knew them. The featureless faces were blurry, and she could identify none of them. Then the terror had come, stark and icy, urging her to flee into the shadows.

Lydia swam to the embankment, unable to shake the feeling of doom. She'd experienced that dream before... But was it a dream? Surely she couldn't have dozed while floating in the water.

Shaking from fear and the cold, she struggled to finish her bath before climbing out of the water. Wrapped in a towel, she stood on the bank shivering, and stared into the water's depths and the slippery rocks, worn smooth from passing water. The breeze, like ghostly fingers rustled the forest canopy and chilled as they gripped her flesh beneath the towel. The afternoon sunlight filtered through the leaves, deepening the light greens to dark, and the browns to the color of pitch. She had been gone too long.

Lydia cast off her towel and her fear and the cold, and slipped into the clothing she had laid out on a scruffy shrub. As she combed her hair, the premonition returned. She could feel it against her skin. The wind had changed. Something or someone was out there. Watching.

She sucked in air to hold her breath as if doing so could keep her unnoticed by an intruder. Still struggling with shaky fingers to fasten the buttons on her bodice, she pressed her back against the jagged trunk of a massive tree, her heart thudding in her chest. The darkening forest loomed.

The crow seemed to warn her, crying out the same moment she spotted the man on the other side of the creek. His dark shirt and trousers nearly camouflaged him within the gnarled vegetation. Without expression, his dark eyes caught a spear of sunlight under the shifting canopy; pupils, like that of a night creature stared back.

He took a step forward, out of the shadows and into a beam of light. Slowly his lips twisted into a sneer, bringing to life the puckered flesh of his jagged scar.

A hand seemed to tighten around Lydia's throat, smothering a scream. How long had he been lurking and watching? Her mind raced with thoughts of what he might have witnessed, the show he might have seen as her naked body descended into the creek and floated in the water.

Neither Lydia nor Willie moved, each assessing the other. A bridge and a creek were between them. Lydia knew there was no security against the tree, no protection within the forest, which was closing in like a tomb.

Her nose puckered with the sharp intake of damp earthy air now turned sour and putrid. She blinked and the creak of old wood and ropes warned that the monster was on the bridge. Approaching.

Run, Lydia. Run.

Turning in the direction of the meadow, adrenaline fueled her legs. She was running for her life. She didn't want to think about his punishment. If Willie were to catch her, she knew his revenge would be swift.

The crack of splintering wood made her head turn. Through the trees she witnessed the old bridge give way, its shattering wood spraying around her pursuer as feet first, arms waving as if he were trying to take flight, he plunged downward some ten feet into the cold moving water of Possum Creek.

CHAPTER 10

Several weeks passed before Joe could find an available room at a reasonably priced rooming house. With Independence becoming a key jumping-off point for thousands of emigrants and miners bound for western territories, lodging was in short supply. The condition would worsen over the next few months as the number of those preparing and gathering for the spring exodus increased.

Once settled into a boarding house, Joe ate the complimentary breakfast with the other boarders, a group of six honest looking men from different walks of life. Joe preferred taking his evening meal at the Regency Hotel where he could avoid conversation, cogitate on accomplishments for the day and plan for the next. He also found that the hotel was a good place to connect with potential candidates to join the caravan. With a set schedule, prospects could easily find him.

Joe was enjoying a mug of beer with country fried steak, collard greens and biscuits with strawberry jam, as he struggled with his budget. In a market where prices seemed to increase daily, so did the stress of completing preparations on time.

Substandard equipment was unacceptable, especially the wagon, which would serve as his aunt and uncle's home during the journey and until a new permanent structure could be erected on their land. Joe had spent the last several days haggling the cost of construction materials and calling in some favors to purchase the lumber at a reasonable cost.

As he took a swallow of his beer, someone slapped him on the back. He coughed and withdrew his pistol, jumped from his seat and knocked over his chair. The flashing weapon brought stares, and gasps from other diners.

"Zachariah, you son of a bitch! You nearly scared the shit out of me. You know better than to sneak up on me like that."

"Sorry," Zachariah shrugged innocently. "I didn't think people carried firearms in here."

Joe returned his gun to where he kept it discretely tucked under his jacket, and motioned for Zachariah Potter to join him across the table.

When Zachariah had settled into his chair, he said, "You shaved your beard. You look too respectable."

Joe waived over the server to order another round of drinks. "Beer okay?"

Zachariah nodded.

"Let me buy you dinner."

When the young server arrived, Zachariah greeted her. "Hello darlin'." His gaze trailed along her shapely form while Joe placed their order.

Eyes cast downward, she smiled shyly under his intense scrutiny and removed Joe's soiled platter. "I'll be back shortly, with your drinks." Her voice was velvety soft with a deep southern twang.

Zachariah's eyes lingered on her swaying hips as she departed their table and disappeared into the crowd of diners.

Joe noticed his friend's fresh haircut and trimmed beard. "Been in town long?" If Zachariah had been on a trail ride, he should look like hell. Maybe he was more interested in the serving girl than the drink.

"Rode in this afternoon. Took some time to freshen up. I've been riding hard for months, checking out some land in Texas."

That would explain the delay in his friend's arrival. "Plan on settling down?" He couldn't imagine Zachariah ever calling a single place home. Himself either for that matter. The two of them were alike in that regard, accustomed to the freedom the west offered.

"I hear cattle ranching is starting to take off," Zachariah said so matter-of-fact, that Joe choked on a swallow of beer.

"You can't be serious. I don't see you as a rancher."

"There comes a point in a man's life, when he needs something more." For a moment, Zachariah's expression turned distant, his gaze unfocused and unblinking. Then he shook it off and leaned back in his chair. "Anyway, I got your telegram about some caravan."

Joe leaned over the table toward his friend and spoke with quiet honesty. "I'm doing this for my aunt and uncle."

"Your uncle? Who didn't even show up to see your mother properly buried?"

Joe had to shake off memories of those lonely days after his mother's death, before his father came for him. "Yeah." He pursed his lips. "I don't have a choice. He's got this idea about settling in California. He's too stubborn to let me talk him out of it. And gullible enough to put their lives in the hands of some charlatan."

Joe had seen it all too often. Emigrants who relied on guidebooks, sold by presumed experts who more often than not, had never ventured west of the Missouri River.

To the uneducated, the guidebooks looked official with maps and route information. In reality, they were little more than instructional pamphlets showing non-existent shortcuts, and didn't differentiate between alkali and safe drinking water. Families were left stranded with broken down wagons and no food. Others could experience a similar fate when joining up with a caravan, by actually trusting a stranger to lead them to the promised land.

Joe had used those same unfortunates to turn a profit for himself. After the death of his grandfather, who had taught him frontier survival skills, he had made a modest living by providing directions or escorting emigrants over the Sierra Nevada Mountains. Zachariah, on many occasions had been right alongside him. The two had met during Joe's trapping days. Zachariah, close in age to Joe had been barely older than a lad and living on his own.

"Aunt Esther deserves better," Joe continued. "Besides, this is the last job I need to pay off my father's gambling debts. Then I'll be free. I'm tired of being hunted, always looking over my shoulder."

When the drinks came, Zachariah whispered something in the server's ear that made her giggle. Joe watched them flirt and took a long gulp of his beer.

After the server had scurried away, Zachariah returned his attention to Joe.

"Someone you know?" Joe asked.

"Naw. But, the possibility is always there." Zachariah grinned, his white teeth a stark contrast to his dark beard.

"I thought you had a woman."

"Not one I'd marry," Zachariah answered with a twinkle in his eye. He tipped up the mug of beer and chugged most of its contents before coming up for air. He sighed and wiped the froth from his beard with a shirtsleeve. "Damn, that's good."

"Didn't you swear your love to Claudette?"

Zachariah frowned. "She was a pretty little wench, great under the covers too. She and her papa got ideas about us getting hitched. I had to high tail it out of town."

Joe had long ago concluded that in many ways, Zachariah, with his charisma and stunning looks was more like Jackson Brice, than Joe himself. At least when it came to targeting the most vulnerable of young women.

"I'm ready for another beer. How 'bout you?" Zachariah asked.

Joe shook his head. "Anyway, I don't want to lead this thing alone. If something should happen to me… I thought with your experience, we'd make a good team."

Zachariah leaned forward. "Men like us don't die taking settlers across the overland trail. We've come through worse scrapes."

Joe didn't want to think of the many times they'd saved each other's necks, either from real danger or simple youthful foolishness. "When I agreed to help my uncle, I had no idea so many would be heading out. Settlers as well as miners. It will be overcrowded come spring, when groups gather to depart with their wagons and animals. I'm concerned about a polluted trail and a shortage of forage."

"Gold fever," Zachariah said. "These fools think that streams overflow with gold in California and that in Oregon, cooked pigs run around with knives and forks stuck in them."

"Then there's cholera," Joe added grimly. "I've seen cholera wipe out whole families within a few days. Well at dawn and dead by dusk."

Zachariah toyed with his beard. "So... Regarding this caravan of fools. What kind of proposal did you have in mind?"

***

Several days and a heavy rain passed before Lydia returned to the creek to collect the belongings she had abandoned. She tried to convince herself that farm duties had kept her away. In reality it was fear. What if she came across Willie's body, bloated and in decay where he had drowned in the creek or mangled as he tumbled down the rocky falls? She had yet to tell anyone about the broken bridge and had not sought any help for Willie. What if she found him alive?

Waiting.

Ready to pounce.

On high alert, she ran through the meadow and into the woods. Hiding in the afternoon shadows, she crept between trees. Her dark sinewy form blended with limbs of twisted vegetation. Bare feet minimized the rustle of damp leaves on the forest floor.

The old bridge greeted her, now broken and dangling from the two banks, its middle section gone. Lydia stared at it only briefly, remembering all too clearly the resounding snap of lumber, the loud splash, the vision of Willie as he plummeted into the water.

She turned her attention to her belongings. They were in the pile where she had abandoned them, soggy and splattered with dirt and debris from the wind and rain. In the mud, she recognized the distinctive hand-like footprints of a racoon rising from the creek bank.

After snatching up her things and wringing out her wet towel, Lydia slinked to the creek bank as if the ground might give way beneath her. She sucked in air as some force made her peer down and into the water. No body. No signs of anyone. Only the normal indications of where the waterline had scrapped along the bank during a storm. She let out a slow breath and followed the creek along its bank toward where it tumbled over the falls.

***

After a full breakfast, Joe left the boarding house and picked his way through the crowded streets of Independence. His nose and eyelashes caught snowflakes as they fell. The stench of burning hair and flesh from branding irons in the stockyards, and clanging of metal upon metal from the smithy were unrelenting. The bustling activity hadn't ebbed, despite the coming of winter.

Joe wondered what Lydia would think of this town. Would she find the chaos exciting or frightening? Intimidating, perhaps, but not frightening. She had more guts than her shy exterior portrayed.

"Mr. Brice! Mr. Brice!"

Joe turned to find a man waving his arms, pushing his way through the crowd. Joe stepped aside to wait for the man to join him.

"Thank you for stopping," the man said, gasping for breath in the cold air. He held out a gloved hand.

Joe shook hands. "Do I know you?"

"I apologize. I don't usually chase people down on the street. I'm Doctor Seth Lively. I've tried unsuccessfully on several occasions to catch you at the hotel. The clerk pointed you out to me."

Joe nodded, and the man continued.

"I hope you don't mind. He told me you're taking a wagon train of emigrants to California. Do you have a few minutes to talk?"

"I have an appointment at the stockyard to purchase some oxen. You're welcome to tag along."

"Perfect. Afterward, I'll treat you to some hot spiced wine or cider."

Joe agreed. He led the doctor past the famous mule market where two men were arguing over the price of a broken-down mule. The stockyard was a noisy, stinking place of milling hooves, squealing animals and the stench of ammonia and manure. Joe took his time running his hands over the animals, examining teeth and hooves and palpating the legs to select the youngest and healthiest oxen with straight limbs.

Among a lot of malnourished animals with runny noses, he found four yoke. He paid the man and then ordered the animals branded immediately. He wanted the same oxen when he returned for them. By the time Joe and Dr. Lively left the stockyard, they were almost numb with cold.

"Let's stop in here." The doctor motioned toward a small inn.

Dr. Lively led them through the room of rowdies and selected a newly vacated table near the fire. The men quickly ordered hot-spiced wine and settled in to get warm. The doctor got straight to the point of their meeting.

"My wife and I are interested in joining your party. Do you have room for one more wagon?"

Joe studied the man. "I'm not accepting just anyone. I only want competent, responsible people. This journey will be mentally and physically grueling, with quick decision making that could mean life or death. It is not to be undertaken lightly."

The doctor nodded.

"Did you introduce yourself as a doctor, a physician?" Joe noticed the man's smooth face and hands. He obviously didn't perform hard labor in the sun.

"Yes, I'm a physician."

Joe kept his features composed. He didn't want to seem overly eager, but a doctor would be a valuable addition to the caravan. He could charge higher joining up fees. "Then as a physician you should be familiar with some of the dangers on the trail. Why would you give up what I presume is a lucrative practice?" And a comfortable lifestyle, no doubt, judging by his clean, stylish suit, and neatly pressed white collar.

The man didn't flinch. "There are many excellent physicians in my home town of Saint Louis. I believe there will be a shortage of doctors during this massive emigration, both on the journey and in California, especially now that cholera is making its way to the frontier."

Their drinks came. The two men leaned back in their chairs, relaxing with the hot drink and crackling fire, the distinctive aromas of cinnamon and clove mingling with the fragrant wine. Joe decided the doctor was not quite forty. There was something down to earth about him that Joe liked. He could imagine the man pushing up his fine white sleeves if the situation demanded, such as if someone's belly was shot full of bullet holes.

"Any family, children?" Joe mentally tallied up how many people in total he might be responsible for.

"My wife and I have never been so blessed."

"How does your wife feel about making the trip?"

"She's apprehensive. Excited. Like me, she grew up in an upper class family with servants tending to her. That's why I've come to you. Neither of us knows anything about trail survival."

Joe sighed. The Livelys could be a burden. But if the doctor didn't join his caravan, he could easily join another. "Everyone must work their own share."

"I understand your concerns. And while I might not be a man who has spent his life toiling in manual labor, I assure you, in my profession, most of my decisions are a matter of life or death. I spend long hours tending to patients, many times at the sacrifice of my own needs. What my wife lacks in physical abilities, she makes up with inner strength. The name of Faith suits her. I would not suggest taking her on such a dangerous trip, if I thought she could not complete it."

"I'm sorry, I didn't mean to imply otherwise. As leader, I am responsible for selecting those whom I deem capable, are suitably outfitted and are as prepared as possible." As Joe continued to fill him in on his background and on how he had been recruited by his uncle for the trip, he thought of Lydia. Perhaps his plans would fall into place after all.

"I know someone who might be able to help you, a young woman who grew up in the Missouri Ozarks. She's very knowledgeable about outdoor living." Joe proposed the idea of Lydia working for them in exchange for her food and supplies.

"This has possibilities. Please tell me more about this young lady."

CHAPTER 11

It started after the harvest.

Small things.

Odd things.

Items out of place.

An axe stuck in the crook of an apple tree. Lydia had to climb the tree to retrieve it.

Sunshine's bridle, buried in the back of the barn beneath some small hand tools. All out of place.

One day, Lydia stepped into the food storage shed to select a pumpkin for pie. Her eyes were not yet adjusted to the dim light, when she toppled head first, belly flat into a pile of goo. A number of pumpkins had escaped their storage bin, and been ripped apart with what looked like a hoe or the claw of a hammer. This was not destruction by a four legged animal.

This was sabotage of a two-legged kind.

Lydia's throat tightened. She sat back on her heels, fighting to shake off the feeling of dread. A cold chill danced through her veins, then turned to anger.

Who would do this?

Pranks were one thing. Destroying a family's winter food supply was another. Neighbors didn't treat each other that way. Possum Hollow was a tight knit community. Residents looked out for each other. If someone was in need, they asked for help and it was granted, without the need for theft or subterfuge.

She raked up the damaged pieces to feed to the hogs, and salvaged what she could of the remaining, grateful that her father had gone into town that morning, and her mother was still in the cabin. Lydia's work would go unnoticed.

Another time, it was the turnips. Then the apples. Until Lydia dreaded her normal tasks of acquiring food and caring for the animals. Every day when she left the outbuildings, she double checked the doorlatches, wondering if the family would need to purchase locks.

Ever since the death of their last hound, about a year ago, Lydia had implored her father to acquire another dog. For protection, she'd argued. A dog could chase away the night prowlers, or at least alert the family to one. They'd kept dogs for many years, but her father stood firm about not replacing the last one, which had a tendency to bray all night and had a propensity for chasing "any varmint" within sniffing distance. He'd grown tired of hunting down the wandering bitch, which always seemed to be in heat and yet never produced any puppies.

A week later, while approaching the chicken coop to retrieve some eggs for breakfast, Lydia found a sight so disturbing, she recoiled as if hit with the ferocity of a storm. She slapped her palms against her mouth to muffle a scream, her basket slipping from her fingers to the ground. Despite the wild clawing fear, she could not pull her eyes away from the bloody, decapitated hen nailed to the door of the coop or divert her gaze from the entry frame, smeared with dried blood. Until her legs crumpled beneath her.

A groan rose from her throat, building in intensity. Like a steam engine ready to blow, the sound became a painful howling from deep within her chest. It was an otherworldly sound she didn't recognize as being from herself. Knees and hands pressed to the ground, she rocked back and forth until the tears came, and then the gut wrenching sobs that twisted her insides and shook her to her core. Then she vomited, violently, down the front of her dress and in the dirt, to purge the evil and shame that she had brought upon them.

She had always feared something like this would happen to her family because of her, of who she was. She accepted that she was a victim of harassment and abuse. But such acts were intolerable against her parents. For all the kindness the Whitleys had bestowed upon her, they were now being punished. She loved them. If it hadn't been for them, she would be dead.

Lydia didn't know how long she continued to rock back and forth on her hands and knees, crooning, nose dripping, tears raining down her face to make pock marks in the dirt beneath her. It could have been an eternity that some force kept her planted, her insides clenched. Or perhaps only a minute had passed when a pair of soiled and scuffed boots stopped in front of her.

"Dear God. Lydia..."

It was her father.

He knew. She couldn't look at him as he scooped up her trembling body, not seeming to care that she stunk with vomit.

"I should have seen this," he murmured. "I should have protected you." He cradled her in his arms and carried her to the cabin. Then he left her with her mother to tend to her as any mother would dutifully attend a sick child.

***

Joe had just settled into bed at the boarding house when the sound of banging bolted him upright. The heavy door of his room shook in its casing and the metal knob rattled in protest. It was well past midnight.

He lay there for a long moment, hoping that if he played dead the obnoxious noise would go away. As the banging persisted, Joe's concerns about waking up all the residents grew. He would certainly hear about it in the morning. The land lady was not tolerant. Reluctantly, Joe slid his feet from the bed covers to the floor. He snatched up his revolver, and by the moonlight seeping through the filmy curtains, he went to the door. Whoever was paying a visit at this hour, it couldn't be good.

"Who's there?" He croaked.

"It's me. Zachariah. Open up."

"It's late. Come back tomorrow." Joe turned away from the door and started back toward his bed.

"Damn it, Joe. Open up!"

Joe stood there in the near darkness, trying to get his bearings, his revolver swinging from the hand at his side, wishing Zachariah would go away. What could possibly be so important at this hour?

The banging resumed. "We need to talk."

As Joe eased the door open, ready to snap at the late night intruder, Zachariah barged past him, reeking of alcohol.

"Come in." Joe waved his revolver filled hand at thin air. He closed the door and shuffled back to the edge of his bed, returning his weapon to his side table. "To what do I owe the pleasure of your company?"

Zachariah stood over him, legs spread, arms akimbo, his dark form barely visible in the light. "What the hell is this I hear about an Indian coming with us?"

Joe pressed his fingers to his temples, feeling the onset of a headache. Maybe he had risen too quickly. "How did you get in here?" The land lady was always careful to secure the locks at night.

"I followed one of the residents in."

So much for security.

"Some of the others are none too thrilled either," Zachariah added.

"About what specifically?"

"Damn it, Joe. Are you listening to me?"

"Can't we talk about this tomorrow? When our brains are clearer." Perhaps he should have passed on that last shot of whiskey.

"Why would you allow some Indian to join the group?"

An odd prickling passed over Joe's skin. "She's going to work for the doctor, in a servant capacity. He needs someone to do the cooking and take care of his wife while he tends patients."

"You know how I feel about them redskins. They murdered and scalped my family."

"I'm sorry. I just don't see how a young woman could matter," Joe confessed. "She's not a warrior. Lydia is a neighbor of my uncle." A woman he couldn't put out of his mind. "White people raised her. She dresses like white people. She acts like white people. She knows less about being Indian than you do."

Zachariah's shoulders slumped and he began pacing.

"Is anyone threatening to withdraw?"

"There's been talk."

Damn. Joe had spent months interviewing and putting together a skilled, well prepared group of emigrants. He'd even secured the services of a physician, which meant he'd been able to charge higher join up fees.

That meant more security for everyone and enough money in his pocket to pay back his father's gambling debts.

Could one Indian maiden unravel the entire operation?

CHAPTER 12

When Joe left Independence with his newly purchased supplies, the month of March had arrived. Spring hadn't. A crust of melted and refrozen snow still settled within the shadier niches of ground.

He was pleased with his accomplishments and the prices he had negotiated. Much of his return journey had been spent reflecting on the conflict which had nearly disintegrated the entire wagon train. It had cost Joe several days and some strategic arguments to convince Zachariah and others to not drop out. Now the problem foremost on Joe's mind, as he rolled into Possum Hollow, was convincing Lydia to leave home.

Tethered to the rear of his covered wagon were Zeus and two oxen. Tar buckets and spare parts rattling on either side of the wagon bed attracted gawkers. Some people smiled and waved while others talked among themselves about the uncommon assembly. A handful of small children, caught up in the excitement, raced alongside on short legs. By the time Joe stopped at the General Store to purchase more licorice, a crowd had gathered.

"Fine looking wagon you got there," someone commented.

"Mighty fine oxen too," another said, stroking the head of one beast.

Joe thanked them and strolled into the General Store, nearly bumping into a large squat woman who was leaving. Her girth filled the entire door frame and did not allow him to pass easily.

"Joseph Brice, well I'll be." She greeted him as she would an old friend by wrapping her chubby arms around his waist and squeezing. "How are ye?"

"I'm fine, thank you." Joe extracted himself from the greasy woman's embrace. He staggered backwards, nearly missing the riser that elevated the building's entrance from street level. To avoid tumbling onto the sidewalk, he clutched the doorframe with his gloved hand.

The woman didn't seem to notice. "You remember me, from the corn shuckin'? I'm Wilma Kincaid, Allison's mama."

How could anyone forget the malodorous, unkempt woman? He'd hoped to never encounter her again. Even on their second meeting, Joe couldn't comprehend how this grotesque woman with puckered mouth, beady eyes, and large bulbous head, could have bred the uncommonly alluring Allison.

"How are you?" Joe asked out of politeness.

"I'm fine. Thank you for askin'." Her wide grin revealed a mouth full of tobacco yellowed teeth. Her eyes twinkled. "And I'm so happy you're back. Now you can make things right with my Allison."

"Make things right?"

Her grin turned into a scowl. "Why yes. In these parts when a man lays with a woman… Well, he's expected to do right by her. So, we'll be expectin' you to come callin' real soon." Wilma Kincaid excused herself and brushed past him, mumbling something about her husband waiting for her.

Joe furrowed his brow with indignation. *What kind of tale had Allison woven?* Obviously, he hadn't been clear enough with her. He would have to set her straight.

***

Lydia was pulling a pie from the oven when the sound of the cabin door closing made her jump. She froze when she saw Joseph Brice. She hadn't heard of his return to Possum Hollow.

"Your father said I could come in."

He looked magnificent bundled up in his leather jacket with a red scarf around his neck, hands stuffed into his pockets. His clean-shaven face glowed pink from the cold. Bright blue eyes danced beneath the wide brim of his hat while a toothy smile lit up his face.

That moment reaffirmed that a part of her would die when he left for California and he would be gone from her life forever.

Joe removed his hat and strolled leisurely over to the table where she was working. His eyes never left her. "Whatever you're baking smells wonderful."

Not half as wonderful as he looked. Not half as wonderful as him being there. "It's pie…" made from last autumn's dried apples. She couldn't take her eyes off of him.

Joe remained unmoving, within arm's reach, his gaze holding hers. She felt the pull of him and wondered if he might kiss her. And she found herself wanting him to.

His mouth opened to speak. Was he going to say how much he missed her? She could easily fall into his arms.

"We need to discuss going to California."

The hot tingles from a moment before turned cold. "California? I thought I had given you my answer."

"We'll be leaving in a few weeks."

Her chest tightened at the thought. She tried to sound firm, uncaring, but knowing that he would be leaving, and she would never see him again was tearing her apart.

Joe withdrew a piece of licorice from his pocket and offered her some. When she politely declined, he pulled off a bite between his front teeth. "I arranged passage for you, with a doctor and his wife."

"You what?" Lydia exploded.

"I arranged passage for you to California. The Livelys agreed to pay your expenses. In exchange, you'll help them with cooking and things." Joe grinned with obvious pleasure at the accomplishment. "The doctor's wife suffers from some blood ailment which weakens her. She's used to servants tending…"

"How dare you! How dare you sell me off like some indentured servant!" Lydia struggled to keep her voice from escaping the boundaries of the cabin to where her parents were working nearby. "Is that what you think of me? A lowly squaw, to be sold off to the highest bidder? And what gives you the right?"

"No, of course not! It's not like that. My aunt and uncle have to sell everything they own to outfit for the trip, with barely enough left to purchase a piece of land. I knew you couldn't afford…"

"Get out!" She picked up the rolling pin and swung it at him.

Joe took a quick sidestep. "Calm down, Lydia. I didn't have a whole lot of choices. I couldn't exactly have you tagging along with me. How would that look? We do have your honor to consider."

"My honor? When have you ever cared about my honor?" Rage burned and spread like fire in her veins. She trembled with the effort to contain her fury. His hands had been all over her. He had cast a spell of lust upon her. She snarled and hurled the rolling pin.

Joe dodged the implement as it flew past his face. The rolling pin landed harmlessly on the floor and rolled away.

"Get out of here," Lydia demanded. "Get out of my life."

"Damn it, Lydia. Will you listen to me?"

"You're the one not listening. I'm not going to California, with you or anyone else." Lydia backed up a few steps. "If I'm not an indentured servant, you must think me a whore or a fool." She glared at him.

Joe laughed. "A whore? You're certainly no whore."

Lydia wasn't sure if that was a complement or an insult.

"Nor are you a fool. What would be foolish about snatching the opportunity to experience a world outside of this suffocating hollow? This might be the only opportunity for you, Lydia. Don't throw it away."

Joe crept to her side of the table, near enough for her to feel his magnetic pull, drawing her to him, diffusing her anger. She felt small and vulnerable as he stood before her, larger than life, exuding power and self-confidence.

Lydia turned her back to him. She wasn't going to allow his blue eyes and air of false tenderness to sway her. "My answer is no."

She heard him shuffle closer to her. A moment later, he placed his hands upon her shoulders. She flinched.

"Don't be like this," Joe murmured.

The feel of his breath across her neck made her quiver. She clenched her fists and closed her eyes. "Leave," she said in a quiet, firm voice.

He lingered there, fanning sparks of deep yearning within her. What power did this vile man hold over her?

Finally, he pulled away. Lydia didn't turn to watch as his boots clomped toward the door. Her shoulders slumped and she let out a long breath as the door closed. She went to the fireplace, snatched up the poker and took out her anger and frustration on some hot coals.

To think, while he'd been away, she'd pined for him. During the months of Joe's absence, her feelings had deepened for him, not lessened. And she'd held onto hope that he might express something more than a passing interest for her, some amorous feelings. How could he expect a woman to leave her home and travel with him, with nothing more than an emotionally detached invitation? Then sell her off like a slave he owned!

Now she only wanted to cleanse her mind and body of him. Her thoughts went to what she still carried in the front pocket of her apron. The tiny red ear of corn, not much bigger than her thumb. She'd kept it there as a reminder of Joe. Touching it often. As if by keeping the ear, a piece of him would remain with her after he left for California.

Like so many things in her life, the ear now mocked her. It had been impossible for her to dance with Joe the night of the corn shuckin'. Now it was impossible for her to have him at all. She withdrew the ear and stared at it before tossing it into the licking flames. She watched with no remorse as the fire quickly devoured the dried ear. There, the deed was done. Now she could be rid of Joseph Brice.

CHAPTER 13

Joe sauntered into the saloon and sidled up to the bar.

Chester Curtis quickly appeared. "Hello, Mr. Brice. Hadn't heard you were back in town. Your uncle with you?"

"No." He quickly regretted snapping at the man. "I came to drink alone."

Chester nodded knowingly and set his customer up with a glass of whiskey. Joe tossed his head back and drained the glass of amber fluid with a couple of swallows. He ordered another drink and began ruminating on the conversation that had brought him here.

He'd never been very adept at understanding women. Lydia in particular baffled him. Mistrustful, wary, ready to flee at the simplest provocation, she was a source of endless distress. And now that maiden was getting more complex. Her bashful nature was becoming bolder and more confident.

What did he have to do to convince that stubborn woman to join his caravan? She'd insisted that she wasn't the sort of girl who gallivanted across the continent with a man to whom she wasn't wed. So he arranged free passage for her… with a doctor. Instead of thanking him, she threw him out!

Joe turned and studied the group of rowdy men at a nearby table. Disheveled piles of money indicated they were well into a poker game. He could almost see his father, Jackson "Black Jack" Brice, sitting there in his fancy suit, twiddling his perfectly groomed mustache. Joe would be alongside him, the "innocent" son counting cards and buying drinks for the men. Between the two of them, they could clean up a table before moving onto another set of suckers.

Joe shook off the vision and returned to his thoughts of Lydia. The memory of her slim body against the length of his and the sweet taste of her mouth brought a spasm to his loins. Her kisses had proven that inside her outward demeanor of innocence and modesty lay a woman of passion waiting to be released from her cocoon.

He took another swallow of whiskey. The drink burned as it glided down his throat, but didn't ease the vice that clenched his innards. He wanted to devour every inch of Lydia's smooth coppery flesh with eyes and hands, to lose his fingers in the tangle of her silky hair spread across his pillow. He wanted her skin, slippery with perspiration, quivering against him, calling out his name.

Joe ordered another drink.

Why couldn't he remain detached? Was it her innocence that so appealed to him? A forbidden fruit? He could never have a woman like Lydia, fresh and unspoiled. He'd seen the tragic consequences of such a relationship. His father had seduced the unsullied Irene Crenshaw at the tender age of fifteen. After his birth, the couple quietly married.

"Black Jack" proved to be neither much of a husband or a father. He used Irene's hospitality as little more than a stop between gambling sprees, returning home drunk and abusive, then sweet talking her into sex and financing his dream of hitting it big at cards with her meager earnings. He always vowed to win them their fortune in *one last game*. Within a few years, Irene was used up, her health failing, no longer the beauty she had once been. His mother had deserved better.

A stab of guilt pricked Joe's heart. He should have done more to protect his mother. His ponderings increased his inner, gnawing torment. With a shaking hand he drained his glass of whiskey.

Years ago, Joe had promised to end his father's legacy. He couldn't trust himself with a woman's heart.

As his thoughts rambled on, he swigged what filled his glass. Chester was so unobtrusive and adept at his job, that Joe lost track of how many drinks he'd consumed. Nor did he notice the room begin to spin until he could no longer focus on the red blur at the end of the bar.

"Howdy handsome," the red blur purred.

Blinking his eyes, Joe found only a temporary solution for his lack of focusing power. When he tried to move away from the bar, he discovered that his legs wouldn't support his weight.

"Easy honey." The red blur glided over to him. "You stay right there."

Joe stumbled awkwardly, plunging forward against the bar as a wave of nausea washed over him. He raised his eyebrows and nodded tentatively in agreement with the red blur. His face heated with embarrassment… or too much drink.

"Now, don't you go worryin' none. Chloe'll be takin' care of you." The woman's smile seemed unusually wide, twisted and grotesque through his swimming vision. She began to lightly massage the back of his neck with well-practiced fingers.

Just the type of woman he needed. Although a little past her prime, she was experienced, expecting no commitments.

"Your neck feels awful knotted up." Her left hand joined her right and she moved her adept hands more aggressively down the sides of his neck and along his shoulders.

Joe's neck prickled with pleasure. Her heavy perfume invaded his drunken senses. He'd gone unsatisfied for too long. Chloe was a tempting morsel, full figured.

When she nuzzled her chest against his back, Joe twisted around, his eyes meeting her heaving breasts. The low cut décolletage trimmed in red lace framed an enticing cleavage of enormous breasts. He grinned and openly leered at them. It was an internal fight to resist reaching out and filling his hands with what he could easily take.

"What say we finish this elsewhere?" Chloe whispered. She nibbled his right lobe and curled her tongue behind his ear. Boldly placing her palm on Joe's upper thigh, she slid her hand firmly inward between his legs, stopping short of his bulging manhood. Then she pulled away, her arm coming around his back to urge him to his feet.

"I wouldn't go messing with that one Chloe," a man's voice came from behind her.

"Wha…?" The woman spun around and scowled at the scruffy young man.

"This here," the man announced, loud enough for everyone in the saloon to hear, "be an Injun lover."

"Is that so? And I suppose then, if I let him go, you'll step right in here without a waitin' your turn?" She placed her feet wide, hands on hips.

"What he says is true," came a deep voice from somewhere in the dark smoky room.

"We seen him with that local squaw a danglin' on his arm," a third voice joined in.

By now, others were taking an interest in the conversation. The overall din in the room quieted.

"We all know that squaw ain't no better than no animal."

"That's right, and we don't want you bedding no man who be screwing animals. We might take our business elsewhere. I'm sure Chester wouldn't like that neither."

Joe slowly comprehended the cackling coming from all directions. He couldn't focus on individual faces, but he recognized a few of the voices. When again he tried to free himself from the support of the bar, a rush of nausea thwarted his effort.

"She ain't bedding no squaw man."

Chloe yelped as the man near the bar seized her arm and pulled her away.

"Let her go," Joe said in a slurred voice he barely recognized as his own. He staggered forward to reach out for his prey. He only grabbed air. After stumbling over a chair, a series of incomprehensible insults hurled his way. All eyes focused on the scene where he stood in front of the bar.

Despite his head swimming, Joe realized that the saloon conflict had degenerated into an attack against Lydia. Not considering that the men might only want to stir up some excitement by flinging harsh words, Joe swung an arm in a futile attempt to punch a dark figure standing nearby.

"I don't want no fighting!" Chester shouted and started around the bar.

"I'll handle him for you," a large man said to the one holding Chloe.

Joe gulped. The disfiguring scar across the face identified the towering man as the one who had beaten Lydia in the street. The same man at the corn shuckin', Willie Kincaid, who had a score to settle. Joe's reflexes were almost nonexistent. In his drunken state, he was no match for this man's bulk. Joe could barely stand. If only he could get the room to stop spinning.

Willie's deep laugh resonated in the saloon. Without warning or taking his eyes off Joe's face, Willie landed a punch in his abdomen. Air whooshed from Joe's lungs; he reeled backwards into another man, who shoved him back into the brawl.

"Looks like you are the goat." The voice belonged to Otis Kincaid.

The sobering realization was like being doused with frigid water. Seems he'd made some enemies in Possum Hollow. Otis, too, had a score to settle. Joe's initial conclusion about the night in the barn must have been correct. Allison must have claimed that Joe had lain with her, if not that night, then another time. And Otis believed her. He'd accused her of being a slut. That's why Allison's mother had practically ordered Joe to *come callin'*.

Words and memories of that night, spun around Joe's throbbing head. He grappled for the support of a chair or table or anything solid. The men were already pushing aside furniture.

Chester Curtis, now red faced, shook his fist and shouted at the men to finish their argument outside. Joe caught a glimpse of Chloe watching helplessly from the end of the bar, anguish twisting her features before Willie delivered a blow to Joe's right jaw.

He heard something pop, and was grateful there was no pain. He tasted blood. A return punch missed Willie. A left fist clipped the edge of Joe's chin to send him staggering backward, shaking his head to stop the ringing in his ears. By some miracle, Joe managed to skitter sideways as Willie aimed a fist at his gut, and who in turn avoided the blow Joe tried to land. Wildly, Joe swung his arms, bringing more laughter from the crowd than offense against his adversary. Three hard blows to his midsection and Joe doubled over, collapsing onto the floor.

The patrons grumbled and returned to their drinks, complaining about a disappointing one-sided brawl. Chloe rushed to Joe's aid, but three men, including Willie, shoved her aside.

"He's ours now," Willie growled.

Chloe stammered a protest as the three men picked Joe up by his arms and legs to carry him away.

One of the men laughed as they stepped outside. "Can you believe our luck? Joseph Brice being stinking drunk this time a day."

"His face is swelling up. We shouldn't have let his face get so messed up. She ain't gonna like that."

Joe didn't know where the three men were taking him and he was too drunk and beaten to care, much less protest. He remembered seeing these men before, but he couldn't recall their names. They dumped him face up into the back of a wagon. He was grateful for the numbness that weighed him down. He tasted blood, and there was a sticky pool forming alongside him in the bed of straw. Overcome with weariness, he closed his eyes against the glaring sun, grateful to be alive.

When semi-awareness next returned, a log-hewn ceiling replaced the blue sky. He was stretched out on a more comfortable surface, a bed, his muddled mind reasoned. And he sensed his nakedness. Through a white haze, he saw several women tending to him. One scolded someone about letting his face get messed up.

A woman with indiscernible features dabbed at his brow. Chloe? Joe tried to ask, but his mouth didn't work. Then a force beyond his control pulled him back into a world of darkness.

Garbled voices. Fleeting glimpses. The real blended with nightmares and flashes of darkness and light.

Three men shoved him into a whitewashed building and dragged him to the front of a room where a tier of candles glimmered like starlight in the velvet night and a man stood cloaked in a dark robe. A woman appeared alongside Joe. Was she an angel wearing red, or was it her halo that was red?

Was he dead? Was this his day of reckoning? Did he now have to justify wrongs of the past?

Strange he should pass from the earth while defending a young maiden's honor. An image focused in his mind of the dark skinned woman with long tresses sitting grandly on a black stallion, her buckskins bleached white, a spectacle of loveliness. Her eyes, like sweet innocence willed him closer. Joe reached out to her.

She disappeared.

Like a dream.

Joe shut his eyes and tried to enter the inviting tunnel of light. A presence held him back.

If he'd found himself at the pearly gates then, yes, he must repent. "I do."

***

"Calico!" Lydia exclaimed when she spotted the brightly printed fabric. She couldn't remember when her mother last purchased fabric from the General Store.

The homespun Lydia colored from dandelion dye was far from the intensity of this calico. Dotted with tiny yellow flowers and green stems the fabric had an overall yellow color. She rushed to relieve her mother of her packages as a cool blast of air swept into the cabin. They walked together to the table and spread out the purchases. Lydia liked when her mother came home with surprises, and she usually had some news to share.

"There is some green here too." Her mother strolled back to the entrance and hung up her cloak. "Unfortunately, we'll have to wait to sew our new dresses and bonnets until we make our quilting squares."

"Who's courting now?"

"You wouldn't believe. I bumped into Esther while in town. She was nearly sobbing when she told me. Allison Seavers and Joseph Brice got married last night."

CHAPTER 14

Lydia staggered backwards, choking for air. Her reaction was irrational, she knew. Joe never wanted her in the way she'd hoped. But he'd been there the day before, telling her he'd made arrangements for her travel to California. He'd implored her to go, his hands placed boldly on her shoulders. She chafed at the thought of him touching her.

Too busy hanging up her cape, her mother didn't notice Lydia's reaction to the news. "Didn't I tell you that man was untrustworthy? Esther said she was shocked to learn about Joe getting 'tangled up in such a mess', getting the girl pregnant."

Pregnant? Allison Seavers was pregnant with Joe's child? All along he'd…? Lydia's throat constricted. How could she have allowed herself to feel anything except loathing for that gun-slinging who-knew-what?

"Esther said that poor Irene would roll over in her grave if she knew. So like his father, that gambling, womanizing, conman, Jackson Brice."

Lydia grabbed the back of a chair, her head swimming, wrestling the assault of tormenting assumptions. Joe had been gone all winter. He must have gotten Allison pregnant in autumn, before he left for Independence. Lydia doubled over as if punched in the gut. That would mean that everything Joe had ever said to Lydia, all the nice things he had done for her, he had done while seducing Allison.

Had he seduced one woman and then the other, back and forth? Is that why he was often so lusty when he came to see her? He'd just been with Allison? Or… Did Lydia leave him so unsatisfied, that he then turned to the more experienced Allison to better meet his manly needs? He certainly must have snickered inwardly at Lydia's inept attempts at kissing. She didn't know which scenario was more disgusting. No wonder he had laughed when she accused him of thinking she was a whore.

Lydia's lips curled back in revulsion as she broke into a hot sweat. Joe had treated her contemptibly, with a false kindness, as if she were a desirable, attractive woman, to seduce, to touch and to kiss. At the night of the shuckin' he had claimed that he felt all warm and tingly inside, like she did. Had that too been a lie? How far would he have taken her, if she hadn't stopped him? Would he have abandoned her for California with a child in her belly?

What a stupid fool she had been. Too easily she had let down her guard and allowed a few kind words to penetrate the wall of armor she had so mindfully built. She was beyond naive to have even considered that Joe might be the one man, different from all others. Mrs. Applegate had offered her hope. In truth, Joe was more like Mad Dog Willie, except this time she had willingly fallen into the snare. Nothing would change for Lydia. She was an Indian. No man wanted her.

Her mother broke through Lydia's thoughts. "I'm relieved you had sense enough not to get caught up with that scoundrel. The way he eyes you with such lust, I could tell he wasn't a proper gentleman. He obviously refused to marry Allison. The Kincaid boys had to beat and drag Joseph Brice to the church."

Her mother's last words drove in the final knife wound. Lydia shuddered and wiped her mouth with clammy hands, as if she could so easily wipe away the memory of Joe's kiss. She ran outside, darting past her father. Nothing mattered except purging herself of the vile man and the evil done to her.

***

Lydia's world continued dismantling as one frosty evening, winter battled to regain its stranglehold. Wind howled over the mountain and into the hollow, seeping into every orifice of their cabin. Her father had spent the afternoon restoring some chinking to the timbers as they had deteriorated over the winter and washed away in the spring rains. Still, the bitter wind seeped into the cracks and made the fire flicker like a ghostly presence.

When the mantle clock chimed out the ninth hour, her father stretched and yawned. "Think I'll bring in some more wood and turn in."

Lydia shivered as cold air swept across her lap. When a second draft made her shiver, she looked up from her sewing and toward the door. A flannel-sleeve reached in and grabbed the rifle propped in the entry.

"Father took the rifle," Lydia said.

"Probably saw that fox again," her mother spoke without shifting her gaze or slowing the rhythm of her stitching. "Maybe your father will finally rid us of that nuisance."

"Poor thing. It must be starving this late in the season." Lydia felt sorry for the creature and didn't wish it dead. Neither did she wish it to kill her father's chickens. They had already lost several to the fox who favored her father's chickens over more elusive prey. Despite the precautions her father had taken to secure the coop, the fox would sneak in during the dead of night. A partly eaten carcass or two with a scattering of feathers remained as clear evidence in the morning.

That was the difference between the predation of a fox and a man. An animal killed for survival. A man… a vandal… decapitated a chicken and spread its blood where an animal could not reach. Not for sustenance, but to terrorize.

Her father had never brought up the incident of the chicken with her. He'd left her with her mother and without word, returned to the crime scene to clean up the mess. The details were still a blur to Lydia, as if she had experienced it out of body or in some nightmare.

Since then, her father made a point of being the first to visit the coop or the barn in the morning, and Lydia, too filled with shame, had never questioned his change in routine. Although, she often wondered about other terrible things that might have happened at their farm in the past or continued through the winter, she never questioned her father about it. She had no idea how aware her mother was, so she certainly didn't discuss it with her, either.

Lydia was staring absently at the door, pitying the poor scrappy fox, when the sound of a gunshot made her flinch. A second later another shot echoed in the hollow. A horse whinnied. Then all fell silent. Lydia expected her father to return to the cabin, cursing and making a big show about how the fox got away. Her father was a skilled hunter, but the creature always remained elusive and caused Lydia to wonder if her father wanted to do anything more than frighten the thing.

Time ticked past. Lydia shifted her attention between the sewing of her new dress, her father, and the fox.

The mantle clock struck the half-hour.

"I wonder what's keeping Papa. He's been gone a long time." With the continued sense of unease, Lydia put down her sewing and strolled to the front window. Only darkness greeted her. "Maybe I should look for him. He didn't take his coat."

"He's liable to catch his death out there." Her mother sounded bothered.

Lydia dressed for the cold, flung her father's coat over her arm and stepped into the awaiting darkness. The crisp night air embraced her, almost taking her breath away. The temperature had dipped lower than she expected for March. The full moon, hanging in a blue haze between clouds, winked.

"Papa!"

There was no answer.

"Papa!"

Only a horned owl responded with its hoot.

A breeze brought an oppressive sense of doom. Lydia shuddered. Something wasn't right. It was too quiet. Her father wouldn't have chased after the fox. Why didn't he answer?

"Papa!" Lydia shrieked on a rising note of fear, and charged toward the outbuildings. When she was certain she'd heard a muffled cry, she paused. The moon slipped behind the clouds to enshroud her in impenetrable darkness. *How could she have been so stupid to forget a lantern?*

A few more steps and Lydia tripped over something soft and fleshy and which moved beneath her feet. She restrained a scream. Was it man or beast? A gentle prod with her foot brought a moaned response.

"Papa, what happened to you?"

Lydia bent to examine the sprawled body, dread prickling her arms at what she might find. Could a coyote have turned on her father to maul him? A fox wouldn't knock a man down. She found a warm sticky mass on along her father's side, but nothing as if some wild thing had ripped him open. He was bleeding and may be dying and she was getting the strange feeling that something was still out there, watching her, as if maybe her father hadn't killed or scared off whatever was out there.

She threw her father's coat over him before tearing a thin, worn section of fabric from the hem of her dress and stuffing it beneath the coat and into her father's wound. She took the hand of the barely conscious man and placed it over the stuffing. In her father's state his effort would be inadequate at best, but she had to leave him to get her mother and a weak hand was better than nothing.

"Hold that," she ordered. "Push as hard as you can."

He groaned and tried to speak.

"I'm getting Mama." She hoped the two of them could carry her father into the house.

Adrenaline propelling her forward, she flung open the cabin door, "Mama! Mama!"

"Close the door, Lydia."

"We must hurry. Papa's hurt!"

"Hurt? How?" Her mother was being much too calm.

"There's a hole in his side. It looks real bad." Lydia closed the door, breathing heavy. She gulped in air.

"Dear God." Her mother stared at her in shock.

The two women grabbed lanterns and quilts and scrambled to where Lydia had left her father, sprawled in the dirt, covered with his coat.

"Help me get him inside," her mother ordered.

The two women rolled up the unconscious man in the quilts, then half dragged, half carried him into the house. They nearly dropped him as they passed through the entry.

They hoisted him up and laid him upon the bed with as much ease as they could before removing his bloody shirt. Her mother went straight to work on her father's wound, pulling out the fabric Lydia had placed there to staunch the flow of blood.

"Lydia," her mother gasped, "he's been shot!"

"Shot?" Lydia's mind refused to register the significance of her mother's words. She watched in bafflement as her mother's shaky hands dabbed at the percolating wound. "I thought some wild animal had done this."

"I can't stop the bleeding," her mother announced a few minutes later, her voice as shaky as her fingers. "I don't know what to do. I've never dug out a bullet before."

"Mrs. Applegate taught me about potions and teas. Nothing like this. I'll get the doctor." Lydia turned on her heels.

"It's not safe. Lydia, come back here."

Lydia didn't even glance backward as she hurried from the house. She ran as fast as she could into the barn, where she found Sunshine and the other animals shifting nervously and kicking at their stalls. Lydia had to calm Sunshine with soothing words as she flung a blanket over the animal's back.

A few seconds later, as Lydia emerged from the barn, a cloud passed over the moon and again enveloped her in darkness. An owl hooted. As she kicked Sunshine into motion, Lydia glanced at the cabin behind her; the fire within cast a warm glow through the windows, belying the life and death trauma occurring within.

***

"It's up to God now," Dr. Adams said.

He stared down at his ashen patient, now resting comfortably. Her father hadn't regained consciousness, even during the surgery to remove the bullet.

"He's lost a lot of blood. We can only hope the bullet didn't do much internal damage. I've done all I can." The doctor handed Lydia some salve and bandages. "Do you remember what I told you to do?"

"I'll take good care of him. I'll sit up with him all night."

"How are *you* doing, Lydia?" the doctor asked.

"I'm fine."

"Why don't you sit down and let me take care of those scratches on your face."

Lydia touched her cheek and found some welts with dried blood. She remembered something scratching her while she rode to Dr. Adam's cabin. She'd been fortunate to find him at home, rather that tending to an emergency somewhere else. Otherwise, her father could have died as she waited hours for the doctor's services.

"Would you like some tea?" Lydia deliberately changed the subject.

105

The doctor openly scrutinized her until she bashfully returned to the stove.

"I'm making one of Mrs. Applegate's teas to help Mama sleep. Can I make something for you?" While the doctor dug the bullet from her father, Lydia had sent her mother up to the loft to rest.

The doctor joined Lydia where the tea was steeping and sniffed the steamy aroma. He wriggled his nose. "Wow. That stuff smells as foul as some of the medicines I force down my patients. Does it work?"

His question of doubt surprised her. "Yes, of course."

"I think I'll pass this time." The doctor packed up his medical items and gave her father a final check.

"Are you sure you don't want some hot tea before you go back out into the cold? I can make you something more pleasing with honey and cinnamon."

Although Lydia never cared for company, she found herself wishing the doctor would stay. He was a man with a pleasant bedside manner, grey hair, perhaps the age of Amos Crenshaw. He had stepped in years ago to fill the role of the aging Agnes Applegate, supposedly having received a formal education from some eastern school. He always seemed knowledgeable enough about diagnoses and modern treatments. Lydia had often wondered how a man of such station had ended up in the backwoods of Missouri. Few came to the region except to escape something else.

Dr. Adams turned as he pulled the leather strap to open the cabin door. "In the morning, I'll stop by the Sheriff's and report what happened tonight, then check back with you to see how your father is doing. Try to get some fluids down him and don't be afraid to give him some of the laudanum if he needs it. In the meantime… if something should… well, you know where to find me."

Lydia nodded and thanked him. She closed the door and listened to the sound of hooves disappear into the lonely night. When there was silence, Lydia shivered and was about to summon her mother downstairs for tea, when her mother climbed down the ladder.

"I've made you tea," Lydia said, "to help you sleep."

"I don't want to sleep," her mother responded. Of a sudden, she looked thin and pale. Her eyes bloodshot. She went into the bedroom and curled up on the edge of the bed beside her husband.

Through the eternal night of loneliness and fear, Lydia's father remained as still as death. The fire flickered as if possessed by spirits and cast haunting shadows across the room. Lydia shivered with each frigid gust of wind that slithered through the cracked chinking.

She jumped from the rocker with every creak or howl of a night creature, often dashing to peer out the window into the inky darkness. She would then return to the rocker and adjust her father's rifle squarely across her lap. She knew how to use the weapon and wouldn't hesitate to defend her family. As long as the gunman was still out there, she could not relax. Her nerves remained on edge. Eventually the world lightened as snow began to sift earthward.

Lydia and her mother were sitting at the table staring at the breakfast of cold biscuits and jam when the sound of snorting horses appeared out front. Cradling the rifle against her chest, Lydia peeked out the window. The sharp reflection of the morning sun off the fallen snow nearly blinded her.

True to his word, Dr. Adams had sent Sheriff Hicks, who was ankle deep in snow, conversing with his deputy. After a few minutes, Hicks strolled to the cabin and banged on the door. Lydia didn't find this man's arrival reassuring.

"Howdy, Miz Lydia." He tipped his hat and smiled, revealing a mouthful of yellowed teeth beneath a full winter beard. A tattered looking man of medium build, maybe forty, Hicks was as much of a backwoodsman as the rest of Possum Hollow's residents. He'd only assumed the role of sheriff because no one else wanted the job and then he pulled his nephew in to serve as deputy. "You don't mind if we have a look around, do you?"

"I suppose not."

"Good. I'll start by asking y'all some questions. Mind if I come in?"

Lydia glanced back at her mother.

"I won't take long." Hicks forced his way past Lydia. He cleared his throat and removed his hat, not bothering to wipe his feet. "How's your husband doing?"

"Not well." Remaining at her place at the table, her mother curled unsteady hands around her steaming cup of coffee.

"Sorry to hear that." Hicks strained his neck to catch a glimpse of the pallid man stretched out on the bed. "He been able to talk yet?"

Lydia closed the door and answered his question. "No."

"That's too bad."

"Do you have any idea who might have shot my husband?" Her mother's lower lip trembled. Long blonde hair tumbled down her shoulders in tangles. Eyes glistening with unshed tears, she gazed up at the sheriff.

"Now, Mrs. Whitley, let's not be jumpin' to conclusions. We don't know for sure that somebody shot your husband."

If the situation hadn't been so dire, Lydia would have laughed out loud from the man's sheer stupidity.

"He has a hole in his side," her mother retorted in the manner of a gentle reprimand. "Dr. Adams pulled a bullet out of it."

"Don't mean somebody shot him. Could a shot himself. Maybe fell on his gun. I've seen men shot and killed just cleaning the thing. What makes you think somebody shot him?"

Her mother shifted restlessly in her chair. She spoke with hesitation, purposely choosing her words with lowered voice. "We've had… some sabotage."

Some… sabotage. Her parents knew about the decapitated hen. Anything else? Lydia thought she had been adept at hiding things from them. Had there been more going on than she knew? Uneasiness crept over her.

"Some of our food stores were tampered with. We thought it was only animals at first," her mother said. "Most recently, we discovered some tools and rope missing. Then one of our chickens…" Her mother's eyes, clouded with concern, caught Lydia's gaze only briefly, then quickly dismissed her. "was decapitated."

Lydia sensed that her mother was keeping something from her.

Hicks scratched his unshaven chin. "Nobody else has reported any thefts. Or decapitated hens."

Her mother focused on her thumb as it caressed the rim of her coffee cup. "No one else has an Indian for a daughter."

A suffocating sensation tightened around Lydia's throat, her ears burning as if she had been caught in a lie. Had her long held secrets not been secrets at all? This revelation shook Lydia more than she wanted to admit. Her mother's words changed everything.

"We don't blame you," her mother said to her.

Lydia shriveled. Her mother might say they didn't blame her. But to even say it, to mention it… the fault was the same. As she had long feared; her presence was endangering the people she loved.

"So what you're sayin' is, your husband was shot when he caught somebody stealin'," Hicks continued. "Wonder who shot first. Maybe whoever shot your husband was defending himself."

The accusation sparked her mother's anger, "That is madness to imply…"

"Well, then I best take a look around."

Lydia pulled herself together enough to escort the sheriff to the door. "I heard two shots," she said. "Find out where the other bullet went."

Lydia watched the sheriff and his deputy make a cursory stroll around the property, hands in pockets, kicking up snow. When they disappeared behind the outbuildings, Lydia decided that Sheriff Hicks was the incompetent idiot her father claimed. Evidence would have had to jump in front of the sheriff for him to actually find anything. When the sheriff rejoined his deputy, they chatted briefly, and then looked upward as if expecting the gunman to actually fall from the clear sky.

A few minutes later, Lydia and her mother were cleaning up from breakfast when the sheriff pounded on their door. "We didn't find any gunman," he announced, once inside the cabin, his wet muddy boots dripping on the entry floor. "If one was here, he's long gone."

Lydia wished his report offered more relief from her anxiety. At least she could safely go about her farm chores. For the moment.

"Looks like the snow covered up whatever evidence there might have been. Didn't find no bullet neither. I'll come back later. Check on your papa."

Lydia decided to put her focus on her father's care, which took priority over finding a criminal or her own personal misery. She watched Sheriff Hicks and his deputy mount their horses with the same sluggish demeanor in which they had conducted their search.

Later that afternoon, Esther Crenshaw showed up at the door carrying baskets.

"Hello, Mrs. Crenshaw. Please come in," Lydia greeted. The sun had melted much of the snow, but the pink cast to the woman's cheeks and nose were a testament to a wind chill that remained below freezing.

Lydia helped her neighbor to the kitchen table with her bundles then took her shawl to hang by the door. Beneath the frayed brown wool, Esther wore her usual working dress. Esther untied and removed her bonnet before presenting it to Lydia, revealing gray hair fastened neatly at the nape of her neck.

With dark haunted eyes, Amanda nodded a greeting at her friend from where she perched in the rocker she had dragged to her husband's bedside.

"This is all so horrible. You should've sent Lydia to fetch me earlier. I only just heard the news from Sheriff Hicks. That dreadful man is going around questioning everyone as if we're all criminals." Esther's eyes widened as she approached Edward lying as still and pale as death. "How is he doing?"

"Not well," her mother's voice cracked. "All we can do is keep him comfortable and force liquid down his throat when he's awake enough to take it."

Amanda looked over at Lydia who was now picking through the bundles. "You really shouldn't have brought all that food. We haven't had much appetite."

With nervous energy and a wavering smile, Esther started sorting through the bundles she'd delivered. "There's enough food to last you a few days. There's corn bread and… Oh, I left the roast out in the wagon."

"I'll get it," Lydia volunteered.

"It should be behind the seat," Esther tossed the words over her shoulder. "Wrapped in cheesecloth."

On her way to the Crenshaw's wagon, Lydia met up with Amos who was on his way into the house. He was pale and hunched, causing Lydia concern that his rheumatism had worsened. They greeted each other before he stepped inside.

Lydia started to reach into the back of the wagon when movement alongside the house caught her eye. A man was rooting through her father's tools. As if he'd sensed her eyes on him, he looked up at her, axe gripped as if ready to strike. With the sudden rush of blood pumping in her ears, Lydia let out a choked cry. The man's bruised and swollen face was almost unrecognizable. When he started toward her with a limp, she let out another cry and bolted toward the house.

"Lydia, wait a minute!" the man called. His grip eased on the axe to let it swing toward the ground.

She stopped, her foot poised to kick the door open. Then recognition dawned on her. The voice sounded as if it came from a heavy tongue in a face stuffed full of something.

"Joe?" Her relief altered into a mix of emotions. She forced herself to look at the man, then regarded him with speculation. Why was he here? Her pulse was not erratic from fear, nor was the tug in the pit of her stomach. Even with all Joe had done, his presence still sparked excitement. Would she ever be unmoved by his nearness?

"Yes." He regarded her steadily. There was no curve to his lips.

"Your face… it's…" A thick lump constricted her throat.

"I know. My nose is broken. Second time actually." He shrugged. "Zeus kicked me the first time. Once the swelling goes down, it won't look so bad."

Lydia knew why his nose was broken. He'd been beaten because he refused to marry the woman he'd gotten pregnant. He'd obviously put up a big struggle. His once handsome face was now as damaged as the character behind it. The skin along her arms prickled and made her shudder.

Joe leaned the axe against the cabin and moved beside her. "You're shivering."

He was too close. She could smell the smoke lingering on his coat, hear the catch of his breath in his throat.

"Why did you come outside without your cape?"

"I… I was getting the roast Mrs. Crenshaw left in the wagon." Lydia pushed passed him and reached behind the wagon seat.

"I'll get it for you." He brushed her arm as he retrieved the roast from between some blankets where Lydia couldn't reach.

"Thank you," she said, and started back to the cabin.

"I'm sorry about your father," Joe said, following her with the roast.

When Lydia and Joe stepped into the cabin, her mother turned in their direction, her hand flying to her gaping mouth.

Joe did not acknowledge or apologize for his shocking appearance. "Sorry to hear about your husband," he said in his nasal voice.

"Esther didn't mention you were here." Amanda gave her friend a brief, stabbing look.

"He came to help with some of the heavy work," Esther said.

"It looks like you could use some firewood split and cut," Joe added.

Her mother eyed Joe up and down. "You don't look in much condition to do heavy work."

"I'm more fit than I seem." Joe handed Lydia the roast and hurried back outside, escaping the discomfort of the room.

While her mother and Esther prepared supper and chatted in the kitchen, Amos offered to check on the livestock. Lydia informed him that she had fed the animals that morning, after the sheriff's visit.

She had devoted most of the day to the care of her father, who had spiked a fever and needed bathing with cold compresses, which caused him great distress. Half-awake, he would moan and thrash in his covers as she laid compresses on his forehead and chest and under his arms. As soon as he was able, Lydia was determined to get him to drink some willow bark tea.

While Lydia continued to tend her father, she couldn't ignore the grunts of the man who was outside splitting firewood. The clang of sledge impacting wedge seemed to go on forever. Slamming against raw nerves. Deafening. Esther and her mother didn't seem to notice. The blazing fire made the cabin unusually warm and oppressive. Although her mother often glanced in Lydia's direction and at her father, she didn't seem to notice Lydia's increasing anxiety until she snatched up the water pail and rushed to the door.

"Where are you going?" her mother asked sharply.

Lydia swallowed as if caught doing something forbidden. "I need some fresh water for Papa." *Yes. And some fresh air. Lured to the man outside whose very presence compelled her there.*

Her mother gave Lydia a warning look. She obviously didn't want her near Joe–as if he would try to molest her on the other side of the wall from her parents–then again, maybe he would. A thrill shot from her stomach to her throat.

Stop it, Lydia. Stop it.

Lydia found Joe a few yards from the house. The day had warmed enough for him to remove his shirt, which was now stretched over the woodpile. Beads of sweat glistened along his spine. She stood mesmerized, watching the play of muscles across his back and his sinewy arms tense and flex, curling her toes into the soles of her shoes. She didn't know how long she had been standing there, when Joe paused in his work to beckon her, causing her face to warm with embarrassment.

"I was on my way to get water for Papa," she stammered, feeling defensive.

"What do you think?" he asked.

What did she think? She thought his body was in perfect form, raw and masculine, that even during times when she thought she could hate him, she could only warm to his smile, and be swallowed into the depths of his deep blue eyes. Each time she looked at the sky, Joe was there, clinging to her mind.

When she didn't answer, he clarified his question. "Is that enough wood to last for the next few days?"

Lydia shook off her previous thoughts and did a mental count of the cut and split logs. "Yes, that should do."

"Good." Joe casually set the sledge aside. He tugged off his work gloves and withdrew a string of licorice from his pocket. Before pulling off a bite with his teeth, he offered some to Lydia. She shook her head no.

"Have you changed your mind about coming to California?"

Lydia focused her gaze across the farmyard. "Why would I change my mind now? Papa might be dying." There was a catch to her voice. "Mama will need me."

"You have to hope your father will get better."

Yes. They must hope. Joe put his arm across her back, meaning to comfort. Instead, his touch sent a wave of longing and loss, intensifying her emotional distress. She pulled away from the man who threatened to destroy what remained of her dignity.

He was married! How could he not act as if he had a wife?

Joe followed her to the well, slipping his arms through the sleeves of his shirt.

"We'll be leaving next week. My aunt and uncle's auction is in five days," Joe reminded her.

"I forgot it was happening so soon." A knot tightened in her stomach.

"I'll put together a list of instructions for you."

She was too tired from the stress of caring for her father to argue with the obstinate man. "I'd better get back inside. Mama is watching me."

Joe looked toward the kitchen window and brazenly waved at the pulled back curtain.

Then, Amos strolled toward them as he returned from the barn. Deep furrows of worry creased his brow. "I heard Hicks stopped by."

"He poked around some," Lydia answered, remembering his pathetic search.

"Did he go into the barn?"

"Papa didn't get shot in the barn."

"So, Hicks didn't mention the trail of blood and prints which lead up the hillside from the barn?"

Lydia felt the blood drain from her face. *Blood. Prints.* She had been in the barn earlier that morning tending the animals. The time she'd spent had been brief, and she hadn't noticed any blood or fresh footprints. Then again, anxious and focused on completing her task, she hadn't been looking. And the snow had melted since then.

Was it possible? The shooter, cold and wounded had holed up in the barn overnight? Fresh prints indicated he could have been there in the morning when she tended the animals. Yes. It was possible. Even probable. She shivered at the thought of how close she might have been to him. Her night of terror had been justified.

"Are the animals all right?" Her voice was shrill with fear. "Are they all there?" Gertie had been lost to them forever, swallowed up by the mountain. She could not bear for harm to come to another. She started to bolt toward the barn sloshing out some of the water in her pail, but Amos reached out and grabbed her arm.

"They're fine," he said and released her.

"What kind of prints?" Joe asked.

"Boot."

"I'm going to have a look," Joe said. "Your father must have gotten a piece of whoever shot him," he said to Lydia. With lips set in a grim line, he headed toward the barn.

CHAPTER 15

Late afternoon the following day, Sheriff Hicks returned to the Whitleys'. Amanda opened the door while Lydia finished checking on her father's bandage. At least blood was no longer staining the clean white fabric, and she'd managed to get some willow bark tea down his throat. She could only pray the tea would reduce the fever and make him more comfortable.

"How's your husband doing? I take it he ain't talkin' yet." Hicks bobbed his head toward the bed.

"He slips in and out." Her mother sounded as tired as she appeared in the wrinkled dress she'd not taken time to change since her husband had been shot. Lydia knew she looked equally as haggard. "Doctor Adams stopped by earlier to change his bandage. He can't do anything more for him."

"Sorry to hear that. I hear folks've been stoppin' by though, to help with chores. You're a brave little lady," Hicks said to Lydia, "ridin' out to fetch the doc with that gunman on the loose."

"I hope you've come to tell us some good news about the man who shot my husband." Her mother said. "We've been on edge with him still out there."

"Well… I've got some good news on that part. Turns out we found a body at the old Applegate place. By the looks of things, he'd been holed up in there all winter." Hicks puffed out his chest.

"Was Joseph Brice the one who found him?" Lydia didn't know why she felt compelled to give him credit. She knew Joe had followed the boot tracks up the mountain, although he had not returned. She hadn't thought much of his disappearance since lately her mother had made it obvious he wasn't welcome there.

"Joseph Brice," Hicks scratched his chin. "Yeah. I guess that was the fella. Showed up late at my office yesterday with his side of the story."

His side? Lydia wondered what the sheriff was implying.

"He claims he tracked the man's boot prints from your father's barn. Said he saw some blood drops too. Now when me and the deputy was here. We didn't see no prints."

"So, the body… Was… he… the gunman?" her mother asked with wavering voice.

"More than likely. We're still sorting through the evidence."

Lydia wondered what evidence had been found.

"So, how did he die?" her mother asked.

"Either bled out or froze to death. Seems he was shot right square in the groin."

Amanda cringed. "My husband shot him in the groin?"

"Well, ma'am, that's where the story gets kind of prickly. That Joseph Brice, rather an unsavory character, in my opinion, claims he found the man dead in the Applegate cabin. I'm thinkin', since me and the deputy didn't see no prints, maybe it weren't your husband who shot him. Could a been Brice, took justice in his own hands or had his own score to settle. Since he's a foreigner to these parts, mind you, nobody knows nothin' about him. Witnesses claim he's had a couple of previous run ins with the dead man."

Blood drained from Lydia's face. She didn't want to believe… could her mother have been right about Joe all along?

"Who… who was the gunman?" Her mother asked.

"William Matheson. Found out he's wanted in Pigeonville, among other places. Numerous warrants. We identified him by the long scar across his face. Supposedly got maimed in a knife fight. US Marshals are still trying to figure out if he killed the other guy in self-defense."

Goosebumps prickled Lydia's skin.

"Ever hear of him?"

"No," her mother answered emphatically.

"He'd been going by the name Willie Kincaid. Guess when the Kincaids found out he wasn't kin, they cut him loose."

Willie. Lydia couldn't say she was sorry the man was dead. Would Joe have killed him in cold blood?

"What was he wanted for?" her mother asked.

"Armed robbery. Horses, saddles, and whatever else he could sell to eke out a livin'." Hicks removed his hat and scratched his head. "The way I figure it, Mr. Whitley probably caught him in the act of stealin' and got shot for it. After that, I can't say much about what happened. We've still got to sort through the evidence. Might make some arrests."

***

The mantle clock's tick-tock, tick-tock, lulled Lydia into drowsiness. Her eyes grew heavy as the heat of the fire seeped through her lap blanket and into her bones.

Getting hotter... as one by one the tall conical structures turned into giant torches. The dark skinned people broke from their ceremony. Dancers no longer twisted in rhythm to the beat of drums, arms no longer flailed in ceremony, but in flight. Wailing song turned to screams.

Propelled by terror at seeing her world destroyed, Lydia took flight away from the fire and the blood which pooled beneath bodies. She tried to scream.

Nothing came out.

Her heart racing, Lydia awoke disoriented and confused, a bright orange glow shining on the dark horizon to mirror the horrors she had escaped. She kicked wildly in an attempt to flee, but the snare of blanket and chair legs held her prisoner and brought her to the ground. A scratchy sound escaped her dry throat. She lay on the wooden floor helpless, trembling with utter terror until blood flowed back into her sleepy legs and she began to comprehend her current situation.

The orange light was only the soft glow from the nearly lifeless coals of a dying fire. She managed to sit up, and with a deep breath, she further surveyed her surroundings. The rise and fall of her father's chest beneath his bed covers was steady and even, indicating that he was resting comfortably. Her mother was sleeping in the rocker by his bed, snoring softly.

Lydia untangled herself and came to her feet. She took a step toward her father. The bullet, which had been removed, now wiped clean, lay among the salves and bandages on the night table, beckoned to her. She toyed with the bullet between finger and thumb, amazed at how such a tiny thing could so disrupt her family's life.

Anguish penetrated the marrow of her bones. The truth was facing her now. Lydia knew with certainty that her presence in Possum Hollow was endangering the two people she loved most. It didn't matter that Willie was dead. There would always be someone. There would always be concern.

She put down the bullet and went to the fireplace where she tossed a couple of logs from their meager supply into what remained of the untended fire. Sparks shot out from the hot coals. Lydia poked at the burning embers, empathizing with the woeful timbers as flames began to consume them, much as the wretchedness of the world was consuming her.

Mrs. Applegate, what would you do?

Lydia's attempt at living by her mother's teachings, being a lady to 'erase any signs of her heritage so society would accept her,' had been an inept failure. She had tried to make it so, but Possum Hollow would never be her home. The shadows of the forest were no longer a safe haven. Like Joe had told her, she didn't belong here.

Moisture in the logs hissed and whistled as they turned to steam. *Ssssoar.* The hoarse aged voice sent prickles along her arms, thrusting her to awareness. Lydia scanned the dark shadowy room and listened for what she thought she had heard.

"Lydia." Like a ghost, a voice crept from the shadows.

"Papa?" She tossed aside the poker and nearly leapt to his bed. "You're awake?" She gently shook her sleeping mother. "Mama, Papa's awake."

Her mother bolted upright.

"Papa's awake."

"Edward?" Amanda leaned over to the man whose eyes now blinked back at her. Tears she'd dammed for days now came in a flood.

Lydia quickly lit a bedside lantern.

Her father tried to push himself into a seated position. He grimaced and fell back into the pillows before the women could help him sit upright and adjust pillows to prop up his head.

"What happened?" His voice came out hoarse and barely audible.

The two women looked at one another, her mother wiping tears from her eyes with the corner of her apron.

"You were shot," her mother answered, "five days ago."

"Five...?" he croaked and swallowed down a thick lump. What color was left, drained from his face. Lydia snatched up a tin mug of water and helped him take a sip. Some dribbled down his chin.

"You've been unconscious most of the time," her mother said. "Dr. Adams did the best he could. The wound festered. Can you remember anything?"

Her father shook his head and closed his eyes, sinking further into the pillows.

"You went out for firewood," Lydia said. "It was cold that night, with snow falling toward morning. When you returned a few minutes later for your rifle, I thought maybe you had seen the fox."

He clutched his chest as if remembering something. "Exploding... burning pain."

"Are you in pain now?" her mother asked, worry creasing her brow. "The doctor left you some laudanum."

"No laud...," his dry voice trailed off. When Lydia offered him more water, he managed to place his hands over hers, helping to guide the mug to his mouth to drink.

"We heard two shots," Lydia said.

He nodded again.

Lydia showed him the bullet the doctor had extracted from his side, wedged near a rib. Her father turned it in his fingers, studying it through squinting eyes and furrowed brow, and then returned it. "Don't remember after that."

"It doesn't matter," Amanda said emphatically.

Her father's eyes widened as if something else came to mind. "The man who... Did he harm...?"

"We're fine Papa. The man is dead." Although the sheriff never admitted as much, that the dead man and the gunman were one in the same, Lydia was certain of it.

"I killed?" He was a peaceful man. He'd never shot anyone before. He made a grunting sound and attempted to push himself further upright. He was too weak to do little more than brace his hands at his sides. The women helped to settle him.

"He died later, up in the hills," Amanda said. "Joseph Brice found him squatting at the old Applegate place."

That information did not soothe her father; his face fell into tight, bitter lines.

"You probably caught him lurking around for something to steal," Lydia added to the story. "That's when he shot you."

"None of that matters anymore. All you need to think about is getting well," her mother said, shutting down the conversation. "Lydia, heat up some broth for your father."

They spent the rest of the night trying to get some broth into her father and keeping him comfortable. He resisted taking the laudanum, but without it, he thrashed in his sleep and awoke from nightmares, moaning. The women feared he would tear open his wound.

Well into the following afternoon, after her father had slept soundly for several hours and taken his first few bites of solid food–mashed sweet potato–Lydia decided to tell her plans to her parents. She approached them from the kitchen, wringing her hands against the physical pain she bore. This was the hardest thing she'd ever done.

Her mouth went dry and her thickened tongue stuck to the roof of her mouth. The words came out bluntly. "I'm leaving Possum Hollow."

Her mother shook her head as if clearing her own thoughts. "What are you talking about?"

"I don't belong here. In Possum Hollow. I am born of another people."

"Lydia, of course you were not born from my flesh. That doesn't mean you don't belong here," her mother said.

"You are our daughter just the same," her father added.

She wrung her hands and paced nervously. "You and Mama have taught me well, but people don't care that I am well-mannered and speak politely. I have copper colored skin. I am ostracized. I cannot walk with my head up. It is often difficult and I am not always brave." She was surprised at how polished her thoughts came out. Her voice never wavered or cracked.

"We know living here isn't easy for you, but you never told us what's inside your head," her father said grimly. His brows narrowed in contemplation.

"Not only am I mistreated, now the farm and Papa…" she choked. "My being here has put you two in danger."

"The man who shot your father is dead," her mother said emphatically.

"What about the next man? Papa might not be so lucky then." Lydia's voice was becoming shrill as she shot reason at them.

"Have I failed you as a father?"

"Have we not treated you well?" her mother chimed in.

"Do you think me so weak…" her father struggled against a dry raspy sounding voice, "that I can't protect my family?"

"Oh no, Papa. Of course not." Lydia rushed to his side and helped him take a drink of water. "I couldn't be more grateful for what you and Mama have done. I'd be dead now if it weren't for you."

"Don't talk of death." Her father shuddered. "We've come too close. You are my daughter. I don't want you to leave."

Lydia hugged him, noting with concern at how thin and frail he felt in her arms. She had to convince herself that he would grow stronger as his wound healed. When she pulled back from him, her vision was misty. "And you are my parents, as if I were born of your flesh." She caught a tear with the palm of her hand as it squeezed from her lashes. "It's not the way you or mama have treated me that makes me wish to leave."

"It's that Joseph Brice." Enlightenment came over her mother's face. "That gun-slinging, who-knows-what has talked you into joining that caravan, hasn't he?" Anger sharpened her voice as she turned and glared at Lydia.

"Why would you think that, Mama?" Guilt constricted Lydia's throat.

"I should have known the two of you were planning something. The other day when he came to chop firewood, you two were outside, his hand was all over your back and he was whispering something to you."

Lydia's face grew hot. The tops of her ears burned as if they'd been singed. She wanted to deny her mother's words, claim that Joe was only being friendly.

"You wouldn't be so disobedient on your own. He's turned you against us. Even the sheriff said he was unsavory."

"Joining the caravan is my decision."

"You're too naive and innocent. Strong men die out west. What do you think would happen to a woman without a husband to protect her?" her mother asked.

"I know it won't be easy."

"We took you into our home and our hearts. Is this how you repay us? Your father is ill and needs you. I need you. The planting season is nearly upon us. You can't abandon us!"

"Don't make this harder," Lydia's voice quivered.

"This is madness. How will you pay for this trip?" her mother snapped.

"I'll work for a doctor and his wife in exchange for passage."

Her father raised an eyebrow. "You've obviously been planning this for some time."

"Well, I forbid you to go! After that scoundrel is gone everything will be all right again," her mother said.

"Everything won't be all right," Lydia burst out. "How can you not understand? Nothing has ever been all right. Your lives are in danger with me here." She turned her back to her parents and moved toward the door.

"Where are you going?" her mother snapped. "We're not finished."

"I'm going to the Crenshaws. Let them know Papa is better." She pulled her cape from off its hook and slipped it on. As she closed the door, she heard her mother pleading with her father to make her stay.

When Lydia reached the Crenshaws' she tied Sunshine to a tree near the cabin. She hesitated to stroll up the hill, despite the welcoming smell of wood smoke beckoning her to the front door. She wasn't usually nervous about visiting the Crenshaws', but today Joe was there. And Allison had moved in. Lydia stood on the porch for a few moments, hesitating to knock.

Then the door opened.

An instantaneous thrill rushed through her. Joe was standing on the threshold wearing his leather jacket, a red bandana tied neatly around his neck. The brim of his hat hid his eyes, and shadowed the bruises on his face. The swelling had gone down.

"Lydia, what a surprise. I was on my way out."

"I…I came by to tell everyone. Papa's better."

"That's great news," Joe said, a smile touching his lips. "Do you need anything? Firewood, perhaps?"

Lydia shook her head. Some of the other locals had been taking turns with chopping firewood. "I've decided to go to California."

"That's wonderful!" His grin spread across his face. Then he glanced over his shoulder and closed the door.

"My parents weren't happy when I told them," she said.

Joe gently took Lydia by the elbow and led her out of earshot of the cabin's occupants. "They must realize that at some point in your life you would leave home."

"Leaving Possum Hollow is one thing. Going to California is another. You know how Papa feels about the trip. He called your uncle a fool."

The front door flew open on creaky hinges to reveal Allison standing there in a calico dress, its thin fabric pulled taut across her rounded abdomen. Red hair hung in shiny curls across her shoulders and accentuated a complexion glowing with youthful freshness. Marriage and pregnancy looked good on her.

It took everything Lydia had to not flee at that moment. Cold reality stung.

"Joe, who you talkin' to?" Allison paused at the entry only long enough to meet Lydia's gaze before striding toward the pair, wrinkling her nose as if Lydia were some foul smelling creature.

Joe released Lydia's elbow and turned to his wife, his smile fading. "It's chilly out here. You should go back inside."

"What she doin' here?" Allison pursed her lips with distaste. "You and me is married now. It's wrong her bein' here." She looped her arms around Joe's elbow and nuzzled up to him.

The sudden vision of the couple with arms entwined jolted Lydia with jealousy.

"Lydia came by to let us know that her father is doing much better. And she's coming to California with us."

Allison glared venom at Lydia. "How dare she! How dare that Injun come?" She lunged toward Lydia but Joe's firm grip thwarted her attack. "How would it look for us to be traveling with a Injun?"

"I don't care how it would look," Joe retorted.

"Well I ain't goin' if she's goin'."

"You are my wife now. You do as I say."

"Yes, I be your wife. But I got rights too."

Their harsh voices exploded within Lydia's head. How could she spend the next few months with a man and a woman who brought her such misery?

PART 2
THE JOURNEY

Gold fever, like cholera, spread across the continent. And gold fever, like cholera, lured multitudes to the western borders. Hard times and restlessness clawed at the young for adventure and a new life. Gold strikes in 1848 enticed many to obtain quick fortunes. Stories were told of mountains and streams overflowing with the precious nuggets.

Publications downplayed trail tragedies of earlier days and accentuated heroism and patriotism. Entrepreneurs responded to the massive emigration by selling provisions for elevated prices. Cattlemen gathered herds of livestock to drive to California or Oregon, where despite heavy losses on the trail, they could receive outrageous profits. Others taught mining or smelting courses. The far west was a place of hope and freedom: hope of economic improvement, better health, freedom from cholera or the law. The far west was Utopia.

Gullible were the 49'ers.

Seeing the elephant*- A popular phrase used to describe facing the unknown. For emigrants, the elephant symbolized both the high cost of their endeavor -- the myriad of possibilities for misfortune on the journey or in California -- and, like the circus elephant, an exotic sight, an unequaled experience, the adventure of a lifetime. Sightings came to epitomize the elephant as something most wanted to "see" but few wanted to "see" again.*

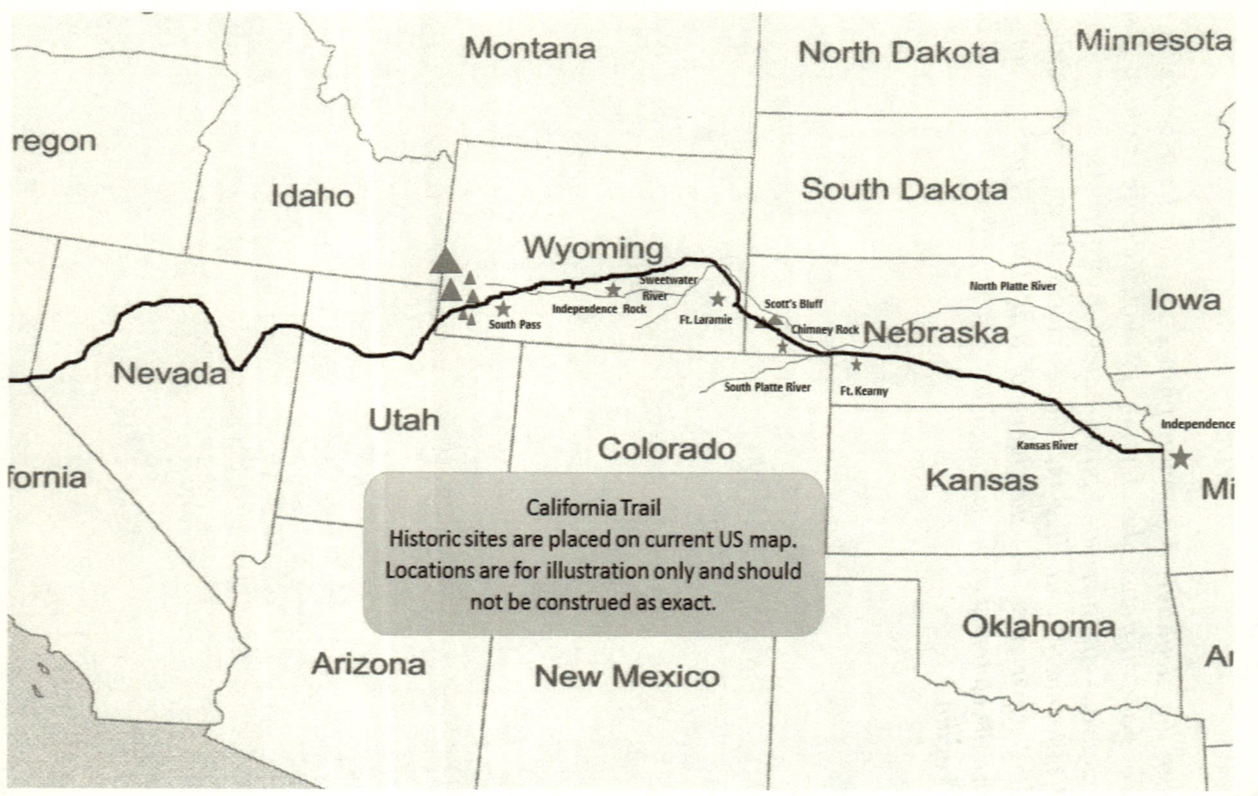

Oregon
Montana
North Dakota
Minnesota
Idaho
South Dakota
Wyoming
Iowa
Nevada
Utah
Nebraska
Colorado
Kansas
California
Arizona
New Mexico
Oklahoma
Missouri
Arkansas
South Pass
Independence Rock
Sweetwater River
Ft. Laramie
Scott's Bluff
Chimney Rock
North Platte River
South Platte River
Ft. Kearny
Kansas River
Independence
California Trail
Historic sites are placed on current US map.
Locations are for illustration only and should
not be construed as exact.

CHAPTER 16

Lydia poked her head from under the rear of the canvas, hoping for some fresh air. Instead, the sharp odors of tar and excrement greeted her. A cool misting rain wet her face, pooled and dripped from her lashes. The hypnotic squeak of wheels and ox-chains were quickly swallowed into the cacophony of Independence, Missouri. Hammers, reverberating with new construction were deafening.

Lydia choked down a rush of panic as her gaze swept across the bustling streets. Sidewalks buzzed with all manner of people, from men in dapper suits, women in fashionable dresses with feathered hats, the likes of which she'd never seen, to more simple folk in sweat stained coats and basic trousers. Along the dizzying labyrinth of brick and stone buildings, trains of ox teams lined the main streets.

Lydia now understood why Joe referred to Possum Hollow as a sleepy backwoods town. It was lifeless compared to the throbbing beat of Independence. She wondered how these townspeople would react to an Indian in their midst. Would they notice her and scorn her? Or could she disappear in their numbers?

Lydia slipped back under the canvas and leaned against the crates.

When the wagon broke its steady rhythm and slowed to a stop, the three women scrambled to peer out the wagon bed and found the sky clearing up to the west. The real attraction lay below the small rise. A sea of canvas, hundreds, perhaps thousands of wagons stretched along the Missouri river. A drowning sensation stole Lydia's breath. Never had she seen so many people gathered in one place, a greater number, she was certain, than all of those who occupied the Ozark hills and valleys she had left behind.

Allison started sobbing, making no attempt to hide her misery. During their last three days of travel, she'd claimed she had been forced on the journey, kidnaped and made prisoner by her own husband. Instead of being surrounded by family and the safety of home when she gave birth, she'd been ripped from her home and thrust into the wilderness. Her continual complaints sparked arguments with her husband and set everyone's nerves on edge. Even Esther's patience wore thin. Although she never raised her voice to Allison, Esther's soft features hardened into a constant grimace of emotional restraint. Joe remained in a grim mood and snarled when spoken to.

A tear trickled down Esther's cheek. She'd spoken infrequently, but freely shared her thoughts on starting a new life in California, with a new homestead. Like so many other women whose husbands yielded to the lure of a fresh life in what was touted as "the land of opportunity", she had relinquished almost everything. Her personal property. Her friends and home. She was nearly fifty, and too old to be starting over, she'd said.

Lydia was determined to focus on the future. She'd had very little to leave behind. Saying good-bye to Sunshine, her one true friend, had been heartbreaking. But she agreed with Joe. The horse was not trail hardened and would probably not survive the trip. Lydia already missed her parents, but not her situation. And their parting gifts would either see her through her mission or be a way home. Lydia choked back a tear at the memory of her father, still pale and weak, leaning on a makeshift crutch as he handed her the gold coin.

"I don't deserve this. You and Mama need this more than I." She'd had no idea her father possessed such wealth.

"Hush," her father said, closing her fingers around the coin. "My ham business has made us comfortable. And we've survived all these years without spending it. Your mother doesn't know. If you get into trouble, use it to get home. Keep it close and tell no one."

Then later, her mother reached into the large pocket of her apron and withdrew a pair of tiny moccasins. "You were wearing these when Edward and I found you. It's all you had."

A rush of excitement surged through Lydia. Despite the dirt and grass stains, and the thin worn soles, they were the most beautiful things she'd ever seen. And in surprisingly good condition. The upper leather was decorated with painted porcupine quills. She squeezed the moccasins as if they might possess some power to return her memories of those days.

"They're beautiful," Esther said.

"I promised myself years ago that I would give them to her when…" her mother's voice caught. "I knew that someday she would leave Possum Hollow." Her lower lip quivered and her eyes glistened with tears. "Maybe they offer some clue to your people."

"Oh, Mama, thank you." Lydia swung her arms around her mother's neck. Both her parents were full of surprises. "I shall treasure them." She broke into fresh tears and the two wept together for a few moments before slowly separating.

With lowered voice, her mother spoke. "I understand now. Although, I tried to make Possum Hollow your home, it never has been and never will be. I've been fooling myself to think otherwise."

Her mother had let her go.

Joe drove the wagon along the river bank until he found an acceptable place to camp, where the crowd was thinner and the grass was less worn. They let the animals drink their fill of water and supplemented their diet with hay, before hobbling them near the wagon, where they could graze. While Allison and Lydia took turns using the privacy of the wagon to freshen up, the Crenshaws prepared their supper over a small fire. The couple would remain at camp while the others dined at the hotel.

It was well past dark, when the hired carriage transporting Lydia and the Brice couple, pulled up to the front of the hotel.

The warm, brightly-lit hotel should have been a welcome to Lydia, instead, she felt as if a hand had closed around her throat. She would soon meet the physician and his wife to whom she had pledged service in exchange for passage. Lydia gratefully took the settee Joe offered before abandoning her and Allison in the lobby to search for their dining companions. Joe had tried to reassure Lydia that the Livelys were kind people, but everything within her core screamed to not trust him.

Had Joe prepared the Livelys for the truth? Had he told them she was an Indian? She could imagine the Livelys' disgust as they discovered the secret of their would-be traveling companion. Concerns of becoming a slave to the Livelys added fuel to her worries about the dangers of the journey itself. The multitude of people milling within the hotel sounded like a swarm of flies with their undulating buzz.

Lydia double-checked that the wide brim of her bonnet shielded her forehead and she tucked her copper colored hands into the folds of her calico dress. She eyed the other patrons, many who looked to be campers tired of the cold and rain and had gathered to dine in one of the few decent establishments in town. None paid her any undue attention. Perhaps, this crowd could be her sanctuary, with her plain dress and simple scuttle shaped bonnet, she could blend in.

The wait for Joe seemed like an eternity. Lydia's nervousness intensified to near panic as if at any moment she would shatter. She broke into a sweat, her heart pumping in her ears, her cape feeling like an iron weight on her shoulders. The air, heavy with perfume and too many bodies made her head swim.

This was a mistake. She should escape now, before Joe came back. Her gold coin could buy her a room for the night and transportation back to Possum Hollow.

She glanced at Allison, who sat in the settee across from her, hands entangled in the strings of her cloth purse and neatly folded in her lap. Her mouth was drawn in a deep scowl of defeat. Dark puffy eyes revealed her discomfiture. Another moment passed before Joe made his way through the crowd toward them, a tall bearded man at his heels.

Before Joe could make introductions, the bearded man pushed his way forward, his raven black hair gleaming in the chorus of candlelight. "Ah, at last we meet." Taking Lydia's hand, he brushed it against his cheek. "I've heard so much about you." He grinned with pearly white teeth that stood out against the backdrop of his dark beard. His dark piercing eyes bore into hers.

She returned a timid, yet courteous smile.

"Zachariah Potter," Joe began, "this is Lydia Whitley."

Zachariah Potter, Joe's old friend and appointed second in command of the caravan.

"Miss Whitley, I look forward to getting to know you better."

"And this is Allison, my wife."

"Your wife?" Zachariah raised an eyebrow. He released Lydia's hand and moved his attention to Allison.

"Yes, we were wed about three weeks ago." Joe smiled and helped Allison from the chair with the arm she offered.

"Three weeks?" Zachariah cast a wry grin at Joe and then at Allison who now beamed from ear to ear. It was obvious that Allison was more than two weeks pregnant. "I thought you'd sworn off marriage years ago. Didn't want to be trapped, you said."

Joe gritted his teeth and said nothing.

"Then congratulations, you old dog." Zachariah slapped Joe on the back. "Allison, you must be some fine filly to hitch this confirmed bachelor."

Allison squeezed Joe's arm, looking smug.

An uncomfortable silence lingered before Joe cleared his throat. "Shall we join the Livelys? I'm sure they're anxious to meet everyone."

"You're the boss," Zachariah answered. Then he offered his arm to Lydia. "Shall we go?"

Lydia hesitated to take the arm of this presumptuous man. So like Joe. His devilishly good looks rivaled his friend's too. Just because she was an unescorted female didn't mean she wanted to be paired up with him. Upon seeing Allison shuffle past her, still attached to Joe's arm, Lydia decided there was no harm in accepting Zachariah as a dinner escort. Indeed, she was grateful to have his support as she walked on shaky legs into the dining hall. And there was something exhilarating about capturing the attention of such an imposing and attractive man.

They stopped at a large table in the far corner near the fireplace. A candle on the table illuminated a couple seated there. *The Livelys.* The man stood politely as the others arrived and was introduced as Dr. Seth Lively. The woman remained seated, smiling only tentatively as the others were introduced, her nose tilted slightly in the air. *A snob.* Light brown hair hung in well-placed curls about her fair complexion. *No hard work in the sun for her.* She was attractive, not a beauty. A bounty of lace embellished the cuffs and low neckline of her dress, and emphasized her long slender neck. A row of expensive looking pearl buttons was sewn down the front.

Against this woman's stylish blue satin dress, Lydia felt like a brown field mouse in her drab clothing. Accustomed to the finer things in life, no wonder this woman wanted a servant to do her bidding.

When all except Lydia had been introduced, the woman lit up. "And this must be Lydia." Faith Lively took Lydia's trembling hand and looked deeply into her face. "Oh, what a lovely girl, Seth! I do hope we can become friends. I've been so nervous about meeting you."

Someone had been nervous about meeting her? It was almost unbelievable. Lydia felt the sincerity of the woman's words and a warm glow flowed through her, releasing her tension. She managed a quivering smile.

"I'm sure we'll all become friends," Zachariah announced, and then seated Lydia next to him, across from the Livelys, leaving Joe and Allison to sit across from them.

A short time later, an attractive young woman arrived at their table with drinks.

"I took the liberty of ordering us some hot spiced wine," the doctor said.

"I propose a toast," Zachariah said.

Lydia picked up her mug as everyone followed his lead.

"To a safe journey and to new friends." Zachariah scanned the group seated around the table, before settling his gaze upon Lydia.

"To health and prosperity," Joe added.

"Here, here." The others clinked their mugs together in the center of the table.

When Lydia tipped her mug to take a drink, the aromatic vapors prickled her nostrils in a reminder that this was alcohol. She'd never had wine before. Since her mother never allowed spirits in the home, the only alcohol she'd consumed was homemade whiskey she'd sneaked during community activities. Instead of the burn of whiskey that scrapped along her throat, the wine warmed as it went down.

This was Lydia's first experience eating in a public dining hall, so she watched the servers come and go, almost to the point of distraction. To have someone do her bidding was strange: to bring the food hot from the kitchen, to replace a fork when she'd nervously dropped one on the floor. It felt unnatural not to get up to serve coffee or pull something from the oven.

Conversation focused on planning for the trip. However, Zachariah frequently changed the subject to less serious bantering with Joe and proved himself to be a lively, energetic dinner companion. He often smiled at Lydia and made a point of bringing her into the conversation, although she would have preferred to remain silent. She often caught Joe scowling at his friend which gave her the distinct feeling that Zachariah's attention toward her displeased Joe. That made her smile inside.

The Livelys were a pleasant couple. The doctor's manner of speech and dress indicated that he was well educated; the other men respected his opinion on matters. He was reserved, but friendly. Every time he laughed, Lydia thought his stiff white collar would crack.

Faith Lively was a most refined woman. She sat erectly, drinking her coffee while neatly dabbing at the corners of her mouth. Pinky extended. And she did it so naturally! The manners of Lydia's mother were more proper than other residents of Possum Hollow, but were crude compared to Faith Lively. Perhaps her mother had acculturated to the backwoods more than she would admit.

They were about half way through the main course when Faith asked Lydia if she were ill. "You've hardly touched your food," she said.

The few bites Lydia had eaten of the lamb chop and the boiled potatoes were delicious. Surrounded by so many strangers and activities, her attention was easily diverted from the act of eating. And her stomach felt as heavy as if she had swallowed a bag of rocks.

"Don't you like your lamb chop?" Zachariah asked. "Try it with the mint jelly."

"Seth, do you think she looks flushed?" Faith asked, pulling her husband's attention from a side conversation with Joe.

"I don't think she looks well at all," Allison quickly chimed in with a derisive grin. "Perhaps she should remain in Independence. What do you think Joe?"

Lydia put down the fork she had been using to pick at the green beans on her plate. "I'm fine."

"I didn't think you were so selfish," Allison continued. "None of us wants somethin' catching. I have Joe's unborn babe to consider."

Lydia felt the sudden urge to leap across the table and strangle Allison. Instead, she shriveled into herself. The barb had been deliberately hurtful. Yet how could Allison know the true depth of her feelings for Joe? She couldn't let Allison discover that truth, of which she was not completely certain herself. Lydia stuck out a prideful chin.

"I appreciate your concern, but I'm quite well."

"She looks fine, dear," the doctor answered before stuffing his mouth with potatoes.

While everyone returned to eating, Allison glared at Lydia with loathing. Lydia had won this little battle. However, it wasn't the end of the war.

CHAPTER 17

During the weeks of camping with the assemblage along the Missouri river, the rumblings in Lydia's camp to "pack up and hit the trail" increased. Every day, other groups headed out. Joseph Brice waited. Timing was critical, and spring seemed to be arriving late this year. The prairie grass needed to be sufficiently high to support the draft animals of his twenty wagons. Too late of a start and the forage would be eaten and trampled by emigrants who traveled before. Lydia was uneasy about leaving the security of civilization, but was as eager as others to abandon the congested, filthy river bank. She had to walk further and further upstream to find uncontaminated drinking water.

Those weeks provided an opportunity for everyone to become familiar with living and working together. Already people were squabbling over who should take responsibility for what, and who should do what kind of work. Lydia discovered that although Faith was eager to help, she was completely incompetent with cooking and camp duties.

"Servants always took care of me," Faith said dejectedly, after the kettle of soup she was preparing fell from the tripod. The soup sloshed out and quenched the fire.

Faith was the first woman Lydia had ever encountered who was incapable of setting up a tripod and performing the simplest task, boiling water over an open fire. The ability to cook outdoors in a kettle was essential for the backwoods housewife who boiled dirty laundry, made soap and scalded hides, among other things. Lydia remained patient and encouraged Faith in her practice as she strengthened muscles to handle the heavy iron pieces.

Joe set up various training sessions to insure that everyone could perform critical duties. Most of the sessions with the men were spent over maps or handling weapons. Zachariah took over teaching the basics of guard duty and conducted small military type drills, much to the unease of the women.

"I don't understand why we need to flash all of this weaponry," Esther commented to Joe over supper one evening. "It makes me nervous."

"Bandits," Joe said simply. He was more interested in mopping up the last spot of gravy on his plate with a biscuit than with conversation. "All sorts of criminals and desperadoes." He stuffed his mouth with the drippy biscuit and then dropped his tin plate into the pan of dishwater.

"He works too hard," Esther said, as she watched Joe round up some men for another of his sessions. "I'm lucky to get him to stop long enough to eat." Esther treated her nephew, as if she were a mother hen. He was putting his own life at risk to take her and Amos to a new home in California.

"And the schedule he's making the rest of us keep is grueling."

Lydia looked up to see Eleanor Fletcher standing behind the group, hands on hips. The brown haired buxom woman was only a few years older than Lydia and already had established a family with four children, the youngest being less than a year. "I hear he wants us lined up to march out each day at seven a.m. Then he says we got to hit the sack at nine p.m. With all he has us doing on this trip, when are us mothers supposed to get our young-uns dressed and fed?"

Faith came to Joe's defense, "Mr. Brice is only doing his best to see we get to California safely and as quickly as possible."

"If'n he wanted us there quicker, he'd have us leaving this hellish cemetery of a camp come morning," Eleanor retorted.

The women drew their gazes to the hillside, dotted with crosses and gravestones marking the hundreds who had already perished, many from cholera.

Early one afternoon, Joe gathered the women for a formal instructional session. "Today, you'll be learning the basics of harnessing and handling a team and wagon."

A chorus of groans followed Joe's announcement.

"Why?" Thelma Lee Purcy asked. "My husband's going to be driving the team."

Joe looked Thelma Lee straight in the eye. "There will be times when your husband is hunting or riding flank. If your husband is injured or killed, who would see you to California?"

Thelma Lee looked visibly shaken, her lips tightening. Some of the other women shuddered. These women were of sturdy build, used to hard living, but none wanted a reminder of the possibility of losing a family member to the overland trail.

"I've got mending to do and a young-un with a bellyache," Eleanor Fletcher complained. "I've been living on a farm all my life. I already know how to harness a wagon."

"Good. Then your lesson should go quickly," Joe responded.

"Wonder when his high-falutin' wife is gonna be taking her turn." Lydia over-heard Thelma Lee speaking to Eleanor. "I ain't seen her at any o' these training sessions."

"She's better'n the rest of us," Eleanor responded. "Didn't you know?"

"I hear Mr. Brice got her a hotel room," Mable Brown spoke in a loud whisper as Joe began his instructions.

"It's a boarding house," Faith corrected.

"It was all that grumblin' she done," Thelma Lee said, "about freezin' to death in a cramped wagon."

"I'm sure he's just being sympathetic for his wife's condition," Faith said.

"Maybe he done us all a favor," Mable added.

For the next couple of hours, the women practiced what Joe had demonstrated for harnessing and un-harnessing. Like Eleanor Fletcher and most of the other women, Lydia already knew how to slip the heavy collars onto the oxen and join the reins, straps and chains. The hardware on her father's farm wagon and workhorses weren't much different than the hardware used on the Livelys' wagon and team of oxen.

Faith insisted on learning the task so she could do her share of the work, but she was not physically fit for the job. Lifting the heavy wooden yokes onto the oxen was especially difficult for her. She required frequent rest periods. When she finally managed to hitch up her team, she sighed and sat down, not caring that the ground was caked in half dried mud.

"If the group had to depend on me to harness up these animals every morning, we'd never get to California," she said.

They were the last to complete their work. Others had already unhitched their team and disappeared to tend their families. Lydia encouraged Faith and told her that she would catch on with practice. Then they sat down together to wait for Joe.

"I can't ever remember being so sweaty or filthy. My undergarments are sticking to me." Faith wiped her dirty, sweaty brow with the hem of her apron, something she would have been aghast at doing a few weeks ago.

Joe praised them as he inspected the connections. "Good. Now let me show you how to grease the axles."

Lydia brought him the bucket of animal fat from where it hung on a nail of the wagon bed. The women watched intently as Joe demonstrated the method of axle greasing. Lydia found her eyes drawn to the tautness of Joe's shirt across his muscular back rather than to the swab.

"It's critical you keep the axles rolling smoothly." When he finished with one axle, he handed Lydia the bucket and swab. "Here, you do the next one."

Lydia hadn't grasped a word Joe had said. She took the bucket and swab in shaky hands and remained unmoving, uncomprehending, staring at the man too close to her.

"This one," Joe pointed, as he strolled to the rear axle.

Lydia dipped the swab into the bucket and tried to work the grease into the wheel as she'd seen her father do on many occasions. She felt frustrated and inept at not being able to stop her hand from shaking.

"You don't want to miss any spots," Joe scolded, "or the wheels will bind up when they get wet."

Lydia grew more self-conscious as he continued to watch her clumsy efforts.

"Like this," he said finally, and came around behind her. He took her hand and the swab in his to assist her.

All too aware of Joe's hand on hers and of his chest brushing against her back with each stroke of the swab, concentrating on the axle became impossible. Despite the cloth between them, she could feel every hot flexing muscle in his chest and arms. His breath across the nape of her neck sent tingles down her spine and tightened in the pit of her stomach.

When finally, they'd completed the torturous task, Lydia pulled away and thrust the bucket and swab at Faith as though the implements were hot brands. Lydia remained at a breath-catching distance away from Joe while Faith finished the two axles on the other side.

Exhausted from their long afternoon of training, Faith and Lydia unhitched the team. Lydia had already formed a bond with the Livelys' oxen. After feeding them, she stroked each one and talked to them. Upon first witnessing this, Faith commented on the oddity of "conversing" with smelly cattle. Nonplused, Lydia introduced the oxen, each with its own personality and given name.

"I'm especially fond of Samuel." The smallest of the team, Lydia found the crescent shaped brown spot on his nose particularly endearing. "It's important to bond with the animals if you expect them to do good work for you. Animals that are happy are more reliable," Lydia reminded Faith of what Joe had told them. "They're the ones who will get us to California."

Faith had become comfortable hand-feeding some of the oxen with long pieces of hay at arm's length. As yet, she couldn't bring herself to stroke and talk to them.

After they completed the care of the animals, Lydia and Faith threw wood onto their smoldering cooking fire and hung a pot of water to boil. Lydia invited Esther, who was camped in the corral circle behind them, for some tea. "Mrs. Crenshaw, would you like to join us for a little respite before we start dinner?"

"Lydia, you must quit calling me Mrs. Crenshaw. We are traveling companions now. Call me Esther. And yes, I'd love to join you."

Lydia nodded and smiled bashfully, before fetching a tin of tea from her collection of herbal blends in the Livelys' wagon. To reach the tailgate from the outside of the wagon circle, where the campfires were, she had to squeeze through a small opening between the left rear of the Livelys' wagon and the front right of the Crenshaws'. The tight ring served as a barricade against bandits and desperadoes and provided protection for the livestock, which were herded inside at night.

The small opening between wagons was an aggravation for doing chores. Larger pieces of equipment had to be hauled in and out of the corral through the open area that was filled in at nightfall with the extra supply wagons. Lydia thought the corral ridiculous so close to civilization. Like other procedures, Joe insisted everyone get accustomed to the arrangement.

Just as the women were getting comfortable with their tea, Joe strolled over to them. "I thought you ladies might like to join some of the men tomorrow on a shopping trip in town. This will probably be your last chance to pick up supplies."

"I don't need anything," Esther said.

"Oh, yes definitely. I still have that list of stuff we need to pick up for Lydia," Faith answered.

"Excellent. I'm sure Allison will love the company. She's been cooped up in the boarding house all week. I'll meet you two here first thing in the morning."

A shopping trip with Allison? What could have been the prospect of a fun diversion, instead, sank Lydia's spirits.

The shopping trip was obviously a surprise to Allison. Her unkempt hair looked as though she'd raked a comb through it at the last minute. She'd thrown a wool cape over her drab brown dress, which pulled tightly across her waist and emphasized her growing belly. Lydia could swear Allison's belly had doubled in size since last seeing her, nearly two weeks prior. Seeing her so large with Joe's child was like being punched in the stomach. Yet, Lydia could not tear away her gaze as Joe helped his wife onto the wagon seat next to where he would be sitting and tenderly wrapped her in a blanket.

Joe dropped the women off in front of a seamstress shop and drove away with the supply wagon and the men. This was Lydia's first trip into town since the day of her arrival. She took a couple of deep breaths and looked around with apprehension at all of the people. She used the hood of her old wool cape to cover her head and tucked her hands into its pockets.

At the shop, Allison tried on one of her maternity dresses, which she and Joe had ordered when first coming to town. "Joe wouldn't buy me nothin' but basic travelin' clothes," she complained to her comrades. "Wouldn't get me one stylish gown for my new trousseau."

"I'm sure you'll be getting some beautiful things when you get to California," Faith said. "Mr. Brice is a practical man. You'll have no place to wear such things on the trail. And they'll only take up space."

"Ach!" Allison growled at the shopkeeper as she stepped from behind the dressing screen wearing a new dress. "This ain't mine! This be hangin' on me like a tent! Tell your stupid seamstress my husband ain't payin' for these!"

"Madame," the shopkeeper responded with her French accent, "your dresses were cut to the standard waist allowance of a lady in your condition. In a few months, you will fill them out. *Qui?*"

Faith and Lydia hid their snickers at Allison's horrified expression.

When the shopkeeper presented Lydia with a new dress, Lydia was dumfounded. She ran her fingers over the crisp fabric. It was a simple dress of inexpensive calico of the most beautiful color, like that of wild periwinkle in the meadows of Possum Hollow.

"This is mine?" she asked Faith, still thinking she must have misunderstood.

"*Qui,*" the shopkeeper answered. "And these too."

Two calico dresses and a third of gray wool were draped over the arm of the shopkeeper's assistant. Matching bonnets and the appropriate undergarments completed Lydia's trousseau.

Lydia's eyes moistened. She'd never owned four new dresses at the same time. They were each different styles, free of lace and embellishments. Perfect for travel and work. She touched the cuff of each new garment and ran her hands along the smooth sleeves.

"*Magnifique!*" the shopkeeper exclaimed after Lydia had slipped on her first dress. "Your gentleman friend was correct," she said to Faith. "I feared the measurement too petite for *mademoiselle.*"

"Your gentleman friend?" Lydia asked quietly.

"Mr. Brice helped," Faith answered with a smile and a twinkle in her eye.

Lydia turned away as her face grew hot. There was a certain intimacy about a man memorizing her shape and size so perfectly. The audacity of the man, so confident was he, to have ordered the items before Lydia agreed to go on the trip. If the Livelys' weren't actually the ones paying for the garments, Lydia would have refused to accept them.

The women left their purchases to be packed up and headed to the cobbler shop where they each purchased sturdy new shoes and some rubber boots. By the time they completed their shopping, it was mid-afternoon. Hungry and exhausted, they began searching for the men.

Joe was loading supplies into a wagon in front of the dry goods store, when Allison rushed up to him. Packages and all, she threw her arms around him, as though she hadn't seen him for weeks. Joe eased her back to arm's length.

The other women were only a few steps behind.

"This ours?" Allison asked, referring to the covered wagon Joe had been loading.

Joe relieved his wife of the packages before answering. "Yep. I bought it from a widow. Her husband had paid for it. He died of cholera before he could pick it up. The widow was anxious to cash out and go back home to family. Look, it has springs."

Joe pushed against the seat to demonstrate its give. The springs would make the ride more comfortable for Allison as the discomfort of her pregnancy increased.

"It's… wonderful," Allison made a miserable attempt at sounding pleased. "Now we can have some privacy."

While Joe helped Allison and Faith onto the seat, Lydia scurried to climb into the back of the wagon before Joe could help her, as she knew he would. She wanted desperately to avoid physical contact with him. The jittery things his touch made her feel were wrong.

The hem of her skirt caught in the hinge of the tailgate and she lost precious time freeing it. One of Joe's hands took Lydia's. The other came around her waist. "I trust your garments needed no alterations?" His moist mouth was much too close to her ear, and his tone inappropriately sultry.

"They fit perfectly," she answered tersely, and jerked her hand out of his. She scurried into the wagon with his other hand still lingering around her waist. She sighed with relief as she sat down and leaned against a barrel.

After picking up the dresses from the seamstress, Joe dropped off Allison at the boarding house. From there, they would rejoin the men with the supply wagon back at camp.

***

They'd camped for a month along the Missouri river, and on their chosen morning of departure in April of 1849, the entire hillside suddenly sprang into life. By the time the carriage transporting Allison pulled into camp, breakfast fires were being doused with water. The smell of smoke and wet ash blended with the stench and decay of camp. Metal clanged against metal as tools and hardware were tossed under wagon beds. Excited dogs barked and ran between legs. Children shrieked with anticipation.

At Joe's signal to begin the march, the corral of wagons uncoiled to expose the bright red letters – California or Bust – painted on their canvas tops. The company's motto would help identify their caravan for any who might become separated. To take the lead, the Brices' wagon, came abreast of Lydia. Allison, sitting alongside her driver, Hank Gifford, was staring straight ahead unblinking, eyes red and swollen beneath the brim of her bonnet. Lydia waved at the Crenshaws as they rode by. Esther sat proud and tall next to her husband, her chin trembling slightly as she fought against tears.

Faith squeezed Lydia's hand as their wagon lurched forward. Lydia turned to look back at Independence, but a sea of covered wagons blocked her view. The pangs of homesickness stung fiercely at her heart.

CHAPTER 18

Never before had so many squeezed onto the Oregon-California trail. Wagons competing for the same space pressed too tightly together and entangled wheels. Inexperienced drivers quickly discovered that the heavy, high profile vehicles were less maneuverable than their familiar farm counterparts. The front axle didn't turn separately from the rear. Too tight of a turn easily toppled the wagons. Emigrants with poor equipment, already experiencing breakdowns blocked paths and forced those behind to maneuver around.

When Amos and her father had discussed the subject, Lydia had been under the impression that caravans traveled in relative isolation, but for wild animals and bandits, she was glad this was not the case. But after a life of seeking solitude, the great number of people was oppressive. Her appreciation increased for Joe's selection of the docile, steady oxen. Each time she heard the crack of a cruel whip cross the back of a half-wild mule, she cringed.

Despite Joe's unrelenting pressure to keep his company moving and to get around the crowds, they progressed a disappointing ten miles.

Lydia sighed with relief as Isaiah Johnson reined the Livelys' team to a halt. After setting the wagon break, he wandered off to see how his sons were doing. In exchange for driving the Livelys' wagon, Faith and Lydia prepared meals for the widower and his four sons. The arrangement worked well for the doctor, who was uncomfortable driving an ox team, and relieved of driving, he was free to travel on horseback to tend the sick and injured. It hadn't taken long for travelers to learn that a physician was in their midst.

The two women freed the lathered oxen from their yokes, and led them outside the corral to where there was abundant forage and running water. Abundant timber lined the stream's edge, but fire-wood had to be cut. Previous campers had gathered and burned what dead wood there might have been.

"Do you need to rest? I can take care of the team," Lydia offered when she noticed Faith walking hunched and stiff legged.

"No. I think moving around will help. I've never traveled over so many deep ruts. Every dip and jolt added a bruise."

"Maybe when the crowd thins out, it will be safer to walk. Without fear of being trampled."

"Aren't you sore?" Faith asked.

"A little. I guess I'm more used to riding in a hard wagon."

"You're too kind," Faith said. "Maybe it's because I've been spoiled with velvet cushioned inner-springs."

While the women were preparing dinner, Esther stopped by. "Have either of you seen Allison?" she asked.

"Not since we stopped," Faith answered. She plopped down on a blanket with a bowl of potatoes and a knife.

"My tolerance for Allison's whining and laziness has worn thin," Esther grumbled.

"She's probably stretched out in her wagon," Faith offered.

"Pregnancy is no excuse for idleness."

Lydia watched as Esther pulled up her skirt to climb into the Brice wagon, when a voice arose from within.

"What do you mean you're gonna stay out there with them stupid animals?" Allison shouted.

The male voice that followed was barely audible, its message indecipherable.

"You can't just leave me in this here wagon all alone! There's all kinds a wild Injuns and varmints runnin' around." The canvas top helped to muffle Allison's words, but anyone nearby could hear her well.

This time the voice of her husband was much louder. "There aren't any wild Indians around here. You'll be fine. The men and I will be standing guard."

"You're just findin' some other excuse for not sharin' my bed!" Allison accused.

Esther was scrambling down from the tailgate as others looked in that direction. The women nearby looked mortified at the subject of Allison's dispute, and her claim, which contradicted her pregnancy.

"What are people gonna think?" Allison whined.

"I don't give a damn what people are going to think," Joe said. A second later, he emerged from the rear tailgate and jumped to the ground.

With knuckles clenched around the handle of an iron skillet, Allison crawled out from under the canvas. "To hell with you!" She thrust the skillet at her departing husband. Joe didn't even dignify her action with a pause, or a glance backward as the skillet plunged harmlessly into the dirt.

As Joe strolled off, the gawkers shifted their attention away from the dispute.

After supper, when the sun was dropping low, Zachariah wandered over to them. "I heard a neighboring group is hosting a square dance. There's a fiddler and a caller. Everyone's invited."

"What great fun. Lydia, let's go!" Faith exclaimed. "Seth and I haven't been to a square dance in years."

"I don't think so. I'm bone tired. I'm going to retire early."

"I'm exhausted too. But it's our first day on the trail. We need to get into the spirit of things."

"I've never learned to dance," Lydia continued with her excuses.

"Don't be such a stick-in-the-mud," Allison said as she joined the group. "I'll be there with Joe."

Lydia cringed at Allison's smirk and at her challenge. It had been Allison's words, which had fueled the threats against her at the corn shuckin'.

"I'll teach you," Zachariah turned on his irresistibly seductive smile.

"That would be wonderful!" Faith exclaimed. "You can be in our square."

"Yes Lydia, do come." Allison's smile chilled.

Lydia swallowed, wondering what Allison had planned. When she opened her mouth to continue with her excuses, Zachariah cut her off.

"I insist." He turned on his heels before she could speak.

Lydia continued to conjure up more excuses as she prepared for the evening. Appearing alongside a man so handsome that women fell over themselves just to be near him, would attract attention. Faced with reliving another evening like the corn shuckin', her stomach knotted.

She changed into a new calico dress and new sturdy shoes. Dr. Lively often had to remind her to wear the shoes, "for safety', he would say. She didn't like them, and they felt especially clumsy with a light cotton dress. But he had purchased them for her. Unlike other young women who fixed their hair special for the evening, Lydia hid hers in its usual knot. By the time she attempted to tie on a clean bonnet, her hands trembled so much she had to ask Faith to assist her.

It was the shy, thirteen-year-old Emma Brown, who made Lydia view her evening's circumstance differently. "You're so lucky Miss Lydia, to be partnering with Mr. Potter. I don't know if anyone will ask me, much less a man as strong and fine looking as him."

Lydia took deep breaths of crisp night air to quell the rising nausea and strolled through the void between camps in the security of a large group. A few people had grabbed lanterns, which cast a wavering light with their shifting stride. Lydia didn't participate in the gay conversation.

Laughter seemed more menacing with each step of her approach to the gathering. It took great personal fortitude to press forward and resist the urge to turn around and flee to her tent. A few torches illuminated the dance area. Heavy shadows cloaked most of the onlookers. When they arrived, the party was in full swing with loud voices, barking dogs and fussy children. Husbands left their wives to their own conversations and hurried to find a jug. Shrinking in her shawl, Lydia moved toward the security of the sideline.

When new squares formed, Zachariah found her. "Shall we?" The heady smell of him nearly made her crumple at his feet. In the flickering light of the torches, his dark hair and beard glistened like the wing of a crow. His eyes were bright and piercing, his emotions, unreadable.

Zachariah's large calloused hand closed around Lydia's. Her pounding heart roared in her ears. She couldn't be certain if she was more nervous about dancing with these people or being with Zachariah. No wonder Emma Brown nearly swooned at his presence. There was no denying his masculinity. As Lydia moved into the torch light, the world closed in. The sound of muddled voices amplified in her head. The press of bodies compelled her to flee. Zachariah's strong hand held hers tightly and he kept urging her forward, into the light, into the dancers.

Everyone was staring at her, weren't they? Were they going to send her away? Only Zachariah was looking at her. He grinned and moved his hand to the small of her back. It was oddly comforting. She hoped he didn't notice her nervousness. She kept her heavy shoes planted in the soft earth.

The fiddler was getting into position when the Crenshaws and the Fletchers took their places in the square around Lydia and Zachariah, the Livelys across from them. Then the music started and everyone was bowing to a partner. A beat too late, Lydia curtsied to Zachariah.

Once Lydia took control of her shattered nerves, she could focus on the dancing. Years of practice with pretend partners paid off. She moved more expertly than those who were made clumsy with liquor and missed a step or a beat.

"What do you mean you don't know how to dance?" Zachariah asked when the tune ended. "You're a natural."

Heat rose to her cheeks and she squirmed under his praise. She wasn't going to reveal that she'd only had pretend partners because she'd never been allowed at public dances.

The confident Zachariah swung Lydia around, his strong arms and shoulders effortlessly lifting her from the ground. The music and the spinning made her lightheaded and giddy. She laughed with abandon, not caring that Zachariah held her tight.

After another dance, Lydia was gasping for breath. Her tired limbs dragged like lead weights. She excused herself and slipped into the shadows away from the center of activity where she could watch.

***

The next morning, during breakfast clean up, Lydia sidled up to Faith. "What do you think of Mr. Potter?" she asked.

Faith raised her eyebrows. "Well, he's definitely very handsome. He's charming. Has a sense of humor. But…".

"But what?"

"There's something… dark about him. And I don't mean his looks."

"How?"

"I can't explain it exactly. He's a very intense man, with a high-powered smile and hard glazed eyes that look straight through you, even when he's laughing. Why do you ask?"

"Oh… I think he might be interested in me," Lydia's face grew hot. "I mean…"

"You mean, as a man likes a woman?"

"Yes. Well…"

"How do you feel about him?"

"Like you said. But he makes me happy when I'm with him. And I've had few men come calling."

"Lydia, that's wonderful."

"But you said…"

"Never mind what I said. That's just my opinion. Everyone else is crazy about him. Maybe I'm just uncomfortable around men like that. What's important is how you feel. And it sounds like you're attracted to him."

For some strange reason, having Faith's affirmation took a great weight off of Lydia's shoulders.

***

Rain slammed against the wagon in icy sheets. A blustery wind ripped the canvas from its fastenings. With exhausted arms, Lydia and Faith battled to hold the canvas in place and scrambled to re-secure the thing to the side boards at the next stop. When not fighting with the canvas, the women sat with backs against the cargo, swaying with the rhythm of the wagon and listening to the pounding rain overhead.

They slogged for days through muddy ruts among wagons that had more affinity for being sucked into the knee-deep mud than for rolling forward. A single stuck wheel could hold up an entire column, so men on horseback rode from one wagon to another helping to pry the wheels from the sticky quagmire.

Overcrowding continued to be a problem. Drivers cut one another off as they jockeyed to pass herds of cattle. Joe's unceasing forward press brought them ahead of a large herd, and numerous slow moving wagons. When Lydia thought they would finally be alone, they crested a ridge,

151

which revealed hundreds of wagons weaving like an endless ribbon below.

Graves lined the trail, for victims of accidents and ailments, mostly cholera. Every day, emigrants, who had lost family or been left stranded with a broken down wagon, turned eastward, having *"seen enough of the elephant"*. Fortunately, under the prudent care of Dr. Lively, particularly for the practice of drinking only clean running water, the members of Lydia's company had thus far, been spared from the ravages of disease.

After days of heavy rain, the saturated canvas top provided inadequate protection. No matter how well Lydia covered her possessions with waterproof tarp, almost everything got wet. She practically lived in her rubberized rainwear, which dragged her down like heavy armor. On the rare occasion, when the sun came out and the sky brightened, the women rushed to hang wet clothes and blankets from every hook or nail punched in the wagon bed. At noon breaks, everyone scrambled for available tree limbs or shrubs to hang out their wet belongings. Lydia and Faith snickered at the sight of all the flapping underwear and at two buxom women as they wrestled with one another for an available tree limb from which to hang their petticoats.

One evening, after reaching her tolerance for dining on cold leftovers, Lydia stood over her skillet with an umbrella when the drizzle resumed. She started a fire with some dried kindling she had stored while others looked on incredulously.

"She's cracked," Allison said.

Much to everyone's surprise, Lydia oversaw the production of hot griddlecakes, bacon, sliced potatoes and a little pie of dried apples. While the Lively, Crenshaw, Brice and Johnson families enjoyed full plates of hot food, others looked on distastefully while chewing cold beans and jerky.

That same evening one man who traveled with only a pushcart came to camp begging for food. Joe refused and tried to convince him to return to Missouri and get properly outfitted. Then he sent the disheveled man away.

"That was cruel," Esther accused. "We have enough. We could've shared with him."

"He needs to learn," Joe scowled. "This is not the place for the ill-prepared. If people would quit feeding his sort, they'd return home and get properly outfitted."

Lydia suspected that the 'pushcart man' was not at the center of Joe's foul mood. His brooding was incessant. He and Allison quarreled constantly.

***

The Kansas, (or Kaw) River, the widest waterway yet encountered, stretched out before them, so swollen from all the rain, its swift and turbid water overflowed its boundaries.

"How will we safely cross?" Lydia asked, more to herself than to the women standing beside her. She chilled with the realization that this was the first of many such obstacles they would encounter in the miles and months ahead.

Isaiah Johnson rejoined them atop the knoll after receiving his instructions. "We'll have to make a raft and float across. The river can't be forded."

"Can't we wait for the river to recede or take the ferry?" Esther asked.

"We don't know how long it'll take to recede. And Joe says there's probably at least a week's wait for the Mormon's ferry. It's too dangerous to camp here. Already, the hillside is barren of forage."

Lydia scanned the large agglomeration of wagons clinging to the hillside and wondered if they would be battling rude drivers and worn out camp sites the entire trip.

"We need to keep moving and cross at another point," Isaiah continued, "Joe says if we don't pick up our pace we won't beat the first snowfall in the Sierra Nevada Mountains."

Lydia shuddered. The constant reminder of being trapped in the Sierra snows and meeting the same fate as the Donner party turned cannibal, served as a motivator for all to press forward.

Despite continued opposition, Joe led them upstream to a more suitable place to cross, where the bank was gentler. They camped in a grassy area lined with cottonwood trees overlooking the river. The work of felling timber and building the raft began in the morning.

153

The first day of crossing proceeded without any major problems or delays. Each wagon was unloaded, driven onto the raft, its wheels removed to prevent rolling, and the cargo reloaded. The canvas top was pulled back and secured so it wouldn't act as a sail. The whole procedure reversed on the far shore.

Well into the second day, Isaiah Johnson drove the Livelys' wagon to the riverbank for Lydia and Faith to unload their contents. Other wagons were either in the process of being unloaded or loaded. Cargo was heaped and scattered on the banks. Wet items were being wiped off and spread in the sun to dry.

"I wish there was another way," Faith said as she knelt facing rearward on the floor of the wagon bed. Her mouth was taut, her eyes wide with fear.

"We'll be fine," Lydia joined Faith in the back of the wagon, her heart fluttering. "The others made it all right. Isaiah and Amos are good oarsmen."

The two men had safely crossed their own wagons.

Seth blew a quick kiss to his wife and shouted, "Good luck," before helping to push the raft into the water. It caught the current and floated away.

Lydia had watched others cross the Kaw and knew that doing so on a hastily made raft was tricky as well as risky. The oarsman had to keep the raft at an angle cross-stream against the current. If the rushing water hit them broadside, the precarious load could tip. Anyone riding horseback to herd the swimming cattle could be kicked by a frightened animal, entangled in the ropes or chains and drown.

To ease her nervousness, Lydia focused her attention on the whoosh of each oar propelling them forward and her eyes upon the southern shore where people shrank into the distance.

They continued without problems until about midway when the wagon suddenly tilted to the left. Faith screamed as she was squeezed between Lydia and a barrel of flour. Isaiah cursed. Amos said something, but Lydia couldn't discern his words over the sound of rushing water.

"I'll see if I can tie it together," Isaiah shouted.

As Lydia started to crawl to the front of the wagon to investigate, the wagon shifted again. Lydia was knocked off balance and thrown hard against the edge of a trunk. More loose items slid against her leg.

"Hold that load down!" Isaiah shouted.

"What's going on?" Lydia struggled to free her leg from where it was wedged.

"A couple of logs came untied. The raft is splitting apart."

Lydia gasped. If the wagon slipped into a big enough gap, it could slip completely into the river. With her heart beating in her throat, she watched Isaiah step precariously onto the edge of the raft. He pulled on the ropes to keep the raft from falling apart. Amos was struggling to keep the cumbersome raft under control. The absence of one oarsman caused the awkward conveyance to veer off course. No matter how hard Amos rowed, without a counter oarsman, the current was forcing the raft sideways against the current instead of at an angle upstream. Men on horseback were some distance away, occupied with swimming the cattle and keeping the confused animals under control.

"A log!" Amos yelled a warning.

A second later, Lydia felt the jolt as the raft hit the floating debris. Hearing Faith's scream, Lydia glanced in the direction of her comrade in time to witness a large bureau topple toward Faith. At the same instant, Lydia was thrown backwards against the wagon bed. A sharp pain shot across her shoulder blades.

"Isaiah!" Amos shouted.

Lydia shook off the pain in her back and came to her knees. Faith was rubbing an elbow, as if she had been grazed by the falling piece. She'd missed the full force of the thing, which was now leaning against some crates. When Lydia poked her head above the side of the wagon, Isaiah's hand reached up from the swirling water.

CHAPTER 19

Lydia scrambled out of the wagon bed and onto the raft, which rocked precariously under her shifting weight. She grabbed the oar Isaiah had abandoned and joined Amos who was stabbing the turbid water.

When Isaiah did not reappear, Amos shouted. "We're moving too fast. Dear God! I'm afraid we've lost him!"

The reality hit Lydia full force. They were floating downstream faster than across the river and further away from the men swimming the livestock. Amos and Lydia were on their own and faced with the decision to end their search for Isaiah in order to save themselves and the wagon.

Lydia began rowing in conjunction with Amos. She had seen trappers navigate canoes down Possum Creek without much trouble, and although she'd never rowed a watercraft before, she didn't think it would be too difficult. She was wrong.

The wagon pressed into the ever-increasing gap between the logs The high profile load continued to tilt, making the raft exceptionally tricky to control. Lydia deftly followed the commands of Amos and soon their arms and breathing settled into a steady rhythm. She trusted the experience Amos had acquired in his younger years of floating crops down the Mississippi on flat boats.

Muscles burning and heart pounding against her chest, Lydia successfully helped to steer the raft around floating tree limbs towards the shore where company members were running downstream along the bank waving their arms and shouting words of encouragement.

When the craft entered some rough eddies, it fishtailed and nearly turned completely around. Faith screamed as a set of ropes holding the logs together snapped apart and the wagon sank further into the river.

"Stand over there!" Amos shouted to Lydia.

Her prompt change of position helped to better distribute the weight. Ignoring the pain of straining muscles in her back and arms, she plunged the oar deep into the water. Reaching forward and pressing the water behind them, over and over, they brought the crippled craft back on course and rowed the last few yards to shore.

Not until she felt the scrape of rocks beneath the raft and the waiting men pull at the guy ropes, did Lydia sigh with relief. Over the rush of blood pulsing in her ears, she heard her name shouted in the chanting. They had saved the wagon.

Several men hurried to assist the weary sailors. Vaguely, Lydia noticed someone lift the trembling, ghostly white Faith from the wagon. It was not Seth. He was still on the other shore. Dazed with exhaustion, Lydia stumbled as she transferred her weight from the unsteady raft to the rocks. She was mentally preparing herself for the inevitable collapse in front of everyone, when strong arms encircled her.

"Thank God you're all right." Joe's whisper soft voice was thick with emotion. "I could never forgive myself if something happened to you."

Lydia caught her breath as his own brushed past her ear like the flick of a tongue. She had been so engrossed in piloting the raft that she hadn't allowed herself to be afraid, or ponder upon her own demise. Safely on shore and in Joe's protection, all the fight escaped her, like steam from an engine. Pressed into Joe's muscled chest, the feel of his arms placed along her back seemed natural. It was the only place she wanted to be.

Lydia raised her head and stared up at Joe. His blue eyes were brimming with tenderness, and for a brief second, all the bad that had passed between them vanished. An instantaneous warmth flowed through her exhausted body. Her face grew hot. The moment she feared she could no longer conceal her body's reaction, Joe released her and pressed her to arm's length. His rejection was like being doused with icy water. She jerked herself to a more solid stance and shook off the emotions that had engulfed her just a split second before.

Curse him!

She thought she'd buried those feelings. She wanted to slap him. Joe had definitely grasped her improperly and in front of all those watching eyes! Her own treacherous body was equally at fault. She glared at Joe in an outrage of self-defense. Joseph Brice was married! Then Zachariah was standing before her and she wished he had reached her first, that he had been the one to scoop her into his arms to prevent her from crumpling.

"We lost Isaiah Johnson in the river," she said.

"Yes." Zachariah spoke without emotion, but his jaws were taut. "I watched. I couldn't get to him."

"We'll set up a search party along both sides of the river," Joe said, immediately taking control of the crisis. The thick emotion in his voice was gone. The warmth in his eyes had turned cold, his expression serious. "We'll halt the crossing of wagons until the raft can be repaired. Right now, I need all the men to help in the search."

Joe left Zachariah in charge of organizing the search for Isaiah Johnson's body while he turned his attention to the Johnson boys who stood alone and pale in the crowd, fear aging their young faces, seemingly having been forgotten.

Gloom settled over the camp like a damp morning fog. People trudged through their chores with minimum conversation, even during the preparation of dinner, which was usually a lively and social time for the women. Whiny children and dogs that usually yapped underfoot seemed to sense the tension and were less obtrusive.

Blaming herself for the death of Isaiah and for the boys being orphaned, Faith had the offending bureau dumped into the river. "It was the only thing we brought with us from Boston, for Seth's new office," she said. Her eyes were bloodshot and puffy. Anguish had etched into the smooth lines of her face. "When he finished medical school I gave it to him to store his medicines and things. It cost a man his life. It has no value now, except to cause pain."

"It wasn't your fault," Lydia continued. "If we hadn't hit that floating debris, Isaiah Johnson wouldn't have fallen."

"He's a strong swimmer," Esther said. "There's still hope the men will find him."

Everyone knew Isaiah Johnson was dead.

The usually self-composed Faith broke down and cried at dinner. "Not even a body to bury."

The men continued searching into evening for the body, returning to camp when they were out of daylight and out of luck.

Lydia gazed absently at the conglomeration of tents and wagons spread out before her, campfires dotting the landscape. At one time their merry festival of music and dance exemplified the emigrant sprit of optimism and hope, now the mood of the emigrants who gathered around the fires was as dark and gloomy as the landscape, the night sounds of crickets, the mournful howls of coyotes and of weeping.

By early evening the next day, when all the wagons were safely across the Kansas River and all members in the Brice party were reunited, Joe presided over a short memorial service. Those who spoke, provided gracious words for the departed, who was praised for his good humor and selflessness. Lydia would especially miss the man and his mealtime conversations. Every evening without fail, he'd helped to set up her tent. Each morning he was there again to take it down and pack it away for her. He'd been a steady, competent driver for the Livelys.

Members of the company vowed to escort the Johnson boys safely to California. Instead, the boys decided to join an eastbound group who had also *"seen enough of the elephant."*

***

They entered limestone country, an almost mountainous terrain with sharp protruding rocks made slippery where vegetation had been stripped bare by the constant onslaught of feet, hooves and wheels. Travel nearly ground to a halt as cargo was secured, wheels locked into place by chaining them to the wagon bed and one by one, wagons were lowered by guy-ropes down the steep embankments. If the load or the manner in which it was secured didn't meet Joe's strict standards, everything was unpacked and repacked. Esther and Lydia were waiting their turns for inspection when Joe admonished the Brown family.

"Why do you still have that stove?" Agitated and sweat drenched from the stress of his job, Joe snarled at the Browns. "You'll kill your oxen dragging that thing! Clive, you know better. No one is going anywhere until you dump that stove. And you might as well leave the rocker too."

159

A bone of contention since leaving Missouri, it had become a running joke among the group that despite orders to abandon the cook stove, the heavy thing kept showing up in the family's wagon. The issue was no longer laughable. Joe's words drew a lot of attention.

Mable's protests turned to tears as she watched her cook stove and heirloom rocker join other trail debris. Lydia helped the distraught woman repack, then later commented to Esther about Joe being needlessly harsh in his manner of ordering the Browns to unpack and lighten their load.

While the men lowered each wagon, the women and children watched helplessly and prayed that all of their worldly goods would not end up a splintered pile below. Each time a wagon slipped and banged against the rocky hillside, everyone gasped.

When the Tate's wagon broke from a guy-rope and sped unimpeded in its descent, it overturned and crashed into the stream. Lydia had joined the frenzy of bodies chasing after the runaway vehicle and its scattering supplies – flour fanned out in the wind like wildflower seeds – when a rock beneath her gave way.

Both feet flew out from under her and she landed on the small of her back, a cry wringing from her throat. Gravity propelled her downward, hips and elbows smacking against hard ground until she could grab a small scrappy tree growing from between the limestone. Shaky and bruised, she struggled to stand and find steady footing among the loose rocks. She felt foolish when Zachariah scooped her up and carried her the remaining distance to the stream and set her on a tree root. Already her ankle was beginning to swell.

Fortunately, the Tate's loses were not as severe as it first appeared. A layover was required to make repairs to a damaged wheel and tongue.

Lydia hobbled through evening chores grimacing on a painful ankle, shrugging off the injury when anyone mentioned their concern. Until Faith summoned her husband for an exam. The doctor's diagnosis was a severe sprain and not a break. He urged her to use a crutch for the next few days. Amos constructed one from hickory branches and leather strips. She hated being made a fuss over. And she hated how the crutch restricted use of her right hand. She could empathize with her father, who confessed feeling like an invalid when he was forced to use a crutch during his recovery.

After dinner, with her ankle throbbing, Lydia collapsed onto her bedroll and removed her shoes and socks. Although it provided support, the high top shoe of her right foot fit uncomfortably tight over her swollen ankle.

"Lydia?" It was Zachariah Potter.

What on earth did he want?

"Yes?" Lydia started to rise. Her stiff ankle slowed her, so by the time she was standing, Zachariah was inside her tent.

"I hope I didn't catch you in the middle of something," he said. "I just wanted to check on you." In the close quarters of her tent, Zachariah's large frame towered over Lydia, filling out the entry. His deep voice seemed to boom.

Suddenly hot and dizzy, she grasped the side of her face and swayed backward.

Perhaps she had gotten up too quickly.

"Are you all right?" Zachariah asked.

"My ankle hurts."

He helped her to her bedroll. "Let me look at it."

Before Lydia could protest, he was sitting beside her and pulling back the hem of her skirt. The outside of the ankle, along the bone, was purple.

"I can't believe I sprained my ankle. I feel so stupid," she said.

"Don't feel stupid. Not after what you've done, helping to save the raft. I've been so occupied with navigating us through this tough terrain that I haven't had a chance to tell you."

Lydia's face heated at the praise and she looked away.

With gentle, nimble fingers, Zachariah palpated her ankle and bare foot. His examination wasn't exactly in the manner of a doctor. The caress wrung a gasp from her.

"It hurts there?" Zachariah asked.

Lydia bit her lip and nodded. She tried to jerk her leg away from him. It wasn't proper for him to touch her like that. He didn't relinquish her ankle.

"I'm surprised the Livelys let you walk around on this. Has the doctor looked at it?"

"He's the one who insisted I use a crutch."

Zachariah continued to massage the tender spot with his right thumb, while his other hand casually drifted up Lydia's slender calf in a light caressing touch. "There's quite a knot."

The pressure of his fingers shot a dull pain from her ankle to her stomach, bringing tears to her eyes. She flinched and grit her teeth.

"It's bigger than a walnut. Should I summon doctor Lively?"

"N… No. It'll be better after some rest." Faith would worry over her, and she didn't want to be a burden to the other women.

"Then, perhaps I should excuse myself?"

"Perhaps." She hated to be rude and insist that he leave, especially after he'd shown her such kindness. Zachariah's presence made her pulse race unnaturally. He was still fondling her ankle and the lower part of her calf with the touch of a butterfly. It was after all, improper for a lady to be alone with a man in her tent. She could only wonder which gossips had seen him enter.

In a blink, his hands pulled away and Lydia's dress was back to its proper position, his quick movement making her shiver. He started to stand, but aborted the action when his gaze fell upon something next to her. "What are those?" he asked.

"Indian moccasins."

"Oh? Where did you get them?"

"I was wearing them," Lydia swallowed a lump, "when my adoptive parents, the Whitleys, found me."

"Found you?" Zachariah picked up the tiny shoes.

"Yes." Lydia went on without thinking. Zachariah was so very easy to talk to. With his gentle prodding, the story of her life in Possum Hollow spilled out. She was mindful however, not to mention how the community mistreated and ostracized her. "It was a stroke of luck that Joseph Brice and the Crenshaws gave me a chance to seek a future outside of Possum Hollow."

"Can't say I blame you. From what Joe tells me, that Hollow sounds like a very stifling place. I need open country."

"Don't you ever feel homesick for some place?"

Zachariah tossed his head back and chuckled his deep throaty chuckle. "I get bored once a place becomes too familiar, so I'm never around long enough to get attached."

He returned the moccasins to her and she stared at them longer than was necessary. She had studied them so many times that she had committed their design and intricate quillwork patterns to memory. It was ridiculous to think they might jog memories or provide clues to her previous life with another people. Finding her Indian family was a silly dream, concocted by a foolish young girl.

"I feel such a sense of loss," Lydia confessed, her lower lip trembling as a wave of melancholy washed over her. She didn't know why she kept staring at the moccasins. She'd been gone from Possum Hollow for about six weeks, but the day of her departure, when her mother had given her the moccasins seemed like years ago.

"Of course. The Whitley's are your family. You can't help feeling homesick and guilty for leaving them before the planting." Zachariah tipped up Lydia's chin and looked into her eyes. "You're a very caring and sensitive person, Lydia."

His eyes tugged at hers until she managed to pull her chin away.

"Do you like to ride horses?"

"Yes. I had to leave my horse Sunshine in Possum Hollow." Misery softened her voice and she looked down at her lap. "Why do you ask?"

"How about if I set you up with one of the mares from the loose stock? That'll be easier on your ankle than having it knock against the side of a wagon as we travel. You can use your injury as an excuse to ride with me."

"I'd love to," Lydia answered with the excitement of a child.

The grin, which filled Zachariah's face reminded her of Joe's similar response when he'd seen her sitting on the back of Zeus.

Using his charm and wit, Zachariah soon had Lydia laughing out loud and thinking of the great adventures she had yet to experience. Then rudely, the flap of Lydia's tent flew back and Joe barged in.

"What's going on in here?" he snapped, his eyes ablaze.

"Nothing's going on. Zachariah just stopped by to check on my ankle, which is more than I can say about you."

Joe grunted. "I could hear the two of you carrying on clear across camp."

Lydia felt the heat rise in her face.

"What is it Joe?" Zachariah asked, the sound of annoyance in his voice.

"Come with me."

Zachariah knew better than to hesitate.

"I'd appreciate it if next time you used more discretion when entering my tent." Lydia glared at Joe who made no apology as he departed.

"Good night, Lydia," Zachariah said.

When out of earshot of Lydia's tent, Joe tore into Zachariah, pointing a firm finger toward Zachariah's chest. "I don't care what the hell is going on between you two. Stay away from her."

"She's a grown woman. You can't…"

"I can, and I will."

"You've been awful protective of her, even before we started this damn trip. What's she to you anyway?"

"Just stay away from her." Joe clenched his fists at his sides and stomped away.

***

The next morning when they broke camp, Zachariah fulfilled his promise by presenting Lydia with a mare from the loose stock, which were normally rotated as pack animals. Lydia thought the cream-colored mare, Sandy, had been named appropriately.

"I feel guilty riding Sandy while you walk or ride in the bumpy wagon," Lydia said to Faith.

"Don't worry about me. I'll be in good hands with Jeb Newlan." Jeb was Pearl's brother. He'd been a widower for about two years, and was now heading to California with his sister's family to start a new life. "I've never been much of a horsewoman. I'd probably fall off first thing. You obviously love horses, so have fun."

Sandy quickly won Lydia over with her mild temper and gentle gait. She was easily managed, although Lydia sensed that within the beast was a wild spirit, much like her own. Perhaps, Lydia reasoned, having served as a pack animal and forced into a methodical pace, she was eager to run.

164

When appropriate, Lydia would loosen control. In the meantime, she remained alongside the Livelys wagon, Faith sitting next to her driver. Seth, as usual, traveled separately on horseback to be available for medical calls.

As Zachariah patrolled with the mounted men, he often slowed next to her to smile and chat, before his duties, or Joe, pulled him away. At first, Lydia thought it unusual for him to be called away to manage such simple matters as keeping the loose oxen under control, since he was second in command, until after a couple of occasions, Lydia realized Joe was deliberately finding excuses to separate them. She seethed inside as again and again, Joe deliberately pulled Zachariah to the rear of the caravan. Joe had tossed her aside months ago and married Allison. Why should he interfere with her interest in another?

She shouldn't have been surprised when during their next break at some nameless creek, Joe announced he would begin tutoring her in Indian sign language.

"I've never heard of such a thing."

"The nomadic tribes developed sign language because they have so many languages and dialects." Joe stepped closer to her, his eyes burning with intent. "I made a sort of vow to you, Lydia."

"A vow?" She didn't remember any vow. She gulped and stepped backwards; he was too close. Close enough for her to smell the sweat and smoke that had settled on him.

"I told you I'd show you how Indians live. So far we haven't seen any. When we do, chances are they won't speak much, if any, English. Indian sign language is the fastest way for you to learn to communicate with them."

Lydia couldn't be sure she was hearing right. His words spoken so many months ago had been sincere? She would have thought that since marrying Allison his words were no longer valid.

"Just you and me?" Lydia asked

"Of course."

"What about your wife?"

"What about Allison?" His face pinched sourly. "How does she feel about us spending time together?"

Lydia wasn't even sure she liked the idea. Having consciously avoided the man during the last few weeks, she didn't want to be in close proximity with him during periods long enough to learn something like sign language. Besides, it was completely improper. The two of them. Alone.

Joe frowned. A look of puzzlement creased his brow, as if he hadn't considered his wife's feelings with regard to him spending time with another woman, especially with a woman Allison made clear she despised.

"Perhaps you should ask her to join us." Lydia grinned. She knew Allison would not participate, nor would she permit her husband to do so. That would be the end of it.

"Fine, I'll ask," Joe grumbled, obviously none too pleased with the idea.

Soon after the wagons were again rattling along their perpetual westward route, Joe rode up alongside Lydia who was mounted on Sandy.

"She said no. Allison is not interested." Joe clenched his teeth as though fighting against swallowing something bitter. "You'll have your first lesson after supper this evening. We'll find a shade tree." Then he was gone.

Lydia later found Joe sitting by the edge of the stream, his form silhouetted against the golden sunset, the water glistening at his feet. She continued watching the glorious sight and the magnificent form that pulled a fresh string of licorice from a pocket. She could have gazed upon him forever, shutting out the rest of the world.

Her stomach fluttered as the longing in her heart renewed.

"I've always thought the sky was clearer and bluer, the sunsets more vibrant out here. Do you think so?" he asked without glancing at her.

"I don't know. I've never thought about it." She wasn't averse to learning sign language. She just wanted to get the lesson over with as quickly as possible. And he was discussing the scenery! How could she appreciate the sunset, or even learn sign language when his maleness distracted her so?

"Come sit," Joe spoke. Then used sign. He held his right fist at shoulder level before lowering it briskly several inches.

Lydia obeyed, sitting cross-legged at a respectable distance from him. When she tried to place her crutch between them, Joe took it from her and laid it aside.

"Sunset," Joe said. He made a semi-circle with his right thumb and index finger, then brought his right hand down to the side. "The movement symbolizes the setting of the heavenly body. Done in reverse, it means the rising of the moon. Now you try them."

"That's silly," she said. "Why would the reverse of sunset be moonrise?"

"I don't know. I didn't make up this stuff," he answered with impatience.

"Then what's a sunrise?"

He showed her. Then Lydia repeated the three signs.

They continued in that manner of instruction as the orange ball of the sun dipped toward the western horizon. Lydia decided she loved learning sign, but the close proximity to Joe made her jittery and pulled her attention away from her lesson, especially when he touched her hands or arms to help her form some of the motions.

"Before long, we'll have you conversing with the tribes," Joe said with obvious glee. "And as much as I'd love to continue this, we should get back to camp. It'll be dark within minutes."

In the growing darkness, they strolled silently back to camp by the glow of various fires. Peaceful tiredness had settled upon the travelers. Children had been tucked into their beds. Conversations muted. As Lydia passed between the wagons and entered into the corral, someone shoved her from behind. She staggered forward a couple of steps, but the crutch helped her balance and she remained on her feet.

"Keep away from him!"

Lydia whirled around to face Allison, whose teeth were barred like a pit bull. Reflecting the firelight, her eyes appeared as if they were shooting flames. "He's *my* husband," she hissed. "It ain't proper you sneaking off with him. Go find someone of your own kind."

Her own kind. An Indian brave.

Allison's prejudice stabbed Lydia with anger. "We didn't sneak off alone. We were sitting in plain view."

Allison kicked up dirt with her heel, spat in Lydia's face and stomped away.

***

The area of the Black Vermillion was distasteful, its river oozy and odorous. Ill fit for drinking, the water had to be boiled or made into coffee. Grave sites were as prolific as weeds. Diagonal paths, worn into the dirt, led to them. Bones of long dead animals scattered on the landscape, whitening in the sun.

Mosquitoes attacked every inch of exposed skin, orifice and eyes on every living creature. Dogs whined and dug at their bleeding sores. Lydia pitied poor Sandy, who became skittish and more difficult to handle. Her swishing tail had little effect against the steady onslaught of biting insects. Unruly mounts bucked strong men. Little children cried and were wrapped in tight bundles and put inside the family wagon. Joe urged them forward at a brutal pace, away from the contagion, away from the cholera.

A day later, they arrived at the Big Blue River valley, which was a great relief from the Black Vermillion. With its groves of sycamores, hackberries and oaks, it was as lush and green as Joe had promised.

"Maybe we can collect some nuts or berries while we're here," Lydia said to Faith while they set up camp for the evening.

"Can you do that much walking? With your ankle?" Faith asked.

"The swelling's down and doesn't hurt quite so much." She relied less on her crutch as the days passed.

A couple of women from a neighboring camp passed by and told Lydia and Faith about a marvelous alcove for bathing. "We're on our way there. We hear the water is clean and somewhat private with lots of trees and brush. It's designated just for women."

After Lydia and Faith completed the pre-dinner preparations, they hurried to inform others of what they'd learned. Eleanor Fletcher was particularly excited about cleaning her brood. Bathing in running water was rare. There were too many people and too little privacy. Sponge baths did little to remove the crusty coating of sweat and stirred up dust which settled on everything and got into every fold of skin and undergarment. And hair washing was nearly impossible. Even with the protection of her bonnet and vigorous brushing, Lydia's hair was more a dull brown than its normal glossy black.

"I've got some more things to do before I can relax," Esther said. "Don't wait for me. I'll walk over with Allison in a short while."

Sounding like an overly exuberant child, Faith appeared outside Lydia's tent a few minutes later. "Hurry up!"

Lydia quickly finished the last couple of stitches near the waist of her petticoat and bit off the thread with her teeth. So far, her tactic of creating a small pocket in each petticoat kept her coin hidden and secure.

She soon emerged from her tent to join Faith with a bundle of clean clothes and a towel. "I can't wait to get in the water and scrub these awful insect welts," she said.

"Don't remind me. "Just thinking about them makes me itch and squirm. That dreadful swarm of mosquitoes managed to find their way under the hem and cuffs of my dress and into my shoes."

"I'm finding them in our food and water," Lydia added with distaste.

"At least the rumors were wrong about them being the size of turkeys."

The alcove with its clear, calm water and overhanging trees was as beautiful as the women had been told; thick undergrowth kept it relatively secluded. The loamy scent of earth and vegetation welcomed Lydia, and reminded her of her favorite spot on the bank of Possum Creek. Away from the alcove, the main body of the stream became turbid and treacherous where it flowed over some rocks.

Small children, some naked, played and splashed in the alcove, while others ran along the bank gathering rocks and other items of interest. A dozen or so women stood near the edge of the bank holding up their skirts while scrubbing not so willing children. For modesty's sake, none of the women in the water had removed their undergarments.

"I don't think we've actually bathed in running water since leaving the Missouri river," Lydia said.

Confidence that the men would use discretion and avoid the women's bathing area did not reduce Lydia's shyness about undressing in such a public place. The look Faith flashed Lydia betrayed her similar discomfort. The two women decided to follow the lead of the others and only removed their dresses.

As Lydia exposed her dark arms and released her raven colored hair from its pins, she expected to receive strange looks, before realizing that the hands and faces of many on the trail were sun darkened and similar in color to hers. She'd seen some daring young women with sleeves torn from their dresses in the hopes of staying cooler on hot days. Their only reward was skin the color of ripe strawberries.

Despite the initial shock of the cold water, Lydia found it refreshing. She immersed herself to her neck, knees dug into the muddy streambed, petticoat swirling around her shoulders. Faith waded up to her knees, then sponged off the worst of the grime with a soapy cloth. She avoided putting her head in the water by using a bowl to dump water over her hair.

"I'm getting out," Faith announced to Lydia, a few minutes later. "I'm freezing. You haven't even scrubbed yet. How can you stay in there?"

"Back home, I used to swim in Possum Creek until nearly winter."

Faith emerged from the water shivering. She used a hackberry bush for cover as she removed her wet undergarments and toweled off. She donned the fresh clothing she'd stretched over a communal branch, then leaned against a rock warmed by a sunbeam and started to work the tangles out of her hair with a comb.

Lydia stretched out in the water and pondered on her current situation. In Possum Hollow, she'd been alone most of the time. On the western trail, where privacy was found only in her thoughts, she often longed for the comfort of solitude to which she was accustomed. Soon a comfortable feeling of home engulfed her. She closed her eyes and took a deep breath. Slowly, the village took form in front of her.

She felt at peace in the village, surrounded by everyone and everything she knew. Loved ones, with skin the color of her own and clothed in animal skins, danced around the fire. Drums beating. Arms flailing. Bodies Twisting. The movement of the feathered headdress, in rhythm with the dancer mimicked an eagle soaring on the breeze and seemed to come to life.

As one by one the tall conical structures turned into giant torches, the people broke from their ceremony. The comforting scene quickly turned into terror. The song of ceremony turned to screams. Women snatched up

small children and fled. Blood was everywhere! Blood puddled on the ground. It puddled beneath bodies lying wounded and bleeding.
    Gunfire cracked in the air.

With a jolt, Lydia rose up, disoriented, ready to take flight, on legs pumping with fear, away from the fire and the blood. Her toes scrapped the muddy bottom of the stream instead of the expected hard ground. She had dreamed that terrifying dream again. How could she have drifted off to sleep in the water?

Lydia spotted Faith on the bank waving her arms and screaming at her. With a rush of panic, Lydia realized she had drifted toward the more turbulent, dangerous part of the stream. Then she saw what had made the crack like gunfire. A tree limb hanging over the stream had broken, and the young boy perched atop was crashing into the water.

CHAPTER 20

ydia's first reflex was to dodge the falling limb, its smaller branches reaching out for her like claws. Before she could react, the branches crashed upon her, scratching her face and threatening to press her under. She sputtered and gasped for air. Half blind with water splashing into her eyes, she groped for a solid hold on the floating branch. Dead pieces broke off in her hands.

The young boy screamed for help. Lydia struggled to see him through the branches, which impeded her view, as well as her movements. Branches snared her floating petticoat and threatened to pull her under. When she finally caught sight of the boy, he was clutching the thickest part of the limb. She continued to grapple with the tree until her garment ripped, releasing her. Then, Lydia realized that a small eddy was sweeping them into the main body of the stream. As the current gave the tree new life, the boy lost his grip. His curly head slipped under the water.

Instead of surrendering to fear or panic, Lydia found new strength. Determined to save the boy, she fought her way along the tree limb to where she'd last seen him, her shredded petticoat catching on small branches. The boy's head bobbed out of the water like a cork, his arms flailing before he went under again.

As terrified as the boy, whose fate she held, Lydia kept her gaze focused on the spot where he'd disappeared until she managed to break free of the cumbersome tree branch. Without its support, she was completely on her own. She was tired and numb with the cold and fighting with her floating petticoat.

Groping to find the boy beneath the murky water, Lydia wished the water were clearer. Despair began to wrench her heart; she'd already watched one man die in a river. Then the boy was there, in the corner of her eye. His head bobbed up. He was coughing and fighting the water. Lydia sucked in air and flung herself downstream. A few strokes later, Lydia was able to grab his shirt and with arms around his chest, she forced his head out of the water. The panicky boy continued to cough and gasp and flail his arms thwarting her efforts to help him.

"Calm down," she told him, as his arm smacked across her face. "I'm here to help you. Don't fight."

When Lydia finally secured him, one arm around his chest, she turned toward shore. Her heart sank. She was in the middle of the stream. The place where the water ran over the rocks like rapids was only a few yards away. Then, for the first time, she caught a glimpse of the people gathering on the shore waving at her, shouting words of encouragement. This rally of support was what she needed to spur on her exhausted limbs and force air into lungs that felt as if they were on fire.

The current was difficult to fight. Eventually the boy relaxed against her. For every length Lydia managed to put behind her, she was that much further downstream, until finally she could grab a low hanging branch that reached out like a helping arm. Several large men rushed into the water, which came up to their necks. One of them took the boy. Another set of arms enveloped her, and she yielded her exhausted body to him.

"Zachariah," she breathed with relief.

"You made my heart nearly stop." He pulled her from the water and lowered her onto the bank where her legs gave out and she flopped down on the sand. "You saved that boy from drowning. You're a hero."

"She done what many men couldn't a done," a thin, gray bearded man said, "taking control like that. She's a brave one."

Lydia squirmed at being made a fuss over. "I just did what I had to do."

"No. You're braver than I am," Faith admitted. "After I heard the limb snap and saw that boy fall into the water, all I could think to do was run for help. I didn't even consider jumping in."

Lydia was settling into camp that evening when a humble looking man with deep lines gouged into his face stopped to speak with her, hat in hands. His patched and worn clothing were covered with the usual sweat and trail grime.

"Don't know how I can thank ye for saving my boy," he said. "I only got the three boys left. Lost my wife and the new babe 'fore we even left Independence. Lost another boy back in the Kaw."

"I'm sorry," Lydia said.

"I always told my wife we should a taught them boys to swim. She was too skeered o' water to let the boys swim. Anyway, Jeremy shouldn't been peeping into the women's bathing hole. I done boxed his ears good. He ain't gonna be doing that no more. Anyway, I just wanted to thank ye for saving my boy. Don't know how I'll ever repay ye."

"I just did what I had to," Lydia said.

"Well, if'n there be anything me or my boys can do for ye, just let us know."

***

Nearly three weeks after leaving Independence, they crossed the Big Blue River without mishap. Then for two days, Joe pushed them toward the Little Blue River through treacherous uphill country without any source of fresh water. To lighten loads, once precious cargo, suddenly deemed useless, joined the refuse of previous travelers, surely to be plundered by later passers-by who dallied to pick through the waste.

All around was the smell of sickness and death. Individual graves merged into a vast cemetery of haphazard burial sites. Travel slowed as wagons deviated around the maggot-infested bodies of dead or dying animals, which lay rotting where they'd dropped. Lydia pressed the palm of her free hand against the scarf which covered her nose and mouth from the stench.

When they reached the Little Blue River, Lydia found renewed spirit in its fragrant groves of wild plum trees and sweet green grass. Cottonwoods lined the stream of pure clear water. At dusk, after enjoying a fine supper of ham, cornbread and pickled beets, Lydia spread out a blanket at the main fire to join the story telling and to learn about the valley.

"This valley is a natural thoroughfare, not only for emigrants but Indians. There's a good chance we'll encounter some," Joe warned.

"I hear them Injuns'll steal the bedroll right out from under ye," Thelma Lee's husband, John spoke out.

Lydia cringed. Why did people have to keep telling those kinds of stories?

"Most will be friendly, usually looking for trade items," Joe responded.

Lydia was considering leaving this uncomfortable conversation when a woman screamed.

Joe was first on his feet, pulling his revolver from his holster and running toward the sound. Lydia and others followed closely at his heels. When they found Allison, a few hundred feet from camp, Joe's arm came around her shoulders.

"What are you doing so far from camp?" he barked.

"Injuns!" Allison shrieked, pointing at the ground.

Half buried in the dirt was the body of a small child, perhaps two years old. Her auburn hair had been ripped away with part of her face. The shredded blanket and mutilated body were evidence that like so many, she'd been hastily buried in a shallow grave without timber for a coffin.

Lydia clasped a hand over her mouth to squelch her own scream. A sickening knot tightened in her stomach and percolated bile. Other women fled the gory site.

"It was Injuns what done it." Allison turned to glare at Lydia as if she were guilty of the atrocity.

Lydia's blood pulsed in her ears. Her empathy for Allison's horror turned to anger.

Joe looked directly at Lydia. "Scavengers," he said loud enough for everyone to hear, "probably wolves."

The tightness in her chest eased. Her anger cooled under Joe's unspoken apology for his wife's accusation.

When Joe tried to steer his wife away, she protested. "We can't leave her! We have to bury her!"

When no amount of coaxing moved the woman, Joe ordered a couple of men to grab shovels and bury the child. Then Joe ushered his wife back to camp.

***

The following day, during their usual "nooning", which was a three-hour respite from travel designated for laundry, cooking and repairing equipment, the men took a heightened interest in their firearms. They cleaned, performed maintenance and counted their store of ammunition. Zachariah set up some areas for target practice and reviewed emergency procedures to follow if attacked.

While Lydia sat against a tree mending her torn petticoat, a neighboring company from Arkansas began performing military type drills. She lost count of the number of times she pricked her finger, flinching every time they fired the small cannon they'd towed across the plain.

The day was particularly beautiful with a clear blue sky and a gentle breeze, so when Joe strolled over to her, he cast a shadow across her feet. A few months ago, she'd been horrified to have him gaze upon her petticoat while she hung it up to dry. Out on the prairie, privacy was rare and she was slowly becoming accustomed to the lack of it, insisting on privacy only when necessary to perform personal hygiene. Now, she didn't even acknowledge Joe hovering over her until he bent and took her hand.

"What is this?" she asked, as Joe placed a pistol into her palm.

"A gun."

"Yes, of course, it's a gun. I don't want it." She returned the weapon.

"Just in case you need it."

"Just in case of what? We get attacked by Pawnee? I've heard others talking about how they treat women captives. But I have no intention of shooting myself like a coward to avoid capture."

Joe frowned. "The gun is for defense," he spoke with exasperation. "I can give you lessons so you won't be afraid to carry one."

"Why do men always assume women are incompetent handling firearms? I've been well trained. I've shot my share of varmints."

"Good. I can show you how to strap it to your thigh so it won't be cumbersome to carry."

I'm sure you would. I'm sure you'd love to run your hand along my thigh.

Lydia stuck her needle into the pincushion and stood up. "I'm not carrying a gun. I'm not afraid of Indians."

"Brave words."

Lydia gathered up her mending supplies and started to stand.

"Well, then, maybe we should resume your sign language lessons, so if a cross warrior does get too close, you can at least send him a few smart remarks."

Lydia held her tongue against some deservedly terse words. She wanted to learn Indian sign language; she just wished that someone else could teach her. Then of course, she had to endure Allison's murderous glares as she met Joe for the lessons.

"We'll meet then, first chance we get." Joe strutted off like a rooster.

***

They followed the sweet clear water of the Little Blue northwesterly for four days, before saying farewell to its banks of cottonwood trees and oaks. They departed the mouth of the river and entered black, sandy bluffs. It was a dry miserable place without running water. After no more than twenty miles, the oxen sagged in their yokes; the heads of horses hung low. The women, who had walked the distance to ease the burden on the oxen, were near to collapsing.

"My Lord!" Esther's voice was muffled from the scarf covering her face, protecting her cracked lips and nose from the sun and blowing sand. "It's desolate."

Gazing over the ridge, Faith added. "There aren't any trees. No relief from the sun."

"It's a desert," Lydia said. "Papa was right." As far as the horizon, there was nothing except low growing brush and tall grass waving in the hot breeze. Except for the sandstone bluffs rising on either side of the valley, there was barely a bump in the landscape.

Mabel Brown broke down and cried. "No wonder Mr. Brice told us we'd be using buffalo chips for cooking."

"Buffler what?" Allison asked, as if suddenly awakened.

"Dried buffalo dung," Esther answered. "There's no wood for cooking. We'll have to start gathering chips into our baskets as we walk."

"I ain't cookin' with no dried buffler dung!" Allison shrieked.

They descended into the valley, the draft animals gaining new energy. No amount of effort from cursing drivers slowed the sturdier oxen from pulling their weaker, more tired comrades toward the smell of water at dangerous speeds. Some of the oxen were chest deep in the river before stopping to quench their thirst.

The emigrants, swept along in the excitement, lost enthusiasm when they discovered the quality of water that greeted them. The wide and shallow Platte River was as wretched as the rumors. 'Too thin to plow and too thick to drink,' it crept like a wounded snake over the scorched prairie. The dark river seemed to ooze rather than flow, dragging along dirt and squiggly things.

After a supper cooked atop dried buffalo dung and washed down with thick coffee brewed from the nasty water, Lydia joined Joe at a peaceful spot along the riverbank for a sign language lesson. Joe managed to sneak in the subject of firearms by making a motion of pretending to shoot. When he pointed to Lydia and then grasped his left index finger with his right hand and moved his hands slightly from the right to the left, Lydia shook her head.

"No," she said. "I won't keep a gun. If you keep persisting, I'm going back to my tent."

He took hold of her arm before she could get to her feet. "Wait Lydia. You can't blame me for trying again."

"Well, stop it. You're not changing my mind."

"Okay, okay. You win this time. Just don't leave. You are full of surprises. I've never shown you the sign for 'to keep'."

As the sun edged its way over the horizon, Joe finished the lesson and they headed back to camp. "In a couple of days, some of the men will be riding to Fort Kearney to purchase supplies. I'd like you to ride there with us."

"Why?"

"Gus Hargis. I hear he now runs the trading post. He used to trap with my grandfather and me. I was shocked to hear that Gus was living at the Fort. I guess he's starting to feel his age."

"So?"

"He knows more about Indians than I do. Maybe he can find some clue to your family in your moccasins."

Her moccasins might actually hold clues? A rush of excitement bolted through her, until thoughts of what she'd been told of fort life dampened her spirit. The fort wasn't a proper place for a lady. Only fur trappers, drunkards and outlaws hung out at forts.

"I don't want to go."

"There will be Indians there," Joe stuck the words out like bait on a hook.

"It's not proper for me to ride to the fort with the men." She'd already been the target of snarky, behind-the-back comments, from the women as she mounted Sandy without a sidesaddle. She could only imagine their criticism if she were to ride to a fort with only male escorts. "And how would Faith handle things while I'm gone?"

"Faith will be fine. You've instructed her well. She can even cook over an open fire now."

Lydia glared at him, but nodded her agreement.

CHAPTER 21

As the men packed up their gear and saddled their mounts, Lydia waited, her skirt hiked up above her ankles, the hem of her petticoat peeking from beneath, sturdy shoes placed firmly in the stirrups on either side of Sandy. With head held high, she endured disapproving looks from the women. After a life time of longing to fill in the missing pieces of her past and hoping that the sight of Indians might trigger memories, she would not let the women dampen her spirit. Whether or not she sat atop a horse in the manner in which the others approved would not change her status with them.

"Ladies don't go ridin' off with men to forts," Allison spoke in a deliberately loud whisper for all who stood within earshot. "And astride, with ankles showin' beneath her skirt."

"Only loose women hang out at those sorts a places," Thelma Lee added.

Lydia's mood turned increasingly somber as she watched Joe kiss Allison on the cheek, while she pleaded for her husband to stay. When they pulled away, Allison glared at Lydia so full of loathing that Lydia was grateful looks really couldn't kill.

The group headed away from the dust of wagons and loose cattle, and without the odors of human and animal waste, the warm breeze refreshed. Sensing the freedom between the dome of blue sky and waves of green grasses, Lydia soon relaxed. She understood now why Joe spent much of his time in the saddle, scouting for clean campsites and forage. They rested only long enough to drink from their canteens and eat a snack of jerked antelope.

"Can you see it?" Joe asked, interrupting the rhythm of squeaky saddle leather.

Lydia squinted. "Yes, the American flag!" She could barely discern the blur of white and red stripes waving proudly against the deep blue sky. And as she approached, the fort took shape against the flat terrain, rising like a monument from the earth.

"I've never seen anything like it," Lydia blurted out with excitement.

"It was made from the earth itself," Joe answered. "Sun-dried bricks. Remember, Fort Kearney is a military garrison established last year to protect emigrants from hostile Indians. U.S. soldiers are stationed here."

As the group continued their approach, a series of long low buildings with flat roofs, much the same color as the landscape came into view. They passed abandoned wagons, most in need of repair, pitched on missing wheels or broken axles alongside abandoned farm equipment and furniture. Torn canvas tops flapped in the prairie wind.

"What are those tall cone shaped tents?" Lydia asked.

Joe smiled at her. "Tepees. They're Indian homes."

As soon as Joe said it, Lydia's heart lurched and a wave of dizziness washed over her. *The same as in her dream*. She waited for the dizziness to pass before she could more thoroughly admire the clean white structures gleaming in the reflected sunlight. They were the most beautiful things she'd ever seen. She couldn't wait to get a closer look at how these Indians lived in their little portable village.

"What are they made of?" Lydia asked.

"Traditionally, buffalo hides scrapped clean of hair and sewn together with sinew. I'm seeing more made of canvas."

As she passed alongside a small circle of tepees, set up outside the walls of the fort, Lydia examined them more intently. Several long straight poles held them up. A hole in the top with a flap allowed smoke to escape. Some of the tepees were brightly painted in the likeness of animals or various geometric designs and patterns, reminding her of those on her moccasins.

Groups of strong, tough looking young Indian men, some blemished with pockmarks, sat cross-legged on the ground smoking pipes and conversing in a strange language. Their garments varied from a leather breechcloth, which brought a gasp from Lydia at seeing men so scantily clothed, to bizarre combinations of emigrant garb, jackets or shirts buttoned backwards or worn wrong side out. She found herself wondering if they had desecrated graves or if the clothing had been acquired by more legitimate means. Necklaces strung with beads and shells or animal claws hung over bare chests. Brass rings encircled biceps.

The "door," or flap, of one tepee was pulled back, exposing the interior. Inside, an old man sat cross-legged on a cot-like structure. His eyes were closed, as though in prayer or meditation. Somehow, Lydia knew that the heavy fur hide draped over his shoulders was a buffalo robe. She'd seen something like it before… in her reoccurring nightmare.

Joe took them close to a congregation of filthy, foul smelling men. They were either drinking from tipped-up liquor bottles or were passed out on their bellies. One brave was eating a hunk of meat with his bare hands, juices running down his chin. He belched loudly as Lydia passed. Then he wiped his greasy mouth on a plaid sleeve and smiled at her with rotting teeth. Another group of braves were casually cleaning themselves of lice and popping them into their mouths. Adding to Lydia's horror were human scalps boldly displayed on the opening flap of several tepees.

Her distress increased with the storm of mixed emotions, tightening her throat and chest. Did Joe bring her here to humiliate her? This scene brought no comfort. She felt no kinship with these vile, disgusting people. Hot tears distorted her vision.

As they entered the gate of the fort, the walls pressed in on her. Without the prairie breeze, the place was hot. The odors of smoke and putrid meat mingled with those of urine and excrement. For a brief second, everything blurred, *except for the Indians who were running and screaming, their tepees on fire around them.*

Lydia broke into a sweat. The hammering of the smithy sounded like gunfire.

When she blinked away her blurry vision, she saw emigrants loading supplies into wagons and onto pack mules. While soldiers lounged in front of the barracks picking their teeth, drunkards staggered out of a noisy saloon. People with crude splints or limbs wrapped in bandages, formed a line stretching out of what was presumably a hospital.

Nathaniel Tate, one of the men with them, said something about meeting them at the Tradin' Post later. "Our throats are awful dry." Then he veered off toward the saloon with another in their group, John Purcy.

"We're heading back to camp in a couple of hours," Joe shouted, "sober."

Joe tied up the horses a few yards away from the wooden doorway marked by the weathered sign "Tradin' Post". Placed in front was a long trough from which the horses could drink.

Lydia realized that the only women in the fort were Indians. Her presence there wasn't startling. But, to be considered "just another squaw," prickled her. She wasn't downtrodden and submissive like these Indian women. For once in her life, Lydia had a connection to a group, but for once in her life, she wished she did not.

"Don't forget your moccasins," Joe said, as Lydia was about to do just that.

As they turned toward the Tradin' Post, a squat, foul smelling Indian rushed up to them. "Trade," he said. "Tobacc." He displayed a pouch of tobacco between his grimy thumb and forefinger.

Joe shook his head. "No thanks. I'm not interested." He took Lydia by the elbow to usher her along.

The persistent Indian continued. "Squaw," he said.

Joe scowled at the Indian.

"Squaw," the Indian repeated. "Trade for squaw."

Joe's eyes twinkled, and he smiled. "I want four horses."

Lydia was stunned. Men traded horses for women? Surely, Joe would not! What right did he have? She was not chattel, his chattel!

"Cook good?"

"She makes excellent pies."

"Scrape hides?"

Before Joe could answer, Lydia burst out. "I certainly can scrape hides! If it's any of your business!" Then she turned to Joe and added, "I ought to scrape yours!"

The Indian scurried off, obviously having changed his mind.

Joe laughed. "I guess he doesn't want such an outspoken squaw."

"I can't believe men trade for women!" She tore into Joe.

Joe continued to laugh. "I was only humoring him. He had such lust in his eyes. Besides, four horses is a high price. I knew he couldn't meet it."

Waves of suppressed anger convulsed and tightened her jaws. *Men trading women like chattel. A high price. Indeed.*

Inside the Tradin' Post, which was lit only by a few oil lamps strategically placed to illuminate the merchandise, the air was stale with smoke, leather and sweat. Lydia's eyes took several seconds to adjust to the dim interior. Her first impression was that the facility was small for servicing so many. Merchandise was crowded onto shelves and counters. Smoked hams and slabs of bacon hung by ropes from the ceiling.

On the way to a counter containing jars of candy and piles of fur pelts, they passed barrels of flour and cornmeal and various vegetables floating in what smelled like vinegar solutions. Behind the counter a large wooden sign read, *'IF IT AIN'T HERE. I'LL FIND IT FUR YE'*, attesting to the proprietor's business connections.

Joe waited for the young man behind the counter to finish negotiating the price of a rifle with a customer. When the customer wouldn't agree to the price, he left.

"Help ye?" the man behind the counter asked.

"I was hoping to see Gus Hargis. Is he here?"

"Haay Guuus!" the man shouted over his shoulder toward a curtained opening behind him. "He'll be right with ye."

Gus Hargis kept them waiting for several minutes before appearing from behind the curtain. A grizzled man of stocky build, his bright, intelligent eyes peered at them through a face full of gray beard. One cheek protruded with tobacco. He wore a simple gray flannel shirt and dark pants, held up with suspenders.

"Can I help ye?" he asked. He seemed slightly annoyed at the interruption.

"Gus. It's me. Joseph Brice."

"Joey?" The man squinted his eyes and studied Joe up and down.

Joey? Lydia would have laughed at the title if she weren't so irritated and flustered.

A smile broke out and Gus's eyes twinkled. "Well, don't that beat all."

Gus came from around the counter and embraced Joe with a firm pat on the back, as a father would do a son. "My eyes ain't what they used to be. I almost didn't recognize ye. Shaved your beard." Gus absently caressed his own gray beard. "What in thunder, brings ye out to these parts?"

"Business. I'm guiding settlers to California. My mother's brother Amos Crenshaw and his wife Esther hired me. You remember me mentioning them?"

Gus nodded. "Settlers eh?" He scratched at his bearded chin. "Well, don't that beat all. Pretty soon this won't be wild country no more. Pelt count's already down. But hey, settlers is what's keepin' me in business."

"Judging by the number of people on the trail, business ought to be booming."

"Ain't doin' too bad for meself. Ye ain't told me who your squaw is." Gus's attention turned to Lydia.

"This is Lydia."

Lydia presented Gus with a polite curtsey, bringing a smile from the man.

"Finally got yourself a pretty little squaw, eh?" Gus eyed Lydia up and down. "He always said he'd never get hitched. I can see why he changed his mind."

Lydia wasn't sure if she should be flattered, or slap one of these men. Or both.

"Well…" Joe stammered. "We're not married."

Gus winked and slapped Joe on the back.

He assumed she was Joe's mistress. *Why didn't Joe set him straight?*

"Say, Joey where's my manners? Y'all must be mighty thirsty. Come on back and have some Kentucky bourbon what just come in."

Gus led them into a small stuffy room. A round table was in the center with papers scattered on top and a lantern straining to light the room. The only sunlight filtered in through a couple of holes in the rear wall which, Lydia guessed, were designed for sticking rifle muzzles out for defense in case of an attack on the fort. A cot, a small chest of drawers and some cooking utensils indicated that this was Gus's private living quarters.

Lydia would have said she'd wait outside, if she could be certain the outside was any safer than the private quarters of a man she didn't know and accompanied by a two-timing gun-slinging…

"Pardon the rough quarters," Gus said. "I don't own much. I'm used to keepin' all my personal effects in the space of a mule pack."

Gus quickly shuffled the papers together and tossed them onto the cot. He seemed flustered as he waved for his guests to sit down. Then he went to a shelf to retrieve some glasses.

Gus gave each glass a close inspection before wiping them out with his shirtsleeve.

"So, what can I offer ye, little lady?" Gus set the glasses and a bottle of bourbon on the table.

"Nothing, thank you." She was thirsty, but would wait for the canteen she left on the back of Sandy.

Gus took his seat and poured out two glasses of caramel colored liquor. He'd tossed back his drink before Joe's reached his lips. Gus sighed in satisfaction and wiped his mouth on his sleeve.

"I was surprised to hear you'd taken over the Tradin' Post," Joe said. "What made you decide to give up the trapping life?"

"Pelt count's dropped years ago. Last couple a summers I couldn't make a livin'. Sides, I'm too old now for that sort of life. Takes me longer to get movin' in the morning and the energy just ain't there no more. And I decided I don't want to die as a lonely ole hermit in some mountain lean-to."

"Alone?" Joe asked. "Isn't your wife, Yellow Bird, still warming your bed?"

"Yellow Bird got the fever. Took her back to her village and the medicine men," Gus said with sadness. "Died last fall. Her people gave her the proper Cheyenne ceremonies."

Lydia couldn't believe what she was hearing. A white man married an Indian? The moisture in his eyes revealed that he thought more of Yellow Bird than just a squaw to service him. He loved her.

"I'm sorry. She was a proud and beautiful woman," Joe said and drank his bourbon in one swallow. He leaned back into his chair and sighed. Lydia hadn't seen him relax since leaving Possum Hollow, the stress of his duties and the lives he was responsible for obviously weighing heavily on him.

When Joe and Gus settled into an exchange of stories about the old trapping days, Lydia relaxed somewhat. Joe rarely disclosed details about that part of his life, even with the men in camp. The more Lydia learned about Joe, the more she realized how very little she did know. The men reminisced on the good days and on the mountain rendezvous with famous men who were among the first to forge the Oregon Trail, like Kit Carson and Colonel Fremont. Gus and Joe and his grandfather had traded with William Sublette who later founded Fort William, now named Fort Laramie.

"Then there was the time we was trapped in the Sierras. We hunkered down in little more than a lean to with snow up to our butts." Gus said to Lydia. "I'd kept tellin' his grandpa to pick up the pace. He'd hurt his foot and was hobblin' purty bad. Anyways, we got stuck for six weeks. Ran out a liquor after two. We nearly starved to death on the short rations. That was the winter Joey became a man."

Lydia thought she detected a blush on Joe's cheeks. He definitely flinched with discomfort.

After what seemed like hours, Joe diverted the conversation to Lydia, explaining that she'd been a neighbor of his aunt and uncle in Possum Hollow and raised by a white couple there. "Her past is a mystery to everyone. Even her. She's got these moccasins."

"I know who you are!" Recognition drew on Gus's face. His suddenly booming voice caused Lydia to nearly jump from her seat.

"You do?" Joe asked astounded.

"Word's out you're some kind o' hero. You're quite a famous lady. And here you are, settin' in my Tradin' Post. Lordy, Lordy, don't that beat all." He continued to study Lydia. "You saved that boy from drownin'."

"We're all very proud of her," Joe added, his eyes sparkling.

Lydia shifted uncomfortably in her seat.

"Sure I can't get you nothin'? Got some stew simmerin' in a pot."

"No, thank you," Lydia said.

"Show him the moccasins," Joe urged.

Lydia retrieved the moccasins from her drawstring bag.

Gus closely examined the child-size moccasins, turning them over in his hands as Lydia often did. "These is good. Whoever made these knew what they was doin'."

"Anything special about them? Color? Pattern? Where they came from, or who made them?" Joe asked.

Lydia held her breath, waiting for Gus's answer, her thoughts a mixture of hope tempered with realistic pessimism.

"Can't say. They're typical moccasins from a plains tribe. Could be from any o' em. You know tribes trade for paint and shells and beads and things. Hard tellin' where any o' this stuff come from."

Lydia's excitement fled. She knew better than to get her hopes up.

"You see, Miz Lydia," Gus went on to explain. "Only the maker knows what the designs mean. This here triangle." He pointed. "Can mean life and health. Could be part o' some prayer for good fortune. Could be why you was found, not left for dead. Can't figure though what a Plains Indian was doing in Missouri, a near babe no less."

Lydia had wondered the same thing all of her life. She'd always known she was not a Missouri Osage. Agnes Applegate hadn't thought so either. The moccasins now confirmed that. But the information put her no closer to her Indian family.

Gus scratched his chin. "This bit 'o yellow might be a bird or some special mountain peak. Or a spiritual vision."

"What about all of this red?" Lydia asked. "What could that mean?"

Gus's face lit up. He looked at Joe with a grin that showed off his missing front teeth. "Arapaho," he said. "They use a lot of red."

Joe nodded with a smile of agreement. "This time of year they should be southwest of here, where there are buffalo. Yes, perhaps we should speak to some Arapaho."

CHAPTER 22

Awakened by the sound of her own scream, Lydia sat up with a start, panting, her heart pounding in her ears. How long had she been screaming?

"Lydia, are you all right?" Faith pulled back the flap of her tent and peered in.

Lydia shivered at the onslaught of cold night air, which swept across her sweat-drenched bodice. "I think I had a bad dream."

"What in hell is going on?" John Purcy grumbled.

Faith let the tent flap fall back into place. "She had a bad dream."

"For crying out loud. We're all out here on alert and some female went and had a bad dream. Go back to bed men!" John ordered.

The men cursed and grumbled as they shuffled back to bed or to their guard posts. Lydia imagined some of them in their long johns or tucking a shirt into trousers hastily pulled up, rifles poised and ready. She hadn't meant to scream. She was sorry and embarrassed that she had.

The camp had settled when Faith again peered into the tent. "Can I get you something?"

Lydia was still sitting up, a quilt pulled to her shoulders. "I'll be fine."

"Are you sure? Your teeth are chattering. I'm going to get you some more blankets and hot tea to help you sleep."

"I don't want to be a bother. And I'm not sure I want to go back to sleep."

"It's no bother," Faith said and disappeared.

When Faith returned with the tea, Esther followed with some blankets and an extra pillow. The two women helped make Lydia comfortable, tucking the blankets around her.

"Please don't make a fuss. It was just a dream."

Esther and Faith remained while she sipped the blend of tea used as a sleep aid. It was bitter, but Faith had obviously remembered Lydia's earlier instructions to add a teaspoon of honey. The hot liquid helped to ease her shivering.

"I had a nightmare the other night about a stampede," Esther said. "We've all been thinking too much about stampedes and Indian attacks."

"Often when I'm sick, I have nightmares," Faith added. "Dysentery is in camp. Then there's the measles and a few cases of chicken pox."

"I don't think I'm sick," Lydia said. "I've had both measles and the chicken pox. And I've had this dream-nightmare before."

"Sometimes it helps to talk about a bad dream," Esther said.

Lydia described the dream of the Indians with vivid detail. "It's so real. Like I know those people. When I wake up, terror and sadness weigh me down. I'd hoped that seeing Indians at the fort would make the nightmare go away. Instead, it's gotten worse. This time, I could hear voices speaking. The language was strange, but I swear, I felt as if I should understand what they were saying. I tried to reach out to what seemed a familiar face. Someone pulled me away. Always there is gunfire and blood." A tremor shot through her.

"A massacre!" Faith exclaimed.

"You poor dear," Esther added. "How long have you been having this nightmare?"

"As long as I can remember."

Esther and Faith looked at each other.

"Are you sure it's a dream and not a memory?" Esther asked.

"I don't know." Lydia's hands wouldn't stop shaking. *A memory*. It had crossed her mind more than once. "The details are getting more vivid. At fort Kearny, I saw a buffalo robe that looked like one in my dream. I don't know how I knew it was a buffalo robe. I don't remember seeing one before. And now Joe wants me to ride to an Arapaho village."

"What could my nephew be thinking?"

"Joe only wants to help. That's why we went to the fort. To show my moccasins to an old trapping buddy." She told Faith about what her mother had given her. "His friend suggested we visit an Arapaho village. They might recognize the design. This is all madness anyway." Lydia looked down into the teacup, she held in her lap. "Mama and Papa never knew anything. And wouldn't talk about it, either."

"Is this something you want to do?" Faith asked.

"No. I don't know. Maybe." She wasn't going to tell them that the Indians at the fort were filthy and disgusting, and that she didn't want to see any more like that.

"Seems dangerous," Esther admitted.

"Riding off on horseback would be scary enough for me, much less away from the emigrant trains," Faith confessed.

"Joe says he knows these Indians. He says he smoked a pipe with the chief."

"I think my nephew has spent too much of his life smoking pipes with chiefs and fur trappers." Esther rolled her eyes.

Lydia talked more about her dream, while her friends listened. Slowly the bitter tea took effect and she drifted off to sleep.

***

"I thought it was settled." Joe came to her the next morning. "We all agreed that the Arapaho village would be the next logical place to go."

"Who agreed?" Lydia stopped her vigorous scrubbing of the skillet to look at him. She brushed back a stray hair that had fallen across her eye.

"You, me and Gus."

"I don't recall agreeing to anything."

"I spotted a small hunting camp to the south yesterday. I don't know how long they'll be there. You can take Sandy and ride out with me."

"Why won't you just leave me alone?" She resumed her scrubbing.

"I thought you wanted to learn something about your heritage. You won't learn much about Indians at an emigrant camp."

Lydia looked Joe straight in the eye. "You know as well as I do, those moccasins don't hold any clues as to my parentage. Even your friend Gus confirmed that."

"I thought that's why you left Possum Hollow."

"Go away." She wiped out the skillet and returned it to the Livelys' wagon. When she climbed out of the wagon, Joe was waiting for her.

"Why are you still here?"

"I'm not leaving this spot until you agree to go to the Indian camp."

Lydia could only stare at the bully, her anger swelling to bursting. He'd coerced her into going to the fort, probably knowing that the moccasins offered no help. He had to know the vile conditions of the Indians there. Joe took her to the fort to humiliate her. Every night since her visit, she'd awakened in a cold sweat with her old nightmare.

"Fine Jooeey, stand there. I'm not going to visit any more filthy Indians." She managed to brush past him and his shocked expression to retrieve some cooking utensils.

"What do you mean, filthy Indians?"

"That day at Fort Kearney, I saw them. Greasy, lice eating…"

Joe shrugged. "I guess… I hadn't thought about it. Indians who hang around forts are more destitute than others. They're not all like that."

"You practically dragged me there to meet Gus Hargis. Like you're doing now."

"It's just that… you can be so exasperatingly inflexible!" Joe followed her back to the wagon where she returned the clean utensils to their place. "I've never heard you speak about Indians like this before."

Lydia thought she detected fatigue and sorrow in his voice. When she remained silent, he continued. "You've been listening to the others about grave diggers and massacres. I thought you didn't believe those stories."

Growing up in Possum Hollow she'd wanted to deny the awful things, but after seeing their wretched conditions at the fort, her beliefs were faltering.

And so the argument went, until he wore her down and she finally agreed to go.

"We need to keep it a secret," Joe told her. "No one will stand for me taking you to an Indian village."

It wasn't unusual for Joe to disappear all day, but her absence would be noticed. The last time Lydia had ridden off with the men, they had nearly caused a scandal. They told only a few in the company, so it they weren't back by dusk, someone would know in which direction to look.

Now, Lydia fidgeted in her saddle as she rode alongside the wagons, waiting for Joe's signal. She frequently glanced behind her as she rode, concerned that their plans for this clandestine trip would be discovered. Despite donning the trousers Esther had loaned her to wear under her skirt, some of the women looked at her as if she were a harlot. *What was keeping Joe?*

When Joe finally rode up alongside her and Sandy, he asked. "Are you coming?"

They did as Joe had instructed, falling back into the dust of the loose cattle, then heading south. Although Faith had given her blessing, guilt for leaving the woman who was paying for her passage settled into Lydia's bones. This was not a short side trip, like to Fort Kearney.

They had travelled no more than a couple of miles at a trot, when a lone rider raced toward them from behind. Joe didn't alter his pace, but his right hand slid along his gun holster. It was a tense few minutes until they recognized the dark horse and its rider. It was Zachariah Potter. Lydia breathed a sigh of relief.

"Surely there isn't something needing my attention," Joe snapped with impatience when Zachariah came abreast.

"I couldn't let you ride into that Indian village alone. And you didn't tell me you were taking Miss Whitley."

"I'm perfectly capable of looking out for her."

"If something were to happen, at least there'd be two of us."

"Suit yourself," Joe said, and shrugged off Zachariah. "One more man won't make a difference against a village of well-trained Indian braves."

A village of well-trained braves… The Indians at the fort had not been warriors. Thoughts of danger beyond an accident hadn't crossed her mind. She clung to her belief that no Indian would harm her.

The lengthy ride to the Arapaho village took them far south of the Platte River. The emigrants with their guns and noisy wagons had pressed the major buffalo herds steadily southward. The various tribes with their temporary hunting camps had followed.

The three riders passed numerous deep depressions, or wallows, where the buffalo en route to their favorite watering places had rolled upon the ground, scratching their hairy hides. A few of these wallows were so large and deep with stagnant rainwater, the riders had to navigate around them. Swarms of gnats and the smell of putrid flesh forced Lydia to cover her face with a bandanna. At least a couple dozen buffalo lay randomly where they had fallen, as though in a battle field, their meat and hides rotting in the sun.

Lydia knew instantly, before Joe spoke. "White men."

Indians would not have wantonly slaughtered the animals that sustained their lives. They hunted no more than they needed, and used all they took. Lydia now clearly understood what Joe had tried to tell her once.

"White people could be equally as brutal to Indians, as though they were vermin to exterminate, shooting them for sport, polluting their hunting grounds. They take over land, which Indians feel is to be shared by everyone. Indians retaliate, even to the innocent. So then do white people. Mostly the two races misunderstand each other."

A mix of deep sadness and bitterness washed over Lydia for the terrible waste. They were strange feelings, unbidden, as though the wind had carried them to her from others of her kinship.

They rode several more miles across the prairie, each lost in their own thoughts, the wind sweeping the grass below them, the air dry and hot under the late morning sun. Lydia spotted the peaks of tepees jutting up from the horizon just as a dozen tough looking braves materialized seemingly from out of the terrain. Sandy whinnied and would have tossed her rider if Lydia hadn't been alert. She halted and shifted nervously as the braves who were brandishing tomahawks quickly surrounded them.

"Stay calm," Joe said. "They're not here to attack. They would have killed us already."

"I thought you said you knew this band." Zachariah made a point of displaying his rifle in front of him.

His movement didn't go unnoticed by the braves, who in turn snatched arrows from their quivers and loaded their bows.

"I do. At least I know the chief. Unfortunately, I don't recognize any of these younger men."

Joe's words didn't comfort Lydia. Staring at the flashing weapons and well-muscled braves, she struggled for air. Naked from the waist up and faces painted with gruesome designs, these Indians looked savage. She didn't doubt that with deft owners, the more primitive bows and arrows could be as deadly as the white man's firearms.

A tough looking brave with a necklace of bear claws blurted out something in a smooth, sweet sounding language, causing Lydia to wonder if she had ever known the meaning of his words.

"We've come to visit Chief Blue Feather," Joe said. He extended the index and middle fingers upwards and together. With all other fingers closed, he raised his right hand in a sign of friendship.

A few of the Indians acted as though they understood Joe. None spoke. One grunted and made a motion toward Zachariah.

"Put away your gun," Joe ordered.

"Like hell!" Zachariah snapped. "This rifle might be the only thing keeping them at arm's length."

"We didn't come here to pick a fight. How do you expect us to get any closer to their village if you don't cooperate?"

"If this is all the greeting we get, then I'd just as soon we return to our wagons." Zachariah didn't take his sharp gaze off the band of braves, who shifted on their mounts impatiently.

"Returning to the wagons is not an option now," Joe said flatly.

"So, what do you suggest? Shooting our way out of the situation is probably not appropriate."

"We've come to visit Chief Blue Feather," Joe repeated to the Indians. "Does he still live?"

The Indians only stared at Joe blankly until he gestured with his hands. The braves consulted with one another before the brave with the bear claws responded back in sign. Joe continued the conversation with his hands.

Lydia was delighted to discover that she recognized some of the signs, although the men's movements were too quick for her to understand more than a few sporadic phrases.

"What's going on?" she asked. "What's he saying?"

"He wants to know how we know of Blue Feather and why we have come." More sign language exchanged between the two leaders, while the dark eyes of the fierce Indians never diverted from the white intruders.

"He said his men will take us to him if we hand them our weapons." Joe presented the Indian leader with his pistol. Zachariah scowled as he slowly relinquished his rifle and pistol.

With one of the braves galloping off ahead to announce their arrival, the small group of emigrants followed the remainder toward the row of tepees. Vibrating with renewed energy, Lydia sat up taller in her saddle as they converged upon the Arapaho camp. She couldn't take her eyes from the tepees jutting up from the horizon. By the time she reached the edge of the village and dismounted, her heart was nearly beating from her chest.

A mob of children and barking dogs rushed to greet the strangers. The youngest children unabashedly stared at their visitors. Lydia cringed in humiliation as several touched her clothing and commented to one another. Some even giggled. Zachariah's face twitched in a snarl. Their standoffish approach said they'd formed an immediate aversion to him. Joe drew the most attention from the women. He tipped his hat and smiled at those who stared. They kept pointing at their eyes and jabbering something to one another.

"What are they saying?" Lydia asked with impatience.

"They've never seen blue eyes before," Joe answered. "And I would bet these children have never seen a white face, or an Indian woman dressed in white women's clothing."

It seemed to Lydia that she was a freak even among other Indians.

Three adolescent boys stepped forward to lead their horses away. The boys would see to the animals' proper care and feeding. A husky brave, wearing only a breechcloth, emerged from a tepee and strode over to the guests with an air of purpose, causing the overly curious women and children to quickly disperse. The brave made what sounded like some kind of announcement, speaking in his native tongue and using signs.

Joe translated. "The men have just returned from a hunt and are relaxing in the lodges. The women are busy preparing the hides and the meat. Chief Blue Feather says that Zachariah and I are welcome to join him in his lodge for refreshment and stories of the hunt. His great-granddaughter will show Lydia around and make her feel at home."

Joe responded to the brave. "We would be most honored to join your chief. We have brought items to trade."

The brave nodded and ushered the men toward the chief's lodge. Alone, Lydia trembled beneath the staring eyes within the sea of copper faces.

An attractive Indian woman, about the same age as Lydia, hastily stepped forward and motioned for Lydia to follow her. A sleeveless kind of shirt made of hide covered her upper body, like the women at the fort. Leggings rose from her moccasins to meet the lower fringed edge of her shirt. Like white women, her covered legs preserved her modesty. The outfit looked soft and easy to move in and Lydia wondered if it was actually as comfortable as it appeared.

The woman's shiny long hair was tied back simply with a leather cord. Lydia detected the sweet smell of herbs as the hostess strolled ahead. While being observed by curious onlookers, the hostess, moving gracefully and soundlessly in her soft moccasins, led her visitor into the circle of tepees. The circular formation reminded Lydia of the corrals the emigrants formed with their wagons. All the tepee openings faced east, she noticed, toward the rising sun.

Within the circle of tepees, women were either setting up strips of meat to dry on racks or were on hands and knees scraping hides. Having scrapped hides for her father, Lydia knew it was a particularly laborious chore, yet the women here were singing and laughing and treating it all as a social affair. These women weren't much different than emigrant women who socialized and gossiped during laundry and cooking chores, much as women did during quilting bees and house raisings in Possum Hollow.

The Indian woman stopped in front of a tepee, which was bleached white from the sun and painted with scenes of buffalo, grasslands and mountains. A flap of animal skin with the hair still on, hung from a lacing pin to cover the entrance. A pair of dewclaws hanging by the opening rattled as the hostess moved the skin aside. Lydia's heart increased its flutter as she entered a real Indian home.

A marvelous aroma of sage and smoked meat swirled up from whatever was cooking over the central fire in a strange looking "pouch", which Lydia could swear was the stomach of a large animal. Furs, placed like throw rugs provided warmth and a barrier to moisture. A sort of curtain, made from skins painted with geometric designs, hung against the interior walls.

The sparse furnishings consisted of what looked like four "chaise lounges" made from mats of willow rods. A tripod of sticks supported the backs, with the lower sections bending against the ground to provide seats. A buffalo hide draped over each back. Rawhide storage cases and other decorated bags hung from the tripods. Beaded saddlebags and pouches hung from poles and the inner wall. A shield and other war paraphernalia were stored near the door beside a small pile of firewood. The home was tidy, with everything organized and in its proper place.

After settling them into chaises, the hostess pointed to herself and carefully enunciated what was obviously her name. Lydia seized upon her cue and tried to repeat the long word, each trial resulting in a giggle from the other. Out of politeness, the hostess covered her mouth with her hand in an attempt to mask the sound, until Lydia chimed in with laughter of her own, easing the edge of tension between them.

After several poor attempts at pronunciation, the hostess got down on her knees and folded back a fur piece to expose the bare ground. With a finger, she scratched out primitive drawings of three flowers, each a different size. Then she pointed to the smallest one and to herself again.

Lydia thought they could be any type of flower she'd seen at home, with their round centers and multiple tear dropped petals. She wondered if the flowers were supposed to be a particular kind of flower or just any flower. And for her to draw more than one, the size must be significant.

Lydia held both hands palm side up, fingers pointed toward the sky, a few inches from the ground. While raising her arms, she shook her hands slightly to symbolize "grass". Lydia added a wide circle from her thumbs and index fingers, and held her hands so that her little fingers were touching. This finished the sign for "flower". By the time Lydia completed the sign for "little", the hostess was nodding her head vigorously.

"Your name is Little Flower." It was a beautiful name, befitting of its trim and graceful owner. Lydia revealed her glee with a wide grin. She didn't understand the spoken word of the Arapaho, but she had figured out her hostess's name from the lessons Joe had taught her.

Little Flower struggled with English words as much as Lydia had with Arapaho ones. Upon requesting Lydia to draw out her name or use sign, she became puzzled as to why it could not be done.

Little Flower went to a rawhide case and withdrew a bowl hollowed out of wood. After dipping something out of the cooking pouch, she presented the meal to Lydia with a spoon carved out of horn in the likeness of a buffalo. Although the aroma was pleasing, Lydia was reluctant to taste the offering. She'd heard stories of strange and barbaric things Indians ate, like grasshoppers. Thinking of the dirty Indians at the fort snacking on lice made Lydia's stomach churn. She would die before eating such a thing.

Lydia took the bowl into her hands and stirred the thick creamy liquid with her spoon. The consistency was much like a thick porridge, but the ingredients were a mystery. She decided the food was some kind of gruel. She swallowed thickly and glanced at the hostess who was signaling for her to eat. When Lydia continued with her extensive examination of the food, Little Flower gently pushed the bowl closer to her. Lydia stared at the food, then, still unable to bring herself to taste it, she handed the bowl back to Little Flower with a shake of her head. The hostess would not accept the refusal. In a gruff voice she again urged Lydia to eat.

Lydia remembered Joe telling her that to refuse what an Indian offered was an insult. So, she cautiously brought a spoonful of the substance to her mouth. She blew across the hot food before tasting it with the tip of her tongue. It had the expected gamey flavor. Those less accustomed to eating wild meat might consider it rancid. The gruel was also slightly sweet with chopped up berries, similar to something Lydia had once prepared, using jerked meat. She'd ground up the meat and re-hydrated it with warm water, using onions for seasoning. Lydia decided she liked the variation with berries. After eating several spoonsful, Lydia politely returned her utensils to Little Flower who then motioned to follow her from the tepee.

Upon leaving the dwelling, Lydia sensed the villagers watching her. When she turned to meet their gazes, each averted their eyes. Some of the women smiled as she passed, while others remained stoic and wary. Lydia shared the same color of skin. Nonetheless she was a stranger and worthy of observation and mistrust.

Sometime later, Lydia was joined by Joe and Zachariah as she played '*Ring Around the Rosy*' with a group of children. Blue Feather emerged from his lodge behind them, moving slowly on his feeble legs like some ghost of the past.

"I trust you've had a pleasant visit," Joe grinned at Lydia, as *they all fell down.*

"Oh, yes!" she exclaimed, grinning. "Little Flower showed me around the village."

Joe glanced in the direction where Lydia pointed and saw Little Flower on her knees cutting buffalo meat into strips for drying.

In a breathless rush, Lydia relayed the events of her afternoon.

"Lydia?" It sounded like a question, but the old man already knew the answer.

Lydia started at the strong deep-throated voice coming from such a wrinkled up old man.

"Yes, I am Lydia Whitley," she managed a timid smile

"I, Blue Feather," his eyes twinkled with uncommon intelligence. His expression spoke of warmth.

Fluttering attacked her stomach. She was standing in front of an Indian chief! Lydia swept into a deep curtsey.

The humble man grinned wide at this formal gesture. His eyes swept over her. "You be fine healthy woman, carry many strong sons."

Lydia's face grew hot. Such topics were taboo among white people, especially with strangers of mixed company. She managed a meek, "Thank you."

"Enjoy visit? We not have visitors for many moons.

"Yes. I've always dreamed of meeting real Indians."

The chief looked at her strangely. "Not understand. You be real Indian."

"I know," Lydia said, bashfully looking toward the ground, "But, I'm different."

"Everybody different, in own way. Look Indian to me, except white man shirt."

"I grew up with white people. I don't know Indian ways. Sometimes I don't understand what or who I am," she confessed. She found it surprisingly easy to disclose her turmoil to this man. His mere presence seemed to pull the words from her.

"We hear of you. Story come to village of squaw who travel with white people. You save boy from river. Show strength. Courage."

"We're all so proud of her," Joe beamed at her.

Zachariah remained stoic.

"Joe is white man, but counted as friend to Blue Feather. He tell, you search for your people. Joe show these." Blue Feather displayed the tiny moccasins clutched between wrinkled fingers. "I meditate on these. Get help from spirits." He returned the property to her. "I find truth for you."

There was a long anxious silence as the chief gathered his thoughts.

"I give advice first. Need be happy of who are, have good life. Be unhappy if always seeking something cannot find."

The chief stared silently and unblinkingly into Lydia's eyes. For a moment she felt as if he could reach into her soul. She shivered with the power of his gaze.

"Search no more. We have many good warriors need squaw. Stay here. Be happy with Arapaho. Not go with white men to new land."

Lydia swallowed down a lump. Stay with the Arapaho? She'd never considered such a thing.

Lydia looked at the only man she'd ever wanted. His eyes were pleading with her. Did Joe want her to leave the emigrant caravan? Is that why he brought her out west, to remove the Indian from white society?

She turned to Zachariah. His face was stone-like and unreadable.

Lydia settled her gaze upon Little Flower who was a picture of contentment as she chatted with her friends, children playing near. Could Lydia actually make a life for herself here, have friends, her own family?

Then, there were the Livelys to consider. They'd purchased all of her supplies for the trip. Faith was strong emotionally; she rarely allowed her physical weakness to limit her activities. Lydia doubted she could survive the trip without someone to help her with the heavy camp chores. And Faith was her friend.

Lydia blinked. She looked at Joe and Zachariah and the villagers who were busy performing duties within their designated social structure. She looked at the gleaming white tepees and out at the endless prairie sweep of grass. Then she looked into the Chief's eyes.

"I am honored, Chief Blue Feather," she said. "But, somehow I know these are not *my* people. If I were to stay, I would be giving up the search for *my* people. I must return to the white man's camp and keep searching."

The chief nodded. "Yes. You too have felt the spirits. Your people are not the Arapaho. Somewhere, I know not where in land of buffalo, your people live."

CHAPTER 23

Lydia was up before the sun had emerged above the horizon to rekindle the fire and put on a kettle of water. This was her favorite time of day, a chance for quiet contemplation before the bustle of camp life began. The air was cool and dewy, not yet baked from the sun and wind. If she were lucky, she could hear the screech of eagles or the final hoot of an owl. A flock of geese honked overhead in a 'V'.

"Your people live." Chief Blue Feather had given her hope.

Could he be right and what would it mean? If she found her people in this impossibly vast land, then what? She'd never thought about that. Would she stop and say, "How is everyone? I'm doing fine." Or would she set up a tent and join the community? Assuming she was welcome. The more time that passed and the more she cogitated on it, the more ludicrous the notion became.

As the sun rose, so did the crescendo of activity. Emma Brown, swinging her bucket, waved at Lydia as she passed on her way to milk the family cow. Dogs ran loose among the fires, barking and nipping at heels and begging for scraps.

"Blasted mutt!" Esther threw a pot at one persistent dog after he lifted his leg to her wagon wheel. The dog yelped as the pot made contact with its hindquarters and scampered off.

One bold pup, which had pulled a slab of half cooked bacon from someone's skillet, dashed past Lydia who was just then getting her own bacon into a skillet. Two women were close behind waving their arms and cursing at the thief. Lydia couldn't restrain a chuckle and reminded herself to closely guard her meal.

A few minutes later, annoyance in her voice, Esther asked Lydia and Faith if either of them had seen Allison.

"No," Lydia answered. She was not in the habit of seeking out the company of someone who gave her so much grief.

"Sorry, I haven't seen her either," Faith said with a shrug. "Allison doesn't usually show up before breakfast."

"I thought as much. I was hoping that by some miracle she'd risen at a normal time." She rolled her eyes and went off in search of her nephew's wife, as though Allison were some child who needed fetching.

Allison's voice soon pulled Lydia's attention from her cooking. "'Taters, 'taters, always I got to be peelin' taters!"

Lydia glanced up to find Esther standing at the rear of the Bryce wagon trying to coax her niece into doing some work.

"Well, I ain't doin' it. I'm brushin' my hair!" Allison continued her rant.

"What's the problem?" Joe strolled over to his aunt. Esther shook her head in frustration and stepped away. Often, it took less effort to actually do the work than to round up Allison and argue. For most everyone else, travel and camp chores had become routine. Even the children were expected to do their share.

"Leave me alone!" Allison screeched.

"Shh. Everyone can hear you," Joe said.

"I don't care if everyone can hear. Since when did you care what people think?"

"Allison, sweetheart, you don't need to brush your hair. You look lovely as you are. Now come on out and help with the…"

Lydia had tried to ignore the conversation, but when Allison hurled cooking equipment at her husband, Lydia's attention returned. With hairbrush in one hand, Allison climbed over the tailgate. Now in her ninth month, her movements were more slow and awkward than usual. Joe helped steady her until her bare feet touched the ground and she flung his hands away.

"I'm tired o' peelin' taters!" Allison glared at Lydia and Esther, as if they were guilty of creating her situation. She brushed past Joe, then reeled around to squarely face him.

"And I'm tired o' havin' wet clothes an' sleepin' in a wet bed, while you're off doin' who knows what at night, and gone all day. I hate livin' out o' that musty wagon in this God forsaken' place with Injuns and wild animals and worrin' about stampedes ever' time it rains. I might be your wife, Joseph Brice, but I ain't like some cattle you own."

Joe threw up his hands and watched Allison squeeze between the wagons and out of the corral.

That morning passed without help from Allison and all too soon, the equipment had to be packed up and the oxen fastened into their yokes. At Joe's signal, the wagons lurched forward.

Within an hour of being in route, the gentle breath of May turned to a gust of wind that kicked up dust and wrapped Lydia's skirt around her legs, hampering her forward steps. The basket she carried to collect dried buffalo dung, swung sideways, almost tossing the contents she had carefully gathered.

Swelling thunderheads smothered the white cirrus clouds of fair weather. Before a drop of rain fell, lightening cracked the blackening sky to send children squealing to their mother's heels. Horses reared and threatened to throw their riders. Zachariah and the men riding flank, signaled for the teams to keep moving, while those in charge of loose stock and the pack animals, tightened up their formation.

"Where the hell are we going?" The words of Jeb Newlan boomeranged in the wind. His hands were full trying to keep the usually docile oxen from running.

The danger of agitated animals stampeding was very real. Hooves would trample and destroy whatever was in their path. Animals in yoke could capsize a wagon, irreparably damaging an axle or tongue, dumping the contents and occupants, who could be injured or killed. Draft animals might get tangled in chains, necks twisted in their yokes. Only some break in the landscape, such as a stream, would bring charging hooves to a halt.

Amos Crenshaw, face in a grimace, biceps straining against the reins, flew past Lydia, cursing at his team. Poor Esther was screaming as she bounced on the bench alongside her husband, one hand on her bonnet, the other gripping the seat. Lydia's heart lurched when the front wheel bumped something on the ground, a large rock, perhaps, and the wagon momentarily became airborne.

Not far behind the Crenshaw's, the wagon containing Allison Brice flew past. Both of her hands clenched the seat against the jarring ride. She screamed for the stupid animals to stop. Having lost her bonnet somewhere, her red hair flew wildly behind her like a banner.

Hugging each other for stability against the wind, Faith and Lydia increased their pace to catch up to their wagon, which had surged ahead. Others in their company were stopping in a slight dip Joe had located in the landscape. After reaching their stopped wagon, the two women climbed up and grabbed opposite sides of the canvas cover, which had been pulled back to air out the musty smell, and began to slide it over the support ribs. A precarious perch, the wagon lurched and halted as the oxen tugged against their yoke.

"Have you seen Seth?" Faith shouted over a boom of thunder.

"No," Lydia answered. A gust of wind caught the cover like a sail. The two women heard the rip. "It'll hold!" Lydia shouted back at Faith who looked at her questioningly. Repairing the torn canvas was just one more aggravating item to add to their chore list.

A blinding bolt of lightning fractured the sky ahead; its resounding crack seemed to vibrate the earth. Lydia's heart slammed against her chest in the same instant the hairs raised on the back of her neck. A tingling flow of current brought a startled cry from her throat. A bright light pulled her attention away from the canvas.

"Faith, look!" Lydia pointed to a wagon, which was stopped not far ahead. The wagon had been struck by lightning and burst into flames. "There are people in there!"

Others near the burning wagon rushed to help a woman who was groping her way down over the tailgate. Someone from inside handed her an infant, wrapped in swaddling, before two more small children were thrust at her. The same group of good Samaritans helped her husband to safety from inside, while others threw buckets of water on the blaze. It was spreading too quickly, and water was in short supply. Efforts to save the family's possessions was in vain.

The rain began falling in thick heavy drops.

Beneath their shelter, the women wrestled into their rubberized rain gear, which helped protect against a lightning strike. Wind buffeted them from side to side. Sheets of rain turned to hail soon pounded overhead.

***

Meanwhile, Allison braced herself against being thrown forward as her team halted just yards from the burning wagon. Too terrified to scream, Allison could only react. In a blind panic, she flung herself from her wagon, landing only briefly on her feet before her heavy belly brought her to one knee. She landed with an "oof".

As she picked up her skirts to flee, something deep inside warned that someone was shouting at her. All that pierced into her mind was a shrill pinpoint of a sound. Not words, not the tone of a human voice. She was no longer there, on the prairie. She was in Possum Hollow, her mind imprisoned in the nightmare of Derek Seavers's death.

The fiery wagon become the burning cabin that she and her first husband had shared. She saw the fiery timber drop and scrape along her husband's back, knocking him to the floor. She screamed as the shirt she had so lovingly made caught on fire, like tinder tossed into an inferno. A nightmare of living flames engulfing the man she loved.

Then his voice rose from the depths of orange light and heat. "Run!"

She couldn't move. She didn't want to run.

"Run!" The voice shrieked in anguish.

She didn't want to leave him.

But she ran.

Like she was running now, away from the fire. Her mouth and throat tasting of smoke, her lungs burning, the sound of her breath raspy in her ears. Even if she willed herself to do otherwise, there was no stopping her course of action. One leg thrust forward in front of the other, as fast as they could. There was no other choice. Panic was an irresistible force.

Until Allison bumped into something solid. She screamed and crumpled to the ground.

When a crack of thunder brought her alert, she found herself flat on her back looking into the green eyes of a young woman who was staring down at her.

"Don't be afraid," the woman said. "You'll be safe here. Out of the storm."

***

When the sky lightened, Lydia left the wagon to inspect the storm damage, her feet sloshing through ankle deep water. Loosely secured items lay scattered where they had been tossed from hooks on wagon beds. Torn canvases flapped in the breeze. She wove her way around the haphazardly set up camp to find Amos tending lacerations on a couple of his oxen. Esther, with a pained expression, glanced Lydia's way before returning her attention to Zachariah. He was standing across from her, legs spread wide in a confrontation with Hank.

"I told you, the last time I saw the crazy woman, she run off," Hank said. "I was busy tryin' to get the team to turn. I don't know where in hell she went after that. I hired on to tend the team. Not baby-sit the wife."

"Joe is missing too," Esther said. "Should we call a search party?"

"No, we'll wait. They can't have gone far in the storm," Zachariah answered. "Let's get the livestock rounded up."

Esther took the few steps toward Lydia. "That girl is going to be the death of me."

A spot of blue had appeared in the sky and campers were dumping rainwater from where it had collected in lard or tar buckets, airing out wet bedding, and sorting through the storm's aftermath, when a covered wagon pulled up. The driver was a burly redhead with a face full of freckles. Joseph Brice, looking tired and wet rode alongside.

"We've been worried about you," Esther said, as Joe dismounted. "I assume Allison is with you?"

"Yes." He sounded as tired as he looked. "This is Patrick O'Malley. He and his wife, Beatrice sheltered us during the storm."

"Nice to meet you," Esther said. "I'm Esther Crenshaw."

The big redhead grinned and acknowledged her with a nod.

"Allison is in the back with Beatrice," Joe said. "She's suffering from some kind of shock."

As Joe and Esther moved to the rear of the wagon, a small head bonneted in pale pink calico popped out and looked in their direction. Joe took her hand and helped her to the ground. She was a tiny thing, with wisps of blonde hair floating around her face. Attractive, with fair skin, pink lips and a pert nose, she appeared much younger than her husband. Less than age twenty. Her checks were drawn and her green eyes sunken beneath the rim of her bonnet. The most remarkable feature was that of her rounded belly, which indicated a delivery date probably within weeks.

Patrick lowered the tailgate and easily helped to deliver Allison's curled up form into Joe's arms. By then, the O'Malleys were swarmed with warm greetings. Joe carried his wet and shivering wife to their wagon, Lydia and Esther following closely behind.

"She's settled down now," Joe said. "She's been crying some nonsense about Derek and a fire."

"Her first husband, Derek, died in a house fire," Lydia said.

Joe tensed his jaws. "I didn't know. She's not said much about him."

"That burning wagon must have triggered some memories of that night," Esther said. "Poor dear. It was such a tragedy. Only been married about a year. Everything was turned to ash. Even Derek's..." Esther swallowed down a lump, "body."

"She's said often enough that she's terrified of dying in childbirth, away from family," Joe said. "She's never told me anything about this."

"We'll take care of her," Esther said. "We'll start by getting her out of these wet clothes."

"Thank you, ladies." There was both relief and worry in his voice.

Undressing Allison was like working with a dead weight, reminding Lydia of the time years ago when her mother was stricken with delirium and fever. Neither patient offered any help pulling arms through sleeves. When they were finished and Allison had coiled herself into her bedroll, Esther offered to sit with her.

"You go help Faith with supper," she said. "Allison is my responsibility."

Eventually, it was Beatrice who calmed Allison and coaxed her into joining the supper fire where they became the center of attention, surrounded with all the sympathy a pregnant woman could want. They sat across from Lydia on a blanket, legs crossed, eating everything that was offered to them. Next to her larger than life husband, Beatrice seemed exceptionally small boned and shy.

Lydia watched in her usual way, suffering in silence with the pain for which there could be no cure. Allison sitting there so obviously staking her claim as Joe's wife, ripping at the tear in Lydia's heart.

Patrick O'Malley explained that it had been only a matter of luck that both parties met. Their own group had left them behind because Beatrice had become too ill to travel.

"Mrs. Brice quite literally bumped into me," Patrick's deep, resonating voice was as large as the man. "I'd just tucked Beatrice inside. The winds blowing. When I went to secure the team, Mrs. Brice collapsed at my feet. I noticed her condition, and figured she must be suffering from some women's malady or other. So, I brought her inside. It wasn't long after that, when the hail started, that Joe here, come looking for her. We all sat out the storm inside."

"When Patrick told me that his wife was ailing, I suggested that Dr. Lively take a look at her," Joe said.

"You, poor thing," Faith said to Beatrice. "Imagine your friends and colleagues leaving you behind because you were ill, and carrying a child besides. You must be near term."

"Not for another six weeks or so," Beatrice answered quietly. "And Dr. Lively has given me some medicines to help my ailments. We'll catch up to our friends tomorrow, or the next day."

"I shouldn't think you'd want to," Eleanor said haughtily.

"Why don't you stay with us," Faith suggested. "We'll see to it that you and your child have proper care and delivery."

"Oh yes, please stay," Allison begged.

"With Isaiah Johnson gone, God rest his soul, we could use another capable man," Esther said.

Despite the continued urging for the couple to remain, Beatrice and Patrick were determined to return to their companions once they were located.

During the next few days of travel, Allison and Beatrice became inseparable. Patrick quickly proved himself an excellent storyteller, captivating everyone with stories of his hometown in Ireland. The children especially, looked forward to gathering around the evening campfire to listen and laugh at his engrossing tales of Leprechauns. Even Lydia was made to wonder if in his youth, Patrick O'Malley really had met up with an old bearded Leprechaun.

In the end, when the O'Malleys departed, they thanked the group for their hospitality. Allison in tears, swore she would see her friend again.

CHAPTER 24

Two months after leaving Possum Hollow, they arrived at the confluence of the Platte's north and south forks. To reach the north fork, the wagons had to cross the south fork. It was a dangerous prospect to cross the nearly one mile stretch of river, braided with islands and channels of mud and shallow water. Joe tested his selected route of crossing on horseback. Then set willow poles deep into the sand bars to mark the way.

Lydia watched the wagons enter the water one at a time, creating a line from one shore to the other. Although most of the river's depth was less than the top of the wheels, wagons often slipped into quicksand or deep holes and had to be pulled loose with great effort from extra teams. Crossing became increasingly dangerous with each passing wagon, as the one before added to the churned up sand and mud. The last half dozen wagons had to be diverted to a slightly different route.

Lydia's wagon was in that final group. When she rolled into the water, she hunkered against the side of the wagon bed across from Faith, fingers crossed, the noise of the water rushing through the spokes deafening. Three exhausting hours after the first wagon rolled into the South Platte river, the final wagon crossed to the northern shore.

Beyond the river, the landscape was a distinct contrast to the route along the flat, treeless Platte valley. After a sharp uphill climb, they traveled at a grueling pace, rationing water from barrels over a barren, waterless plateau. After lowering wagons by guy-ropes several hundred feet to the North Platte valley, a wooded glen greeted them. They camped in the sweet, earthy smelling Ash Hollow alongside a clear spring and gave thanks for the absence of casualties while crossing the South Platte and descending into the blessed hollow.

***

A woman's scream sliced the crisp silence of the night. Allison sat up with a start, grasping her taut, distended belly. Had she been the one screaming? The men would soon congregate outside her wagon to admonish her. And where was her husband? He should be with her when she suffered nightmares of an agonizing labor in the wilderness, away from family. In her nightmares, she always pulled herself awake after giving birth, never seeing the face of her child.

The scream came again, pained and tortured. Icy fear twisted Allison's heart. She snuggled tightly into her bedroll, trembling, envisioning wild Indians plundering neighboring camps, ripping scalps from victims and plunging tomahawks into their chests. She clutched at her own chest, feeling her heart race beneath her engorged breasts.

Her husband should be here. He should be comforting her when there were screams and other sounds of terror in the night. Fury bubbled in her throat. It was his fault she had to endure this suffering. It was he who had torn her away from home and family into this God forsaken land.

She watched silhouettes of men pass outside her wagon, lanterns swinging. Someone rode into camp. The galloping hooves stopped a short distance away. *A message of warning, no doubt.* The guards greeted the visitor.

She didn't recognize the voice of the man who spoke, "…might be breech. The women don't know what to do."

The moment she recognized Faith's soft soprano voice respond to the man, Allison pulled herself from bed and waddled away from her wagon, her hips paining her much these days. She joined Faith and the group of armed men, which included her husband and Zachariah. None gave her more than a glance. A leather pouch of medical supplies was slung over Faith's shoulder. She held a lantern in one hand.

"Seth left hours ago to see a patient." Faith stared out into the black void between camps with her usual look of worry when her husband was gone. "I'll have to help with the delivery on my own. I've helped Seth turn babies a couple of times."

Faith only confirmed what Allison was beginning to fear. She swallowed a thick lump. "It's Beatrice, ain't it?"

"How did you know it was Beatrice O'Malley who was laboring?" the man on horseback asked.

"The baby is early," Faith said.

"Yes ma'am," the messenger answered. "It's a shame. Probably won't have much chance anyhow. Grieving what done it."

Allison felt as if a hot knife pierced her womb. "Grieving?"

"For three days now. Lost her husband after he got kicked by a mule. Right in the head. Knocked him out cold. Died a few hours later. Terrible shame. Everybody liked him."

He'd been so happy and full of life. Allison filled with grief and rage.

"If everbody liked him, why'd they leave him and Beatrice when she was sick?" Allison snapped.

"Allison, dear, they've come asking for help." With teeth clenched, Joe moved beside his wife and grasped her arm as if to steer her away from the group.

Allison knew the sign when her husband was displeased and admonishing her. She pulled away from him. "I'm coming with you," she said to Faith. "She needs me."

"What do you mean she needs you?" Joe asked.

"I promised Beatrice I'd be with her durin' the birth. She's got no family."

Joe frowned. "How could you have promised such a thing? What were the chances you would ever see her again?"

"I've got to be with Beatrice."

"Allison," Joe continued, "What about your own baby? Should you be riding atop a horse when you're so far along in your own pregnancy?"

"She's the only friend I've got." Allison's voice cracked as she fought back tears. If Joe tried to stop her, she was prepared to fight, both with words and action.

Joe turned to the guards. "Saddle another horse."

***

Word of Patrick O'Malley's untimely death and Beatrice's premature labor travelled quickly through camp. And most remarkable of all was the

212

story of Allison's selfless act. When Allison, Joe and Faith returned to camp, the sun was high in the sky. Lydia dashed alongside others to greet the three riders, eager for news. She froze when she spotted the bundle Allison carried. Allison had claimed the baby. Beatrice must be dead.

Faith was hunched in the saddle, exhaustion and despair etching her face. The front of her dress was smeared with blood and birthing fluid.

"We had trouble getting out the afterbirth. I think it tore. She lost too much blood." Her choked voice revealed her desperation and defeat.

"I couldn't leave him," Allison said to the gathering crowd. "They didn't care nothin' about the babe or Beatrice. Ain't little Patrick beautiful?" Grinning with pride, as if the child were her own, Allison held the swaddled baby so that everyone could see.

Lydia stifled a gasp. She hadn't seen many babies up close, and her only experience with birthing was with farm animals. But she knew there was something not right with this child, the tiniest she'd ever seen. His lips were greyish-blue. His breathing was shallow and irregular.

Eleanor Fletcher provided the expected compliments with "ooos and ahs" at the newborn. Then, as if it were Allison who had given birth, Eleanor escorted her to her wagon to rest.

Seth Lively rode into camp as Eleanor was leading Allison to the wagon. When he saw his wife's soiled clothing he dismounted and rushed to her side. Faith sagged against him, fighting back tears.

"If only you'd come back a couple of hours ago," she started to sob. "The baby was breech. I had to turn him. The stench of burning oil and sweat and fear made me nauseated. I almost vomited. Those women tried to help, but they didn't know what to do."

"I'm sorry," Seth's voice was heavy with his own weariness and sadness. "The line of patients was endless. I had to amputate a gangrenous leg." The usually stoical man wrapped his arms around his wife.

"Allison watched her friend die," Joe sounded as tired as he looked, as if he too were carrying a great weight.

Lydia had never known Allison to do something so selfless. She could only imagine what had gone through Allison's mind. Terrified, she probably pondered on how easily it could have been herself lying there dying in that stuffy tent.

"I tried talking her out of keeping Patrick," Joe said. "I doubt he'll live long."

"I'll go check on him," Seth said. "See if there's anything I can do."

"Faith, I'll help you clean up," Lydia offered. She took her quivering friend by the arm.

Too weak to suckle, his cries a pitiful mewling, the baby survived only a day. In the morning, Joe found Allison sitting upon her bedroll rocking the cold body of little Patrick in her arms. Sometime in the night, without a sound, he'd passed away. Only when the doctor came and took Patrick did Allison cry.

Out of respect, the camp held a simple service in memory of Patrick and Beatrice O'Malley and their babe. Wrapped in a blanket in the tiny coffin, which Allison had insisted upon, they buried the newborn near the river, against the red burst of the rising sun. There was not a dry eye among those who attended the service. As surrogate father, Joe took the honor to place a tiny wooden cross as a headstone, adding to the collection of those already scattered along the unforgiving plain.

***

Lightning severed the sky with a crack like cutting glass, shattering the air with its thunderous retort. The humid air sizzled and raised the hair on the back of Joe's neck. Dark angry clouds roiled and churned in their rapid approach from the west. The wind picked up and suddenly grew cold. Joe turned Zeus around to face the row of emigrant wagons. Senses alert, he stared at the eastern horizon. The pounding he felt was not from his heart or from the thunder. It was from the ground beneath him. Anxiety gripped Joe like the claws of a wild beast.

"Stampede!" he shouted to the scouts riding alongside and signaled the men to follow him back to their wagons.

They rode on lathered horses at an exhausting pace, until they were forced to rein up, their path blocked by the wall of stampeding buffalo. The horses whinnied and reared back in alarm. Helpless to reach their families, the three men waited in the blinding, choking dust for the seemingly endless stretch of pounding hooves to pass.

Joe watched anxiously as a couple of drivers, poised to take the full brunt of the stampeding hooves, took charge of redirecting the crawling wagons. Zachariah and a couple of men riding flank sped toward Joe in an attempt to turn the lead buffalo. Nothing except a river or a bump in the landscape would halt the giant beasts, but they had to try. As the buffalo overtook the wagons, both the loose stock and those oxen in yoke joined the stampede, quickly blending their drivers and wagons into the melee.

Joe might as well have been in prison. The buffalo entrapped him like bars. His gloved hand tightened on the reins and his boots pressed into Zeus's ribs to control the skittish energy of the horse. Heat from buffalo bodies warmed the humid air around him, tasting of fetid wild animal flesh. He pressed his scarf closer to his nose and mouth as protection against the continual onslaught of thick tangy alkali dust. Somewhere along the wall of snorting beasts the blasts of gunfire sounded.

When the last animal passed, Joe and his men caught their first glimpse of the devastation. The scene was surreal. The wagons, some overturned and their contents dumped, were no longer in neat columns. Clothing was ground into the dirt. Shoes had become separated from their owners in flight. A dozen or so buffalo were dead, either having been trampled by their comrades or shot by emigrants. Horses, dogs and oxen lay among the dead or dying. Squawking chickens fled from overturned coops.

People hovered over injured family members and comrades. Others crept from within or behind their wagons, or barrels where they'd sought protection from the multitude of hooves and horns. From within the cloud of irritating dust, stunned mothers clutched crying children and choked out names of loved ones.

Joe wiped his burning, watery eyes on a clean inside corner of his bandana and slid from Zeus. He tripped over an axe as he hurried to help the Fletchers who were struggling to upright their wagon. One final shove and the Fletchers' wagon was righted. Joe caught sight of Esther in her yellow bonnet helping a little girl to her feet. A few steps behind her, Amos emerged from the dust. The Livelys and Lydia filed out from where they had sought protection behind a wagon.

"Joe!" a man shouted from behind. "Thank God you're here. We need you! This way!"

The two men wove through debris and the settling dust cloud toward a circle of people hovering near an overturned wagon. His wagon. Sick feelings of dread gripped him as they pushed through the circle. Nothing could have prepared him for the twisted, distorted form stretched out before him. His throat constricted.

Filthy, bloody and sickly pale, the fire extinguished from her hair, Allison's terror- darkened eyes reached out to him. "Can't move," the words sputtered with a spray of blood from her mouth.

"Allison, I'm here." Joe knelt beside her and slipped the bandanna from his face. "Someone get the doctor," he ordered to the handful of onlookers.

Allison smiled weakly as he took her frail, clammy hand. He squeezed it as though he could transfer some of his own strength.

"What happened?" he asked.

Her driver, Hank Gifford, ghostly white, spoke for her. "There was three of 'em. We tried to divert 'em, even turn the wagon. That's when it happened. They hit us right-square. She got throwed. Then one a them bulls… meanest thing…" Hank stammered. "I ain't never gonna forget that bull just picking 'er up and tossing 'er in the air, goring 'er with his huge set of horns." Hank made a motion with his forefingers at his temples to mimic the bull's horns. Then he pointed to the spot on the side of his body, in the same location where bright red blood percolated from Allison. "Must a broke ever' bone in 'er."

Joe pressed the heel of his hand onto the gaping wound, in an instinctive and wishful attempt to staunch the flow of blood, despite knowing the act was hopeless. He watched bright red ooze around his fingers and seep under his nails.

"I shot that buffler," Hank continued. "Got him right-square in the neck. Only made him meaner. Rolled her over and over. I ain't never gonna forget her screams."

"Allison, what can I do? How can I help you?" Joe asked. Hank and others, who had gathered, respectfully slipped away.

Allison shook her head. As she tried to speak, her voice made a strangled gurgling sound before she coughed up blood. Joe fumbled with his free hand for his bandanna and wiped the blood that dribbled from her mouth.

"Oh, God! What have I done?" He looked into her face and scooped her limp, broken body into his arms. "What have I done," he moaned. "I should have been here for you. I should have never dragged you from Possum Hollow."

Tears trickled from her eyes. "Don't blame... I was stup..." More blood bubbled up, silencing her voice in the depths of her throat.

"Hush." Joe swallowed a lump. A great spasm raked her body as Joe rocked her in his arms. The life drained from her eyes and her breathing stopped.

CHAPTER 25

Lydia tossed off her covers and sat up, fighting for breath in the suffocating tent. Another restless night, filled with visions of stampedes and little Hettie Brown crying for her mother.

"We'll find your Mama," Lydia had shouted over the deafening thunder of hooves. The tangy cloud of alkali dust burned her throat, lips and eyes. She took little Hettie's hand in hers and pulled her behind an overturned barrel.

Hours later, Lydia still had been unable to wash away the mix of dust and spent gunpowder that clung to her throat and lungs. She'd tasted the wild animal flesh, felt the heat from the snorting beasts. And there was Allison's mangled body.

The story had shocked everyone. Lydia's dislike for Allison hadn't lessened with time, but she'd come to feel sorry for her. The prideful exterior and constant complaining hadn't won Allison any friends. But to die such a horrible death, gored and trampled by a raging buffalo, and the poor unborn child, Joe's child. There was no justice.

During the brief memorial service, Joe had clung to Allison. Lydia watched him place her in a coffin with a farewell kiss. *How in love with her, he must be.* Zachariah closed the coffin and with the help of others, lowered it into the tidy grave. It had been a pitiful sight as methodically, without expression, Joe tossed dirt into the hole that contained his wife and unborn child. The only words on the cross he left were simply their names, *Allison Brice*, and *Baby Brice*.

Lydia finally surrendered to her insomnia and left her tent. A cool breeze, brought the scents of smoke, cattle and hay. An eerie wail drew her attention to a fire where a featureless man sat on a hunk of rock, hunched over, elbows on knees. More than once, she'd joined Zachariah and others in the wee hours around a fire, listening to stories. The flames shifted. It was Joe. Disappointment swept over her. She turned to leave.

"Lydia?"

"I didn't mean to disturb you. I was just leaving."

"You don't have to go." His voice was a deep croak.

"I couldn't sleep," Lydia defended herself for what Joe might construe as snooping. "I should get back to my tent." She wrung her hands as she turned, feeling exceptionally awkward alone with him as he was obviously grieving for his wife and child.

"You came here for a reason. Don't let me stop you. It's a nice evening."

Disregarding the voice inside telling her to leave, Lydia knelt onto the ground at a distance from Joe. She shifted her attention to the fire, where they both stared in silence for several minutes.

"Earlier… I didn't get a chance to say how sorry I am about your family, losing your wife and baby."

Her words must have set something off inside him because he put his head in his hands and made a dry hacking sort of sound. "I killed her. I killed her just as surely as if I'd gored her myself."

"Don't say that," Lydia said. "You can't blame yourself for what the buffalo did."

"I should have been by her side."

"You were doing your duty, as Captain."

"I dragged her out here. I had no right." Joe stood and began to pace.

"You had every right. Allison was your wife."

"No. You don't understand. It wasn't like that."

"I understand. She loved you. And you loved her. She was carrying your child." The words were thick in her mouth like molasses.

Joe shook his head. "The child was not mine."

His words hit Lydia like a fist to the gut. The air whooshed out of her. How could he be grieving for his wife and deny his own child? She pondered on his earlier claim of having been beaten and forced into the marriage. After all these months, even after their deaths, what kind of man denied his own child? He was a monster.

"I won't listen to this anymore." She stood to leave.

"Wait Lydia, don't go. I need to talk… we need…"

"No. We don't." She refused to be sucked into more of his lies. She hid her pained expression and walked away.

In the dull, mindless routine of breaking camp, the men hitched up the teams while the women reloaded the wagons. Dirty clothes were piled with other laundry. Combs and personal items were placed into handy pockets sewn inside the canvas. Tar and grease buckets were returned to their hooks on the outside of the wagon bed, tools placed underneath. Everyone assumed their positions, either to ride atop the wagon seat, on horseback or on foot. Joe signaled to begin the march. The rattle of chains and swaying buckets, the crunch of wagon wheels, the occasional command of cattlemen, resumed their familiar rhythm.

Lydia, Faith and Esther with baskets in hand, dragged their skirts through grass and mud, staring into the monotonous landscape.

"I hate to admit it, but I can understand Allison's point of view," Faith spoke. "I'm having more difficulty adjusting to the trail than I'd thought. Sometimes, I wonder how much more of this I can endure."

"One never knows what one can endure until faced with the challenge," Esther said.

"People die out here every day from illness or injury, or drowning. Strong men and little babies. Seth works so hard to help people. I worry about him. He returns to camp late, exhausted and dirty, and devastated by those he could not save."

Some time passed before Faith spoke again. "Lydia, do you ever wish you hadn't come on this trip?"

"When my bed is wet and I have to choke down cold beans for the third time in a day."

Faith and Esther nodded in agreement, all too familiar with the frequency of it.

"I know I shouldn't pry," Faith glanced at Lydia who stood on the right side of her. "Women only desert their homes and friends because their husbands desire it, not because of their own choice. Can I ask why you came out here?"

Lydia was a long time answering. Even Esther, who had known her family for many years, did not fully understand the extent of what Lydia had endured in Possum Hollow, or what was in her heart. Faith had shared many things with her, and she deserved some sort of answer.

"Without a husband or household, I was free to leave to seek a life of my own."

"What is that life, Lydia? What do you seek?" Faith asked.

Esther looked at Lydia intently.

"I'm not sure," she answered truthfully. "I only know I haven't found it yet."

They resumed their silence until Faith spoke again. "Seth and I have been talking. When he sets up his practice in California, he's going to need an assistant. We'd like for you to consider the position."

"A doctor's assistant?" Lydia was flummoxed. "I wouldn't know anything about that."

"You know how to treat people with those tea recipes. And you're good at applying salves and bandages. Seth could teach you the rest."

"Lydia, what a wonderful idea!" Esther exclaimed. "And how gracious of the Livelys to offer."

"I don't know." How could Lydia tell her friend that except for bandaging simple wounds, she doubted that anyone would let her touch them? She struggled daily to convince herself that not everyone thought her filthy or soiled.

"You don't have to decide now, of course. You have until we get to California."

California. The end of the line.

CHAPTER 26

The following evening, Faith helped Lydia dress for a wedding feast hosted by a neighboring caravan; everyone within hollering distance of the ceremony was invited. Faith made some last minute adjustments to Lydia's clothing and then started to work on her hair.

"Why can't I wear my hair as I always do, so it stays out of my face, like when I'm working?" She didn't want to draw any attention to herself.

"Tonight you're not working. Why not look your best? I've been meaning to show you other ways of wearing your hair."

The woman created a simple flattering style, which allowed Lydia's hair to drape loose with finger curls around her shoulders. Faith loaned her a couple of ornate tortoise shell combs to help keep hair out of her face.

"I've never worn rouge before," Lydia said, as Faith approached with the little pot. Lydia thought only harlots wore rouge. She wasn't going to say that to her friend.

Reluctantly, Lydia let her friend apply the rouge. Then Faith handed Lydia the mirror. "Just a dab well blended," Faith said. "See how it accentuates your cheek bones?"

Just what Lydia needed, to call attention to one of her Indian features. She handed the mirror back to Faith and followed her out of her tent, hair sweeping her lower back. She felt as if all eyes were upon her and the rouge, which seemed to lie thickly on her cheeks.

They passed Zachariah and Joe who were involved in a discussion. Zachariah spied her first. He winked and grinned. Joe just stared.

Lydia shriveled under the scrutiny.

"So, what do you think?" Faith asked Esther.

"Lydia, you're breathtaking. Faith, you've done a wonderful job."

Lydia followed the group of women to the neighboring camp, dining utensils clinking in her small basket.

She'd never seen so much food at one gathering. Alongside meat and fruit pies, fresh breads and cakes and corn relish, an assortment of pickles lined a long table. There were green beans, stewed carrots, boiled potatoes with onion, and candied yams. Lydia's mouth watered at the aromas of corn pudding and sweet potato pie. A choice of black coffee, tea or whiskey would wash it all down. Lydia added her fresh skillet bread to the collection of food.

After the bride and groom had been served, Lydia shuffled in line behind the other guests who descended upon the tables. Lydia ladled small scoops onto her plate, wanting to taste as many of the mouth-watering dishes as possible. Too quickly her plate was overflowing. Someone poured thick black coffee into her tin mug. Somewhere in the melee surrounding the tables, Lydia lost track of her friends.

"You look lost," Zachariah joined her.

"The others disappeared."

"Let me help you," he said, taking her plate. "I'm sitting over there. Would you like to join me?"

"Yes. Thank you," she answered, relieved that she would not be eating alone.

He led her to a grassy spot away from the crowd where they could enjoy their meal. She settled herself on the ground among the folds of her skirt, smiled and thanked him as he handed her the plate.

"I'll replace this coffee with something more suitable to quench your thirst." Knowing that she did not care for coffee, he took her mug and poured the thick black liquid onto the ground. A short time later, he returned with her mug full of diluted whiskey.

The wedding festivities continued with square dancing. With the help of whiskey, Lydia relaxed and danced with Zachariah. She even accepted some invitations from the abundant number of gold seekers. Several times she caught Joe staring at her from across the crowd. Once for spite, she scowled at him and stuck her tongue out. He frowned and turned away.

Bachelors, as well as married men who had left behind wives to seek gold in California outnumbered the women, so finding a partner for dances was not an issue for the women, even the homely ones. But women eagerly waited a turn to partner with Zachariah. His popularity had not diminished. With his wide smile that made hearts flutter, he could easily sweet-talk even the shyest maidens into dancing. When he led the shy Emma Brown to the dancing area, Lydia thought the poor girl would faint.

Lydia expected to feel the same rush of jealousy she had experienced when Joe ushered Allison to the dancing at the corn shuckin'. Instead, relief washed over her for the chance to collect her wits made cloudy by the whiskey.

Eventually, Zachariah caught up with Lydia as she relaxed against the skeleton of an abandoned wagon. Its useful parts had been pilfered. The shell left to rust and meld with the landscape.

"I thought I might find you here, away from the action," he said.

Through a whiskey fog, Lydia gazed up at the imposing figure. At more than six feet tall and broad shouldered, he could make any women's head spin, including her own.

"I would have been disappointed if you'd returned to camp," he continued, "before saying good-night." He sat on the ground next to her and coiled up his long legs. "You look stunning this evening. I can hardly believe you're the same shy woman we dragged into the dancing a few weeks ago." He squeezed her hands and leaned into her until his rough beard moved across her cheek.

Lydia's heart increased its rhythm and her stomach went to her throat.

"May I kiss you, Miss Whitley?" The next instant, his lips touched hers, moist and warm. He tasted sour with whiskey. No doubt she did too.

Lydia giggled and pulled away.

"What's so funny?" He asked.

"N… nothing." Except for the whiskey she had consumed and the headiness of the moment.

She hadn't considered kissing Zachariah, and was surprised he wasn't overbearing as again his mouth came down to hers, caressingly soft. Curious if this man could make her feel as Joe could, warm and tingly inside, she allowed his lips to do as they willed. She could understand why so many young women, like Emma, were drawn to him. The pressure of his mouth increased on hers, and his hand eased across her shoulder and down her back to press her closer.

Lydia felt nothing. No leap of flames. No pulsing in her loins.

She pulled back slightly and turned her head away from him, freeing her lips. Zachariah in turn, dragged his prickly beard, which felt like thistle, across her cheek, to nibble on a sensitive earlobe. A tiny gasp escaped her.

Some voice inside her head told Lydia to repel him. Instead, she concentrated on the warm strong body, the muscular arm embracing her. She longed for a spark of those wild ardent feelings she felt for another. Why couldn't she summon those feelings for a man who obviously wanted her? Why did Joe have to keep creeping insidiously into her life, and into her thoughts, destroying what pleasure she yearned to find?

In an act of pure rebellion and desperation to rid Joe from her thoughts, she squeezed her eyes closed and sought out Zachariah's mouth with hers, urging him to recapture her lips. He took them eagerly to explore with increasing pressure until his tongue teased the inside of her upper lip and pressed against her barred teeth. She remembered what Joe – curse him for always being at the front of her mind – had told her to do and allowed Zachariah to enter the cavity of her mouth. All the while, his hand continued its unfaltering path of caressing circles across her back.

She was barely aware when he was forcing her to the ground, until his solid body collapsed on top of her, crushing her beneath him, trapping her hands between their bodies. When his mouth slipped from hers, she took in a big gulp of air.

"Mr. Potter, what are you doing?" Her heart was beating in her throat.

While he propped himself on one elbow, his other hand slid to her throat and began unbuttoning the front of her dress.

"Please, let me go." Her voice was a soft pleading as she tried to sit up and twist sideways in an attempt to wriggle free.

"I can't," he moaned, gazing down at her, his eyes like deep dark pits trying to swallow her. "I think I've fallen in love with you."

Startled by his words, she quit thrashing. She allowed him to untie the drawstring lacing at the neck of her chemise before his calloused hand deftly slipped inside her garments to cup a breast.

He loved her? Is this what loving was about? Where was the searing leap of flames? The only explosion of senses she felt was of raw panic, a need to escape.

His hand released her breast and began to work its way under her crumpled skirt and layers of petticoat. He eased through the opening of her crotch-less drawers and settled on the moistness between her legs. She cried out.

"Shh," he was eye-to-eye, nose-to-nose.

She needed air! She couldn't breathe! She continued to squirm in protest, but her action only seemed to fuel him. Everything was happening too fast! She tried to bend her knee to separate them, to get some leverage for escape, but he outweighed her several times.

"Mr. Potter, please stop. If you love me."

"I can't stop now, love. It's too late. I'll be gentle, I promise."

What had she done? Tears pooled in her eyes. She bit her tongue to keep from crying out; if she was found in this position, her reputation would be shattered. How could she face anyone again?

In one smooth movement, he eased the full weight of his body from hers as he reached for the buttons of his fly. Lydia took advantage of the brief reprieve to fight for freedom, burying her nails in his forehead and gouging deep scratches down his nose. With an upward thrust, her knee made contact with something fleshy.

Zachariah yelped and reared back on his heels.

Lydia managed to wriggle her way out from under her captor and onto hands and knees. She was about to scramble to her feet when his hand snatched her ankle and dragged her back to him. She clawed at the ground and kicked her heels backwards. When she heard a pop, she knew she'd made contact with his chin or jaw. He growled and tightened his grip, twisting her ankle until she thought it would snap. Every movement she made to escape, he increased the pressure.

"What game do you play? A second ago you were a vixen in heat. As much as any savage whore, you wanted it. And now you toss me aside like some rejected plaything you tired of."

Lydia didn't know what she'd done wrong, to provoke him. She'd only wanted to love and be loved. He'd called her a savage whore. Is that what she really was, just wanting to be loved? She didn't understand.

"You can't have it both ways. Which is it? The tease or the innocent maiden?"

"You said you loved me," she choked. Surely a man who loved her would not treat her this way or force himself on her.

"Ah, you use those words against me. You're so naive. Those words are meaningless, except for the moment." He flung his entire weight upon her, pressing her into the ground.

A whoosh of air rushed from her lungs. If she hadn't turned her head at the right moment, her face would've been buried in the dirt. Something gritty caught on her tongue and she struggled to spit it out, her lips catching a taste of grass which fluttered against her mouth. Her hands were free and above her head, but useless in that position. His hot breath moved along the exposed part of her neck where the fabric of her unfastened bodice fell away.

Maybe this was her fault. She'd been playing a daring game, dressed to entice with rouge and her hair in soft curls, dancing with the men. She'd wanted Zachariah's affection and to feel ardor for a man other than that blue-eyed gun-slinger.

Then a voice came out of the darkness. "Who's there?" It was Joe. He was swinging a lantern around, obviously looking for something or someone.

A rough hand pressed against her mouth while the weight upon her increased its pressure. Panic rose as she gagged and struggled to get air into her lungs.

"Shh!" her captor hissed, droplets of saliva spraying onto the exposed side of her face.

Lydia thought she would be sick. Before she could decide whether to attract attention for help, or hide in shame, Joe and the lantern drifted away.

When again in darkness, Zachariah slid from her and disappeared into the night, leaving her utterly alone and shaking. She sucked in air and sat up, her pulse racing. What had just happened? How could anyone be so cruel, to abuse the words of love? Her mind tumbled with a mix of fear and humiliation. Had Joe known she was there? Should she be grateful? She shouldn't be surprised he knew her whereabouts; the way he always kept a close eye on her. Had he seen her kiss Zachariah? Her embarrassment mingled with raw fury.

With slow trembling fingers, she managed to refasten her dress. Maybe she really was a whore. But as long as she loved a man who didn't love her, she was doomed to eternal maidenhood. Shaken, mentally and physically exhausted from the ordeal, she pushed herself to her feet and staggered on rubbery legs to the security of her tent. She curled up like a fetus, shaking as violently as if she'd fallen into an icy river.

The following morning, Lydia left her tent to find her traveling companions standing in a semicircle. Mable and Oscar Brown were on one end, Mable leaning against her husband for support. Zachariah stood alone in the center of the semicircle in what looked to be a confrontation.

Something wasn't right.

Faith leaned in close to Lydia and whispered. "No one can believe it. Seth tried to examine her. When her mother found her this morning, she was all curled up, just staring straight ahead. It was the longest time before they got Emma to talk."

Lydia's chest tightened. A dizzy sensation came over her. Perhaps she had gotten up too quickly, or drank too much whiskey the night before.

"Such a shame," Thelma Lee clucked. "Emma is ruined. No man will want her."

Lydia's eyes darted among the cold staring faces before settling on Zachariah. She choked when she spotted the vivid streaks of red along his nose. A glance at her fingernails revealed the evidence she'd neglected to wash away. She tucked her hands into her apron pocket.

So it had been true. She hadn't dreamed it.

Were her lips as swollen as they felt? Did people know? She wanted to shrink away and crawl into a hole.

Zachariah stood tall and handsome as always, in a defiant sort of way, as though daring these people to accuse him of wrongdoing. His dark stealthy eyes caught hers and warned her not to speak out against him. At that moment, Lydia knew he was guilty of whatever crime he was being accused.

Joe held the commanding position directly opposite Zachariah. "Why did you do it, man?"

"I didn't molest her," Zachariah said. "We were together. So what?" he shrugged. "Everyone knows how she plays the innocent, willing maiden with her coy expressions. The way she lowers her eyes when I approach."

Molested? Lydia slapped a hand to her mouth.

Clinging to her husband, Mable began to tremble with quiet sobs as Zachariah threw out accusations against her daughter.

"How many of these women can deny wanting my affections?" In a smug sort of way, Zachariah turned on his bright white smile, which was a stark contrast against his raven dark beard. He motioned at the women standing in the crowd. Even some of the married ones blushed and looked away. None of them spoke a denial.

Awash in torment, Lydia heard little of the ensuing discussion. Had Zachariah really desired her so much that he used Emma for his lustful release when Lydia turned him away? A wave of paralysis seized her. An invisible noose tightened around her throat.

Zachariah had said he loved her, then called her a savage whore. Was she really a whore to want a man's affections? Emma called it molestation.

Joe just stared at the accused. "There is a difference between willing and molesting. Emma was not a willing party." Joe's voice was chilling. "Her clothes were ripped and there were marks on her. Pack your bags, man, and get the hell out of here!"

"Who made you judge and jury?" John Purcy stepped forward and protested.

"Help him get packed," Joe shouted back at the man, and evaded the question. "Give him one rifle with ammo and whatever provisions his horse can carry."

"Don't you think you're being too quick to condemn?" John asked. "How's he going to manage out here alone with so few provisions?"

Joe stared into the crowd. "Ask Emma. Ask Mable and Oscar Brown. Ask anyone who has young daughters if they agree with my punishment."

Tension in the air was like a tight-rope, the crowd looking each other over, waiting for someone to disagree. Or perhaps, daring their comrades to allow acquittal. With expressions etched of anguish, mothers pulled their daughters close. A couple of the fathers with pinched faces stepped forward and nodded at Joe, then a couple more stepped into the semicircle and nodded. No one spoke. Then one by one the group dispersed.

As soon as her limbs could move again, Lydia fled to a discrete place to heave up the contents of her stomach. She needed to cleanse herself of Zachariah, the whiskey taste of him and the liquor that had soured inside her. The memory of his scratchy beard, his hard manhood, and the wet tongue which had left its trail along her throat was now especially repugnant. If Zachariah had raped her, would Joe have sent him away? How could she have ever thought she wanted such a man?

Faith was not far behind Lydia, catching up to her as she heaved another time.

"Are you all right?" Faith asked, handing Lydia a handkerchief to wipe her mouth.

Lydia nodded her head. "I'm better now."

"I know it was quite a shock. It was to all of us. And I know that … you and Mr. Potter… you mentioned it once."

"Maybe all that liquor I drank last night didn't agree with me."

After rinsing her mouth and wiping her face and neck with a damp cloth, Lydia had regained enough composure to help with the morning camp chores. She kept one eye on Zachariah and the men as they prepared him for expulsion. There were frequent and animated discussions as to exactly what provisions were his to take. Not until the man was set to depart did Joe take him aside.

***

Battling a kaleidoscope of emotions: outrage, disappointment, guilt, Joe stared at his longtime friend. The two had been through some tough times together, each having put their life in the other's hands. They'd often been bonded closer than most brothers could claim.

"I trusted you," Joe said. "I thought you were over this. I vowed to protect these people. How could you do it, right under my nose?"

"You don't have to send me away," a demonic smile twisted Zachariah's mouth. "It's not too late. You only need to say so and the others will abide."

"I can't defend you this time." With jaw clenched, Joe handed Zachariah a small leather bag. "Here's your share of the profits."

Zachariah slapped the drawstring bag out of Joe's hand. Coins spilled onto the ground. "I don't want your damned payoff."

"It's not a payoff."

Zachariah mounted his horse and looked down at Joe. "After all we've been through, you would humiliate me like this? Expel me?"

"What the hell got into you? Was our friendship so worthless?" Joe couldn't come to terms with Zachariah's poor judgment. Joe was as much to blame for what happened to Emma.

"This might be the end of our friendship, but it's not over between us," Zachariah threatened. He spat at the dirt, then clicked his horse into motion.

Joe watched his long time friend disappear, then barked out orders to break camp.

CHAPTER 27

"Pin-cushioned with arrows," Esther said. "I can't imagine such a horrible thing."

Lydia wouldn't have believed such a thing either. Except Amos Crenshaw had seen it.

"There was a two mile path worn from the main trail. People were viewing the gruesome corpse like some circus side-show," Amos said.

"It's terrifying. Some wild Indian is out there shooting arrows at people." Eleanor Fletcher was pounding laundry with the other women alongside the Platte River.

Lydia jumped as more cannon fire shook the ground.

"Someone is going to get killed with all of these practice drills," Faith said.

"I'm glad the men and the weapons are here to protect us," Eleanor said. "I wish we had a cannon."

Lydia was more concerned about skittish livestock and stray cannonballs than any Indian attack. As she tossed her last garment into her basket, she noticed Joe strolling in her direction. She snatched up her basket for a quick retreat.

"I need to talk to you," he said.

"This load is heavy."

She brushed passed him, bouncing the basket on her thigh when he attempted to take the basket of wet clothes from her. Despite her chilly reception, Joe continued his pursuit.

"It's about you sleeping in my wagon," he shouted louder than necessary.

Lydia turned to face him, her face hot. "Sleeping in your wagon?" she choked.

"Yes. I think that under the circumstances, and well…Since Allison's gone. My wagon's empty."

"You do think me a whore." Lydia ground the words between clenched teeth.

Joe tossed his head back and laughed more freely than she had seen in many weeks. "Oh, Lydia." He wiped tears from his eyes. "You know I always sleep outside, under the stars. Except during the worst of weather. Then I unroll my blankets in the tent with the men doing turns at guard duty. Except for a few barrels of food, my wagon is literally quite empty."

"Oh, of course."

She knew that. He'd embarrassed her on purpose. There had been a running joke among the men that Joe always slept outside, never with his wife. Even some of the women had noticed and made comments on the subject, wishing their husbands were as considerate while they carried.

"I like my tent. I'd rather sleep there."

While Lydia draped wet clothing over the roof of her tent to dry in the warm afternoon sun, Joe sputtered out the advantages of taking up residence in his wagon.

"As long as someone is out there shooting arrows into people you'd be better protected in a wagon. Besides, you wouldn't need to set up this thing every night."

"Mr. Gifford helps me set *this thing* up."

They continued arguing back and forth, Joe reminding her that everyone's security was ultimately his responsibility. "I'm going to insist, for your safety. I already failed Emma."

"Zachariah Potter is gone now. You don't need to worry about him any longer."

"Bringing him out here was my mistake," Joe's voice reflected disappointment and weariness. "I shouldn't have trusted him."

"I'm going to keep refusing," Lydia turned to face him. She wasn't going to let him persuade her. She was always giving in to what he wanted. Not this time!

Joe's expression was of pained indecision. He grumbled something about stubborn women. Then he reached into the pocket of his trousers.

"I found this. I believe it belongs to you." He handed her a tortoise shell comb.

Lydia had forgotten about the comb. She shriveled with humiliation. *He knew.* He knew she'd been with Zachariah. She watched Joe's back as he walked away, a chill of comprehension lifting the hairs on the nape of her neck. Of course Joe knew. He knew Zachariah better than anyone. That's why he found trivial excuses to keep them separated. No wonder Joe had laughed when she accused him of calling her a whore. She was a naive stupid fool.

That night, during a fearsome storm, the worst they had yet experienced, Lydia found no comfort in sleep. Despite quilts pulled up to her chin, she shivered. Her teeth chattered in the unrelenting cold and dampness which penetrated to her bones. Rain pounded overhead and seeped as a fine mist through the saturated canvas. When lightning lit the interior and a clap of thunder cracked the air, she sat up with a start. Moisture dripped from her face and lashes. The tarpaulin beneath her had trapped the rain like a pool. Her bedding and clothing were sucking up the rain.

Lydia knew she needed to get to higher ground. She shuffled to the rear corner of her tent where the ground cover was pulled up a bit. Water hadn't pooled there, so she scrunched up as tight as she could, arms across her knees, knees up to her chest, to wait out the storm. But the rain was unrelenting, slamming against the canvas within inches of her back. And the water continued to rise. Lightening shattered the sky.

She bent her head to her knees and prayed for the rain to stop.

Without warning, it was upon her, like a large heavy hand. Suffocating. Pressing her to the ground. She tried to cry out, but the sound was swallowed by the storm. The wall had collapsed inward, imprisoning her under the heavy canvas that was her tent. Disoriented, her heart racing, she groped and splashed in the standing water to tunnel her way on hands and knees to freedom. She had to escape. Or she would drown.

After recovering from the initial shock, she decided that either the stakes which held the ropes in place had dislodged in the mud, or that part of the roof had collapsed under the weight of collected rain. When finally, she found the entrance to her tent, she stuck out her head, gasping for air. She pulled herself to standing and stepped barefoot into the soggy night.

A sheet of rain struck her squarely, its accompanying gust of wind nearly knocking her backward.

She had to find shelter. The canvas top of a wagon, no matter how well-oiled would leak, but at least the bed would be above the flooded ground. Where could she go? The Lively's were at the far end of the circle. She was closer to the Crenshaws.

Her dress molded to her like glue, and although it would weigh her down, a nightgown would offer little protection against the weather, and even less for her modesty. She'd made the right decision to wear her dress at night.

She stumbled along in the ankle deep mud, which sucked at her feet and thwarted her forward progress. Fear gnawed at her about being be trapped in the mud. No one would hear her cries for help. She could imagine the anger in John Purcy's voice about how they had to rescue a stupid female who got herself stuck in the mud like a cow.

Lydia pressed on, lightning bolts illuminating her path well enough. Raindrops attacking her eyes like pellets, she staggered to the nearest wagon and braced herself against its wheel. She doubted she could make it as far as the Crenshaws. She glanced up to see who the wagon belonged to... maybe it was the Fletchers... maybe they would let her stay. But they had a whole passel of young uns. She couldn't bother them.

Then Lydia recognized it. The wagon belonged to Joe. *Don't go in there*. She glanced back at the mess of her tent. *Don't go there.*

She gripped the wagon wheel as another gust of wind brought a sheet of rain that threatened to topple her. She gazed up at the wagon seat, her portal to shelter. It seemed as high as the heavens. Joe had told her that he never slept there. Even Allison had complained about it. Lydia hated to, more than anything. No one would have to know that she'd been there. The storm wouldn't last forever. She could sneak out before sunrise.

The effort she spent climbing onto Joe's wagon seat in the driving rain and wind was like that of scaling a muddy hillside in Possum County during a deluge. Her feet and hands kept slipping from their holds; her soaked dress kept binding her legs. After scraping her knuckles on the wood sideboard and bumping a knee, she finally pulled herself under the canvas flap.

With slow deliberate steps, she searched for a blanket or quilt until her foot made contact with something solid. She lost her balance and tumbled forward, screaming as a pair of hands reached out to break her fall. Arms came tightly around her and she fell solidly against a hard body. A whoosh of air escaped her lungs.

"Joe! What are you doing here?" she shrieked and tried to pull away from him. He held her fast.

"I should ask the same of you. This is *my* wagon."

"You… you, offered it to me."

"You refused."

"You always sleep outside."

"It's storming, Lydia. And my wagon was unoccupied," his voice was a little too sultry.

Lydia added the feeling of stupidity along with that of surprise, and the rapidly increasing urge to leave the place. *Of course he'd come here.* She was still lying on his bare chest.

"Yes. Yes of course. All I could think of was fleeing my wet tent."

She noted how warm he felt beneath her; his arms were bands of heat across her back. She was torn between the desperate need to escape and giving in to the desire to cuddle up with him. She made a weak attempt to push herself from his chest.

"The wall of my tent collapsed."

"You poor thing," Joe said. "Your hair is dripping wet and you're shivering. Your dress is soaked. Let me help you take it off." He sat up and while he untangled himself from his blankets, she shrieked and scrambled on all fours away from him.

"You can't stay in that wet dress. You'll get sick," he said as she reached for the canvas flap. "It's dark. I won't see you, if that's what worries you. You can cover up with a blanket.

"No. I'll just go to the Livelys and wait out the storm."

"Nonsense. You don't need to bother them. There's more room in here."

Lydia couldn't disagree with his logic. She didn't want to bother the Livelys. With all of their possessions, sleeping quarters for three became very cramped. Going back outside and tromping through a flooded camp had no appeal. Her shriek from a clap of thunder brought her back on her heels. Joe handed her a blanket.

Lydia kept her back to Joe as she put her cold numb fingers to work unbuttoning the front of her dress. When she struggled to slip her arms out of the wet garment, Joe crawled to her. A delightful shiver ran through her as he reached out to help, his hands coming around her, easily slipping her dress over her head and raised arms.

"Do you always sleep in so many layers?" he asked.

"I never know when I might need to go out into the night." Her heart increased its pounding, hammering loudly enough in her ears, that she thought for certain, he could hear it. She wanted him to touch her. How could she want a man to touch her after what Zachariah had done? She hadn't thought she would ever want a man to touch her again. And certainly not Joe. His wife just died. He was not a gentleman.

When she was wearing only a chemise and thin petticoat, Joe draped the blanket around her shoulders. It smelled like him and felt good around her. Lydia continued to shiver, her teeth chattering. Neither of them spoke. While she waited for the storm to die down, she kept her back to him, sensing his eyes boring into her. The heat radiating from his body jumbled her nerves. Every time she thought of venturing outside, a crack of thunder made her decide to stay. Where it was warm. For just a few more minutes. Her teeth eventually ended their chattering. She laid down and curled up in the blanket.

When she sat up screaming from her nightmare, Joe scooped her into his arms. "What is it?"

A few seconds passed before she regained her bearings. She kicked and clawed at whatever held her so tightly. Then she started shaking.

"Is it the storm?"

Joe wrapped her in the blanket she had tossed aside in her fight. "Please, talk to me. I hate seeing you in such misery. We used to talk. Can't we again?" His voice was husky with emotion.

She wanted to trust him. She was so full of loneliness and despair, and he seemed so full of compassion. "It's silly. It was just a nightmare."

"It's not silly, if it frightens you."

Lydia tried to laugh. "Only children get frightened over nightmares."

"Nightmares can upset anyone."

"I suppose. This is the second time tonight I've awakened feeling utter despair, as if I'd been ripped away from my home and all that I know."

"That makes sense. You're probably homesick. You left Possum Hollow and all that you knew."

"Sometimes I feel homesick." Zachariah had said as much. "This same nightmare has haunted me for years."

"Years?"

"Yes. I don't remember the first time, but ever since we've been on the trail, especially after visiting the fort and the Indian village, it's gotten more real and more terrifying. The details more clear. The feelings more intense." Lydia pulled the blanket tighter before explaining her reoccurring nightmare, of the Indians and of the burning tepees.

"I can practically smell the smoke, and feel the heat of the flames."

"There's been too much talk of Indian attacks. It's put fear into everyone."

"I've never been afraid of Indians."

"Right. I didn't suppose you would be."

They sat there, staring at each other through the darkness, in an awkward silence, listening to the rain above their heads.

"Well," Lydia said. "I think the storm has died down. I'd better go." She shuddered at the thought that someone might have seen her climb into Joe's wagon. She certainly couldn't be found here in the morning.

"Go where?" Joe moved toward her. "What about your flooded tent?"

Reluctantly, she handed him the blanket, swapping it for her wet dress. "I'll manage." In truth, she had no idea what she would do. She only knew that she couldn't stay in this man's wagon. When she opened the canvas flap, a blast of rain pelted her. A loud clap of thunder made her screech and sent her back on her heels. Joe was there to cradle her in his arms.

For a brief second, Lydia relaxed into his embrace. She ached to stay with him, to shut out the rest of the world, to have him smother her fears with kisses. *No!* She had to leave. Being alone with a man in his sleeping quarters was terribly wrong. And the things he made her feel… She had to be anywhere except with Joe. This attraction only brought her misery. Lydia snatched herself away from him.

"You can't leave. Your hair is still damp. And you're shivering with the cold."

Was she shivering from the cold? Or from the effort it took to fight her internal desires?

"Lydia," his voice was pleading. "Why must we go on like this, pretending as though we're little more than strangers?"

"What do you mean?" She couldn't hide her indignation.

"We used to talk… not so long ago. Now you avoid me. As though you think I'm loathsome."

How could he suggest she find him loathsome? How could he not know how much she desired him? How wildly her heart beat for him? His mere presence turned her into a quivering mass of nerves. His kiss, his touch was forever burned into her memory.

"What about Allison?"

"Allison?" Joe shook his head as though he were shaking off something offensive. "What has she got to do with us?"

"She was your wife."

"Allison is dead." His curt matter-of-fact words stung Lydia. "She has nothing to do with you and me."

"How can you say that? You should be mourning her, not inviting women into your sleeping quarters. It's not proper for me to stay here." Lydia lifted the wagon flap to leave. Joe grabbed her arm.

"Lydia, you're not just any woman. And I never loved Allison."

"Let go of me!" she exclaimed, loud enough for others to hear if it hadn't been for a well-timed clap of thunder. "How can you still deny loving your wife, even after her death? You refused to claim the child and were forced into marriage. What kind of a man are you?"

"It's the truth, Lydia. The child wasn't mine. Allison and I never consummated, not before, not after the marriage."

When he released her arm, Lydia clamped her hands tightly over her ears and shook her head to block Joe's words.

Joe pulled her hands from her ears and held them tightly. He looked at her squarely, within inches of her face. "Allison was pregnant before we met."

"I don't want to hear any more of this." She pulled against his hands which bound her wrists. "You're hurting me."

"Listen to me, Lydia. It was a farce. For some reason, Allison got it in her head that she wanted me for a husband. When she found out she was pregnant, she made up the lie that I was the father. Of course her family believed her and expected me to do the right thing. When I refused, well… in the meantime, I got drunk at Chester's and into a brawl with Willie Kincaid."

Lydia shivered at the memory of Willie's putrid breath and his hands on her.

"Willie beat me senseless; I'm embarrassed to say, much to the luck of Allison's brothers. They finished me off and dragged me half-conscious to the marriage ceremony. I was barely aware of what was happening. Later, Allison admitted that the child belonged to a Jimmy Evers." Joe released Lydia's hands. He'd said what he needed to say.

A voice inside Lydia warned her that Joe's words were all lies. But he'd mentioned Jimmy Evers. Everyone in Possum Hollow knew about Allison and Jimmy. Joe had been a newcomer. He wouldn't have just come up with the name unless he'd known. Was it possible? Lydia searched Joe's face through the darkness for some hint of truth.

"Do you believe me Lydia?"

The whole story seemed too incredible. "You were still her husband."

"In name only. I swear to you, I never loved her."

"Why didn't you get an annulment or something?"

"Allison was beautiful on the outside," Joe continued. "Inside, she was full of fear and insecurity. I felt more pity for her than anything else. The guilt of her death now weighs heavily upon me. At first she thought leaving Possum Hollow would be a great adventure. When reality set in, she wanted to return home. By then she was my responsibility and I couldn't just send her back, pregnant and alone. I'm ashamed to admit; I suppose I wanted to punish her for what she'd done."

All this time. "Does anyone else know? Amos and Esther?"

"Yes, they know."

"Why didn't you tell me before?"

"I tried. You didn't want to listen."

"I'm listening now."

"Would it have mattered? Would it have changed anything between us if you had learned sooner?"

"I don't know." Her mind hurt to contemplate the significance of his words. Just because he hadn't loved his wife didn't mean he had any interest in her, other than as a traveling companion.

CHAPTER 28

Joe couldn't resist touching Lydia's bare shoulder where the chemise had fallen away. "Does it make a difference now, Lydia?"

"I'm not sure what to believe."

He sighed and brushed away the damp strands of hair that fell across her face. "Can you believe that I want to be here with you now?"

He kissed her cheek lightly. Then again. His lips meandered along her neck to her ear, where he whispered. "You have no idea how often I have longed to hold you."

A crack of lightning illuminated the interior, and sent Lydia back into his arms. He felt her twitch before she melded into his embrace. He laid her on the blankets next to him, his chest pressed against her back, arms wrapped protectively around her.

"They are right," she said.

"Who is right? Right about what?" His fingertips stroked her temple as she relaxed.

With nothing between them except her thin chemise and petticoat and his lightweight trousers, he could feel the rise and fall of her chest with each breath. He knew it wouldn't be enough, to simply hold her. He nuzzled his face in her damp hair and breathed in the smoky scent and warred with the voice inside his head.

She is too innocent. You are too much your father's son. Just like Jackson Brice destroyed your mother, you will destroy Lydia.

"I am a savage whore," she answered.

"Just to be here with me like this?"

She rolled over to him, her face inches from his. "No. Not just that I'm here with you. I want you to kiss me. I want to feel that leap of flames, the burning in my veins."

Joe widened his eyes. The gnawing in his loins grew. From the moment she'd climbed into his wagon he'd wanted to make love to her. "Where have *you* heard of such a thing? Is this the talk of your female companions?"

"Ladies don't talk of such things, certainly not to other ladies."

"Zachariah…" Joe clenched his jaw and his chest tightened. "I know that you and he…you've been together on occasion. Did you develop some feelings for him?" It tore his insides up to speak of it, but he had to know. That night before Zachariah's expulsion it had been pure selfishness that sent him looking for her. He hadn't wanted to embarrass her. Since then, he'd tormented himself about the decision to not break them apart.

"No. He and I never!" She sat up. "He told me he loved me, and when I wouldn't…"

"Did he hurt you Lydia?" A band tightened around his chest.

"He called me a savage whore and tossed me aside."

Joe hated that Zachariah had hurt her in such a way. "I wish I had never asked him to come. I would never have forgiven myself if he had… I will always carry the guilt of Emma."

"He's gone now," she said. "He can't hurt us anymore."

Joe took her in his arms. Then he kissed her as she had asked. They clung to each other, lips entwined, feeding the other's passion until they were no longer just smoldering embers, but ignited with an explosive fury. They kissed deeply, hungrily, with all the longing and urgency they'd suppressed during the passing months.

His hands were all over her, wishing he could rip away the barrier of undergarments which kept him from touching her skin. He had to proceed with caution. Let her decide how far she wanted to go. When she slid the chemise over her head and pushed her petticoat below her knees, surrendering to him, he thought he would spill his seed right then.

Joe sat back on his heels, hastily removing his trousers, not caring if he ripped off buttons in the process. Lightning flashes illuminated fleeting glimpses of Lydia's full length of smooth copper skin stretched out on disheveled blankets. Her chest rose and fell like a winded cougar. Her glassy eyes narrowed. Disheveled strands of silky hair spread out from around her head. Her skin glowed with beads of perspiration. She was the most beautiful woman in the world. In the past few months he'd come to love her strength and courage more than anything else.

She was there with arms outstretched waiting for him when he returned. Their bodies came together flesh-to-flesh for the first time.

***

Lydia had ached for months to be with the man she loved. His kisses had only fueled her appetite. Now she hungered for the meal. She didn't care that he might discard her and find another. All that mattered was to sate the pulsing in her loins. She'd become a writhing thing, out of control. She clawed at Joe's back and the swell of his buttocks. The sound of pounding rain overhead had long ago faded into the pounding rhythm of their hearts.

When Lydia felt his hard manhood against her thigh, she thought of Zachariah and the night he had tried to take her. She broke out of her clouded brain and pushed her hands against Joe's chest.

"What is it?" Joe dragged his lips across her shoulder and to the dip between her breasts, leaving a trail of steamy moisture.

"That. That." She pointed at his manhood.

"My organ?"

"It's so large!" Surely Joe didn't expect to get such a large organ inside her. She would be ripped apart. The only human male organs she'd seen were unplanned glimpses of men relieving themselves in the brush. Their organs had been small limp things.

"It swells up," Joe explained, "when a man desires a woman."

"It's too big!"

"It'll only hurt for a moment the first time. I promise."

Panic continued to rise within her and she tried to squirm away.

Joe put a finger to her lips to quiet her protest. "Shh. We don't have to if you don't want to."

She gave her answer, pressing upward into him, her hands grabbing the back of his head.

CHAPTER 29

In the aftermath, they lay tangled in a heap of blankets, skin glistening with perspiration, panting as if they'd run a long race. A deep feeling of peace washed over Lydia. Her breath became even and shallow until she drifted off to sleep.

She next awoke to the gentle rocking of the wagon to find Joe pulling up his trousers. "Is everything…"

"Hush," he cut her off and grabbed his rifle before leaving. He didn't have to tell her to stay put.

Lydia pulled the covers to her chin and waited with anticipation for Joe's return. The storm had passed. Nothing except the sound of crickets pricked the silence. Her eyelids were growing heavy when a gunshot fired and brought her alert. As per their safety training, she remained hunkered down unmoving, although some skittish guard had probably shot at a resident night creature that was snooping for dinner leftovers. She hoped it wasn't another skunk.

A few minutes later, Joe returned.

"What happened?" she asked.

He dug through his things, collecting ammunition for his rifle.

"Clyde says he saw something inside the corral. With feathers sticking out."

"One of the chickens probably got loose from the coop. Did he kill it?"

"Taller, he claims. Whatever it was, he chased it off."

"Indians?" Lydia's throat tightened, as she remembered the man who had been pin-cushioned with arrows.

"Don't know. Shadows can play tricks on the eyes. I'm going to scout around the perimeter for a while. It'll be light soon. I suggest you get dressed."

Lydia pulled herself up onto her elbows and gazed at him. "Joe?"

"Yes?"

She wanted to tell him how much she loved him. "Nothing."

As she slipped into her damp dress, she warred with the niggling concerns of an intruder in camp, and with the need to be invisible. If she were spotted sneaking from the sleeping quarters of the recent widower, by a single tongue wagging witness, she would be ridiculed.

Her toes sank into cold, viscous mud and rain-filled wagon ruts en route to her tent. Wet, muddy dogs scurried between fire pits whining and sniffing ashes, looking for food scraps or fat drippings. On this washed-out morning, most of the dogs would be disappointed

She halted in front of her tent, the scene quickly bringing to mind the events of the previous night. The left side of her tent had collapsed inward, while the other remained relatively intact. As she had suspected, the ground beneath the stakes had softened and washed out in the rain. Without support, the stakes and ropes had given way under the wind and rain.

Tugging on stakes and rope, Lydia struggled to reset the tent enough to retrieve her things, when Joe joined her. The two completed the task just as Joe was called away again. As soon as she entered her tent, Lydia knew something was wrong. Her trunk, which was sitting on the right side of the tent and should not have been affected by the collapsing of the left side, was opened, its contents scattered on the flooded tarpaulin.

The trunk had been closed when she'd gone to bed. She'd laid her clean apron on the lid. *Someone had been in her tent!* She shuddered, feeling as violated as if the hands that had picked through her trunk had actually searched her person. Why would someone go through her things? The only thing of value was her gold coin. She double-checked that the disk shaped object was still in a pocket sewn at the waist of her petticoat.

Lydia dragged the hem of her dress through the standing water to reach her trunk, watermarked from storms past, and sifted through her scattered belongs to see what might be missing. Her Indian moccasins were gone. And only her moccasins. Why would someone steal her moccasins? Few knew she had them. Neither Esther nor Faith would go through her things. She'd been with Joe. Except after the shot was fired. No. If he wanted her moccasins, he would have had plenty of other opportunities. Although he was the only one who knew her tent was unoccupied… Zachariah. No. He was long gone.

As she turned to leave her tent in what was now a desperate search for Joe, she bumped head-long into him where he stood just outside the entry.

"Joe!" she cried out. "My moccasins are gone! Someone stole my moccasins." She struggled to keep her shrill voice low.

"Anything else missing?" Joe stood as aloof as if he was talking to anyone. Not the woman he had made love to. Had he found her unsatisfactory? Had their night together meant nothing? She didn't know how a man or a woman were supposed to feel or act after making love. Surely there should be some warmth between.

"No. I have no valuables."

"Maybe it was just a prank. When they couldn't find anything of value, they took something of interest."

"It's creepy." She wrapped her arms about herself.

"All the more reason you should sleep in my wagon. It's safer there."

"You didn't take them did you? So, I'd adjust my sleeping arrangements?"

"No, Lydia. But that would have been an interesting ploy." He cracked a fleeting smile. "I did stop by to tell you that I have no more information on '*feather man*'."

"And we have a thief in our camp."

"Which is disturbing. So, I'm going to insist you move your things into my wagon. I promise you privacy. I won't sneak in and accost you."

She nodded.

"There is something I want to show you today. Saddle up Sandy and ride out with me and the scouts."

Later that morning, in the company of five men, Lydia found herself following the semicircular ridge of rocky knobs, of which Chimney Rock was the eastern most point. This architectural feature had been the latest in a series of great natural monuments that rose from the flat and desolate horizon. Riding side by side, Lydia and Joe bantered like children in their game against boredom and the monotonous rhythm of creaky saddle leather, to name architectural shapes in the large pile of sandstone they followed.

"That one looks like Chester's Saloon," Joe pointed. "See that funny piece sticking out? Just like the sign hanging in front of Chester's."

"I don't see a saloon."

"At least we agreed that Chimney Rock looks like a chimney," Joe said.

Lydia nodded. She'd chilled as she'd gazed upward at the towering spire. It reminded her of burned out chimneys she had seen all too often in Possum Hollow, a remnant of a family home in the rubble and ash.

They continued along the trail, left the river, and entered into a smooth valley. Joe led the group to a small spring of frigid water where he stopped to rest and water their horses. The men were just beginning to roll up their tobacco, when Joe gave out his orders.

"We'll noon in this valley. I want us to reach the Platte and the end of the bluffs by nightfall." He sent two of the men to regroup with the wagons while the other two were to remain in the valley to claim their campsite. "Lydia and I are going to scout out ahead. We'll rejoin you later."

Joe and Lydia veered away from the trail of wagon ruts to follow a path which ascended the bluffs.

"Where are we going?" Lydia was uneasy about leaving the security of the group. The path had become too narrow to ride side-by-side.

"I want to show you something," Joe shouted over his shoulder.

They continued to ascend the bluffs for some time. A glance backwards and she could no longer see the men they'd left in the valley. "Should we be going so far from the others?"

"We're almost there," Joe said.

Lydia couldn't comprehend the importance of taking her from the safety of others and the valley. Any would-be attacker could easily hide where the hillocks met and formed shadowy, depressions.

After a short while, they reached the extreme height of the dividing ridge. Joe came to a stop and dismounted. Looking out, Lydia instantly knew why they'd come.

"The Rockies!" She gasped.

Their ominous height made the Ozarks seem like foothills. Beneath a cerulean sky, the tall peaks were a breathtaking bluish gray along the horizon. Another landmark to lure them forward

"Come and look," Joe said. He augmented with sign language, something he had taken to doing when the opportunity arose. Lydia joined him near the edge of the ridge. "Over there is Laramie's peak." He pointed. "It's maybe 100 or 150 miles away. I've heard some brag about seeing Pikes Peak 300 miles away to the southwest. I've never seen that far."

"Can we sit here and rest for a while?" Lydia returned in sign, easily remembering to fist her right hand at shoulder level, then to lower it briskly.

Staring at those mountains, far away across the plains, yet seemingly close enough to touch, she understood why Joe found freedom in that wide open space. So different from the cool green canopy of her woodland home in Possum Hollow, the rocky landscape had its own appeal. Sitting on that ledge, away from the trail, and the push of people, the air was clear and scented with sweet wild flowers. A warm breeze tickled.

Across the plains, Lydia saw those same alluring mountains looming like an adversary, eager to swallow those who attempted to tackle their tall craggy peaks. Mocking. Daring. Only the most cunning would survive.

"Can we get the wagons through? Is there really a pass?"

"Yes Lydia, there is. I can't promise it won't be difficult. There's a lot of obstacles. The ten or so days travel between Fort Laramie and Independence Rock is particularly nasty. I can promise, I'll do everything I can to see everyone and their wagons safely to California."

Lydia could have gazed at the mountains all day, contemplating their beauty. But, apprehension and melancholy were gnawing travel companions, always eating away at her fortitude. For the first time since leaving Possum Hollow, she fully grasped how far from home she'd traveled and how dangerous was their trail yet to come, but there was no turning back.

"What's after the mountains?" she asked. "What's that part of the trip like?"

"Desert mostly, until we get into California. And I mean an arid, rocky basin of sagebrush and other scruffy vegetation. The sun reflects off the white salt sands and surrounding mountains. It's blinding and bakes everything and everyone. Some believe the area of the Humboldt, or 'Hellboldt' River is where the devil resides."

"It sounds horrible."

"The water in the Humboldt is not fit for drinking. We'll need to get our drinking water from wells and springs and transport it in barrels. The few hot springs we see are interesting to watch, but can be dangerous. Once, I saw a dog run toward one as if it were going to lap up the water. The poor thing slipped in and yelped as its hair scalded off."

Seeing Lydia's horrified expression, Joe squeezed her hand. "The most difficult part for me will be controlling everyone's fears. The last time I went through that area… well, I don't want to bother you with my concerns."

"Please Joe, tell me what bothers you."

"You'll just get worried."

"No I won't. If you share with me, maybe I can help."

"Sometimes worry and sleeplessness causes madness. The animals frighten easily. People shoot their dogs because of the incessant barking. I rescued a family who had lost everything when the wife set fire to their camp. Her husband had refused to turn back. I predict a lot of dead animals and hungry people begging in the desert. There's not much wild life to eat. Snakes and scorpions maybe."

Lydia crinkled her nose. "Guess we'll be rationing beans."

"Are you pleased I brought you here? I wanted you to be the first to see the mountains." Joe scooted closer to Lydia so their thighs touched, making her all too aware of their aloneness on the bluff and Joe's muscular body, and the hot flesh beneath his clothes. Then he took her hand, which was innocent enough.

"Oh yes, Joe. I am." Her eyes began to water. "And I'm glad you shared your stories with me. I won't be afraid. Not when I'm with you." Was he actually here with her, his hand firmly claiming hers? As she looked into his eyes, he leaned over and kissed her briefly, ever so tenderly and pulled her to him.

"Last night…" her voice nearly trembled. She loved him so much. "I don't know what I would do without you."

"Shh. Just think about the moment. We never know what the future will bring."

She swallowed down a lump and forced a smile. "I know." *No. Not fully*. And she wasn't sure she wanted to. Dangerous days lay ahead and already they'd seen as many graves on this trail as there were stars in the sky. Life was short and unpredictable. She had to cling to the moment.

Joe tightened his hold on her and kissed her fiercely, igniting a flame between them. As their passion intensified, they knew that neither could be satisfied with only touching. They pulled away from each other in frustration.

"Why did you have to touch me?" Lydia's lips were parted and receptive. She was shocked at how quickly her body came alive at his touch.

Joe was already tearing at the buttons of his shirt.

Ruled strictly by her body's enflamed desires, Lydia took Joe's cue. She stood and removed her garments. Neither showed concern with the possibility of being seen by other passing emigrants. The risk of being found in a compromising situation did add a certain excitement to the moment.

They tossed their garments aside with no regard for tidiness. By the time Lydia had struggled with shaky fingers to remove her under clothes, Joe had discarded his trousers and boots. When she returned her attention to him, he was eyeing her. Hungrily.

This was the first time Lydia had seen the full length of Joe in the light of day and she unabashedly eyed his nakedness. The western sky framed him gloriously. His hair was tousled casually, in a most appealing way. He stood there completely vulnerable, his manhood bold and swollen.

They rushed to each other, pressing naked flesh against naked flesh. Joe's hands were all over her, making her tremble and her legs weaken. He pulled her closer, increasing his grip on her to keep her on her feet. Then his hand was between her legs, sending currents of raw heat through every nerve. She gasped and reached out for something to grab as her knees buckled. She found his taut buttocks.

Joe eased her down onto the ground away from the edge. She was losing all awareness of the bluffs, the view, and the scratchy vegetation. His arms and legs were all over her as if they had multiplied a hundred-fold. Wild and savage, they clung to each another, legs and arms entwined.

The sound of men's laughter brought a curse from Joe and brought Lydia aware. Her eyes widened with shear panic. Joe pulled away and snatched Lydia to her feet. He led her to an outcropping protected from view by vegetation.

All Lydia could think about were the men in their scouting party finding them in this situation. She could never live with the shame and humiliation. "What if they…"

Joe clamped his hand over her mouth and forced her to the ground. Rocks and brush scratched them as they slipped under the outcropping. Only after they had stretched out on their stomachs, did they realize Joe had left his gun and holster with his clothing. When the small group moved to where Lydia could see them through the vegetation, she couldn't identify any of the six scruffy men, each with a horse and a pack mule loaded with furs. She sucked in her breath, heart racing, as the men quieted and looked around. They must have seen Zeus and Sandy who were hobbled along the edge of the trail.

One of the men dismounted and probed the vegetation with the butt end of his rifle. Another picked up her dress for the others to see. He said something Lydia couldn't understand. Realizing they'd interrupted a lover's tryst, the men laughed, before discarding her dress. They scrutinized Zeus and Sandy, but left them alone.

Lydia sighed with relief as the men passed from sight. "Oh Joe, what if they'd seen us? It was bad enough they found our clothing." Joe helped her from the outcropping as she continued speaking. "What if they had taken our horses or my dress just to be cruel? I'd be walking naked back to our camp."

Joe wrapped her firmly against his chest. "Perhaps, we got a little careless."

Lydia pulled away. In an attempt to hide her modesty, she turned her back and began to redress. "This was a mistake. We can't just stop in the middle of the day and… and…" she couldn't say the words. What had happened to her, to let her body's desires rule over clear thinking?

"You are the company's Captain, still in mourning. And I'm supposed to be a lady. Just for riding with five men, I'll be facing the scorn of the women.

They dressed quickly and rode in silence back down the mountain.

CHAPTER 30

"Is it true the Bluffs is haunted, Mr. Brice?" One boy asked at the evening community fire. Weeks had passed since Joe had joined the evening fires and the children especially had missed hearing the stories of his youth when he was on the trail with his grandfather.

"We heard some kids down at the river talkin' about how Scott's Bluff is haunted."

"It ain't haunted," the sister scoffed. "Is it, Mr. Brice?"

"Well, now." Joe's eyes brightened. His lips turned upward into a sly grin as he leaned toward the semi-circle of children. "There was a man who died up on that bluff." He pointed in the direction.

Like the wide-eyed children, Lydia stared into the inky darkness where Joe pointed.

"His name was Scott."

"Like the bluff," one of the children said.

"Yes, like the bluff. There are several legends as to why the bluff takes his name," Joe began. "This is my favorite."

Lydia knew he had them hooked.

"A group of men who worked for the American Fur Company were on their way home from the mountains when Scott became sick. For some reason, his group joined up with another party. Some say it was because Scott's group lost all of their gunpowder in the river and so had no way to hunt for food."

Flames shot skyward from the fire, which served as a kind of barrier between audience and story teller, adding to the ghostly mystique. Joe's eyes glowed orange, as if fueled by some other worldly spirit. His voice skillfully lured the listeners into the ebbs and flows of the legend. They were there, with Scott and his comrades, on that ghostly mountain. With a great up swelling of love, Lydia gazed at Joe with adoration, knowing her expression mimicked that of the captivated youngsters.

"Anyway, in order to catch up with the other group, the leader of Scott's group went ahead with his men, leaving two men to bring Scott down the North Platte in a boat. The agreement was to meet at what is now called Scott's Bluff."

Despite the evening chill, Lydia warmed at the way these children adored Joe. For weeks, the stress of leadership had weighed heavy on him, and burdened with the responsibilities of a wife he did not love, he had been short tempered and distant with everyone. Watching him now, their charismatic and confident leader, his stony scowl was only a memory. This was the man she had fallen in love with.

"The boat carrying Scott wrecked," Joe continued.

He caught Lydia looking at him from across the flames. His eyes held hers, speaking more than words could say. Then he smiled his bright white smile that lit up his entire face and could send any woman's heart skittering. It was meant only for her.

"Finding no easy way to transport him, the two disloyal comrades abandoned Scott, thinking that he would die anyway. So, they hurried ahead and joined the rest of group reporting that Scott had died. So, the entire company left the bluff and returned home.

The following summer these same men visited the bluff and came upon the bones and skull of a human skeleton. They believed these bones to be those of Scott. But the place they found the bones was 60 miles from where they had abandoned him. Somehow, in all of his suffering and agony, Scott had crawled there before his death, only to find his comrades had abandoned him. These bluffs have borne his name ever since."

Lydia shivered. To think, a dying man had crawled 60 miles to the very spot where she and Joe had crossed.

"His bones still there, Mr. Brice?"

"Can ye show us the bones?" One lad asked eagerly.

"Yea, we wanna see the bones."

Pearl Clemens, who had three of her children by the fire, came and shooed all the children off to bed, saying it was past their bedtime and that they should not be bothering Mr. Brice with such foolishness.

***

Lydia watched the men saddle up and prepare an empty supply wagon for their expedition to Fort Laramie. The fort had been built on the left bank of the clear Laramie River, which emptied into the North Platte a short distance away.

Lydia handed Joe the letter she had written to her parents. He added it to the stack in his saddle bag for delivery to the fort's Post Office. After mounting Zeus, he adjusted his pistol in its holster and seated the assembly more comfortably about his waist.

"Please be careful," Lydia said, rubbing Zeus's silky nose.

"I promise." Joe leaned over to her and added breathlessly. "I'll miss you. Wish I could take you with me. But, unlike Fort Kearney, a military fort, Fort Laramie is a trade center for Indians and trappers. Too many gunfights and outlaws."

As the men rode off, Lydia thought of the heavy burden Joe carried. Along with her letter to her parents and Esther's bundle of letters, he carried one to Wilma and Walter Kincaid, which notified them of their daughter's death. He'd been torn between telling the Evers about the loss of the unborn grandchild they didn't even know was theirs, or perpetuating the lie that the child was his. In the end, Joe decided not to be the bearer of grief for two families, and let the lie rest."

As the women dispersed and returned to their chores, many grumbled about their "good for nothin'" husbands they were certain were going to drink and gamble away the family's last cent. Lydia was glad she didn't have that worry. But she couldn't shake her concerns about Joe and gambling and other shady dealings. There was so much she didn't know about him. He could handle himself in rough situations, although that knowledge did not completely reassure her.

It was well after dark when the men straggled back into camp, laughing and whooping it up, disrupting everyone's sleep. There was no end to the arguments; wives berated their husbands for what they had gambled away or for being "stinking drunk". Thelma Lee made a production of tossing her husband his bedroll and refused him entrance to the family wagon. Even camped several miles from the fort, Lydia heard drunken miners, gunfire, and Indian war whoops well into the night.

Joe came to breakfast moving slower and stiffer than normal. Lydia said nothing about it. He was not her husband and not in her charge. He was in better shape than some of the other men who had dark circles under their eyes, hands pressed to their heads and seeking black coffee. Ned Elders was nursing a black eye.

"What supplies did ye get?" Amos asked Joe.

"I learned that the US government is going to purchase the fort later this summer and turn it into a military outpost. All the men I knew who worked for the fur company are gone."

"What about the supplies? We still got two horses that need shoeing."

"I know," Joe grumbled, and rubbed the sides of his head. "I managed a handful of nails and a couple of shoes. Supplies are scarce, even at exorbitant prices." Joe took a sip of black coffee. "There's about ten thousand people already ahead of us."

"Ten thousand?" Esther asked.

"That's the number someone scratched into the registration book. I'm not surprised, but more than I expected."

Lydia doubted that many lived in all of the rural Missouri county that included Possum Hollow. No wonder it was a constant battle for fresh water, clean campsites and grazing.

"Add in those taking the Santa Fe route and those behind us; there could be as many as fifty thousand people out here," Joe added. "Then of course, all the animals that go with that great a number."

"What are we going to do?" Esther asked.

"Don't look so worried, Aunt Esther." Joe dumped out the last dribble of coffee and grounds from his cup, and went to refill. "Nothing is different from yesterday, or the day before. We just have to keep pressing westward."

***

Lydia grimaced with each agonizing step in another seemingly endless skyward climb. Loose and abrasive rocks created unsure footing. Heels rubbed raw into blisters; some she knew were oozing. Nothing she'd experienced in the damp forested Ozarks compared to the barren, dusty ground of the Laramie Mountains. Sharp precipitous turns. Wagons lowered by guy ropes. Lengthy stretches without water meant storing it in barrels for rationing.

Lydia was beginning to second-guess her motives for leaving Possum Hollow. Perhaps she had overestimated the danger her presence caused her parents. She had been naïve to think life as a farmer's daughter would have prepared her for this perilous journey. How could they get through the Rockies, if these smaller mountains were breaking everyone in both spirit and body?

An avalanche of rocks pulled Lydia from her thoughts. She shouted a warning over her shoulder to Faith and leapt sideways to avoid being pummeled, grateful to a pine sapling shooting out from between rocks to prevent a downward summersault. A fine, silver mare tumbled past with a great scream to fall to her death.

Lydia looked back to find Faith, a grimace on her face, leaning into her husband's lean frame. One hand gripped her side, her chest heaving, she looked on the verge of collapse. Lydia wondered how long Faith's husband, unaccustomed to hard manual labor, could support his wife this way.

Relief didn't come soon enough when they stopped at a cool spring to rest the animals, now slumped in their yokes, and let them drink. Seth handed out ointment to soothe blistered feet, scraped knees and elbows. The women cut up whatever kind of hides they could scavenge to make bag like shoes to tie around the ankles of animals. Even the dogs were given "moccasins" to wear during the next leg of the trail.

Six days after leaving Fort Laramie, sore and exhausted, tempers flaring, they were within view of the North Platte crossing. The animal hide shoes had worn thin, or were completely shredded and falling off. Lydia knew she would have to replace her own pair soon. She looked forward to resting her blistered feet for a day or two while they waited for a ferry.

Instead of resting, Joe ordered them to continue following the river downstream, to a shallower, calmer part of the river where they could cross on their own.

"The operators are charging the outrageous fee of four dollars per wagon and fifty cents per draft animal," Joe reported. "With both banks sprawling with customers, there's no incentive to negotiate their prices down."

The men complained about the extra effort to build their own raft, but no one wanted to camp among human and animal waste left by previous campers at the bottleneck. None could disagree with the tactics of Joseph Brice, whose constant press forward kept them on schedule.

Grumbling and arguing increased with each passing mile and the more unsanitary the conditions became. This area of the North Platte was a natural thoroughfare for Indians and migrating buffalo. Seemingly clear lakes, sparkling sapphire in the distance, were actually stagnant ponds where rain water had collected in buffalo wallows. A concoction of excrement, mosquito larvae and other floating debris, which had warmed for weeks in the hot sun was too foul for humans and their animals. At one such place, which reeked like spoiled meat, children delighted at throwing rocks into the pit, watching them float and then slowly sink into the jiggling gelatinous fluid.

They crossed the North Platte without incident and were rewarded with an extra day of rest before embarking on another hellish stretch where for the next three days, the sturdiness and perseverance of every living thing was tested.

The trail left the river and entered a barren, sandy country, destitute of timber, where again, water had to be stored in barrels. Sprouting from the white crusty soil, forage was insufficient and the livestock, especially those in yoke, tired easily. Churned up alkali dust choked and blinded, coated ears, eye rims and nostrils. Wild-eyed and skittish, the thirsty animals tugged on their restraints, taxing the stamina and tempers of their handlers, as each spring or small lake, appeared on the horizon, the animals moved to stampede. The alkali water was poisonous to humans and animals.

Alkalied!" Joe's call brought Lydia to attention.

She followed him to a group assembled around a half dozen oxen. Two men were attempting to restrain one, which was coughing. Its forelegs and abdomen were swelling. Amos Crenshaw was holding the head, John Purcy steadying the frame, while Ned Elders began to force large globs of lard down its gullet with a stick. The animal stomped and twisted his head and coughed up the grease. Without the antidote, the alkali would destroy the lungs.

Lydia knew what to do. Calm the animal. Her rapport with frightened or injured animals had been called into use many times. With her words and soothing touch, he eventually swallowed the lard and drank down the vinegar wash. Meanwhile, treatment on another began.

Travel continued in fits and starts, everyone focused on directing the thirsty oxen away from the pools of alkali water. Every time an ox, usually along with its companions in yoke drank the toxic water, globs of lard had to be stuffed down its throat to neutralize the alkali. By the time the misery finally ended at the Sweetwater River, a half dozen had been lost.

After a grueling day of travel and supper clean up, Lydia wanted nothing more than to spread out a blanket in view of the river where she could work on stitching her yellow calico dress. She was walking to her selected spot with a basket of sewing supplies when Joe approached, Zeus and Sandy in tow.

Lydia wasn't sure what he had in mind. She was bone weary. Her blistered feet were sore, despite salves and tight wrappings.

"You know it's not appropriate, you and me riding off alone." *Together.* "Things happen between us." To remain impassive and aloof, as though they hadn't become lovers, was becoming increasingly difficult.

"There's nothing inappropriate about us riding to Independence Rock. Have you looked toward there lately? We'll hardly be alone."

Lydia gazed in the direction of Independence Rock, the latest landmark to lure the emigrants westward. For days, she'd watched the small bump grow into the massive rock, which seemed to have been plunked down in the middle of the prairie. Named by a group of trappers who had partied there on July 4th, 1830, the landmark at least wasn't struggling to resemble something.

"Everyone who is able is already there," Joe broke into her thoughts.

Lydia couldn't deny that the population in camp had thinned out after dinner. Dozens of people, mostly on horseback, were coming and going in all directions to and from the rock. In truth, riding on Sandy and escaping the confines of camp did have its appeal.

"As much as I'd like to have my way with you right here and now, I'm not going to accost you in public view," Joe added with a roguish grin.

Lydia's heart tripped. She wished she could deny it. But she felt that tug too. Her body responded to his nearness.

Against her better judgement, she agreed. She stowed her supplies and let Faith know she would be going for a short ride. In the past several weeks, the seriousness of Faith's blood ailment had revealed itself. The strenuous climbs, the lack of water and oxygen at higher altitudes had left her with extreme fatigue. Except for the most menial of tasks, she was often more hindrance than help with camp chores. Each evening, Lydia, with Seth's insistence, sent Faith to their wagon to rest after supper.

"Do you need anything before I go?" Lydia asked.

"No. Seth will take care of me. He's around camp somewhere. Have fun."

After Lydia and Joe mounted up, Joe said, "There's a freshly painted cross stuck in the ground at the bottom of the rock. You'll see it."

"How do you know the cross is freshly painted?"

"I was out there earlier, remember? Now, whoever returns to that point first, after going around the rock once, wins. It's about three miles from here, with another mile around the rock."

"What would I win?"

"What difference does that make?"

"I want to know if it's something worth racing for."

"How about…" Joe's face lit up with mischief. "If I win, I get to accost you!" he shouted and kicked Zeus into motion. True to form, in the blink of an eye, the hooves of the strong stallion dug into the earth and the sturdy animal sped away, to leave Lydia and Sandy in the dust.

The mare needed no command to bolt after the speeding Zeus and his rider. Wherever Zeus went, so did Sandy.

Accost her, after he promised. She'd give him a piece of her mind. Then again, if she lost, maybe she'd still win. A shiver ran through her at the thought of his hands on her.

By the time Lydia had gone the three miles and reached the giant rock, the mare was lathered. Lydia saw the painted cross, which no doubt marked the grave of someone's beloved family member. She rode past the onlookers milling around the base of the rock, who turned at the sound of hooves galloping at full speed.

By the time she'd returned to the cross, Joe was climbing up the side of the rock.

"Come on!" He waved.

The steep, smooth surface of the rock forced Lydia to crawl on her knees, tangling her legs in her skirt. She scrambled for handholds, but found few.

"Wait!" she called.

Joe climbed like a mountain goat, while Lydia kept sliding backwards. Mothers were yelling from below for their children to get down. How easy to fall and break an arm or leg. Scooting on her fanny backwards, Lydia was about to give up when Joe reached out his hand and helped her to her feet.

"I don't want to go to the top," she protested.

"You've come this far. You can't stop now. I want to show you something."

They continued skyward, discovering who had journeyed before them. Like a registry, names had been recorded on the surface with whatever they had on hand: wagon paint, axle grease or gunpowder mixed with various liquids. The amount of failed attempts at carving names or initials into the rock was a testament to the solidity of the granite-like surface.

"People brag about either witnessing the highest name on the rock or inscribing it themselves. As far as I know, Cicero Dowd of Ohio is the highest. I've seen it." Joe began his instructive commentary. "Damn it."

"What's the matter?"

"It was supposed to be here."

"What?"

"What I came to show you." Joe left Lydia to wait while he continued his search of the rock. Finally, he waved to her with a smile, the white of his teeth gleaming in reflected sunlight.

Lydia struggled to follow the path, which Joe had taken. He saw her frustration and went to her and took her hand. By the time he stopped, Lydia was breathing hard and gulping in great mouthfuls of air.

"There it is." Joe pointed.

Lydia could only stare dumb struck. Chiseled on the side of the rock, taking a commanding place were the letters…
J B
L W

CHAPTER 31

Lydia swallowed a lump, staring at the carving. "When? How?"

"I paid some Mormons. They've got a business going." Joe was still grinning from ear to ear

Her eyes misted over and she scrambled down the smooth surface of the rock. Nearly blinded by the flood of hot tears flowing unimpeded down her cheeks, she stumbled on some loose stones at the bottom. Her toe caught on something half-buried and she wound up face down in the dirt.

Joe followed closely and helped her up. "Are you hurt?"

She brushed herself off and shook her head, feeling more clumsy and stupid than anything.

Joe eased her against a pile of rocks near the base of the main rock. "Rest here a few minutes." He removed his gloves, and with a calloused thumb, brushed away the dirt clinging to her wet cheeks. "No hanky," he said quietly. "Can't keep them clean out here."

Lydia's fight against tears, reminded her of when they'd first met. He'd gently scooped her from the mud and held her soiled body against him while he cleaned her face with his hanky. She was so full of love now, rather than fear, as she gazed at him through glassy eyes. Her lips trembled. She didn't mean to cry. In honesty, she wasn't sure how she should react. Joe's carving was a wonderful thing. But what was the significance? There had been no 'love'. No 'forever'. The names and initials she'd seen carved on trees by lovers back home, usually contained hearts or other symbols of love.

"Are you not pleased?" Joe asked, sounding disappointed. He kept looking at her, obviously as unsure of her reaction as she was. "If I had had more time or more money, I would have carved our full names."

"It's lovely." She looked at him with a tentative smile.

"Now everyone will know that we passed this spot together."

Joe was obviously pleased with himself and wanted praise. Is that all the carving of their initials meant to him? That they were just travelers, registering their names like so many before? Did he see no permanence to their relationship, like that of their initials carved in the rock?

Joe replaced Lydia's bonnet, which had slipped to the back of her neck during the ride. He tied a fresh bow neatly under her chin. With a heavy heart, she allowed him to take her hand, and they strolled silently along the base of the rock.

"Looks like a storm is moving in," Joe said. "We'd better round up the horses and head back to camp. The crowd has already begun to thin."

She raised her nose to the changing wind. She could smell rain.

The horses were nowhere in sight. When Zeus didn't respond to Joe's calls, he mumbled, "Where can that horse be?"

Joe and Lydia called in different directions. As the horizon became darker, other emigrants scrambled to pack up their picnics or gear to return to camp. With increasing ferocity, the wind carried debris and dirt in little swirling masses and blew Lydia's skirt about her legs. Walking became difficult. She had to hold down her bonnet to keep it on her head and shield her eyes from the swept up dirt. As the air took a sudden chill, heavy drops of rain left little craters in the bare ground.

"Zeus is not one to wander and lose his way," Joe shouted over the wind.

"Could they have been stolen?"

"They'll come back. They must have gone around to the other side of the rock. We'd better find shelter before this storm gets worse." Joe studied the sky. "It'll only be minutes until the clouds completely open."

"Where are we going to find shelter?" Anxiety intruded in her voice. Lightning bolts shot out of the western sky, each with a hair-raising thunderclap.

"Maybe one of these crevices will be big enough to protect us from the worst of the storm."

While Joe scrutinized the surface of the rock, the rain became blinding, blowing against them in sideways sheets out of a blackened sky. Lightening surrounded them. Lydia shivered as the fierce wind and rain penetrated her undergarments and pasted her wet clothing against her.

"What are we going to do?" Lydia's fear was escalating, as again and again, Joe rejected each crevice. Out here, they were completely exposed. Even the giant rock was no help.

"Here," Joe said at last. He still had Lydia tethered by the hand when he slipped into the rock.

After passing through several feet of near darkness, her eyes adjusted enough to see the large crevice, which opened up to an area where daylight seeped in. Rain rushed through the same hole like a waterfall and splashed onto the smooth earth below. The inside surface and dome-like ceiling looked as if they had been scooped out by a giant claw and were of the same smooth granite as the outside of the rock. The charred remains of a campfire and some small animal bones were evidence that others had once occupied this shelter.

"Looks like we're not the first ones to find this place. They spent some time here, at least overnight." Joe pointed to two areas on opposite sides of the charred firewood. "Two men, I'd guess. That's where their bedrolls were stretched out."

Lydia wondered who might have discovered this place before them. Someone trapped in a storm? Hunters maybe? More likely, outlaws.

"Did you know about this place?" Lydia asked. "I would've never seen it."

"No. Just dumb luck."

"And I thought you were super human," Lydia teased.

Joe grinned. "I'm just an ordinary man who would go to great lengths to see to your comforts."

"The only comfort I need is warmth and dry clothes. A fire would be nice. I don't think even a super human could deliver that right now." Lydia wrapped her arms about herself, trying to minimize the shivering.

Joe kicked the remains of a fire long quenched. "I wish those blasted horses hadn't run off. I had a blanket packed in Zeus's saddlebag, and some matches too, for emergencies. I'm going to have to give him a good talking to."

"Maybe those men left something we could use." Lydia started picking around in the dark recesses where the scooped out dome of a ceiling met the dusty floor.

"Here's some firewood scraps." Joe picked up what amounted to an armful, and tossed it alongside the remains of the previous fire. "Unfortunately, we have no matches or flint."

While Joe kicked the dirt with his boots, making a lame attempt to search for anything, Lydia continued more diligently on hands and knees. When she was about to give up, she spied something sticking out of the ground. She pulled at the object, which refused to budge.

"Joe! Look!"

She clawed with fingers to unearth whatever it was. It didn't matter that the discovery might not help her situation. Having located something buried was exciting enough for the moment.

Joe hunched under the slopped ceiling as he approached her. "What is it?"

"I don't know. It feels like a piece of leather." She pulled at the object, which had about two inches of length sticking out of the ground.

With Joe's help, she exposed a large enough section of the buried item so that with one great tug, Joe lifted it from the loosely packed soil. "Looks like whoever was here intended to come back," he said.

"Pelts," Lydia said in awe, as she stared at the tight bundle neatly held together with rope. "Why would someone leave this here?"

"Maybe the owner lost one of his mules, and couldn't carry this bundle any further. For that matter, maybe there is another one buried here somewhere. Maybe he knew he'd never make it over the Laramie Mountains and to the fort without enough pack mules. My grandfather was forced to stash a load of pelts once. We went back for it a few weeks later."

"You don't talk much about those days," Lydia said. "Why not?"

"Right now we need to get you warm." Joe retrieved a knife from his pocket and cut the rope, freeing the pelts from the bundle.

Lydia gasped as beautiful buffalo hides uncoiled before them. They were winter hides with fur, well scraped and supple. Someone had invested a lot of time to preserve them. No wonder the owner had buried them.

"Now we can get you out of those wet clothes."

Joe dragged the cumbersome load, with Lydia's help to the center of the area, where they could both stand up straight. After they dropped the load, Joe unfastened his shirt, Lydia watching.

"Aren't you going to slip out of that dress?" he tugged against the buckles of his gun holster.

"N… No," she stammered with teeth chattering.

"As much as I'm stirred by seeing you in that clingy dress, you need to get out of it. You're shivering." Joe reached out to help unbutton her bodice, but Lydia stepped away.

Joe's eyes raked boldly over her, making Lydia devastatingly aware of how her rain-soaked dress molded and accentuated every curve. She put her arms protectively across her chest to discover her nipples threatening to poke through.

"Your lips are turning purple. We need to get you warm."

"I just feel kind of strange, undressing here, like this."

"In front of me? It's not like I haven't seen all of you."

Lydia thought Joe seemed smug at the concept of knowing her so intimately. Lydia turned her back to him. "What if someone should see?"

"Out here?" Joe chuckled. "Nobody can see. And besides, have you forgotten about that day on Scott's Bluff? You were in a hurry enough then to remove your clothes."

Lydia's face grew hot and she turned to give Joe a friendly slap on the arm. Joe grimaced and rubbed the bicep as though she'd actually inflicted pain.

"Ow."

"Have you forgotten how that ended? Those horrid trappers found us. I still shudder when I think about it."

"I haven't forgotten. My mind dwells on how your damp skin gleamed in the sunshine."

Lydia wondered which fate was worse, having some strangers find her all naked and wrapped in pelts, or having Joe devour her with his every thought and glance.

Lydia turned her back to Joe and undid the buttons of her dress. Cold, almost numb fingers made the task take longer than normal. She pulled her dress over her head and tossed the thing in a crumpled heap onto the ground. Then she removed her rain soaked undergarments.

"Happy now?" Lydia asked, turning around, arms akimbo.

"Quite." Joe stood boldly naked observing her with his devilish grin. His blue eyes had turned to dark pools that threatened to drown Lydia as he stepped within arm's length of her. Casually, he ran his hands along the curves of her body, gliding them upwards, thumbs making small circular movements over pert nipples. Lydia quivered with the pleasurable sensation of the gentle act.

When she attempted to retrieve a pelt which she needed all of a sudden, a large hand ensnared her wrist and put a stop to her idea of covering herself.

"I have a better idea of how we can get warm," Joe said, his eyes burning into hers.

"And how might that be?" Lydia asked coyly, quivering beneath his gaze.

Joe captured her free wrist and pinned her arms behind her back. In a similarly quick movement, he brought her body against his. She was helpless to free herself from his embrace.

"Allow me to demonstrate." His husky voice was a whisper.

Then his mouth swooped down on hers with a fierce animal desire that sent an instant jolt of arousal cascading through her core. His kiss was all consuming, sensitizing every nerve of her body with wanting. Her breasts were instantly alert and eager for his touch, lost horses and fierce storms dissolving into the dreamy world where the only thing of importance was the hard muscular body imprisoning her.

What happened to their agreement to behave as a lady and a gentleman? She was powerless to deny him and to pull away. The slightest touch from this man could cause a savage passion to erupt within her.

Raging with desire, Lydia molded her body to Joe's, pressing her breasts against his hard furred chest. He in turn crushed her against him, his mouth demanding more. She ached to throw her arms around him, to clutch his shoulders and feel the raw manly power of him, but Joe did not release her hands. It was exquisite torture.

Joe's manhood, grown large and firm, had cradled itself against her thigh. Lydia groaned and writhed with the agony of penned up frustration and yearning until finally Joe freed her with a quick release that sent her back on her heels.

"We must stop this." He was bent over, hands on hips gasping for breath. "It cannot end well."

"You would leave me wanting?" She needed him to be as wild as she was. Nothing mattered except satisfying the throbbing in her loins.

They stared at each other hungrily, assessing each other, waiting for the next moment of attack. Then Lydia leapt at him, legs coming around his waist, arms encircling his chest, the aggressive move nearly knocking him over. She kissed his neck and the side of his face.

Joe put his arms around her to support her thighs and buttocks. Almost effortlessly he eased himself to his knees with Lydia still clinging to him like some wildcat. Blindly, he felt for one of the hides and stretched it out onto the cold hard ground where he lay down with her, cradling her head in his palm. He kissed her, sweetly, gently.

Why was he tormenting her? Why was he depriving her? The yearning inside had become a painful restraint. She needed him like an opiate.

Joe's eyes, dark and dilated, reflected his own burning desire as he eased his body upon her.

In the afterglow of their heated passion, their energy spent, Lydia nestled her face in Joe's hard chest, breathing in the scent of him, her hair falling in disarray across them both. His arm draped over the curve of her slender waist. Filled with quiet contentment, she sighed as her lids fluttered open to meet Joe's. He had that distant, brooding look about him. His mouth was tight and grim.

He released her and slipped from under the hides.

"Where are you going?" she asked.

"I thought I heard something."

They both listened. The sound came again. A soft whinny.

"Zeus," Joe sighed. He boldly strode to the entrance.

"You're not going out there?" Lydia asked in a rising panic. She grabbed another hide and pulled it to her chin

"I'm going to see if they're all right."

"Like that?" She gasped, wide-eyed at his nakedness.

"No one is out there. The rain is falling in sheets." He slipped into the shadows and disappeared.

Alone, Lydia rolled over to face the entrance. She shivered and sank deeper into the fur pelts. Joe was gone for only a few minutes. It seemed like an eternity. He was carrying the saddlebag when he returned.

"They're fine. I hobbled them outside. Against the rock, they'll get some protection from the storm and won't wander."

A rising ache of disappointment surrounded her heart when he didn't immediately return to her.

"What's wrong?" she asked.

"We need to get our clothes dry," he started to sort through the abandoned fire wood.

"Have I displeased you?"

He stiffened. "Why would you ask me that?"

"Then come back to me."

"We can't very well return to camp dressed in buffalo hides."

Lydia propped up her head in the palm of her hand to watch Joe work. "Since when did you ever care about such things, as you prance around here with your man parts hanging out?

"Can't say I ever have, now that you mention it. I just don't want other men feasting their eyes on *your* nakedness." He sounded like Joe, but there was no humor on his face, no twinkle in his eyes.

As Joe worked on the fire, Lydia admired his long powerful form and the strong sinewy muscles that flexed as he walked. His broad shoulders tapered to a narrow waist which a short time ago she'd been clutching. Just watching his naked form gave her a rush of excitement. She quickly found herself yearning unquenchably for him to return to their cocoon, to touch her, to caress her.

Joe managed to get a small fire going, using some dried moss as tinder and a match, which he'd stowed deep in his saddlebag. He stretched out their clothes as close to the fire as he dared.

When he returned to Lydia's side, she was sitting up, legs crossed, staring into the flames. Her hair hung in tangled masses.

"I'm trying to picture the gossipmongers if we were to ride back to camp covered only in fur," Joe chuckled. "Can you imagine the look on Thelma Lee's face?"

"It doesn't matter. I think she already knows."

"Already knows what?"

"That we're lovers," Lydia stared at the growing flames. "She watches me. There's gossip, and I can tell the way the other women look at me. Or the way their conversation changes when I pass. What else would we be doing out here in a thunderstorm? We've been out here since late afternoon. It's already past nightfall."

"Which means everyone will be worried. We should get back soon, before they send out a search party."

"And find us like this? In such a compromising situation? I'm starting to wish we never had to go back."

"Because of people like Thelma Lee?"

"No, not just that. It's difficult to explain. Among the others, it's different. It's not just you and me." She looked away to hide her melancholy.

"It doesn't have to be different."

"You know it has to be. We certainly can't be lovers with the whole camp constantly on watch. I'm not even sure what we can be. Is it proper to be friends? Mama never taught me anything about relationships with men. She would probably faint from shock if she knew what you and I have done. She said that lust was only for whores. Sexual activity was only for the procreation of children."

"Do you think your mother and father didn't?"

Lydia cringed. "I know Papa loved Mama. He would have done anything for her. But I can't picture Mama and Papa as lovers. Mama was always so proper."

Joe chuckled. "I suppose it's hard for anyone to picture their parents that way."

Lydia wrapped a fur around herself and moved closer to the fire. "My parents didn't let themselves get caught up in some wild country, doing as they pleased, uninhibited or unencumbered by social expectations."

"Is that what's bothering you?"

"I only know that out here away from camp, it's just you and me and this wild country. I don't need to worry so much about what other people think."

"You've said yourself, how I never worry about what other people think. Perhaps you should try not to worry."

"If only I could, I would. I have to concern myself with such things as, how close is too close for a man and a woman to stand. How familiar is too familiar? If I touch you, or look at you, am I seen with savagery in my heart? After we came back from the fort that day, there was no end to the wagging of tongues. People watch. It's better to slip into the background and be unnoticed. You don't know what it's like to be ostracized by the community or forbidden entrance into places or activities simply because you're a different race."

"Like at the corn shuckin'."

"Yes. You have no idea how many times I've wished I could wash away this copper skin, or lighten my hair. They mark me as an Indian, a race that is loathed."

Joe wrapped a pelt around his shoulders and joined her by the fire where he enveloped her in his open arms. "I know your life's not been easy. It tears at me to see you so tormented. Isn't it better since leaving Possum Hollow?"

"I suppose." She leaned her cheek into Joe's shoulder. "Most of the women treat me nice enough. Although, I've never been fully accepted into their social circle. Since I'm single and childless and the hired employee of the Livelys, I'm at the bottom of the social status. The men show mild indifference. They're too wrapped up in their families and their work to pay me any mind."

"What about Faith? Doesn't she treat you well?"

"Faith is the best friend I could have ever wished for. But there are things I can't talk to her about. Like what I've shared with you about being Indian. It makes me feel shame."

He tilted her chin upwards and looked at her. "Never feel shame for who you are, Lydia."

They stared wordlessly at the small struggling fire, willing it to warm them.

"I'd hoped your situation would improve," Joe said after a few moments. "It seems then, I must confess something. I've been selfish."

"How?"

"I talked you into leaving Possum Hollow, so you could be with me, despite having a wife. It wasn't fair to lure you out here with dreams of a better life. I'm sorry we haven't found any clues about your tribe. And I'm sorry you lost your moccasins."

"Finding my tribe was a foolish, childish dream. For as long as I can remember, I've wanted to learn more about Indians. There's a huge part of my life that's missing from my memory, part of what makes me who I am. I left Possum Hollow of my own accord. For the moment, you are my reality. The past no longer matters. It can't be changed."

His hold on her eased, the lines in his face growing deep. "The past does matter. You are right that the past helps to form who we are. It sets us on a path into our future. I can't erase my past, the imprint of my father and his gambling, womanizing ways, any more than you can erase who you are."

Lydia shook her head absently. "I don't understand. I can't change that I'm Indian, or that I grew up as the daughter of a poor farmer in the Ozarks. We can't predict the future. But we can change our forward path by the decisions we make."

Lydia sensed there was something more to Joe's line of thinking that he was not letting on. She probed him some more. "So, who are you, Joseph Brice? Gunslinger? Outlaw? Gambler, like your father?"

The muscle in his jaw tightened.

"Mr. Brice! Miss Whitley! You in there?"

"Shit," Joe said.

He fumbled among the tangle of heavy pelts to toss Lydia her soiled, damp clothing. Then he scrambled to dress. Still fastening the belt to his pants, Joe called out.

"We're in here!" He glanced at Lydia before disappearing into the rock opening. "Thank goodness you found us," he said a moment later, his voice, overly loud. "Lydia! Amos Crenshaw and Hank Gifford found us. They've got lanterns so we can see to get back now."

"Thank goodness," Lydia shouted back. "It was terribly frightening." She kicked ashes and dirt onto the fire to extinguish it. When Joe returned, she asked. "Should we take some of these pelts?"

"No. We'll save them for some other stranded souls."

"We'd a never found ye, if'n ye hadn't hobbled your horses here," Hank shouted into the crevice. "Good thinkin' on your part."

"If I'd been thinkin' good, I'd have hobbled the horses somewhere else," Joe mumbled.

CHAPTER 32

Lydia took her final look at Independence rock as the caravan of wagons braided its way along the Sweetwater River. The rock was no less of a marvel as they passed by it, looming tall on her right. She strained her neck to catch a glimpse of the carving Joe had left for all eternity, then remembered with disappointment that the carving was on the other side.

The next leg of the trail took them close to Devil's Gate, where the ancient force of the Sweetwater River had chiseled its way through the rocks to form a cleft about 30 feet wide at the base and several hundred feet at the top. Impassible to wagons, they followed the mountainous range around the curious feature while hikers disappeared into the cleft for an adventurous short cut. A swarm of mosquitoes greeted Lydia. Thousands of swallows took flight in a great squawking and flapping as their nesting places at the base of the walls were disturbed.

They crossed the river several times, taking advantage of little beaches on either side of the zigzagging river, in order to avoid bad road and the rock walls. The cool clean Sweetwater was a pleasant reprieve from the alkaline water of the North Platte.

The following morning, Lydia was scrubbing a greasy breakfast skillet when a group of five Indian braves caught her attention. They boldly rode to the encircled wagons before dismounting. Waving rifles and pistols, John Purcy and a group of men approached the Indians. Lydia's curiosity surged as the scene unfolded. She discarded the skillet to toy with the dishrag, wondering what brought these men to her camp and which tribe they belonged to. They wore animal skins and headpieces with brightly colored feathers. Warriors, not weak from hunger and begging like those at the fort, they reminded her of the lean, muscular Arapaho. She wished that Faith and Esther hadn't gone to the river. They would want to see these Indians too.

None of the braves flinched at the approach of men with rifles or reached for knives strapped to their sides. Erect stances signaled that flashing weaponry did not threaten them. The brave in charge spoke with John Purcy who quickly became frustrated with the conversation. Joe appeared, pushed his way through the group and conversed with the visitors, each augmenting their speech with sign. Lydia couldn't hear their conversation, but she picked up the gist of it with the help of sign. The Indians had come to trade.

One of them offered a beaded bracelet, which Oscar Brown accepted for a pouch of tobacco. This activity continued for several minutes as each Indian offered something of value for trade. The leader eventually dismounted and stepped forward to present a tomahawk to Joe, who studied it at length, then shook his head.

When Joe waved for her to come, Lydia's nerves had stretched taut, her pulse was beating erratically. She tossed aside the dishrag and hurried to join the group. The Indian in charge caught Lydia's gaze with keen dark eyes. They dilated slightly when she stood before him. His expression otherwise was without emotion and unchanging.

A silver and turquoise band accentuated the chiseled muscles of his upper left arm and combined with the leather string of bear claws dangling against his smooth copper chest gave him a savage appearance. Despite having ridden on the dusty prairie, his long black hair, which was pulled back and fastened with a beaded tie actually shone. Lydia thought, with a pang of embarrassment that her hair always seemed to attract dirt and except after a fresh washing, never looked as glossy as this Indian brave's. Did he notice this as he studied her?

Wildness strained against his calm controlled demeanor. The lengthy scar, which marred his hairless chest from beneath his arm to just below his breastplate, attested to his ferocity. This Indian had killed men, Lydia knew. The thought was chilling. Yet her skin tingled with the thrill of standing within arm's length of such contained power.

The colorful quillwork of his leggings and moccasins reminded her of Little Flower's beautiful creations, signifying his wealth and marital status, for he surely had a wife to make such things for him. This fine specimen of a brave could not be a bachelor.

Joe stared into the eyes of the warrior, with no more expression of emotion than the man staring back, each assessing the other's thoughts, to extract some clue to gain an edge in the negotiations. Neither clenched his jaw or twitched an eyelid or furrowed a brow. Both seem made of stone. Joe had confided in Lydia that he'd learned this skill from his father at the poker table.

"This is my woman, Lydia," Joe said. "Is she the one you speak of?"

The mention of her name pulled Lydia from her thoughts.

"You squaw who travels with white men," the leader spoke with a broken combination of words and sign.

"How do you know of Lydia?" Joe asked.

"We hear. She pull boy from river. She brave."

In a quick, fluid motion, the Indian leader pulled his knife from the sheath fastened at his waist. The large metal blade flashed with sunlight and brought a gasp from the onlookers, who stepped forward with their weapons. Joe waved them back before carefully and graciously accepting the trade item for examination.

It was a beautiful knife, with a six-inch metal blade. The walnut handle was polished to a sheen that brought out the rich variations in the wood. As fine a knife as any Lydia had seen. Joe slid his thumb down the blade and nodded his approval at the deadly sharpness before swinging the weapon about to test the weight and balance. Finally, Joe shook his head and returned the knife.

"No." He replaced his arm around Lydia. "This woman is not for trade."

When had she missed that she was wanted in trade?

The brave motioned at one of his comrades, who brought forward a fine looking brown and white painted pony.

"Trade," the leader said. "Horse for squaw."

Lydia bit her lip to stifle a cry of outrage.

Joe studied the horse for what Lydia thought a much too lengthy time. "No," he said finally.

Again the leader motioned at one of his comrades, who brought forth another horse.

"You offer fine horses. But, this woman is not for trade."

Lydia thought she saw a frown on the Indian's face, but any change in expression was fleeting.

"We offer fair trade," the leader said. "Why you not trade?"

"White men don't trade their women." Joe emphasized his words by signing.

"She not white woman. She squaw," the Indian said. "Squaw belong with Sioux." Lydia cringed as he made an exaggerated emphasis on the sign for Sioux, or Dakota nation. He held his right hand horizontally palm down, just below the chin and moved it quickly to the right. Throat Cutter.

A long silence stretched between the men before the leader fearlessly turned his back to Joe and the five riflemen. Before mounting his horse, the warrior reached into a leather bag and withdrew a shirt-like dress, similar to what Little Flower and the other Arapaho women wore. He held it before him for Lydia to see. It was short sleeved with fringe along the bottom and simple beadwork at the neckline.

Lydia scoffed at the thought that this brave might hope to persuade a deal by presenting her with gifts she could not refuse. She'd give this Indian credit; he was definitely creative and persistent.

Instead of adding the dress to the items already for trade, the brave shoved it at her. "Take. Gift for squaw. Sioux need soft buckskin. Not ugly cloth of white women."

Ugly cloth? The dress was one of her older, shabbier ones, but she'd died the yarn and woven the cloth herself. A rush of panic made her pull back and shriek, "No! I don't want it!" She ignored Joe's hand waving to not anger the Indian.

"Take." The Indian again shoved it at her. "Squaw wear. Next time I see."

"I think you'd better leave now," Joe said. "The trading is over."

The Indian leader shrugged and calmly replaced the garment into his bag. His comrades mounted their horses before he again spoke. "I come back. Bring more horses. You trade then." With wild war whoops, the Indians galloped off; the extra horses, meant as a trade for Lydia galloped freely alongside them.

The men sighed, their shoulders slumping with relief. "I'll organize a watch," John Purcy said to Joe, "in case they decide to come back."

"Good idea," Joe said. "Tell all the women to get back to camp. No more wandering off without an armed escort to pick flowers, or whatever else they do."

Lydia didn't wait for the Indians to disappear from sight before fleeing back to the center of camp and to the only place of security she knew. She was sitting inside the wagon clutching a pillow when Joe peered in.

"You all right?" he asked.

"I never thought I'd be afraid of an Indian," she said woodenly. "That brave terrified me, insisting I take that garment from him. I've spent my whole life hiding in the shadows. Why would I want to call attention to myself by wearing one of their cast-offs?"

Joe made a move to climb into the wagon and then stopped himself. Fuel for gossips. They were no doubt being watched. "It's not just about wearing that garment, is it?"

"They didn't come here to trade for tobacco, did they? They came to trade for me. They'd planned for me to wear that dress when I returned to their camp with them." Her voice became shrill as her throat tightened around her words. "Then I would have belonged to them, and who knows what they would have done to me."

After seeing those fierce warriors up close, fearful images built in her mind; she could for once understand the terror other women expressed at the prospect of being kidnapped.

"I won't let that happen. If it's any consolation, had he been a white man, I would have slugged him. It's offensive for another man to offer you gifts."

"It was degrading to be considered as nothing more than chattel."

"Their offer was very generous. They obviously believe that you're worthy of a high price. Those horses would have made up for some of our own losses. And that knife was difficult to turn down." He grinned devilishly.

"I suppose I should be flattered," she said, unaffected by his attempt at humor. "Other Indian women would be flattered. But I'm not like other Indian women."

"No, Lydia. You're not like any other woman."

It was times like this when she felt suffocated under her old thoughts, torn between worlds. She knew that only her copper skin and dark hair made her Indian. Wearing the clothes of white women did not make her belong to the race of white people into which she had been thrust.

"I've put everyone in danger."

"Because you saved a boy's life?"

"Maybe. Mostly just by being here."

"Quit blaming yourself. It's not your fault," Joe said.

"If I wasn't Indian, those braves wouldn't want me so badly."

"And they didn't even ask if you could cook or scrape hides."

"The way their leader looked at me, I doubt that's what he wanted me for." A shiver shot down her spine.

"I promised I wouldn't let anything happen to you. I'd die if something did."

"Why, Joe? Why did they come? We've never seen them before."

"I'm sure it was like he said. Gus Hargis had heard about you before you two met, so had Blue Feather. You know how stories, no matter how true, travel like dysentery from one campfire to the next. The Indians were obviously impressed with what they heard and came here to check it out for themselves. If you were strong and brave enough to save a boy from drowning, then they believed you would make a good wife. I wouldn't worry about them."

"Do you think they'll come back?"

"I doubt it. I'll add extra men to the guard. In a few days, we'll enter South Pass and the Continental Divide. Then we'll be out of this Indian Territory."

Joe was nowhere in sight when Lydia crawled outside. And much to her chagrin, the entire camp was buzzing about the Indians' visit.

"Lydia, is it true?" Faith asked. Both she and Esther were out of breath from scrambling back to camp. Each set down their buckets of water with a thud.

"Thelma Lee just told us that some half-naked Indians came to camp," Esther said. "They tried to trade some horses for you."

"That wasn't the worst of it. They came here *specifically* to trade for me."

Esther gasped. "How horrible! What kind of people trade chattel for women?"

"At first I didn't think they were such terrible Indians. They were clean and fine looking. I wished you could have seen them, too. But when the leader tried to force me to accept his buckskin dress, I was terrified. Now I'm angry."

"Thelma Lee said the Indians were going to return with more men to steal our horses," Esther said.

"Joe doesn't think they'll come back," Lydia said.

"Thelma Lee is just trying to stir up trouble. If Joe increases the guard, we'll be fine," Faith spoke with confidence.

CHAPTER 33

Lydia's gloved hand grabbed the edge of the wagon seat to keep from being thrown forward, her heart catapulting to her throat as Hank Gifford reined the oxen to a sudden and unexpected halt. The column of wagons ahead had stopped. Judging by the distance of the sun hanging above the horizon, this was too early for the mid-day break.

She paused from swatting the vicious mosquitos to lower her bandana that protected her face. The vision from under the brim of her bonnet, brought prickles of fear. A band of Indians were swooping over the southern hillside to block their path. The Indians had known exactly where to trap the sluggish wagons against the rock wall with no escape or time to form a protective circle. Their erect postures told Lydia this was the same group of Sioux braves, now twice in number, which they had encountered earlier that week. She wished Joe were sitting next to her, instead of the man now reaching for his rifle.

While her driver slid from his seat, Lydia crawled into the wagon bed. Although its canvas had been rolled back to air out wet belongings, the wooden slats provided the best protection from stray bullets or arrows.

Hank took his position alongside the wagon. "I won't let nothin' happen to ye Miz Whitley. Any o' them bastards gets in range, I'll waste 'em."

Lydia gave the man a quivering smile of thanks, although not sure what she was thankful for. She'd never been afraid of Indians or had a desire to kill them. She didn't want to believe now, that any would harm her, or that they were vicious savages who attacked innocent women and children. But she sensed that these braves had come to cause trouble. Now that her own life was threatened, it no longer matter who was on the other side of the bullet. She curled up in the musty wagon bed to wait, like the other women and children.

Time stretched taut as she listened to her own breathing. The tight quarters of the wagon amplified the incessant buzzing of mosquitoes. Without a breeze from the moving wagon, the hot sun beat down. Her long sleeved dress, worn to protect against sunburn and insects held in heat like an oven. Somewhere in the near distance an eagle screeched. The sudden cry of an infant was quickly stifled. Was this what it was like for people in the stories of Indian attacks, their hearts racing, their palms sweating, their nerves stretched taut? She could smell her own sweat and fear.

Hank remained poised with his rifle.

Chains rattled under the shifting weight of the restless oxen. A horse snorted. Several men on horseback, Lydia counted three, rode back and forth the length of the wagon column. When she heard the cock of rifles, she expected the thick steamy air to fill with the cry of war whoops as the Indians swept in for attack. Doom sank deep into her bones.

She couldn't squelch the urge to peer over the edge of the wagon, despite the possibility of meeting her own death head on. She squinted against the bright sun to observe the mounted Indians. They were outside rifle range, surveying the column. The cocking of weaponry by the men in her company was obviously only for posturing, if not for a warning. After the band had made their appearance known, it had become a standoff between the two groups.

Then, as if they were statues coming to life, the poised band of Indians turned and rode with all their usual shouts and whoops into the rocky hills.

***

"Should've sent her back to where she come from," Thelma Lee spoke overly loud, as she and her gossipy friends strolled outside the corral during their mid-day stop near where Lydia was working.

"We could've got something for her, too."

"Joe came to her defense quick enough," Mable remarked.

"Claimed she was his squaw."

284

"It's wrong, she and him. That Injun's gonna bring him shame," Thelma Lee said. "She should stick to her own kind."

"Joe would come to your defense too," Faith said to the group, now standing in the opening between two wagons, hands on hips.

"Faith!" Thelma Lee gasped. Her hand went to her chest, feigning surprise and turned to stare at Faith with wide-eyed innocence. "You startled me. We didn't realize y'all was over there." With lips twisting into a smirk, she peered at Lydia.

"Sure you did," Faith said flatly.

Lydia stared at the women through the same opening, her expression remaining passive, emotions unrevealed. Did they think so little of her? Thelma Lee's remarks didn't surprise her. Faith had once said that if gossip spreading was an event at the county fair, Thelma Lee would win a blue ribbon. But what about Mabel? Lydia had kept her youngest daughter, Hettie, safe during the buffalo stampede.

"Need I remind you greedy women," Faith said, "since my husband and I are paying for Lydia's expenses, it is we who should collect on such a loss."

Thelma Lee gasped and strutted away in a huff with her companions, except for Mabel, who stepped between the wagons to speak to Lydia and Faith. "They didn't mean nothin'."

"Then, perhaps they should hold their tongues," Faith retorted.

The mid-day stop was brief and without fires, allowing only enough time to eat a quick meal of cold beans and cornbread. The oxen were kept in yoke, and watered in place.

While everyone was occupied with tossing gear into the wagons, or adjusting saddles in preparation to march, Joe took Lydia aside.

"I'm concerned about this band of Indians," he said quietly. "The Sioux are a strong warrior race. They find ways to get what they want, by blood shed if need be."

Lydia couldn't stop her knees from shaking as Joe described the earlier encounter, the way the band quietly and stoically assessed the caravan.

"Why are you telling me?" Her voice cracked. There was something special in that Joe had chosen to confide in her about his worries, although she would have rather remained blissfully ignorant of the dangers they were in.

"I don't want to scare you Lydia, but I thought you'd want to know. So you can prepare yourself." The lines in his face pulled tight, his eyes had dulled and the orbs sunken into dark sockets. She'd rarely seen fear in them.

"Prepare myself for what?" Dread knotted inside her. Did he want her to reconsider carrying a firearm? Or did he expect an imminent attack?

Joe's mouth and jaw twisted as he struggled to put words together for an answer.

"They are checking for weaknesses."

"For an attack?" Lydia's mind conjured up all sorts of gruesome visions.

One by one the teepees turned into giant torches, reaching for the sky. A gory backdrop for women running in panic, snatching up small children. She could hear their screams. Hear the gunfire. Blood puddled on the ground. It puddled beneath bodies lying wounded and bleeding.

"Lydia!" Joe's voice broke through the screams in her head. His strong hands pulled her upright from buckled knees. "Lydia! Are you all right?"

The vision cleared, but left her confused to find herself inside a wagon circle, Joe holding her upright. The din of travel preparations: metal on metal, chains rattling, voices shouting commands, pounded in her brain.

"An attack? Shouldn't we tell everyone?" Her voice came out shrill.

"The men have been put on alert, the guard increased. I don't want to needlessly worry the women. We don't have much further to reach South Pass and the Continental divide. Then we'll be out of this Indian territory."

"Why, Joe? Why are they…" she struggled to find the right word, "stalking us? Because we wouldn't trade with them?"

"Perhaps." His lips pinched together. "I'm worried that something more is going on."

"It's my fault." Her voice choked. She fought down the rising bile. "I shouldn't be here." She wanted to flee.

"Quit blaming yourself."

Joe had released his grip on her, but she could sense he wanted to enfold her in his arms, eyes sending a message of comfort. He couldn't reach out to her because of the promise they had made, of reputations to protect. He a grieving widower. Her a proper maiden.

Sometime that night, curled up on top of blankets, alone, caged in the tight quarters of Joe's wagon, Lydia awoke to the sound of screams and wails of terror. She bolted upright, disoriented and confused, pulse erratic, gasping for breath, unable to shake the images of smoke and fire. She needed to breathe. Desperate to escape, she clamored on all fours over blankets and crates and household wares to the rear of the wagon where she threw open the flap. She sucked in a great gulp of air. A harsh wind slapped her sweaty face and filled her lungs with acrid smoke that did not refresh.

In a blind panic, reality indistinct from nightmare, she jumped into the protected circle of camp. A sharp pain from the hard landing spiraled from her ankles to her lower back and gave her pause to stare out at camp and into the darkness. With no moon, the camp was exceptionally dark. The campfires had burned down to smoldering coals.

Not thinking about where she was going, Lydia groped her way along the wagons and tent stakes, careful not to trip on ropes pulled taut. She'd managed to avoid strangling herself on a rope holding up a tent fly, when she heard a strange thwap noise, a grunt and a thud. With a quick turn she headed in the direction of the thud. A few steps later, she stumbled into a soft, fleshy heap, nearly spearing herself on the stick like projectile protruding from it. And then she was there again, standing over her father's wounded body as he hovered near death from a bullet wound.

A gruff voice of warning came out of the darkness. "Go back insi…" Only to be cut off by another thwap.

The need to get help propelled her forward, toward the falling man who was now screaming, "Injun!" His rifle discharging.

There was no time to twist away. Pain shot through Lydia as something pierced her right leg, sending her off balance. The world slowed down, each moment seemed an eternity. Her hand found the sticky mass of blood oozing down her skirt where the arrow shaft stuck out of her thigh, its point imbedded in her flesh. Terror clawed at her chest as a large powerful arm scooped her up to keep her from collapsing. A hand slapped over her mouth to muffle her scream. Raw heat and the smell of animal grease emanated from the Sioux warrior. She flailed her arms and legs in the air, fighting against captivity and the searing pain, as if her leg were being ripped in two. Fighting the urge to vomit, her world closed in on her.

A cold sickening shadow of darkness overtook her.

PART 3
CAPTIVITY

CHAPTER 34

Thunderous hooves propelled Lydia through the darkness, the warrior's arm, like an iron-band pinned her arms against her sides to keep her captive. Each stride brought a jolt of pain where the arrow was imbedded in her right thigh. The horse's rhythm thrust the warrior's hardened manhood against her hips. The flimsy loincloth and her sweat-dampened dress did little to shield her modesty. She wondered if by accident or by cleverness they had put her into such a defenseless state.

The warriors had attacked at night, obviously taking the guards by surprise. They all believed what Joe had told them. Indians usually attacked at dawn. Could he have been so wrong? Or were these Sioux exceptionally cunning? And why did they want her so badly?

Lydia tried to keep her mind from drifting to thoughts of Joe being injured or… killed. If he was able, he would come for her. But with each passing mile, hope of rescue faded into resignation. She was on her own. She would have to find her own escape when the time was right. She closed her eyes, pondering on the events that had brought her to this world turned upside down.

During their brief and infrequent stops, they guarded her closely, although they never bound her hands. The band of about fifteen braves, led by the one who had attempted to trade for her, never physically abused or threatened her. It was during one such respite along a river that she became aware of a brave who remained slumped over his horse. She realized later that the only care he received was the periodic check of the leather strips holding him into place. She decided he must be dead. Probably killed during her kidnapping. Her heart hardened without sympathy. How many of her companions had been killed in the raid, shot with arrows, or scalped, or clubbed with tomahawks?

Lydia lost count of the days. After the first day, her injury become inflamed and a fever set in. One of the savage braves broke off the arrow's shaft and attempted to dig out the sharp head lodged in her thigh. Then he wrapped her wound in soft deerskin and fastened it around her thigh. The injury remained gaping and oozed a sticky yellow fluid. She decided the savages were either ignorant of how to treat her or were deliberately leaving the arrow in place to increase her suffering and continued confinement.

Thrust into a dreamlike state, veiled visions and mumbled voices blurred reality. Despite the burning, which seemed to lick like flames from her injury, she frequently shivered with chills. No amount of water quenched the heat, or satisfied her thirst. Her parched lips cracked and bled. She tried eating the strips of dried buffalo meat the men offered. None of it stayed down. Eventually, she could not sit up without help and rode slumped over the horse and held in place by that iron-like band of an arm.

***

"Mama! Is that you?" Lydia sat up with a jerk from where she lay, crying out with words she didn't recognize.

A copper-skinned woman urged Lydia back upon the pile of soft furs before vanishing again.

"Mama! Come back!" *Why couldn't she form the correct words?*

She was floating, hovering in that gray layer between life and death, unable through the misty blur of delirium to sort out the real from the unreal. There were fleeting glimpses of an Indian woman changing the dressing on her leg and forcing some bitter fluid down her throat. Drums and rattles often disturbed Lydia's already unsettled slumber, while witch-like creatures garbed in beads and dangles of animal flesh chanted shrill incantations. Grotesque shadows danced upon the walls, lending a nightmarish quality to the savage proceedings.

"No!" Lydia screeched. It was too late. Blood spewed as a searing pain tore through her leg and plunged her back into the dark foreboding depths of unconsciousness.

A familiar face of a man hovered over her. It was a haunting ghost from a dream past. He was older and more wrinkled now. *Papa? Are you there, Papa?*

She tried to understand his soothing voice. The words were indistinct and muffled.

"Papa?"

Something cool and wet touched Lydia's face and made her shiver. It eased the searing heat within her body.

A familiar face returned, arms stretching out to her as she tumbled backward into the dark bottomless abyss. Too weak to reach out to him, the face faded quickly as she tumbled, until the face collapsed to a point and disappeared.

"Joe! Joe!" she screamed.

How pretty she looked, standing tall and proud, beautifully adorned in an embroidered and fringed shirt. Two long braids fastened at the ends with narrow strips of leather framed her face. Through thick dark lashes she peered with curiosity. Lydia reached out to touch the figure in the mirror. Then, as she slowly rose to the startling level of consciousness, an indescribable terror swelled within her. Had she gone to a place where the great Indian spirits awaited her passing?

There was no looking glass.

Lydia's blood-curdling scream frightened away the vision. Disoriented, with heart racing, she stood up and staggered a few steps.

Two Indian women rushed to keep her from falling, and urged her back to bed. Adrenaline, not strength fueled her resistance. The women spoke with soothing voices, in an incomprehensible language. Was she supposed to understand these women? She caught a glimpse of the vision that shared her face as it peeked inside the fire-lit room.

Exhausted from the effort of standing, her legs wobbled under her weight. Blackness washed over her as blood drained from her face. When the women eased her back into the warm soft furs, Lydia wilted into the serene world of darkness.

When she next awoke and reoriented, she wondered what demons awaited her. Only the warm glow of the inner tepee greeted her. She stared upward to where the lodge poles funneled into the smoke filled opening.

What events had brought her to this place?

The memories crashed upon her. The agonizing pain in her thigh. The choking smell of gunpowder and the wild animal smell of the warrior who had snatched her. She sucked in air and moved a shaky hand to examine the vile wound. Hadn't there been a vision of hacking off her leg? Her fingers grazed the sides of her thigh, and she nearly sobbed out her relief. Her leg was still intact. Moss stuffed into the wound indicated she'd been well cared for. The arrowhead had been extracted and the tenderness had eased. Evidenced by the state of healing, she concluded that she must have been with these people several days, perhaps a week.

Realizing that she was completely naked under the fur covers, she shuddered. Who had witnessed her in such a state? *The gold coin!* Unless she could get her clothing back, hope of returning to Possum Hollow vanished. She was about to sit up to see if her clothes were nearby, when a hand touched her shoulder. With a start, she turned to face a woman whose face had lost the smooth softness of youth, but the dark eyes were as bright and alert as those of younger women. She smiled a toothless smile and offered Lydia something in a wooden bowl.

Lydia eased to a sitting position with her own power, clutching the coverings to her throat. Her injury did not pain her overly much as she leaned back against the pile of furs. She waited for her head to clear from sitting up before she accepted the bowl. The aroma made her realize how famished she was. She couldn't remember the last time she'd eaten. The bowl contained a brown colored fluid that looked and smelled much like beef broth. No doubt, buffalo. She took a tentative sip. Seasoned lightly with herbs, the liquid was warm and helped to fill the emptiness in her belly. The hostess remained near as Lydia took in her nourishment, and each time Lydia glanced her way, the elder smiled with warm approval.

After Lydia returned the empty bowl, the old woman returned to her seated position near the fire and resumed sewing on some skins. A bit rejuvenated, Lydia relaxed against the backrest and studied her surroundings. This tepee was not much different from Little Flower's home in the Arapaho village with its furnishings and a scattering of furs and skins. A small fire near the center produced a soft orange color upon the skin walls, indicating that it was evening. The sweet smell of hickory pervaded the air.

"Where am I?" Lydia didn't recognize her own voice made croaky from lack of use.

The old woman answered with a wide-eyed look. So, Lydia repeated the question, utilizing what knowledge she had of signs.

The woman gave no response, not even an acknowledgment; she simply hurried from the dwelling. Upon her return a few minutes later, she was closely followed by that figment from a recent nightmare. Panic rose within Lydia, beads of sweat broke out on her forehead and for a moment she thought she would hurl the meal she had just enjoyed. What was this figment, which shared her face? As the pair drew nearer, Lydia blinked. The vision did not disappear.

When finally beside her, the elderly woman, using both sign language and crude English spoke. "This be your sister, Pretty Moon."

CHAPTER 35

Lydia's lifelong dream of returning to her Indian family was reality. She should be as elated as Pretty Moon and Woman-Who-Laughs. The two women were laughing and chattering incessantly as they helped to bathe and dress her. Instead of elation, Lydia felt empty. In a sort of numb existence, saying little, she went through the motions of what was required of her. Weak from fighting the infection, standing was fatiguing and moving too quickly made her head swim and the world turn dark. She remained on the backrest as much as possible and allowed the women to do what they willed. Chief Flying Eagle, her father, was paying her a visit and she must look her best.

Drowsiness seeped through her bones and her head bobbed as Pretty Moon washed her hair in suds of yucca root to make it glossy. Woman-Who-Laughs gently combed out the mass of tangles with an implement made of a porcupine tail and let her hair hang loose. They helped her into a snow-white buckskin shirt, which obviously belonged to her sister. It was modestly decorated with porcupine quills and feathers. Some makeshift moccasins would serve Lydia until she could make her own. Finally, they adorned her with a necklace made of small brightly painted animal bones.

She had to admit that after having been bedridden for so many days, the fresh bedding and clothes helped her become more comfortable in her surroundings, yet she needed time to get accustomed to the new outfit. The soft leather felt strange against her bare skin. The lack of petticoats and undergarments made her feel vulnerable and naked. Where the fringe dangled, it tickled her arms and legs.

After they returned Lydia to bed and tucked her legs comfortably under a fur, Woman-Who-Laughs and Pretty Moon left to summon the chief. When he was ready, he would talk to her privately. Lydia waited alone in silence, waves of hot and cold washing over her, causing her to wonder if the fever had returned. She gazed sleepily at the surroundings and thought how foreign this world was compared to the one she'd come from. Yet, this world had once been her home. Pretty Moon, her identical twin, was proof of that.

Lydia took a deep breath and closed her eyes, relaxing against the backrest. She had many questions to ask her father, to fill the many blanks in her life. She was finally meeting the father who'd given her life! It was difficult to think of him as her father. Edward Whitley was her father. This Chief Flying Eagle was a complete stranger.

She wasn't sure how long she'd dozed, or how long he'd been standing there. As she awakened and felt a presence near her, she bolted upright. Her gaze first fell upon a shaggy buffalo robe. When she peered upward to discover the face of an aged man, she let out an involuntary gasp of complete astonishment. This man was not a total stranger. Although many years older and more wrinkled, she recognized him. Standing above her was the man who haunted her nightmares. This was her father, Chief Flying Eagle. She had at one time felt safe with this man, so why did she tremble as he stood before her now?

He was the epitome of a regal chief: erect, proud, with a hint of defiance. No doubt by his own merits he was a man in charge. Lines worn into his visage served as a semi-permanent record of the trials and tribulations of his arduous life. Lydia wondered at his age in years. He didn't seem young enough to be her father, grandfather, more likely. He stared at her for a long while, unmoving, saying nothing. For a moment, his features softened and Lydia was certain he was about to shed a tear. Then he stiffened, pulled himself together, before returning to his more stone-like demeanor.

"Have prayed every day, Great Spirit, bring my daughter back," he said in crude broken English. He used the motions of one arm to emphasize his words, pointing to himself and the heavens while the other hand held his robe in place.

Lydia could have sworn that a twinkle came to his sad looking eyes and fleeting smile. Then they were gone. His greeting was certainly more aloof and formal than the welcoming embrace she'd received from her sister. Perhaps it was just as well; she didn't want an emotional confrontation. She wasn't even sure of how one was supposed to act when reunited with a father who was essentially a stranger.

"Knew you return one day. Now bring us much joy." His flat, emotionless voice contradicted his message.

Lydia had to bite her tongue to keep from remarking that she hadn't exactly dropped in voluntarily. She'd been brought here after being wounded in a brutal attack. Some of her traveling companions had probably been murdered.

"How was I found?" Lydia asked meekly.

"Hear squaw camp with whites on land of buffalo. Moccasins lead."

"You stole my moccasins?" Lydia asked. How could he have known about them?

"No."

Then, as if a stone came to life, he moved to the backrest beside Lydia. In one fluid motion he seated himself in the usual style, with knees to his chest. Then he tied the robe across his legs to hold the pose in place. His arms dangled unencumbered.

"Child moccasins match ones of Pretty Moon. Have message to good spirits, watch and protect from evil ones."

So, the designs on her moccasins did have symbolic meaning as Gus Hargis had suggested. All along they'd held information about her family.

"Does my mother live?"

Her father held his finger to his cracked lips. "Tell you once. Then say no more. Sioux not speak of dead. She murdered when you taken from village." He spoke with a bite of anger.

A pang of sorrow struck Lydia. She tried to envision the woman in her mind, grief and loneliness accosting her. And then the memories washed over her full force, as though it were that day again. Lydia trembled.

"I remember." She looked at her father through glazed eyes, barely able to focus through the horrible memories now replaying before her.

Strange men with faces the color of winter grass. Emerged like evil apparitions from the cloud of hooves.

"They shot our mother. I saw it! I was near her. As the white men fired, I ran." Lydia's throat tightened.

Sounds of thunder from their smoking sticks. Fleeing bodies crumpled into bloody heaps: women, children, old men. The smoke of burning tepees blackened the sky.

"There were no warriors?" Lydia asked.

"Warriors away hunting buffalo. White men have no honor to kill women and children. When warriors return, village burn, many dead. You missing."

The clutch of darkness descended upon her like a claw of fear. She trembled wet and cold through the night without sleep. Until the blush of dawn. The once white tepees were now black remnants of their former selves. Their life forces now extinguished. They haunted like spirits of the damned.

"I was hiding in the reeds along the river."

She heard her name called. But she couldn't move. Paralyzed. The sound of leather leggings brushed against the dried reeds and sent her further into the water.

"I was too terrified. I was only a child. Everything I knew was gone."
Her father nodded. "After tend to dead and wounded, braves move village. We came back for you. We try to find. Could not. You always good at hiding." The sound of sorrow and bitterness hung in his voice.
"I don't know how long I stayed in the reeds. A large man came."

Green eyes. Gray beard. Dressed in buckskins. Horses loaded with pelts.

"I kicked him when he scooped me up. He took me with him. I was very hungry."

The vivid memories were fading. She had to concentrate.

"He took me across the prairie and many rivers to a forest. I remember thinking how dark it was, that the trees blocked out the sunlight."

From the darkness came a growl and angry claws slashed the air. The crack of his smoking stick only angered the beast, which pressed forward from the darkness. Then came a great roar and screams and the ripping of claws into flesh. And then the man lie unmoving.

"He had taken me to his cabin. And that night when he went out to get firewood he was attacked and killed by a bear. I heard his screams. I saw it out of the window. After that, I just wandered around on my own."

As sorrow descended, a great weight eased. The answers had been within her all along.

"I go now." Her father untied his robe and came to his feet with surprising ease for a man of his years. "You sleep. Morning come soon."

Lydia wanted him to stay. There were so many unanswered questions and she was impatient to learn more. Pleading with a powerful man like this chief was probably not a good idea.

"Tomorrow we make feast, in honor you come back." He actually showed excitement at the prospect. "Think can walk?"

"Yes."

"Did not want harm you. You too quick. Get in way." That was the closest thing to an apology Lydia had gotten concerning her injury. How ironic that her own people had nearly killed her.

"Please, before you go," she said, as he once again turned to leave. "What name was given to me?"

"Most beautiful flower on land of buffalo, Prairie Rose."

"Prairie Rose." The name was pleasant on her tongue. She could have wished for nothing more beautiful. "The white people called me Lydia."

"L-y-d-ee-ah," her father pronounced the word slowly and distastefully. "No more. Now, be Prairie Rose, sister of Pretty Moon, daughter of Chief Flying Eagle."

***

Several smaller tepees had been combined into a larger one, for the tribal chief and the great warriors to consult and feast. Among the nearly fifty attendees, only six were female. The chief's three wives sat quietly on their heels in front of large kettles, which hung from quadripods over fires. Lydia, attending as the guest of honor, and her two escorts, Pretty Moon and Woman-Who-Laughs, shared an elevated backrest. Everyone else sat cross-legged on the ground.

The warriors displayed their achievements with feathers arranged in their long glossy hair. Full ceremonial attire included leggings and a shirt of buckskin decorated with beads or paint, and fringed with scalp locks, which still made Lydia shiver. She was becoming accustomed to the ferocious looking faces painted with vermilion and ochre along with the wild array of bead necklaces, brass and bone bracelets, earrings and strings of bear claws.

Although less gruesome than the men's, the women's costuming was no less splendid. Pretty Moon wore a simple buckskin shirt, having loaned her sister an impressively beaded garment, which she used for formal occasions. The dress-like garments came to just below the knee with fringe dangling from them. Intricately decorated moccasins with matching leggings covered their legs up to their knees, so, like the attire of white women, their lower limbs were not exposed.

Lydia thought the outfit she was wearing one of the most beautiful she'd ever seen. The craftsmanship of the intricately sewn beads and shells surpassed anything she had seen white ladies wear, even those of wealthy status Lydia had encountered in Independence. Woman-Who-Laughs and Pretty Moon had taken much care to see that Lydia looked her very best. Only reluctantly, she had allowed them to paint her face with cakes of powdered colors mixed with grease. Painting, they'd told her was essential for the properly dressed Sioux, who seldom left the lodge without it.

Lydia wished she felt as regal as she looked and was being treated. After an entire day of feasting and entertaining at various tepees, she was physically drained and frustrated at the need for others to help her from backrests and to walk.

Lydia gazed at the sea of solemn faces, which patiently waited for the medicine man to begin a prayer. She recognized many of the guests, having been introduced to them earlier. She'd quickly forgotten most of their long and difficult to pronounce names. Her gaze settled upon the warrior who had kidnapped her. She couldn't believe she now sat as guest of honor among his band.

Following the opening prayer, Chief Flying Eagle stood to address his guests. He'd looked distinguished when Lydia first met him. That vision paled to mediocrity when compared to the vision he presented now in ceremonial regalia. She couldn't subdue the swell of pride that she had blood ties with this great man who was loved and venerated by his people. Much of that love poured onto her as his daughter. The people welcomed her into the tribe and into their hearts. She'd been lost from them for many years, but not forgotten.

Except for the hand and arm gestures her father used to emphasize words, Lydia comprehended little of his opening oration, spoken in their native language. Once, pointing to Pretty Moon and herself, Lydia thought she picked up something about the village being whole again and that her return was a sign of good fortune. Her father and some of the others blessed Lydia with renewed protection from evil.

Following the speeches, one of the chief's wives took a small coal from the fire and lit the long slender ceremonial pipe. She delivered the pipe to the chief, who presented the stem to the spirits in each of the four directions, north, south, east and west. Then he pointed the pipe toward the ground and finally upwards, to the Great Spirit who was creator of all and giver of life. After saying a few words in prayer, the chief took a deep puff from the pipe, allowing the smoke to curl above his head. He then passed the pipe to the entire group of men. None of the women participated in the smoking.

The chief cleaned the pipe by respectfully placing the ashes in a pile on the sacred altar, signaling the feast to begin.

Another of the chief's wives dipped out a small portion of the stew-like substance, which had been simmering in the kettles, and poured it onto the ground in the sacred fire circle as an offering to the Great Spirit. Although Lydia had attended many such gatherings throughout the day and her appetite was gone, she watched the ceremony ready to receive her share. As the chief's wife placed a bowl of gravy-like substance with hunks of meat in front of Lydia, a whiff of odd aroma accosted her nostrils. She recoiled as the aroma summoned the unwelcome nausea that had plagued her since captivity.

Lydia swallowed a thick lump that had formed in her throat. "What is this?" She signed to Woman-Who-Laughs, when the server had moved her attention to someone else.

"Dog," she signed back and smiled with a toothless grin, pleased with the cuisine.

Lydia fought back the bitter bile. Protocol required her to at least sample the dishes offered. To do otherwise was insulting. Wanting to postpone the inevitable, she took a moment to observe the other quests. They used spoons, sculpted from horn or wood into the likenesses of animals, to drink the thickened broth. Fingers and knives speared the morsels of meat. Lydia wondered how they could still be so hungry after having dined most of the day.

Woman-Who-Laughs' nudging elbow finally forced Lydia to participate in the hideous meal. With a trembling hand, she lifted a spoonful of broth to her mouth. Knowing that it would be rude to hold her nose, she resisted the overwhelming urge. She sloshed the vile fluid to the back of her throat, which at first constricted in protest. Then down the fluid went. Miraculously, nothing came back up. She placed the bowl in front of her to signify that she'd eaten all she cared to. What she didn't consume was passed among the others to eat.

After completing the feast, the elite group of guests joined others gathering around the large bonfire in the center of the village for the ceremonial dancing. Those not invited to the feast had prepared themselves in their very best attire, no less varied and glorious than those who enjoyed higher status. Several of the men wore large masks of animals and covered themselves in the corresponding skins. One man even wore the heavy head of a buffalo with massive horns. Lydia was escorted to a group of women and placed next to her sister and Woman-Who-Laughs. Her father and the other men sat across from the women.

Fighting against the ache of bone weariness, Lydia watched the dancing in a sort of numb state. The leaping flames, the shrill flute and drums were almost hypnotic. The villagers sang and hummed with high-pitched strained sounds as if their voices would crack. There was no harmony, nor melody. The monotone flute of hollowed bone and pounding drums kept the contorted bodies of the dancers vibrating in the firelight. Forward and backward, over and over, the bodies shook wild and furious.

The pelvic gyrations were more vulgar and barbaric than what she was accustomed to. However, the event itself was not much different than the dances in Possum Hollow. The youth took the opportunity to pair off for the evening, often their elders arranging or encouraging them. Watching these young people gave Lydia a twinge of homesickness for her white world of Possum Hollow and emigrant trains.

Time and space separated them. North was still north and south was still south. The stars and the prairie were the same. In-between the two worlds was a bottomless void. Twice, Lydia had passed between them. And each time she passed through the void, she lost more of herself. Was she a white Indian, or a red white woman? Was she Lydia Whitley or Prairie Rose?

Then of course there was Joe.

Sorrow congealed in her throat. Was he dead? Did he care enough to come for her? Were these Sioux clever enough to outwit Joe, an expert tracker, trained by Indians during his trapping days with his grandfather, by leaving no trail for him to follow?

Lydia had wanted to believe that since they had become lovers, there was some permanence to their relationship, but Joe had made no promises for the future. He hadn't even said that he loved her. She closed her eyes in a war against the pounding in her head, the nausea, and the throbbing in her leg. She could now claim a clan with aunts and uncles and cousins. She had a twin sister, born of the same womb at the same time. Her dream had come true!

Why then did she feel so empty?

Thanks for favors, Great Spirit.

***

The following day, Lydia was certain she would faint when Pretty Moon introduced the man with the scared chest as her husband. During Lydia's convalescence, the tribal elders were expecting her to share a dwelling with her sister, Pretty Moon's small daughter, and of course, the brother-in-law. Lydia offered Proud Bull no greeting. She could only stare at him as a kaleidoscope of emotions enveloped her. Proud Bull grunted.

How could she reside in the same tepee as the man who had kidnapped her? How could she quell her anger and resentment toward him? She didn't want to hate her brother-in-law. Shamefully, for a fleeting instant upon their first meeting, she'd been attracted to him. Shouldn't she be grateful that he'd brought her to the family she'd dreamed about? But Proud Bull snatched her from the only world she knew and from the man she loved.

Although the tribal elders were pressing Lydia into a very awkward living arrangement, it was actually a logical one. They expected her to learn the necessary skills for running a household, to become a contributing member of the tribe. This would be especially challenging for a woman who had lost a childhood among her people, a time when little girls trained to be wives and mothers. Not only was there a language barrier, there were nuances of a completely different culture to learn. The gap between this Indian world and the white world seemed to increase every day.

Pretty Moon was a patient and eager teacher, taking genuine joy in Lydia's accomplishments. Using a combination of crude English and Sioux, each teaching the other, and supplementing with signs and ad-libbed gestures, the two managed to communicate adequately. Lydia never felt more grateful to Joe for his perseverance in teaching her sign language. And she surprised even herself as the words and phrases of her native language gradually popped from memory.

Pretty Moon instructed Lydia in the necessary skills alongside her four-year-old daughter, Spotted Doe. Pretty Moon never angered, even when Lydia committed a horrible gaffe, like stepping into the sacred fire circle. The Indians were very superstitious and believed that some tragedy would befall the residents if such customs were violated. Pretty Moon got on her knees and prayed to the spirits to overlook the ignorance of the *"lost one"*. Although Lydia didn't quite understand, she was grateful for her sister's protection. She didn't want to insult her people. She knew it would be a long time before she could embrace their beliefs, if ever.

Pretty Moon's daughter was delightful. Spotted Doe enjoyed playing with her aunt, and even called her Mommy Two. She proudly showed off her dolls and the things she was learning to make. Each evening, while the men told stories, Spotted Doe joined the adult women by the fire with her own sewing projects.

Although Proud Bull treated Lydia with aloof indifference, each encounter made Lydia desire to slither away. If he had any feelings for her at all, it was impossible to discern behind his stony wall of emotionless features. To her relief however, he didn't spend much time near the lodge scrutinizing the women.

Lydia learned that Proud Bull was one of the wealthiest, most respected warriors in the tribe. The women quickly accepted her into their circle and reassured her that she was most fortunate to be under the protection of such a great warrior. Rumor was he was destined to succeed Flying Eagle as the tribal chief. Proud Bull's name fit his air of supremacy well.

Pretty Moon adored her husband, although he didn't outwardly betray any affection for her. Lydia thought her sister pitifully eager to do him favors, like an overly humble servant groveling to please.

"Here," Pretty Moon said as she escorted Lydia to a grassy area where an antelope skin was stretched out on stakes. Not much had been done to the raw piece. Hunks of reddened flesh still clung to it. Urging her sister to join her, Pretty Moon got down on her knees and picked up a bone scrapper.

This was Lydia's first real project. Making a pair of moccasins. Despite the arduous chore ahead, she undertook the project with enthusiasm. She'd begun to feel guilty puttering around the tepee while Pretty Moon toiled with heavy chores. Although Lydia's wound was healing as expected, she remained cursed with low stamina, frequent dizziness, and nausea.

When Lydia's energy was spent and her hand cramped, she longed for the clunky shoes Faith had given her. Or to go barefoot, as she'd done much of the time in Possum Hollow. However, Pretty Moon had informed her that the second option was not civilized. And the first was impossible. Lydia's clothing had been burned shortly after her arrival. Not only did she not have shoes, she had to wear the hateful dress Proud Bull had presented. The horror of that day lingered like musk.

When Pretty Moon later joined her, she brought some nuts and dried strips of meat for snacking. They sat together and chatted.

During that first week of Lydia's convalescence, the twins quickly become best friends. Time and distance had not severed their natural bond. Despite years of separation within different cultures, they discovered remarkable similarities.

Pretty Moon kept her up to date on all of the scandal and gossip. When she told Lydia the story of Cut Nose, Lydia was horrified, even more so to learn that her story was not unique. Cut Nose was an adulteress, discovered by her husband with her lover. Her husband humiliated her by publicly beating her and then whacking off the tip of her nose. This maiming was to remind other men of her infidelity and to make her appearance less desirable to them.

Although the story of Cut Nose made Lydia shiver, her sister's stories usually brought delightful giggles. Her explicit details left nothing to the imagination. The two sisters sat together for long moments shamelessly overcome by girlish laughter. Sometimes, behind cupped hands, they scrutinized the physical endowments of passing braves.

"What do you know about our mother?" Lydia asked one afternoon.

"Shh. Sioux not speak of the dead."

"Oh please, Father told me that too. But I must learn something about our mother."

Pretty Moon went into the tepee. She tossed some dried meat into the fire and said a prayer to the spirits.

"I say once. We talk no more," Pretty Moon said in a hushed tone. "I know not much. Father told me long ago. Her name was Morning Star. Good wife and mother. Looked like me… and you. She killed when you taken by white men. Many died. Father loved her much."

"You say father loved our mother, yet he has three wives now. Did he forget her so easily?"

"No. Wealthy men, like chiefs, need several wives to run the household and entertain. No more children. Silently mourns our mother." Then a look of enlightenment came over her. "You not mourned. Father knew you return."

The two sisters settled into their own thoughts, nibbling on some dried meat.

"Is she an adulteress too?" Lydia asked quietly as a joyless young woman passed without a smile or a word of acknowledgment.

Lydia had seen the woman before, a deplorable sight. Her face was smeared with mud and ash, her hair cut haphazardly. Deep gashes marred her arms, the blood left to dry.

"No. She be widow, Dried-Up-Stream. Widows must cut body and rub in ashes. Give all property away. Not attend feasts. Mourn one year."

Lydia shivered at the senseless brutality of the self-inflicted wounds.

"Husband of Dried-Up-Stream died in your rescue."

So, he was the dead warrior who'd been slumped over the horse. The man was dead because of her. And how infuriating that these people referred to the attack as a "rescue". Lydia hadn't been "rescued" from anyone. She'd been kidnapped in a violent attack. She ripped off a bite of the dried meat with her front teeth and chewed distastefully.

"What like to live with white people?" Pretty Moon asked. "Did they torture you?"

Lydia should not have been surprised by her sister's questions. "No. I was not tortured. I was often treated cruelly. I lived as the daughter of a childless couple and they treated me well."

"When you sick, you call out for our 'mother' in Sioux. You remember your family?

Lydia gazed into the distance, fighting against the strangling memories of her life among the whites. What had only been a passing of two weeks in the village, seemed more like months or years.

"No. But I often wished to know if my family was alive." Her eyes grew moist.

"You did not forget. Deep inside, you remember."

Several minutes passed before Pretty Moon spoke again. "I would hate living with white people. They wicked. Not be trusted. They beat their children."

"I was only a small child when I was taken from my home. It might have been different had I been older."

Indeed, how very well she knew.

***

Lydia pulled the furs over her head to muffle the soft moans and cries from Pretty Moon and Proud Bull as they made love. In public, they seemed little more than acquaintances, not even touching one another. Under the cloak of darkness, they conducted a very passionate relationship. Since there were no separate bedrooms, every member of the household could hear, including Spotted Doe, who slept unperturbed.

Lydia wondered with embarrassment if she and Joe made that much noise. Her throat tightened as she fought back tears. She had to quit dwelling on Joe. He didn't love her. He was part of her past. Lydia's future belonged to her Sioux village.

In the morning, a sleepy serenity encompassed the Indian village. Conversation was muted as men sat in meditation. Yawning children emerged from their homes rubbing crusty eyes with fists and dragging their toys. The spirits had blessed them with another day. With a renewed light came renewed life and all of its gifts. Lydia didn't share the villagers' feelings of contentment. She felt half alive with a hollow heart.

Despite the peaceful beginning to the day, Lydia had the strong desire for solitude. At no time since her captivity had she been truly alone. Even while on the trail with the emigrants, she had occasionally been able to escape the mobs of people.

"Pretty Moon, I know I ask a lot. I wonder if I could borrow one of Proud Bull's horses to go riding."

"You not happy here."

Pretty Moon's frank observation hit Lydia like a shock wave and placed a tense distance between them. She swallowed the lump that had congealed in her throat.

"Father will not permit," Pretty Moon stated. "You might get stolen."

Stolen? Who exactly had stolen whom? The reality of her situation suddenly sank in. Although not in chains, she was a prisoner among her own flesh and blood family. Would she never be able to leave the village of her own free will? The confinement was choking. She wanted to make her life with her family work. But they behaved as though nothing had changed in her 15 years of absence, as if she was supposed to pick up her life where it had left off. She was not the same person she had been 15 years ago.

Lydia gathered up her tools and leather pieces to resume her assigned work on the moccasins.

Later that day, while preparing an aromatic meal of sage hen, wild turnips and onion in the pit of hot rocks, Pretty Moon rushed up to her.

"Prairie Rose, Prairie Rose. Good! Good!" She urged Lydia into the tepee by lifting up the skin door covering.

Lydia couldn't imagine what her sister was going to tell her. It was obviously a private matter, and made her very happy.

"Good news!" Pretty Moon squealed.

Lydia had never seen her so excited and the emotion overflowed. "What? What?"

"It is Proud Bull. He wishes to take you as wife. Father has agreed!"

Lydia felt the color drain from her face. Her sister's face blurred. Lydia fumbled for something to support herself as her knees started to buckle. Her sister noted her distress and helped her onto a backrest. While Pretty Moon disappeared to retrieve a bladder of water, Lydia's equilibrium restored.

"Drink," Pretty Moon ordered.

Feeling very thirsty of a sudden, Lydia complied.

"You not pleased," Pretty Moon stated with her characteristic bluntness.

"I'm just surprised, is all."

Pretty Moon returned the bladder to its proper place before rejoining her sister. "Proud Bull is a good husband. He is kind and generous, respected warrior and hunter. He has many horses and will provide well for you."

Lydia was also aware of Proud Bull's other achievements, including snatching her from the man she loved. How ironic if that same fierce brave were to become her husband. She'd loathed him that day, but her hatred had softened with the passing of time.

"What kind of wife could I make for such a man? I would be unworthy. I have just begun to learn about running a Sioux household and I doubt I shall ever acquire your skills for embroidering quills and making moccasins without a pattern."

"Proud Bull will be patient, and I will teach you. We become equal wives."

Lydia knew that any normal Indian woman would be honored at such an offer. But as she'd once told Joe, she was not a normal Indian. To marry a man of Proud Bull's status would assure her a solid future with the tribe. To become an equal wife to the first, who was usually the undisputed head wife would assure Lydia a stable home.

"You would want to share your husband with me?" How could any woman desire such a thing, especially if she loved her husband as much as Pretty Moon? Lydia couldn't imagine herself wanting to do so.

Pretty Moon took Lydia's hands in her own. "Yes. You are my sister. We are twins. We shared the same womb together."

Lydia's throat thickened with emotion. At that moment she'd never felt closer to another human being. There was a bond between the two sisters which would never be broken.

"I do not love Proud Bull," Lydia admitted, taking a sudden interest in her lap. She didn't wish to see her sister's face.

"Does not matter. When Proud Bull took me as wife I not love him. Father arranged the marriage with Proud Bull's parents. Proud Bull asked for you. Someday, you will love him as I do."

Lydia couldn't be as certain as her sister. Lydia would have to forget one man before she could give her heart to another.

CHAPTER 36

Joe had yet to form a detailed plan for Lydia's rescue. It would take an army of men to wage a full attack and take her by force. He had to rely on stealth to recapture her, then ride like the wind and disappear into the mountains.

Over the last two weeks, the trail continued to fade with each passing day, and Lydia slipped further and further away from him. With each passing hour, a part of him died inside. In three days, Joe would turn back to rejoin the others who would have spent a week waiting for him at South Pass. A longer delay would put everyone at risk for getting through the Sierras before the first snowfall.

Until he'd met Lydia, his life had been a mere existence, restless and without focus. If need be, he would winter in California and resume his search next spring. He would spend forever, if need be, to find her.

Joe squinted into the blinding sun toward the top of the hill. Damn the sun! He'd lost sight of the man who'd been following him for days. When Joe moved his hand toward his gun, a spray of bullets surrounded him. Nerves on edge, breathing in short gasps, he pressed his back tightly against the hill for protection, an avalanche of fist sized stones and a boulder thundering toward him. He scrambled clear of the mayhem until he lost his footing and his weapon. His pistol bounced off rocks in its decent toward the valley.

Joe slid feet first on his stomach downward, rocks slipping beneath his weight until he gained a foothold on a rocky protrusion. Among a tangle of bramble a few yards further down the hill, the pistol gleamed back at Joe in the reflected sunlight. When he reached for his weapon, a shot rang out. A bullet ricocheted off a rock between his hand and the gun.

Then he dared take another look upward. "Is this how you get even?" Joe shouted.

A dark silhouette emerged from the brush. The fringed buckskin and feathers sticking out of the head were unmistakable. When the culprit moved out of the shadow, the less he looked like an Indian and the more he resembled a white man. A rifle was slung over his left shoulder. A scalping knife and tomahawk slapped against his thigh. At least he'd had enough sense to shave off the beard.

"Posing as a renegade," Joe stated bitterly. "I should've known. Clyde kept ranting about seeing something with feathers."

"He's a better shot than I gave him credit for. He barely missed me."

"You killed that innocent man. Pin-cushioned him with arrows."

The sudden realization shook Joe. He'd forgotten that when the Indians attacked Zachariah's boyhood home they pin-cushioned his father with arrows. They raped his mother and slaughtered her alongside his two sisters. The fact that he watched helplessly still ate at Zachariah.

"Trying to start an uprising?" Joe continued. "Let the white men think an Indian killed one of their brethren, so an attack on innocent Indians would be sanctioned. You know, then, Indians kill innocent white people?" Joe's mind raced with horrible scenarios. "That's how you get even with me? Seems a bit extreme."

Zachariah's laugh was demonic. "You think too much of yourself. Killing that man has nothing to do with you."

"Okay, so, why not shoot me now and get it over with? Why prolong it? You've been following me for…"

"Damn you," Zachariah snarled. "Shut up. If I'd wanted you dead, I'd have shot you when I had the chance. No. I've got something else in mind."

CHAPTER 37

Lydia Whitley was dead.

Prairie Rose put her past behind her, to undertake a new life with a new path. Proud Bull, she decided, would make a good husband. When he became chief, she would hold alongside her sister, one of the most esteemed positions in the tribe. Perhaps one day, as Pretty Moon had suggested, Prairie Rose would come to love her husband too.

So why wasn't she content?

Turmoil raged inside her as she stood alone in the shadows away from the other villagers who were assembled around the evening fire listening to stories by the old warrior. Her own thoughts drowned out his words.

"Why so soon?" she'd asked her father when earlier that day he had informed her that her marriage to Proud Bull would occur in three days.

"Custom. Have whole lives, get to know each other," he answered in his broken English.

She wasn't ready.

Despite satisfaction with her decision to marry, events were moving too quickly. Once the status had been altered between her and her brother-in-law, Proud Bull had begun to take notice of her. He acknowledged her when they passed and frequently made small requests of her. To fetch this or that. He offered no thanks. When she asked her sister about this, Pretty Moon told her she should not be distressed at his coolness toward her. His requests were a good sign and should be taken as a compliment. If he were ever displeased with her, he would not hesitate to inform her.

A deep masculine voice sliced through her thoughts.

Prairie Rose gasped. "Proud Bull, you startled me." *What could he need at this hour?*

With an air of aristocratic pride, the looming figure strode over to her, babbling something in Sioux.

"I don't understand." He always spoke with a gruff tone of urgency and usually without helpful gestures, although in the darkness they would have been useless.

As Proud Bull slowed his approach, his voice changed to a soft lilting tone. Prairie Rose shook her head in frustration. She wanted to please. She didn't know how. For him to have sought her out, he must need something important. Then he quieted, and simply stood in front of her, making her increasingly jittery under his intense scrutiny. The light of a full moon flickered in his eyes eerily, and branded her with their heat. Proud Bull was a powerful man, a head taller than her, a perfect specimen of raw masculinity.

Prairie Rose forced her gaze from his face to glide along his neck and bare chest to his waist. Because it was a warm evening, Proud Bull wore only a breechcloth from which hung his usual weapons. A tomahawk and knife. His near nakedness in such close proximity made her acutely aware of her vulnerability. During the long ride with him on horseback, she'd learned that his arms and massive chest were as powerful as they looked. Prairie Rose choked back the knowledge that he had killed men with his bare hands.

She held her breath as he stepped close enough for her to feel the heat of his body. Her nose tingled with his wild animal scent. A calculating smile touched his lips. As a hungry lust began to smolder in his eyes, Prairie Rose's apprehension slammed into panic. She knew what he intended to do.

"Please, I am not your wife," she protested. He had never mistaken them before. "I am Prairie Rose." She took a tiny step backward, feeling as fragile as a frightened kitten. "Prairie Rose…" her voice drifted off in Sioux as their gazes remained locked.

Proud Bull didn't relinquish his gaze. It caressed her mouth and the long column of her neck, then sought more of her. As if stung, she held her breath when his delighted eyes lingered upon her heaving breasts. He casually reached out and cupped her right one. She gasped and jerked away at his boldness.

She obviously wasn't deterring his attention. His right hand firmly attached itself to a breast, while his other swung around to bring her fully against his chest. She stiffened at the intimate embrace, immediately engulfed in that terrifying memory when this same savage brave had snatched her from her comrades. Only now she discovered that beneath the flimsy breechcloth, Proud Bull was ready for her.

Alarm, like a tidal wave washed over her, knowing from experience she could never escape his grip. As Proud Bull's betrothed, he had certain rights to her. As his wife, she would be expected to be intimate with him. It was frighteningly obvious that this man was so virile that he needed two wives to satisfy him.

While she grappled with this new situation, Proud Bull's mouth lowered onto hers. Instead of the expected bruising, searing kiss, the sensuous, almost hesitant caress with his lips was a sharp contrast. His hands gently roamed her shoulder and glided along the contour of her waist and hips. He had the magnificent ability to restrain his brutal strength. Prairie Rose pulled her lips from Proud Bull's.

It seemed wrong, kissing her sister's husband.

He said something to her in a soft tone, but his embrace did not ease. But neither did Proud Bull claw and ravage her like a possessed beast. When he held her in his arms, the stern warrior brought back the memory of a different man.

Joe...

CHAPTER 38

"Lydia!" Joe shouted with unreserved joy. After two weeks of searching, he had found her. He stared in disbelief at the Indian maiden, now dressed in customary native garb. She was in the midst of the other spectators who had gathered, no doubt to witness his entrance into the village. He thrashed and kicked against the two brawny warriors who pressed him toward the people with his arms held behind his back. Next to him, Zachariah was being shoved forward the same way. *How could Zachariah have thought they could easily ride into this hostile group? And why?*

Although the woman was painted and dressed in beaded buckskin and her unrestrained hair draped across her shoulders, he did not doubt her identity. She was the woman he had searched for relentlessly. The one he feared he had lost forever.

A prideful streak gripped the woman's expression in the set of her jaw and the high contour of her cheeks. She was a stunning portrait, her complexion aglow in the firelight, her lips moist and inviting. Yet, there was something oddly different about her, something not quite tangible. For a fleeting moment he felt as if he didn't know this lovely goddess, as if his memory of her had been a dream. Had he never traced his fingers along that creamy skin, never tasted those sweet lips?

"Joe!" came a frantic cry from within the crowd.

Then, before his eyes one figment paused beside another. He blinked several times. The double vision didn't meld into one. The brief deprivation of his Lydia must be driving him to madness.

Had he imagined the calling of his name too?

Then, as the first figment vanished, the second separated from the other and started to rush toward him. Joe's heart pounded with a leap of joy. Then, the same brave who'd tried to trade for Lydia materialized from nowhere to roughly grab her arm and forcibly jerk her away. To see that man now in control, touching his Lydia, twisted his stomach.

Joe growled and cursed at the warriors. He squirmed and tugged against their grip like a nervous horse pulling against its reins. Taut muscles strained against muscles. Joe could only watch helplessly as the crowd swallowed up the mysterious pair of women.

"What goes on here?" the chief, wrapped in a buffalo robe appeared and bellowed at the group.

"What have you done to her? What have you done with Lydia?" Joe felt the veins pop from his neck and forehead as he snarled.

"Great Chief Flying Eagle," Zachariah addressed in a cool mockery of respect. "Your warriors accosted us while we were approaching camp." He scowled at the chief with obvious resentment for being so brutally manhandled.

"Traitor!" the chief accused, his eyes flaring. "You told bring no one here!"

"I can explain," Zachariah said.

"We had bargain."

"What the hell's going on here? What bargain?" Joe asked Zachariah.

"He try to steal horses," the chief answered. "Braves catch him, find child moccasins."

"I should have thrown them damn shoes away," Zachariah grumbled.

"Same moccasins of daughter, Pretty Moon," the chief continued. "Two pair, for twins. We make white man tell where come from. For this we spare life."

"Lydia's moccasins?" Joe faced Zachariah. "You stole her moccasins?"

Zachariah shrugged. "Call it counting coup."

"I suppose then, you had something to do with the ambush on our camp." It was fitting that Zachariah too be taken prisoner by these Indians.

"I only showed them the location of your camp. You and Lydia should be grateful. Isn't that why you brought her on this little trip? To reunite her with her family?"

Joe hissed through clenched teeth and again struggled for release against his captors. He wanted nothing more than to sink his fist into Zachariah's smug face.

"Enough!" the chief bellowed. "You had chance to return our Prairie Rose. You not take our offer. We take what belong to us. White men no good. We spare your life no more!" he snarled. "Traitors both!" Then he signaled for his men to take the prisoners from his sight.

"Wait a minute!" Zachariah barked at the chief. "Joe is the man you want. He's the one who held Lydia prisoner."

"Hear no more," the chief said with finality. "Prepare for punishment."

CHAPTER 39

"What's going on? What ceremony?" Prairie Rose pleaded for answers as she followed Pretty Moon and Proud Bull into the tepee where they changed their garments and applied more body paint. After grabbing a few ceremonial tools, Pretty Moon and Proud Bull ordered her to remain in the tepee. She started to protest, but their looks, warned her not to.

Worry for Joe clawed at her like sharp talons as she churned up stories of rape and torture. She'd never believed those stories, thinking they'd been told only to humiliate her. And she certainly wouldn't have considered her own family harming her, even as it turned out, they were members of the Sioux tribe with a reputation for cutting the throats of their enemies. After living with these people and witnessing their chilling ceremonies and ferocious face paint, she was no longer certain of her beliefs.

She wished Joe had not come.

And why was he with Zachariah Potter?

Cold shivers spiraled down her spine as she remembered the icy faces of Pretty Moon and Proud Bull making their exit. With renewed determination—she would not be a coward—she decided to find Joe before something horrible happened to him, if it wasn't already too late. Joe's safety was worth any retribution her fiancé might bestow upon her.

Before stepping outside, Prairie Rose snatched up a nearby bladder of water and a small parfleche of dried meat. Chances were no one would pay any attention to her; she was after all, the daughter of Chief Flying Eagle and fiancé of the great warrior, Proud Bull. If anyone asked, she was going to offer refreshments to the prisoners.

An eerie silence had settled upon the camp. Even the dogs had become silent. The children no longer ran about the village.

Prairie Rose crept through the seemingly deserted village. The small sacred fires burned inside the tepees like luminaries spread before her, their flames flickering with a yellow glow. The skin linings inside the tepee walls made it difficult to discern the details of interior shadows or signs of occupancy. She had no idea where prisoners might be kept.

Well-practiced at stealth in the shadows, she wove her way through the village as secretively as any other Indian. When entering the center of the village, she remembered that the council and society tepees were always kept void of inhabitants and furnishings. What better place to keep prisoners? Making her way in that direction, she discovered the glow of a small fire within the council tepee.

She took a deep breath and approached. There were no sentries, which made her mission seem too easy. Unsettling. Perhaps she was wrong about the location of the prisoners. Boldly narrowing the distance, her heart increased its rhythm. She paused at the entry, listening over the sound of her pumping heart and the blood swishing in her ears for some sign of activity in or around the tepee. There was nothing. If neither prisoner was there, she decided, she would simply supply the excuse to any occupant that she had mistaken the place for another. With shaky fingers, she pulled back a corner of the hanging door covering and peered in. The discovery hit her like a cold slap in the face.

A man was curled up on the floor, unmoving, his arms bound tightly behind his back. The hat she had come to easily recognize was shielding his face from her. His clothes were splattered with a mix of dried blood and mud.

"Joe…" at the sound of her soft voice, the body uncoiled, tilting his face to hers.

The cold hard eyes softened. Despite the smile attempting to brighten his face, she couldn't believe his sorrowful appearance. Even under the harshest conditions of the westward journey, she hadn't seen him look so beaten down. He was unshaven, and his shirt was ripped as though he had tangled with a cougar. Her throat tightened with guilt and sorrow at the hours she had spent in self-pity, never stopping to consider how her disappearance might have affected him.

***

Joe decided he must be going mad when he turned to look at the figure standing above him.

She knelt and withdrew the leather gag from his mouth.

"Lydia, it's you?" A dry scratchy sound came out.

She nodded and helped him sit up and take a few sips of water from the bladder. Then she started to untie his wrists.

"I thought I was going mad, that I was seeing things…" he fought back a dry cough. "There were two of you."

Joe watched helplessly as she clawed with fingers that were becoming raw. The warrior had used wet leather strips, which had begun to shrink and tighten as they dried. The strips were still damp and slick and nearly impossible to undo. He wished he could slice the leather strips with the knife they had confiscated.

"My sister," she answered simply. "We are twins."

Once his wrists were untied, Joe snatched her hands. "A sister. You found your family."

He couldn't have been more elated for her.

She avoided his gaze and looked at his hands. "You're hurt," she winced at the red slices marring his wrists.

Joe shrugged off his wounds, and worked on his ankle restraints. "They treated you well?" His throat and mouth were dry and scratchy from the gag.

"They are my family." She returned the bladder of water to him.

He sat back and drank deeply. When he'd had his fill, he wiped his chin on the cuff of his shirt and handed back the bladder.

"You look wonderful."

He was still in disbelief that he had actually found her. She was just as he would have imagined, dressed in buckskins and face paint, her hair falling in long braids down her back. A band of silver encircled her exposed upper arm. She smelled of smoke and leather. He devoured her with all his senses, half fearing that like the wild doe she so emulated, she would disappear in a blink.

"I didn't think I would see you again," she said. It was a simple statement, spoken with no hint of emotion.

He had searched for her for two weeks, putting his obligation to the wagons on hold, and with very little sleep, following the convoluted trail the braves had laid out, no doubt to confuse him. Frankly, he'd been surprised they'd credited him with enough skill and intelligence to follow the signs. He should have known they had just been crumbs to distract. If he hadn't been outwitted by their clever tricks, Joe would have reached this camp days ago. Then Zachariah had intervened with his own scheme.

"You had to know I'd come for you. I've been so worried. Everyone's been worried."

"How is everyone? The Livelys? The Crenshaws?"

"The Livelys are fine. Six men were hit during the attack, including uncle Amos, who took an arrow in the arm. All should recover."

Lydia frowned. "I'm sorry for all of it." She looked at the fringe of her dress and rubbed it between two fingers.

Joe paused his work on the leather strip, which was chaffing his calloused hands as it had done to Lydia. He ached to hold her, to relieve her of her burden of guilt. He wanted to taste her sweet mouth. But there was a dark chasm between them, as if they were strangers talking over a great abyss, as if one of them were to reach out for the other, they would both plunge into deep nothingness.

"You are not to blame."

"The warriors came for me. They said they'd heard the story about me saving the boy. Everyone else just got in the way."

"Zachariah is to blame." Joe resumed clawing at the slippery leather strip, which had dug a red trench into his ankles.

"Zachariah Potter? How? I saw him with you." She shook her head. "What does he have to do with this?"

"When the warriors caught him trying to steal their horses, they found your moccasins in his pack. They recognized them. The chief gave Zachariah his life for the information on your whereabouts. He betrayed both *you and me* when he led the warriors to our camp."

"Zachariah stole my moccasins? I should have known. Only a few people knew I had them. I was foolish to trust him."

"You aren't the only one to have foolishly trusted him." Joe took another sip of water and kept the bladder next to him. It pained him to tell her what happened to Zachariah's family. "Young and alone, Zachariah buried his family and became a drifter."

Joe finally freed his ankles and groaned as he stood to stretch his cramped legs. He glanced around the empty lodge, wondering where his boots had gone.

"He eventually met up with me and my grandfather while we were on a trapping expedition. Despite knowing that Indians had killed the Potters and his history with young women, I invited him on this caravan. I had no idea the pain ran so deep. I trusted him." His jaw tensed and the bitterness in his gut tightened and roiled. The woman he had come to rescue just blinked at him, expressionless.

"On our way here, he revealed some things to me, terrible things from the past. He said he would do anything he could to work against the Indians. That night when he stole your moccasins – an impromptu decision, he admitted – dressed like a brave, he'd come into camp to punish me for expelling him. His plan was foiled when he was discovered and shots were fired. Zachariah killed that poor man, pin-cushioned with arrows, just to stir up trouble."

"And I am both Indian, and a woman. What must he have been thinking and planning from the beginning? He was kind to me when you were distant."

"And by bringing me to their village, Zachariah has betrayed the Sioux, for which he is sure to pay with his life."

"And you will no doubt pay with yours." Energized, she stood and snatched up the bladder of water.

Joe slowly came to his feet, realizing how stiff and bone tired he was from the relentless journey to the Sioux village and from the fear gripping his heart.

"I'm sure that's exactly what Zachariah expected when he brought me here. He told the villagers I kept you captive. I think he expected to be released."

"We need to get you out of here."

"I'm not leaving without you, Lydia."

"I am Prairie Rose," she said mechanically, "daughter of Chief Flying Eagle, sister of Pretty Moon. The Sioux never speak of the dead. Speak of Lydia Whitley no more."

"What are you saying?"

"These people are *my* family. And *you* are the enemy."

"Enemy?" He scoffed. "Lydia, ever since that brave snatched you away from me I've been in torment. Hope of finding you was all that kept me from being swallowed up by desolation."

"Prairie Rose," she corrected.

"Prairie Rose, then," he added with impatience. "You don't belong here."

"That's what the white people told me too." She spoke with melancholy. "It's wrong you being here. You shouldn't have come."

"I need you. I love you. I want you to be my wife." His eyes roamed over her intimately, undressing her. It was painful to be so close to her, where he could reach out and touch her, knowing it was impossible.

The air was still with her long pause. She stuck out her chin. "I was under the impression you'd sworn off marriage. How am I to believe you now?"

She raised a good point. Joe hated how he had let his father's legacy rule his life. "I realize now, that just because I'm the son of my father, doesn't mean I have to be like Jackson Brice. Denying my feelings and pushing you away is more hurtful. I need to spend the rest of my life with the woman I love."

It took all his strength to suppress the urge to take Lydia into his arms. He hungered for her reassurance. He hungered for the woman he'd fallen in love with. Not this stranger with fearsome paint and eyes glaring with challenge. He stared into Lydia's dark eyes, pleading for them to brighten with devotion. "I want you to marry me."

"I cannot," she answered woodenly.

"What do you mean? Cannot or will not? You aren't a prisoner here." He threw up his hands in frustration.

"I am to marry another."

A pain of disbelief ripped his chest apart. "What?"

"It's my father's wish." She stared blindly past his shoulder.

"Your father? Chief Flying Eagle? What does he have to do with this? He's a stranger to you."

"He's still my father. I've given my word that the wedding will take place. Proud Bull is a great warrior, destined to become the next chief. I will hold a place of honor here." Her words sounded pre-rehearsed and unconvincing.

"Proud Bull," Joe moved the words around in his mouth distastefully. "He's the warrior who came to trade for you. He's the man who snatched you away in the crowd." Joe felt as if a great hand had scooped out what was left of his insides.

"Yes," she answered quietly, gazing down at her hands.

"Has he harmed you, Lydia? Threatened you?" Joe grabbed her shoulders and forced her to make eye contact with him. "So help me, if he's hurt one hair on your head, I'll kill him! You can't imagine the hell I've been through trying to find you. Each passing hour… a little more of me died inside. I thought I lost you. And now, I have to beg you to return with me."

She tore her eyes from his.

"Look into my eyes," he commanded, "and tell me you don't love me. Tell me you would rather choose this brave over me. Tell me Lydia."

"It would never work," she said, still managing to avoid his penetrating gaze. "You and me. It's wrong. I'll only bring you shame."

"Stop saying that. Our loving each other isn't wrong."

"We are from two separate worlds. You are white. I am Indian. I belong with Indians. You know I've never been accepted by white people. I hear the terrible things the women say about me. Thelma Lee. Even Mable, whose daughter I kept safe during the stampede, wished I'd been traded."

"Don't sell them short. The men spent days trying to find you. The women held prayer circles asking for your return."

"You must find a woman of your own race. My life is here now."

"You're talking crazy. I love you. We belong together." He couldn't believe this nightmare.

Lydia pulled back from him. "These are my people, my family. I must stay. I've wanted nothing more my whole life. Can't you understand?"

"I've spent my entire life searching for something I didn't even realize I was missing until I found you."

His lips were upon hers hot and bruising, demanding that she respond to him. As his arms closed possessively around her, she struggled to escape his grasp. Then gradually, she yielded to him, her body contradicting her words and betraying her need. Their bodies seemed to merge, their hearts beating in rhythm. Then, Joe tore his mouth away, deliberately leaving her breathless and trembling.

"Can your warrior do that to you Lydia? Make you feel the way I can?"

She pulled away from his embrace. Sternly, she said, "I'll discuss your release with my father."

***

The sudden thud of a drum and shrill tone of a pipe caught the attention of Prairie Rose. She slipped into the darkness, curiosity forcing her to watch shadowy figures gather around a fire. They led a man into the circle, or rather, dragged him naked, against his will, and thrust him upon the ground, then stretched his body taut and staked him down by his hands and feet.

Prairie Rose slapped her hand over her mouth to keep her voice from joining the howls of the man who writhed on the ground. Zachariah! What were they going to do to him? Some morbid force kept her attention drawn to the horrific scene. Madness seemed to drive the spring-like limbs of the dancers. Featureless bodies stomped with feral cries to the beating drums, furious and faster, like demons from hell in the flickering flames.

When the women took up long spears and thrust them at the prisoner, Prairie Rose turned away, choking on bile. She couldn't believe the women were committing this atrocity. These were the same women who nurtured the sick and mourned the dead. The men were the ones primed for killing and war.

How could her people, her family do this? No wonder her sister hadn't spoken of this evil to her; Prairie Rose was still a newcomer to these ways. She couldn't accept this. It went against all the good she'd ever learned. Zachariah had done some vile things, but did he deserve this?

On numb limbs, her head swimming, Prairie Rose staggered away from the ceremony. She came face-to-face with her sister.

"Where go?" Pretty Moon asked tersely. "You told stay."

"I saw them…" She couldn't say the words. "Zachariah Potter."

"The prisoner?" She took Prairie Rose by the elbow and led her to the privacy of their home. "You told not go outside. We know you not understand."

"What is there *to* understand?" Prairie Rose's numbness faded to anger.

"White man traitor, must be punished."

The entire situation was making her feel faint. Grabbing her temples to steady her head against the dizziness, she stumbled into her backrest and hunched over her knees, willing herself not to vomit.

Pretty Moon followed closely. "How long you keep this up?" She snorted. "Cannot keep hiding."

Prairie Rose jerked her head up. "What do you mean?"

Pretty Moon knelt beside her sister and spoke gently. "I know why you sick so much. Like me with Spotted Doe. No need to be ashamed. Proud Bull forgives."

"You told Proud Bull I am with child?"

She knew she couldn't hide her pregnancy forever, but she wanted to reveal the information when she was ready. She was mortified that her sister had shared such a private matter with Proud Bull. Previously masked by her illness, Prairie Rose only recognized the signs herself a few days prior. *Who else had heard this gossipy tidbit?*

"Need not fear. Proud Bull will still make you wife. You not live in shame for what white men did."

"I suppose I should be grateful for Proud Bull's kindness," Prairie Rose spoke with false sincerity, choking down the bitterness that was boiling inside her. "Would Proud Bull acquire a fondness for my child?"

Her mind drifted to visions of her child growing up and playing around the lodge with Proud Bull's own flesh and blood children.

"Oh no! The baby is not to live," Pretty Moon said.

The blood drained from her face. "Not to live?"

Pretty Moon's answer came at her as if the two women were a far distance from each other. "Proud Bull will not raise that white man's child. Woman-Who-Laughs will give you potion. Make baby stop growing inside you."

"What kind of horrible people kill babies?" Prairie Rose choked. "I thought the Sioux loved children."

"White men took you from your people and kept you prisoner. Killed our mother and defiled you. White men the enemy."

"But I love this baby," Prairie Rose gripped her stomach possessively.

"I not understand. How can you love white man's child?"

"The baby's father had nothing to do with taking me from the Sioux. He was good to me. I love Joe."

"Joe?" Pretty Moon shook her head. "That is name you cry out when sick with fever. He have same fate as other one. He die, too. Then we move village."

"No!" Prairie Rose clasped her palms over her ears, shaking her head. "They can't! They can't!"

Must she again lose everyone she loved? Her stomach knotted and twisted, and she fought back the bile percolating in her throat.

"It is right of widow, Dried-Up-Stream, to avenge death of husband who died during your rescue."

"We were the ones attacked," Prairie Rose retorted. *Why did they keep calling it a rescue?* "We must help Joe escape. I love him!"

"Shh. Learn to love Proud Bull. He be husband soon."

"I won't let Joe die! They can't do this! Father will set him free."

Her steadfast determination to save Joe drove her. She raced out of the tepee and through the village in search of her father. She overlooked those who stood between them. She ran headlong into the ceremonial gathering, disregarding the group of important men wrapped in buffalo robes.

"Father!" she shouted.

When he turned to look at her, Prairie Rose had to swallow back a choking lump of dread. Despite his age and wrinkles, Flying Eagle was a fierce spectacle, standing as straight and tall as any younger man, his eyes flashing like tiny torches. The formal attire and regal headdress highlighted the deep grooves of his face. The crown of eagle feathers fluttered in the warm prevailing breeze as if in preparation for flight. Enemy scalps fringed his shirt and seemed to mock her plight. Dangling bear claws threatened.

She was his daughter, she reminded herself, as she stood before the regal chief. The knowledge that he was a fatherly and generous man who loved his people and they him, did not ease the quaking of her limbs.

"Please, you must help me," Prairie Rose gasped.

She was sweating and out of breath when she stopped before him. She ignored those who scowled at her uncouth intrusion of their informal council.

"What is it?" her father asked with disdain.

"I beg a favor of you."

"Prairie Rose no beg," he said gruffly, "only poor and helpless beg. No daughter of chief."

She apologized for her gaff and then continued with her request. "You must let the other prisoner go."

Firmly, with fatherly gentility, he wrapped his tired old fingers around her arm and led her away from the group of men. "Why you ask this of me?"

Prairie Rose gulped as she thought of the best words. "Joseph Brice was one of the few white people who treated me with kindness. Most hated me, only because I am Sioux." She used the cut throat sign.

Flying Eagle's features remained stony and unaltered. "I can no help."

"Oh please, Father. I beg you." Tears welled up.

"In hands of women now," he added tonelessly. "It is widow's right."

Tears dripped from her lashes. Unmoving and unblinking, she didn't bother to wipe them away. The indignity of shedding them had already been committed and couldn't be undone.

***

The words of Flying Eagle's daughter had not fallen on unsympathetic ears. To reveal how her tears moved him was not the Indian way. To see her cry tore at his insides. Prairie Rose was not the woman he wanted her to be, the woman that she should have been. He did not blame her for the wickedness, which had come to her. The white men had wronged the entire village.

He'd promised himself to be patient with her, to accept her for who she was. He could not understand how his daughter wished for anything except to avenge her mother's death, her own captivity and her stolen innocence. How could she ask him to free the prisoner?

"Go now!" he said. The longer she stood there sobbing, the more distressingly obvious it became that his daughter cared for the prisoner more than she admitted. "Go to Proud Bull. I talk no more." He shut his lips tight and arranged his arms across his chest.

"I will not! I won't go back to Proud Bull. I won't marry a man who wants to kill my baby!" In a streak, she was gone from his side.

***

When Prairie Rose returned to the council tepee, she slapped a quivering hand across her mouth to muffle her scream. Too stunned to move, through blinding tears, her eyes remained transfixed on the heap in front of her. Joe's hat was placed precariously on the back of his head, which was turned away from her. The familiar trousers and bloody shirt were stretched taut across the broad backside of the crumpled up body. They had already killed him.

A raw primitive grief overwhelmed her. She collapsed to her knees and broke into a sob. She'd been ready to escape with him and to become his wife. Now everything was over. Despair ripped her heart. She was truly alone, with no one to turn to. She hated herself for having scoffed at his proposal and his affections. He would be alive now; she was convinced, if she'd agreed to marry him.

She rubbed the brim of Joe's hat between her fingers, letting her tears flow. She thought of the few wonderful weeks she'd spent with him as his lover. She didn't regret any of it. He'd helped her mature from a shy sheltered maiden into a woman. She loved him. But he was lost to her forever.

Through the blinding deluge of tears, she summoned the courage to look at Joe's face.

Lifting his hat, she reached down to roll him onto his back, then laughed at the trick unwittingly played upon her. Joe had managed to stuff his clothing and hat with animal skins and pieces of what looked like Zachariah's stolen clothing, before making an escape. Joe must have had help. She dropped the distasteful items of a dead man and readjusted the clever decoy to the manner in which she'd found it. Then she fled to her sister's tepee.

"Pretty Moon," Prairie Rose gasped, as she nearly collided with her twin.

In a rush, Pretty Moon began talking in broken Sioux, something about having been looking for her. "Come, Come!" Pretty Moon said excitedly and urged her into the tepee.

Her heart surged when she stepped inside and spotted the counterfeit Indian standing there, dressed only in a breechcloth with a few feathers sticking in his hair.

"Joe!" She rushed to him and flung her arms around his waist, not even considering that he might no longer want her. "I thought you were gone. You didn't leave! You didn't leave without me!" Her eyes glistened with tears of joy and love as she gazed into Joe's blue eyes.

"Of course not, silly," he chuckled and wrapped his strong arms about her shoulders. "I came here to bring you back with me."

"But… but I told you I didn't want you any more, that I'd chosen to marry another." Prairie Rose wiped away a tear that had squeezed from between her lashes.

"Since when have I ever taken 'no' for an answer?" He pecked her forehead with a light, reassuring kiss. "Besides, I could tell by the way you looked at me that you cared for me." Then he whispered for only her to hear, "And you could never have kissed me like that if you loved another."

Lydia's face burned. *Was it so obvious?* Her sister must have thought so too.

Then he released her and stepped back. "Your sister helped me to get away. Do you like the new outfit? We thought it made a better profile for escape."

Another wave of heat spread across her face. The man she loved was nearly naked in front of her *and her sister*. His stance emphasized his broad muscular chest that tapered to narrow hips and flat belly, all of which she had traced with seductive fingers. Long strong legs shot out from below the breechcloth. She knew what lay beneath that strip of leather. Her body reacted, a quiver of longing surging from deep within her belly. How could she have ever thought to deny the love for this man and turn to another?

Pretty Moon smiled bashfully as she observed the reunion. "I do not understand how Prairie Rose can love a white man," she said. "I know what is like to love a man, and to risk everything to save him." She slipped outside to leave the couple in private.

"What made you decide to come back to me?"

"These are my people, but I don't belong here. You are right. You are the only man I love."

Joe gave her a sweet, gentle kiss on the mouth.

"And the baby," the sight of Joe had made her forget briefly. Now the memory brought new urgency to the situation. "They want to kill my baby!"

"Baby?" Joe's eyes widened.

"Yes. It would have been all I had left of you." She broke into a sob. "Proud Bull will not raise a white man's child."

In the next second, Joe's eyes lit up like the summer sun, his mouth forming a clownish grin.

He clasped his large hands over her shoulders. "Lydia, why didn't you tell me before?" His face beamed with love.

She cast her eyes downward. "I… I've only been certain for a short time. Only since I've been here. I… I guess I was afraid to tell you earlier."

"Afraid of what, my love?" Joe gently tilted her chin up so he could see her face. "That I might reject the child? Even my father was not such a cad. It's my own flesh and blood, conceived by our love."

Joe's moist lips closed upon hers, taking her breath away with its sudden and passionate sting. Then it became a long, sensual kiss, bringing to mind warm sunny days and the smell of sweet grasses.

"I love you," he whispered, as he pulled his mouth from hers.

"Must hurry!" Pretty Moon barged into the lodge. "Alarm sound! Must leave!"

"Our friends have discovered my absence," Joe coolly stated the obvious.

"What will we do?" Prairie Rose asked in a shrill voice. She glanced at her sister, then at Joe.

"Follow me," Pretty Moon said.

Joe took Prairie Rose by the hand and followed Pretty Moon out of the tepee. As if by magic, a horse had materialized and was waiting for them. A bright-eyed lad who had been assigned the task of packing, stood proudly alongside, obviously pleased with his labors. The horse was burdened with only the barest of provisions: blankets, pouches, and skins of water. Pairs of matching parfleches hung from each side.

A thrill of excitement increased Prairie Rose's already heightened state, as she instantly recognized Joe's black stallion. She turned to thank her sister, but Pretty Moon interjected.

"Have gift for baby." Her sister presented a beaded cradleboard. "Keep baby safe and happy with warm soft furs. Make strong back."

"Oh no, I couldn't." She would feel guilty taking such a wonderful gift.

"Take… Please." Pretty Moon added the white man's courtesy word to stress her own desires.

Joe shot Lydia a look to remind her that Indians did not refuse favors. They accepted gifts graciously.

"Thank you." She allowed Pretty Moon to strap the cradleboard across her back.

"It's lovely," Joe commented with a twinkle in his eyes as he admired the device.

Lydia hugged her sister. "I hope you're not punished for helping us."

"No worry. Proud Bull not beat."

"I wish we were departing under better circumstances. But we must hurry," Joe said.

Pretty Moon pulled away from her sister and looked pleadingly into her eyes. "Please, do not hate us for what we have done."

"I do not hate. You have returned a piece of myself that has been missing. I wish I had a gift to leave with you."

"Piece of you stay in heart." Pretty Moon motioned to her heart and then to the village. "In all of us."

"We must go," Joe said with urgency. "The warriors are coming."

Lydia nodded. Then strong arms came around her and hoisted her onto Zeus's back.

Joe gave a startled Pretty Moon a quick kiss on the cheek. "Thanks," he whispered.

A second later, he swung his leg over the side of his stallion. The lad presented him with Zachariah's rifle and Joe's own gun belt.

"Let's go!" Joe kicked Zeus into motion.

Lydia glanced over her shoulder and caught a glimpse of moisture in her sister's eyes. Behind her, the warriors were running through the village retrieving their bows and arrows and whooping it up with their ominous war cries.

Pretty Moon hurried into motion, stirring up the corralled horses and setting them free. Camp quickly became a cloud of dust and chaos as the beloved war ponies stampeded through the village.

When two gunshots fired, Joe urged Zeus into a full gallop, passing the last tepee. There was no turning back.

***

Somewhere in the flickering firelight, a chief ordered his warriors to throw down their arms. This time he knew. She was leaving of her own free will.

EPILOGUE

Sitting high atop the hillside, Lydia watched the construction of her new house. Despite hardships in the Rocky Mountains and the dry Humboldt Valley, the five months as Joe's wife had been more like a dream.

She couldn't have imagined a wedding in a more picturesque mountain valley, with hundreds of joyous onlookers. The women had fussed over her and helped her into her yellow calico dress. Faith loaned her a hat, a beautiful creation of silk and feathers by a famous milliner in Philadelphia. Someone gifted her a bouquet of blue and yellow wildflowers. A large antelope anchored the customary feast and a fiddler and a banjo player provided the entertainment.

"I've been looking all over for you," Joe said. He sat down alongside her to rest. "I don't know how long you expect to keep this up. This hike wears me out."

Lydia smiled, thinking of something similar her sister had once said when confronting her about the pregnancy. When was that, about four months ago?

"Sometimes, I just need to get away from the hammering. And the breeze is nice here."

Joe put his arm around her shoulder. "I bumped into the Crenshaws while I was in Sacramento. They decided on that piece of land along the creek. They'll have a beautiful view of the mountains. I invited them for supper soon. I hope that's all right."

"Of course it's all right. I haven't seen them in weeks."

"By the way, Seth is set up in his new office. His practice is booming, I hear. He and Faith have started building their home on that small tract of land just outside town. Seth wants me to bring you in for a check-up."

She'd been putting it off as long as possible. "When do you think it will be finished?" she asked.

"The baby?"

"Our house, silly. I know how long babies take."

Joe's deep blue eyes sparkled. His face lit up with that wide grin that made Lydia nearly swoon. "Oh. It will be quite some time yet."

"Before winter? Before the baby comes? Living in a wagon with you is cozy, but that thin bedroll and hard wagon bed are getting more uncomfortable. Maybe the house doesn't need to be so big. It wouldn't take so long to finish."

"The main living quarters might be complete before Christmas. In the meantime, I'll look into getting a thicker mattress."

"Thank you." Lydia gave Joe a quick peck on the cheek. "You spoil me."

Their house was going to be larger than any she'd seen in Possum Hollow. Made of real bricks and stones. And the gold coin, which her sister had secreted away in a pack, had been used toward purchase of their first tract of land. With Joe's small mining claim turning into a modest gold strike, he had made more than enough money to repay the debt his father left him. He was planning to start a business of breeding horses, using Zeus as the first stud.

"Licorice?"

"Yes. Thank you."

He tore a long string off between his teeth and gave it to her.

After she took a bite, Joe chuckled. "That's the first time I've seen you eat licorice."

Lydia smiled, the string of licorice held between two fingers and two front teeth. "I think I've acquired a taste for it." She'd tasted it on Joe often enough.

"Maybe that mean's the baby will be a boy," Joe placed a hand on Lydia's swelling belly.

"I can't help wonder. How will our half-breed child be accepted into this world?"

"After all this time, you should ask me that?" Compassion filled his eyes as he stared at her. "The two of us will give our child more than enough love." Hungrily, Joe's lips crushed Lydia's and instantly the two were swallowed up in their love.

ABOUT THE AUTHOR

Linda Chalk grew up in Cincinnati, Ohio where she graduated from the University of Cincinnati with a degree in chemistry. She dreamed of becoming a published author since she could first write. Some of her earliest stories were romances. Of course, studying chemistry left little time for creative writing or reading fiction of her choice. But the premise of *Torn Between Worlds* was born during this time. The old west had been subjects of interest since early childhood and days of watching *Gunsmoke* and *Bonanza*. After college graduation, she gave up studying weighty text books to read fiction of her choice and to research her book. Since she lived near the university with access to their library, she could spend evenings combing through personal diaries written by actual immigrants who had traveled the overland trail to Oregon and California.

Over the next few years, while she worked for a major consumer products company, married and raised two daughters, Linda continued to hone her craft, networking with other authors and those in the publishing industry. She published her short story, "Titanic Love", (based on a real story with real people, during the sinking of the Titanic) in collection of short stories, *Love's a Beach,* with her local writers' group. Meanwhile, the book of Linda's dreams sat on the back burner unfinished until she retired, and her two daughters were grown.

Linda lives in a suburb of Cincinnati with her husband and Shetland Sheep dog. She enjoys retirement and travel in their RV, golfing, sightseeing, photography and writing.

Follow Linda on facebook:
Linda Chalk Author@lindachalkauthor